Library of Congress Control Number: 2015918258

ISBN: 978-0-692-75413-9

First Edition: July 2016

Dedication

This novel is dedicated to the lasting memory of my childhood friend, and brother in religion, Hasaan Brooks . . . you are one of the most influential leaders, 8th and Jefferson, and our entire neighborhood has ever witnessed. May our Creator raise your status in Paradise and put you amongst the righteous (Ameen). Insha Allah, I'll see you when I get there.

(City of Secrets)
10-book Series

PHILADELPHIA TEARDROPS

Chapter One

"Brittany, you an ungrateful, little bitch. You know that?"

"I am not! Aunt Tanya, why you just sittin' there, lettin' him talk to me like that? You just gon' sit there and not say nothin'?"

"Me and Marvin was downstairs in your apartment, while you was at work, Brittany. We read one of your diaries."

"What?! Why?!"

"Ay, bitch, look here! Ya aunt ain't gotta do no goddamn explainin' to you about why we did shit up in this mu'fucker! Bitch, don't forget, this . . . whole goddamn buildin' belong . . . to . . . me!!"

Brittany ducked, then shielded the front of her face with her pocketbook, when Marvin, her aunt's boyfriend, shifted his three hundred and forty-three pound body on his couch, and hurled her diary across his living room at her. The lavender pages on the pink diary flapped in the air, until one of the spinning blades on the ceiling fan in his kitchen, clipped it, and sent it sky-diving down into his kitchen sink, that was full of sudsy-water and dirty dishes.

"Why-Marvin, why would you do that?!"

"What?! Bitch, you lucky that's all I did!"

While Brittany went scrambling through her aunt's boyfriend's kitchen, in her attempt to rescue her book of secrets, her aunt, with an evil expression on her face, rose from where she had been sitting at the kitchen table. Muttering words that were incoherent, Brittany's aunt raised the chair she had been sitting on up over her head, and went charging at Brittany's back. The things that Brittany had said about her in her diary had hurt her, and had even caused her to cry in her boyfriend's presence.

Brittany's aunt was a plus-sized woman. She outweighed Brittany by one hundred and twenty-two pounds. Due to this, when Brittany's aunt violently struck Brittany on the back of the head with the wooden stool, Brittany immediately lost consciousness, and melted down to the kitchen floor at her aunt's bare feet.

"Tanya, go in her pocketbook, and see if she got some money. I feel like goin' over Atlantic City, and doin' some gamblin'."

"This bitch stay with some fuckin' money."

"And get her car keys, too. I gotta stop I wanna make, before we get on the highway."

Brittany's existence had come at the cost of her mother's own. After ten and a half hours of labor, Brittany's mother had died on the delivery table, seconds after pushing Brittany out of her womb. Shortly after that, Brittany's father had gotten into a bloody scuffle with some of the hospital staff, which, then led to his swift arrest, after several packets of crack cocaine, a butterfly knife, and two crack pipes, had fallen out of a torn jacket pocket of his, while he had been in the process of cutting Brittany's umbilical cord. Following that chaotic incident, a host of Brittany's family members had shown up to the hospital. However, when the moment had come for someone from amongst them to step forward, and speak to the counselor from Child Services, to claim guardianship of Brittany, only an aunt, who was the younger sister of Brittany's father, had the moral decency to step up and accept the responsibility.

All of Brittany's childhood, and a majority of her teenage years, had been spent in West Philadelphia. She was raised on Chestnut, between the intersections of 63rd and 62nd. Over the past summer, Brittany and her aunt had moved across the city, to live with Brittany's aunt's boyfriend, who had recently inherited a funeral home from his deceased grandfather. The funeral home was located in North Philadelphia. It was on the corner of Franklin and Master, below two apartment units, that were also a part of the three-story, 98-year-old property. The funeral home was currently under foreclosure.

Brittany was twenty-two, gorgeous, and extremely goal-driven. She was passionate about her dream, which was to one day become a national, best-selling author, and she would share her ideas with anyone that was willing to listen to her. Minus the hair, because hers was much darker, and a lot longer, Brittany looked like she could be the younger sister of the CNN news anchor, Soledad O'Brien. Brittany's last boyfriend had gotten killed by an off-duty police officer, after the two men had exchanged stares inside of a West Philadelphia Chinese store. It was a tragedy that Brittany's heart was still trying to heal from.

At a few minutes shy of two in the morning, Brittany blinked her eyes open and let out an agonizing groan. She was surrounded by complete darkness. Aside from the painful fact that she had an excruciating headache, the back of her neck, and right shoulder, was feeling like they both had been the targets of a brick throwing contest. Pain was inspiring Brittany to remain as still as she possibly could. She was lying on her back. Just as her eyes were adapting to the darkness, Brittany closed them, and began to think about how she had ended up in the position she was in. As she slowly started to remember, teardrops began to trickle out of her closed eyelids. There, on her back, Brittany realized her path of mistakes. A car passing by outside gave her a reason to open her eyes again.

"Don't they know I'm the one bitch you don't cross?" Brittany thought, while struggling to bring herself to a sitting position. Her diary was inches away from her left hand, but the darkness prevented her from seeing it, or the other miscellaneous items from her pocketbook, which had all been dumped on the kitchen floor, in her aunt's haste to find her car keys and money. "Watch what happen to them two, fat motherfuckers now. Watch . . . watch."

After patting the kitchen floor a few times, Brittany found her cell phone. Tearfully, she called the one and only person, who she trusted with her life. That person's cell phone rung six times, before Brittany got an answer.

"Hello?"

"My dad up, Miss Olivia?"

"He right here sleep. Why? You okay? What's wrong?"

Up on her feet, and moving around, Brittany located a light switch on the kitchen wall, and flipped it up. The sudden flood of light caused her to squint, and immediately increased the intensity of her headache.

"Brittany?"

"Miss Olivia, can you wake him up, and give him the phone, please?"

"Okay, baby, hold on."

It was August 18th, 2012. The time on Brittany's cell phone read 2:11 a.m. Up above the dark city of Philadelphia, dozens of clouds were releasing a steady downpour of drenching rain. The rain had been falling non-stop, since earlier in the afternoon. In other parts of the United States, in places like Mississippi, rivers were gradually drying up, due to it being a lack of rainfall there. Out in the mid-west, there were several states suffering from it being a shortage of wet weather as well. It was because of this shortage of wet weather, and dry heat, that was causing a lot of their forest areas to experience wildfires, which, at the moment, were burning out of control.

"Doll baby, what's wrong?"

Brittany let out a sob at the sound of her father's voice. He was a super hero to her; a defender of her name and honor. Inside of her heart, his promises meant more than all of the money in the world.

"You okay?"

"Daddy, they jumped me. They hit me with a chair and knocked me out."

"What? Who?"

"Aunt Tanya and Marvin."

"Tanya and Marvin?"

"Yeah, Daddy. They . . . They was in my apartment, goin' through my stuff and everything. They was reading my diaries. When I got off work, Aunt Tanya called me, and she . . ."

"Hold on for a second, Doll baby. Let me get dressed."

"Okay."

Brittany and her father were as close as any parent and child could ever be. Brittany's father's sobriety had glued their hearts together, and had put them both on common ground. After promising Brittany, on her thirteenth birthday, that he would never smoke crack ever again, Brittany's father had stood true to his oath. He had even helped Brittany land her first job.

Brittany was employed at a famous nightclub, in the 'Old City' section of Philadelphia. Brittany's boss' name was Tianna Barnes, and she was one of the most ambitious women that Brittany had ever met. At work, Brittany's job description covered a wide range of responsibilities, which, at times, even required that she sometimes watch her boss'

15-month-old infant son. However, out of all of her duties at work, being her boss' eyes and ears, was really how Brittany earned her pay.

A lot went on at Gossip Alley. It was a nightclub that was always packed to its full capacity, and the home of some of the best parties ever thrown in Philadelphia. Weeknights were crazy, and the weekends were a lot crazier. On the weekends, at the stroke of every midnight, male and female, exotic dancers, became a part of Gossip Alley's night life experience. It was a tradition that had been started, since its grand opening night. Gossip Alley was owned by the husband of Brittany's boss. He was currently incarcerated at a Philadelphia county prison, fighting a murder charge. In his absence, his wife had been keeping his business alive, and thriving. Gossip Alley was so popular, people had to make arrangements to reserve space for their private parties, months in advance. Just recently, Brittany's boss had launched an adult calendar, featuring all of the exotic dancers, who were all on the payroll at the club. Over the 2012 summer alone, the adult calendar had grossed more than sixty-five thousand dollars. The bulk of those sales had come from Gossip Alley's business website.

"Doll baby, you still there?"

"Yeah, I'm still here."

"Where that gun I gave you for your birthday?"

Brittany walked out of her aunt's boyfriend's bedroom, and went back into the kitchen. Teardrops were still flowing down her face.

"It's in my closet," Brittany answered, after putting all of her things on the kitchen floor back inside of her pocketbook. Noticing that her car keys were missing, she walked over to a nearby window and took a look outside. "Daddy, they took my car. All my money gone, too. I had a little over two thousand dollars."

"They'll replace every dime. Doll baby, right now, I just want' chu to get that gun outta the closet. Use it, only if you have to, okay?"

"Okay."

Innocent.

Sinners.

"Daddy, hurry up."

"Doll baby, I'm on my way. Stop cryin'. Here, talk to Oliv-"

"Daddy, it's gone."

"What's gone?"

"The gun . . . it's not here. It's gone."

"Son of a bitch."

Brittany switched her cell phone to her other ear, as she wiped her face clean of her teardrops. She was beginning to have a bad feeling in the pit of her stomach. Once more, Brittany checked the right pocket of her white, mink vest, hanging in the back of her bedroom closet. Her gun was definitely missing. Brittany spun around and looked around at her bedroom. It was a complete mess. Her bedroom had been ransacked by her aunt, and her aunt's boyfriend. Her entire apartment looked like it had been turned upside down. Out in the living room, every thing was in disarray, as was the case in her kitchen, and bathroom.

"They here, Doll baby."

"Who?"

"Tanya and Marvin. They sittin' in ya car, parked behind mines. Olivia, go back in the house."

Brittany stood still when she heard a car door slam on the other end of her cell phone. She suddenly began to feel fearful for her father's safety.

"Daddy, go back in the house, too."

"I wish I would. She might be my sister, but-"

But . . .

The gun that Brittany had been looking for was in the left hand of Brittany's aunt's boyfriend, and being pointed at Brittany's father. The gun's chrome frame was wet from the rain falling from the night sky. The gun was a 9mm Smith & Wesson.

"Daddy, go back in the house with Miss Olivia."

Brittany's aunt's boyfriend had a cryptic plan, of how he was going to unbury his funeral home from the debt it was in, and rescue it from foreclosure to the bank. His goal was to bring Brittany's entire world crashing down to her feet, by revealing the stories in Brittany's diaries to her family members, friends, and co-workers, starting with some of Brittany's most personal, and juiciest secrets first. Marvin, Brittany's aunt's boyfriend, wanted to have as much leverage against Brittany as he possibly could get. Once he had Brittany backed into a corner, wanting no more, and having no one to turn to, or any place safe to go, he, with Brittany's aunt's help, was then going to force Brittany into starting a bloody drug war, with some of their neighborhood drug dealers, so that the deadly results of the drug war could help with revitalizing business at his funeral home.

While Marvin's plans were ugly, and methodical, and at least to him, well thought out, Marvin had the slightest idea that Brittany was on the other end of her father's cell phone, listening to what was going on.

"Daddy, please, go back in the house."

"Doll baby, this fat motherfucker gotta nerve to be walkin' up on me wit' the goddamn gun I gave-Ay, Marvin, so, you some gangsta now, nigga? You better watch where you aimin' that . . ."

Brittany flinched and dropped her cell phone when the sudden sound of gunshots exploded on her father's end of the cell phone. It was déjà vu all over again. The gunshots

8

had sounded like there was someone shooting inside of her bedroom, standing directly beside her; just like before.

Frantically, Brittany placed her cell phone back to her ear. The gunshots hadn't ended. They seemed endless.

"Daddy?!!"

Brittany's scream came from her gut. Once more, a loved one of hers was being shot on the opposite end of her cell phone, while she could do nothing but listen, with a feeling of complete helplessness, that was almost paralyzing. Crying hysterically, Brittany released her cell phone yet again, dropped down to her knees, and screamed, until there was no breath left in her lungs. Her only hope was that her father wouldn't meet the same fate as her boyfriend, because if so . . .

Who was going to save her soul now?

Chapter Two

Six days later . . .
Tuesday, 1:56 a.m.

Every so often, a thin patch of clouds would appear in front of the bright, full moon, then casually vanish away into the night. The clouds were being swept by warm winds, coming out of the northwest corner of Chestnut Hill, Pennsylvania. The sky was lit with stars, and as blue, and as beautiful, as the waters surrounding the coasts of St. Croix. Even while it was almost two hours past midnight, temperatures still hadn't dropped below the mid-70s,which made the weather nice enough for some people to still enjoy.

In the gigantic backyard, that belonged to Tianna Barnes, the light sound of crickets, was blending in with the soft hum of R&B music, joyful laughter, talking, and the occasional sounds of splashing water, that was coming from Tianna Barnes' large, in-ground swimming pool. The mood was a lot less jovial inside of Tianna Barnes' master bedroom.

"Brittany, that wasn't just some random misunderstanding," Tia explained, after taking a generous sip of her grape Moscato. As she returned her glass of wine back to her nightstand, she looked into her assistant's watery eyes sympathetically. "Brittany, Detective Konn was following your boyfriend that entire night. I know this, because the person I hired to kill his crooked ass was on the phone with me the entire time. I heard the gunshots and everything, Brittany. All nine of them. Mind you, this was months before you and I even met. Now, I could've still went ahead, and had Detective Konn killed, like right then and there while he was shootin' your boyfriend in that Chinese store, but I let my curiosity get the best of me that night. Brittany, I started thinkin'. I wanted to know who your boyfriend was. What was his beef with Detective Konn. His story. More importantly though, I wanted to make it my business to find out what he did to cross Detective Konn. And that's exactly what I did. Now, before I tell you what I found out, I want'chu to come with me. I wanna show you somethin'."

Tianna Barnes was twenty-seven, rich, beautiful, and insanely dangerous. Her 15-month-old son was her savior. If not for his existence, death would have been snatched her soul out of her body months ago. Her son's life was keeping her balanced. God had rewritten her destiny more than five times, but the deaths of loved ones, and the intimate betrayals of others, had blinded her from seeing all of the blessings she had to be thankful for. Tia only displayed softness around her son, and when she was in the company of her husband, when she visited him on Mondays, at a Philadelphia county prison. In the presence of her husband and son, Tia was able to let down her guard, and become who she so deeply, and honestly, truly wanted to be.

Herself.

Tia owned gray eyes that were angry on most days, and while she could easily get by as being Hispanic, or some other Latin ethnicity, Tia was actually just a mixture of some Italian, and black DNA. When they were seen together, a lot of people often thought that her assistant was her younger sister, because of their similarities in how they looked. Both of them stood 5'9" tall, had the same complexion, and was of equal beauty. Internally, however, Tia and her assistant were as opposite as the summer and winter. Few women could compare to Tianna Barnes. Some men didn't even have the heart that she had; or the ambition. Everyone out in her backyard admired her, and knew that she was the alpha-female.

"God, please don't make me regret doin' this," Tia thought, before turning on the lights in her walk-in closet. As her Pomeranian poodle, and her assistant, followed behind her closely, she chewed on her bottom lip with a sense of anxiety, that was soon followed by a feeling of ease, and much-needed comfortability. "Tia, all you have to do is keep trustin' your instincts. The only person that don't like her, is Rhonda. Splash gave her two thumbs up. Sooly love her. Snookums like her. Everybody at work do. So far, she ain't never disappoint you. And not only do she remind you of Camay, but you all she got. She look up to you. What if she turn out to be another Jen, though? Well, here goes nothin'."

Trust.

"Brittany, me and my husband used to kill people for a-Snookums, move."

With her left foot, Tia moved her small dog from in front of the all-glass door, that stood between her and her expensive shoe closet. Her walk-in closet had the length and width of an average-sized bedroom. Walking into it, there was a center path of soft, peach carpet, that came to an end at the rear wall, where there was a window, overlooking Tia's two-lane driveway. Tia's walk-in closet had been renovated into four private spaces. Each area had an all-glass door. There were two on the left of the carpeted aisle, and two on the right.

A feeling of pride and accomplishment swept through Tia's veins as she opened the door to her shoe closet, and walked into it. The cold surface of the hardwood floor chilled the soles of her bare feet, as Tia squatted to pick up her poodle.

"So, like I was sayin' . . . Brittany, step back. Me and my husband used to be professional killers, and we used to make a lot of money doin' what we did."

After pressing the panel beneath the glass shelf, displaying her various styles of Christian Louboutin shoes, and sneakers, Tia quickly took a step back, and stood shoulder to shoulder, beside her assistant. As Tia's wall of shoes slowly began to revolve, Tia's assistant's eyes grew wider and wider.

Brittany had been staying with her boss, since the night her father, and her father's live-in-girlfriend, were murdered. The death of her father had Brittany miserable with grief, and sick to her stomach with depression. All Brittany had motivating her now, was a single promise that her boss had made to her, as the two of them had been going into the Philadelphia police Headquarters, six nights earlier.

"Brittany, our lives are a lot alike," Tia spoke, while blinking back a few tears. All sorts of memories began to bombard her mind, as she returned her dog back down to the floor, and walked into her secret, customized-vault. "I've been where you are, more times than I can count. I know disappointment, like I know the back of my hand, Brittany. What I'm about to share with you, is nobody's business at the club. If it ever becomes someone else's business, I'm going to hold you responsible. Brittany, we clear?"

Brittany nodded her head.

"My mom was my dad's mistress. When she got pregnant with me, he bought her this house. He told her to start planning for their wedding. Problem was, he was already married. Brittany, my dad's wife didn't like the fact that, my, um, that my dad had filed for divorce, or that he was tryna start a new family. She stabbed him to death, while he was sleep. Then, her crazy ass swallowed a bottle of pain pills, got into bed with him, and died right beside him. Retarded, right? The story don't end there, though. It gets better."

"Tia, why you tellin' me this? Why you showin' me this room?"

"Because it's time that we take our trust in each other to another level, Brittany."

"Does this have anything to do with why you told me to lie to the cops, and not tell them who really killed my dad, and Miss Olivia?"

"Part of it does. Sit down."

Sometimes . . .

Revenge solves everything.

"I know what it feel like to get betrayed by an aunt, too, Brittany."

At seeing that her boss' gray eyes were filling up with tears, Brittany lowered her own watery eyes, and stared at the hardwood floors, surrounding her Prada sandals. Brittany didn't want to see her boss cry. However, she was deeply touched to see that her boss was allowing herself to become transparent in her presence, because her boss had never done so before. As Brittany continued to keep her eyes down on the floor, she was feeling entrusted with a piece of her boss' true self, that no one else at work would ever be privileged to witness.

"Way before she even crossed me, my aunt had crossed my mom and dad," Tia confided, while she used the palm of her left hand to catch the teardrops falling from her eyes. Speaking on the skeletons in her family was always an emotional, and psychological hurdle, for her. "Her and my dad's wife didn't like each other, and from what I've been told, that's puttin' it nicely. Out of spite, my aunt had hooked my dad up with my mom, who was my aunt's best friend. The whole time, though, my dad was already creepin' with one of my aunt's other friends, and my aunt, or my mom, didn't have a clue about it. That's how me and my brother, Malcolm, is related. So, um, yeah, so anyway, my dad and my mom started messin' around, and when she had me, to throw it in my dad's wife's face, my aunt sent her all these pictures of my dad, my mom, and me, when I was first born."

"So, that's why ya dad wife stabbed him up?"

"Yup."

"I guess everybody was mad at'cha aunt, after that, huh?"

"Nobody knew she was the one who sent the pictures, Brittany."

"Not even your mom?"

"Not even my mom," Tia echoed, staring blankly at the cabinet of machine guns, against the wall, behind her assistant. Unconsciously, she touched the gold locket on her necklace that held a tiny picture of her father. "Would you believe, they had the nerve to bury my dad beside his wife? Brittany, they didn't even let my mom go to the fuckin' funeral. How does that make sense? Bury him beside the woman who put him in his grave, but deny the woman that he wanted to marry, and be with."

"Yeah, that don't make sense. Not to me, at least."

"My dad side of the family didn't accept me. Just my aunt."

"The one that sent the pictures?"

"Her . . . my mom died, thinkin' my aunt was her best friend, when the whole time, she really was just her frenemy."

"How ya mom die, Tia?"

"She was in one of the World Trade Centers on nine-eleven, havin' a business meetin'."

"Can I ask you somethin' else?"

"Brittany, when we walk outta here, I want our trust to be beyond where it's at now, like I said earlier. So, how about we do this. You can ask me five questions. I'll answer them all honestly, no matter if I like them or not."

"So, I can ask you anything I want, and you not gon' get mad at me?"

"Brittany, I can promise you honesty. I can't guarantee that I won't get mad at what you ask me."

"Can you guarantee that I won't lose my job?"

"Your job is safe, Brittany."

For a long moment, Brittany looked tentatively at her boss, considering what she wanted to ask her boss first. There were so many things about her boss that she wanted to know. The woman was intriguing. At work, there were whispered-rumors going around that her boss' husband was in jail for killing an aunt of hers, two of her best friends, and several other people. Feeling a little indecisive, Brittany used a few seconds to look around her boss' hidden room, while her mind slowly began to prioritize her five questions.

As Brittany thought, and quietly looked around at the tall, money safes, and all of the machine gun racks, and large, footlockers, Tia was casually sitting in her chair, using her left foot to play with her poodle. When a ball of dust moved over in the corner, near a small pile of her bulletproof vests, Tia was reminded of the last time she had done some cleaning in her secret room. There were so many responsibilities, demanding her attention, and pulling her in different directions, that she rarely ever had any time to think, much less relax. Tia never had time for herself. Her infant son was spoiled rotten, which was solely her fault. From the moment he opened his gray eyes, until he closed them, and went to sleep, he ran her wild. Life as a mother was taxing, but life as a wife, to an incarcerated man, made all of Tia's days uphill battles.

"Okay, I have my first question. Why that cop killed Sean?"

"To prove a point."

"To who?"

"Several people, actually. Brittany, did your boyfriend ever tell you how his mom ended up in that wheelchair?"

"He was little when that happened," Brittany recalled, remembering what her boyfriend had told her. While she knew what she had been told, she sensed that her boss was about to reveal a different version to the story she was aware of. "His dad started shootin' when the cops was doin' a drug raid on they house, and his mom got caught in the middle of the shootout, right? That's not what happened? His dad, and one of the cops died, and Mrs. Maxine got paralyzed. Sean said he was next door at a neighbor house, Tia."

"Well, maybe his mom never told him the truth. She could've been tryna protect him, I guess."

Brittany's eyes became watery.

"That was Detective Konn and his partner, Brittany. That wasn't a drug raid. That was Detective Konn."

Brittany's tears became rain.

"Your boyfriend dad got double-crossed by Detective Konn,"Tia quietly explained, saddened at the sight of her assistant crying. In a couple of hours they both would be attending her assistant's father's funeral, and she couldn't help but to feel a little concerned with how her assistant was going to deal with coming face to face with her aunt, and her aunt's boyfriend. "They had a deal, that your boyfriend dad was supposed to kill Detective Konn's partner, in exchange for fifty thousand dollars. Your boyfriend mom knew the whole scoop. She the one that opened the door, and let them in. It was never a drug raid,

Brittany. Detective Konn and his partner wasn't even on duty. Now, only ya boyfriend mom know what really went wrong in that house that day, but as soon as ya boyfriend dad shot Detective Konn partner in the face, Detective Konn remixed they whole agreement, and flipped out. He killed ya boyfriend dad, then he shot ya boyfriend mom, when she tried to jump outta the second floor window."

"And she been keepin' this to herself all this time? Why didn't she tell?"

"Brittany, your guess is as good as mine. You know the lady better than I do. I only seen pictures of her. Brittany, this is what I do know . . . she tried to blackmail Detective Konn for some money, that I assume she feel like is still owed to her. Detective Konn killed her son to make a point. She know that wasn't some chance encounter in that fuckin' Chinese store. Trust me, as soon as she found out the name of the cop that shot her son, she knew exactly what the fuck was goin' on, and what it was about."

Tia stopped talking to let out a yawn.

"My other questions can wait,'til tomorrow, Tia. I'm tired, too."

"Okay, but I wanna make some sense of a few things for you," Tia said, yawning again, and stretching her arms up over her head. She felt exhausted. "My husband in jail, because of Detective Konn. Detective Konn put a body on my husband that I did. I have another brother, and him and Detective Konn are in cahoots together, some kind of way. It's a lot to that story. I'll let you know about all of that tomorrow. More importantly, though, Detective Konn will be dead by Halloween. We're going to get him to come to the club for our Halloween party."

"Are you serious?"

Tia nodded her head, smiling devilishly.

"You gon' kill him at the club?"

"Yup . . . while the party goin' on, and everything. Honey gonna help us get him there."

"Honey?"

"She owes me a huge favor, Brittany."

"She owes everybody, from what I hear."

"True, but here's where things get complicated. I'm gon' need you to move back with your aunt, and her boyfriend, tomorrow."

"What? Why?"

The confusion in Brittany's eyes, and the sudden disappointment that came out with her questions, sliced and diced Tia's heart into quarters.

"Brittany, it's the only way I can fulfill my promise to you."

"But-But I don't understand," Brittany cried, feeling betrayed by the only person she had left to count on. Hurt had her heart in its hands. "How can you-Tia, don't make me go back there. Not there. Anywhere, but there, Tia. Anywhere, but there. You know what they did. They killed-Tia, they murdered my dad and they got away with it. Tia, I didn't tell them cops what I knew, or said anything, 'cause you told me not to."

"Look at this, Brittany."

On the rear, exposed-brick wall, hanging in between a machine gun cabinet, and a cabinet stocked with countless handguns, there was a 22 inch, flat-screen TV. When Tia thumbed the screen of her iPhone, the flat-screen TV lit up, and came to life. For a moment, the flat-screen just showed a blue screen, but in a matter of seconds, it then produced four, split-screen images.

Wiping the tears from her eyes, Brittany stood up, as the familiar images on the flat-screen TV began to slowly register in her head.

"I had cameras put in there the other day, while they was out," Tia spoke, touching the screen of her cell phone, once more. Doing this, gave the flat-screen TV an audio sound. "I got this app from the security company, that'll let'chu bring up those surveillance cameras, on any TV that'chu near. We gon' download the app to your cell phone tomorrow. Brittany, I gave you my word, and I'm goin' to stand by it. Won't nobody ever get away with hurtin' you, Brittany. I hold grudges for life. Your issues are mine."

Brittany stepped closer to the flat-screen TV with watery eyes that were amazed at what they were seeing. Right there, on the bottom, left corner, of her boss' flat-screen TV, was Marvin, and her aunt, spooning in bed. They were asleep, and snoring like bears.

"We gon' make them pay for what they did to you, Brittany. That wasn't some empty promise I gave you."

Brittany let out a sigh as she looked at her boss. There was conviction in her boss' sentiments.

"Brittany, Marvin gran'father used to be a big trick. He was strung out on heroin, too. That's how his funeral home got into so much debt. He was borrowin' money from any, and everybody. So, anyway, a while back, Detective Konn came to him with this crazy scheme. You see that room right there?"

Brittany cut her eyes to the top, right corner of the flat-screen TV, where her boss was pointing her finger. Brittany squinted her eyes at what appeared to be some sort of operating room.

"You seen that room in the funeral home before?"

"No."

"It's in there."

"I never been inside of the funeral home. Marvin keep it locked anyway. Since we been stayin' there, I only saw him go in there like once."

"Brittany, Detective Konn, and Marvin gran'father, got this Jamaican guy to get in on they scheme," Tia revealed, suddenly feeling a little unnerved at the creepy story she was narrating. A week earlier, she had experienced a nightmare, because of what she knew. "The Jamaican guy was they bootleg mortician. He used to be in that room, stealin' bones out of dead people, Brittany. He was a fuckin' monster. He was replacin' they bones with rusty pipes, and shit, like,fuckin' mop sticks, and crow bars, and . . . whatever he felt like puttin' inside of people, Brittany. And they families never even knew. They still don't, Brittany. Just think about it. Who examine they family members, after they go to the funeral home? We trust them people to cut they hair. Do the makeup. Dress them. All we do is look down on them in a coffin, and that's about it. Brittany, they was even stealin' dead people skin."

Crying for people she didn't even know, Brittany turned and looked at her boss, with eyes that were wide with shock, and disbelief. She was horrified at what she was being told.

"They was sellin' dead people skin to burn victim centers, in places like Brazil, and third world countries."

"Oh, my God. Tia, that's so wrong."

"Blame Detective Konn. It was all his doin.' He master minded the whole operation, Brittany. When people wanted to have they family members cremated, they would give them urns filled with kitty litter, and cement mix."

"I wanna check my dad body tomorrow."

"I would, too."

Brittany shook her head sadly.

Yawning, Tia squatted down and picked up her poodle. This got her a few licks to the face.

"Brittany, I gotta private investigator all over Detective Konn. That's how I know all the shit that I know. I been doin' my homework on him for the past two years. That's how I know all about what happened to ya boyfriend mom.

Brittany, that's the real reason why I hired you, and made you my assistant."

"So, it ain't have nothin' to do with my dad, and ya uncle bein' friends in high school?"

"Brittany, that was just fate smilin' at us. That's how I saw it. I been wantin' to talk to you about all of this for months, but trust is a major, major issue for me. Then, all of this happened. It was just about Detective Konn in the beginning. Now, with what Marvin did to your father, he put himself in the line of fire as well."

"It's like it all just came full circle."

"Karma."

Brittany let out a long sigh.

"Brittany, Marvin called Detective Konn yesterday."

"How you know?"

Tia nodded her head at her flat-screen TV.

"Oh, yeah."

"He tryna start business up at that funeral home again, Brittany."

"How?"

"The same way his gran'father did. His plan is to use you to start up a drug war in that neighborhood, so when they start dyin', they peoples can bring they dead bodies to him. He even thinkin' about tryna get muslims to come there, so they can be doin' they Janazah services there."

"But I thought muslims wash they bodies, and-"

"Oh, he don't plan on doin' nothin' wrong with any muslim people, he just tryna bring in money any way that he can. His ass not stupid. I'm just wonderin' how he can do all that other shit in there, without it lookin' suspect."

"What other shit?"

"Brittany, he asked Detective Konn to find that Jamaican mortician, and to set everything up, like his gran'father was doin' before."

Brittany shivered as she placed her eyes back on Marvin's giant, sleeping body. Her aunt's boyfriend was more sadistic, than she had even imagined. She had underestimated his temperament. However, as Brittany stood beside her boss, and continued to stare at Marvin as he slept, she felt no fear. What Marvin had done to her father, and to her father's girlfriend, had her compulsively wanting redemption.

"From what I heard, Detective Konn is all for goin' into business with Marvin. Ya aunt not. After Marvin left out, she did a lot of cryin', Brittany."

"Fuck her . . . she might as well go along with what he tryna do. It ain't no use in not likin' shit now. You can watch him kill ya brother, but'chu got morals about what's gon' be done to people you don't know? Fuck her. I want her to get the same thing he got comin'."

"Okay, so, Marvin told Detective Konn all about'chu, Brittany. He told him he was gon' approach you, after ya dad funeral tomorrow. So, you just gotta go along with whatever he say . . . not so easily, though. Act like you unwilling at first, but—"

"I got this, Tia."

"Brittany, this our opportunity to kill three birds with one stone. We can get revenge for so many people by doin' this. You just have to be on the inside, for this to work, though."

"Fine by me."

"You sure, Brittany?"

"They killed my dad, Tia. That fuckin' cop killed Sean. I never felt so fuckin' sure about anything in my entire fuckin' life."

"Brittany, this won't be no cake walk."

"Gettin' revenge never is."

Chapter Three

Bloody.
Beginnings.

It was early in the afternoon when the black, GMC Yukon, and the maroon, Range Rover,pulled across the entrance of the Southwest Philadelphia cemetery. After a little driving, and the making of some right, and left turns, both of the SUVs pulled over and parked opposite one another, on the cemetery's wide, cobblestoned path. Oddly enough, the September weather was beautiful, and still displaying subtle signs of the summer. Temperatures were in the mid-70s,and expected to gradually increase as the day went on.

The Southwest Philadelphia cemetery was currently the resting place for the older sister of Kyzer Rogers, a young man, who had just been released from a Pennsylvania state prison a day earlier. Kyzer was sitting in the passenger seat of the GMC Yukon. Kyzer's mother was behind the steering wheel of the Range Rover.

"Drees, what the fuck was he doin' up Frankford, anyway?"

"Kyzer, everybody been tryna figure that shit out for the past two years. I'm still losin' sleep over that shit. I miss the shit outta Saan."

Lies.

"And who the fuck is this young girl, Rock 'n Roll Rhonda, I keep fuckin' hearin' about?"

"Nobody."

More.

Lies.

"Drees, man,I don't know who the fuck you think you talkin' to, but'chu can save that arrogant bullshit for somebody else. Nigga, this me you talkin' to. Who is she?"

"Kyzer, she only like nineteen, or twenty. She ain't nobody."

"Fuck her age mean? It's little mu'fuckers out here in fifth grade that's runnin' around bodyin' shit."

"Naw, don't get it fucked up. I ain't tryna say she ain't out here catchin' a little wreck. She just not on ya level,though."

"Alright, so since you sayin' that . . . let me ask you this then. Was that her and Maniac that rocked Saan?"

"Fuck no. We would've been heard some shit like that, if that was them. Kyzer, Maniac crazy, but that nigga ain't that throwed off."

"This nigga gon' take that secret to his grave,"Kyzer realized, staring directly into his cousin's eyes. His cousin's betrayal was sickening him, and had a cold spot forming in a corner of his heart, where his evil intentions for his other enemies resided. "You was there, Drees. I know you was. You set Saan up, and some kind of way, you helped Maniac get Marshall and Jefferson back. Neef told me you be speakin' to them niggaz and all 'lat. Yeah, shit gon' come to light. It always do. When it do though, I'm gon' rock you personally, Drees. Think niggaz ain't been keepin' tabs on ya moves, huh? I'm all-"

"Ay, yo, not to get off the subject or nothin' like that, but'chu remember ol' head, Marv, right?"

"From the funeral home?"

"Yeah."

"What about him?"

"His gran' pop left him that jawn. He came at me a few weeks ago about lettin' us have access to it, if one of our folks check, and we need somewhere to wash they body, and do they janazah. I ain't give him no answer, 'cause I wanted to run it by you first, since I knew you was about to touch."

"That nigga tryna capitalize off of death, huh? His fat ass still owe me from when I stopped Skinny Lou from stabbin' his dumb ass."

"Just give it some thought, though. Knowin' you, once he see you home, he'll give you the keys to that shit."

Kyzer began to think as his cousin pulled out his cell phone and made a phone call, which lasted just a few minutes.

"Ay, you know Aunt Trina worried about what'chu gon' do, now that'chu home, right?"

Dragged out of his thoughts, Kyzer exhaled an unsettled sigh, as he shifted in his seat. Where he was, and why he was there, gradually brought him back to focusing on another painful reality; his older sister's death.

"She just concerned, Kyzer."

"I know," Kyzer acknowledged, staring through the tinted windshield of his cousin's truck. His heart started to tremble in his chest, as he forced himself to cast a sideways glance at his mother's Range Rover. "We talked last night. For a real long time, too. Felt like one of the best conversations me and her ever had. We both got to air out our differences. And what's crazy is, we did that shit wit'out even arguin'. That shit would've made Cam proud of us. Drees, my mom whole thing is, like, and this shit between me and you . . . like, she agree wit' me that, what Sabia did to Cam was some nut ass shit, and all'lat, but'chu know how my mom is, Drees. She on some shit, like, we should just let the cops do they job, and let shit play out like that. Just play the sidelines. Don't get involved or nothin'."

"And let me guess . . . that's where you and her disagree?"

"You know me well enough to know that ain't the page I'm on. Drees, I got my own fuckin' justice league. It ain't a fuckin' cop, or a judge alive, who can give my fuckin' sister the revenge, or the justice she deserve. You seriously think I want Sabia to go to fuckin' jail for what he did to Cam? Nigga, I'll never be in a courtroom, and root for the prosecution. The way I'm bombin' on mu'fuckers, I ain't gotta worry about, if a nigga gon' spank his case. Once I'm on a nigga top, he guilty, and his soul flyin', as soon as I lay my fuckin' eyes on him."

"Kyzer, Philly hot as shit right now."

"Good."

"I'm serious, Kyzer."

"Man, do I look like I give a fuck about how hot it is? When that shit ever mattered to me, Drees? I shot mu'fuckers, while the cops was right around the fuckin' corner. Nigga, my sister over there in her fuckin' grave, and you tryna talk to me about how hot Philly is. Nigga, so what! The cops can get everything they lookin' for, fuckin' wit' me! Everything, Drees!"

Kyzer was younger than his cousin, Idris, by six years. The two of them both came from a close-knit family. Their mothers were sisters.

"Kyzer, shit ain't how it was five years ago. I know you was watchin' the news while you was down all that time. You had to be. Yo, a whole lot of shit changed out here, Kyzer. A lot of shit. These mu'fuckers got cameras everywhere now. All up and down Broad Street. On Girard Avenue. Up Lehigh. On fuckin' Alleghany. Kyzer, as soon as them jawns hear the sound of gunshots, the fuckin' cameras zoom right the fuck in to where they comin' from.

Then, the mayor started up this nut ass, rat program, where, now, mu'fuckers that's out here rattin,' can jump on they cell phones, and just anonymously send fuckin' text messages to the cops. This shit deep out here, Kyzer. That's all I'm tryna tell you. Yo, just for tips, they cuttin' these rat ass niggaz husky ass checks."

"Yeah, well, like I said, fuck the cops. The mayor, too. That nigga keep shuttin' down all the rec centers, like he want the little kids to be in the streets anyway. They gon' need more than some fuckin' cameras, and some nut ass text-messages to put fear in Trina son. Let me guess, that's the reason why you let Maniac and them 10th and Thompson niggaz, get Marshall and Jefferson back, huh? Drees, you family and all 'lat, but I know bitches that got more heart than you. That little bitch, Rock 'n Roll Rhonda, definitely do."

With those parting words, Kyzer angrily hopped out of his cousin's SUV, and slammed the passenger door behind him, without looking back. Being in his cousin's company had caused a lot of emotions in his chest to catch fire. As his cousin's GMC Yukon pulled off, Kyzer tried to calm himself down by taking some slow breaths, but this didn't work. Knowing that his face was reflecting what he was feeling in his chest, Kyzer pulled the hood to his black, zip-up, Loden Dager jacket, over his head, and started walking over to his mother's Range Rover. To keep his mother from seeing the tears that were beginning to stream down his face, Kyzer lowered his eyes down to the cobble stones beneath his black, Aston Martin sneakers. The closer he got to his mother's truck, the hotter the emotions in his chest became.

Kyzer was twenty-four, and notoriously known for being a person that had a toxic temper. Kyzer didn't look like a threat, or carried himself like one, but he was the kind of young man that could turn a peaceful atmosphere into a full-blown riot, at the drop of a dime. His passion sometimes overruled his heart, and his intellect. Kyzer was highly intelligent, and even while he shared his mother's last name, and like her, had a talent for writing music, and had a love for traveling, everything else about Kyzer, from his strikingly, handsome face, to his golden brown complexion, and the confident way that he walked, and talked, all mirrored his Panamanian father, who was currently serving three life sentences, in a Mexican prison.

Two years earlier, Kyzer's older sister was murdered by a family friend. That family friend was once a very close friend of Kyzer's. Several other people had also gotten killed at Kyzer's sister's house that day, including Kyzer's sister's boyfriend, a male cousin of hers, one of her best friends, and some other people, who were unknown to her or Kyzer's family. The small massacre had made local, and national news; in total, eight people had died in, or near Kyzer's sister's home.

At the time of this tragic loss, Kyzer had been confined to a Pennsylvania state prison, serving a 26 to 53 year sentence, for a Southwest Philadelphia kidnapping, that he actually had been innocent of. However, because of his violent history, his own mother had believed that he was guilty; so did twelve jurors. Camay, Kyzer's older sister, was the only person who had believed in Kyzer's innocence. Months before her untimely death, Kyzer's sister had hired one of the best appeal attorneys in the state of Pennsylvania, who went ahead, and had taken a closer look at Kyzer's case. After the unearthing of some vital, newly-discovered evidence, it had taken Kyzer's appeal attorney just one year, to get Kyzer an evidentiary hearing, exonerated of all charges, and subsequently released from prison.

"Tia just called. She five minutes away."

Kyzer kept silent for a moment as he pulled the passenger door to his mother's SUV shut, and removed his hood from his head. Still crying, Kyzer followed the rear of his cousin's truck with watery eyes, until it disappeared out of sight.

"Drees happy you home?"

"Yeah."

"Why don't 'chu look like you was happy to see him. Those don't look like happy tears to me."

After letting out a heavy sigh, with the help of his mother, Kyzer wiped his face clean of his tears. It was a bonding moment that both of their hearts needed.

"So, you leavin' your hair like this, or you gettin' it cut?"

"Leavin' it like this,"Kyzer answered, instantly reminded of his days as a child, as his mother inspected some of the long, individual braids, hanging from the left side of his head. His mother's show of affection brung fresh tears to his eyes. "When Camay used to come see me, she used to always tell me that my hair reminded her of when you used to have my hair like this when I was little. I'ma just keep it like this, and get shape ups whenever I need one. Plus, I don't want everybody recognizin' me right away, anyway."

"I think they look nice. You look like your dad."

"Mom, I did a lot of self-inspection when I was locked up," Kyzer shared, remembering all of the nights he had spent in his jail cell, sleepless, searching his heart for the personal flaws, that he felt kept sabotaging his own success. He was proud to know that he was no longer the man he once was. "I'm different in a lot of ways now. It might not seem that way to you right now, but I am. You ain't gotta worry about me standin' on a corner ever again, Mom. I wanna office somewhere. Like, I'm tryna travel to Paris. Mecca. All over. Mom, I wanna breathe air in Dubai. I wanna get married, and settle down, and all 'lat. I'm just-

Mom, it's just that, like a lot of that stuff gotta get put on the back burner, and gotta wait, 'cause I ain't gon' never be able to enjoy nothin' I do, until I find Sabia, and make him pay for what he did to Cam. I can't do nothin' until then, Mom. I can't. Mom, I'm home 'cause of Camay. I owe her."

Shaking her head sadly, Kyzer's mother looked away from him. Her eyes swept over to the area of the cemetery, where her first child was buried; her daughter. The child of hers, who saw good in everybody.

"Mom,at least I'm bein' honest wit'chu."

"Kyzer, your honesty feel like breast cancer."

"Don't say that, Mom. Why you gotta say somethin' like that?"

"That was my honesty. Here come Tia."

Kyzer followed his mother's gaze through her rear passenger window, and rested his eyes on the approaching, slow-moving, silver Jaguar XJ. The windows on the luxury vehicle were masked with a dark tint, causing them to be impossible to see through.

"Okay, well, give me a hug and a kiss before you go."

"Mom, why you gotta sound all sad like that?"

"Sadness is all I'm feelin' right now, Kyzer. Come here."

"Mom, I'm gon' replace all 'lat sadness wit' a lotta happiness, watch,"Kyzer promised, while giving his mother a warm hug. He felt terrible for him bringing more sorrow to his mother's all-ready, aching heart. "Mom, I'm not gon' be out here, wearin' my war paint everyday."

Kyzer's mother interrupted her and Kyzer's hug, and grabbed Kyzer's face by the chin, forcing him to meet her stare. His words had been devastating her spirit. Kyzer's eyes were glossy with tears, just like hers. Both of them were still mourning the loss of Kyzer's sister. There was a contrast to how the two of them were grieving.

Kyzer's mother wanted peace.

Kyzer wanted war.

Camay, Kyzer's older sister had been shot eleven times; seven of those bullets had struck her beautiful face, and had mutilated it.

"Kyzer, Sabia is long gone. It's been two years, and there's no telling, if he's even still in the United States, for that matter. He could be anywhere with all that money he has. Now, like I said last night, don't for one second think that I don't want justice for your sister, but Kyzer, I want'chu . . . to . . ."

Still holding Kyzer's face, with her free hand, Kyzer's mother wiped away some of her falling teardrops from her face, then sighed, before finishing what she had to say.

". . . listen to me, okay. I don't have the strength, and I damn sure don't have the heart, or anything else left in me, to step inside of another damn morgue, and identify another one of my babies. You hear me, Kyzer? I don't have it in me. You didn't see how Sabia did your sister. I did. If it wasn't for Tia talkin' me out of it, I would've left Camay's coffin open, just so everybody could've seen how evil Sabia was. Kyzer, Camay loved you more than any sister could ever love her little brother. It shows how much she had you on her mind when she sat down with that lawyer, and had him draw up that will for her. Kyzer, she left you everything she owned. You got her big house, and over a hundred thousand dollars in the bank, to do whatever it is you want. Why jeopardize your freedom, and all of that, for an opportunity at revenge, that you may, or may not get?"

Kyzer had no answer for his mother as she released his face and looked into his eyes. There was nothing that could be done about his mood for vengeance. Kyzer's mother was well aware of this. Violence was in Kyzer's veins. It was hereditary.

"Why is it so hard for you to honor your sister's memory, by doing something constructive with yourself?

Kyzer, show me how different you are, by making different choices. That's what'll remove my sadness. Give me something that I can honestly be proud of. Go over to your sister's grave with me."

"Mom, I already told you, I'm not goin' over there, until I find Sabia."

"Ain't nothin' changed about you, but the length of your hair, Kyzer. Lie to someone else about being a changed man. I'm your mother. I know better."

Kyzer climbed out of his mother's truck with his heart feeling like a two ton anchor in his chest. He wanted his mother to understand what was motivating him to feel the way that he felt, but it seemed impossible. His emotions were ablaze again. While the warpath that he was about to travel down was unknown to him, and, in fact, could possibly be the one path that expedited him to meet his own demise, Kyzer's only true concern was that he completed his sister's revenge. It meant more to him than his freedom.

"Hey."

"What's up, Tia?"

After pulling the passenger door to the Jaguar closed, Kyzer regarded his older sister's best friend, Tia, with a smile, then he turned and showed the same smiling face to the pretty, young woman, and the sleeping baby, who were sitting behind him in the backseat. The sight of the infant boy asleep in his Yves Saint Laurent, upholstered-carseat, started pulling on every heartstring in Kyzer's chest. For a second, Kyzer even wished that the adorable little boy was his own.

"Kyzer, that's my assistant, Brittany... Brittany, that's Kyzer, who I've been tellin' you about. And that's my son, Sooly, Kyzer. We tried keepin' him awake for you, but he fell asleep as soon as we got off the expressway."

"Yo, he look just like you. He got'cha eyes, too?"

33

"Yup . . . Kyzer, I brung you some stuff. Brittany, can you hand him that bag that's back there on the floor, please?"

Kyzer had an eye for beautiful women, and he definitely knew when he was in the company of one. Brittany's beauty not only had Kyzer impressed, but he was intrigued to a point where it had him feeling distracted. As Kyzer was accepting the white, Ralph Lauren duffel bag from Brittany's hands, he fought himself to appear casual as he met her stare. In Brittany's eyes, Kyzer spotted a similar struggle, which he sometimes saw when he stared into the eyes of his reflection in the mirror.

I'll.

Cry.

Tomorrow.

"Those two keys in there are from Splash. That ain't coke. It's heroin."

Kyzer placed the mid-sized, leather, duffel bag across his lap, and unzipped it, to get a good look at its contents. When Kyzer saw what was actually inside of the duffel bag, his heartbeat sped up.

"He told me to give you them two hand grenades, too. The money and them guns from me."

"How much money is this ?"

"Fifty thousand. You can spend it on your car."

Mildly impressed, and far from feeling any true satisfaction, Kyzer examined one of the thick stacks of money, then dropped it back down into the duffel bag.

"Kyzer, that's not me, or Splash's way of making what happened to Cam seem okay."

"It fuckin' better not be."

"Don't come at me like that, Kyzer."

"Or what?" Kyzer asked, quickly becoming angry, as he removed the duffel bag from his lap, and placed it down between his feet. As he turned to face his sister's friend, for the sake of her sleeping child, he purposely kept his voice low, and his temper in check. "Or what, Tia? You act like I'm the one that did something wrong. Like, if you and Splash wanna really show me how sorry y'all is about what happened to Cam, gimme a fuckin' bag wit' Sabia fuckin' head in it. Tell Splash that. Until then, ain't shit y'all do ever gon' satisfy me, Tia. For you to even say y'all ain't givin' me this shit, because of what happened to Cam, make me automatically think y'all is. That could've went unsaid, on some real shit."

"Brittany, can you give me and Kyzer a few minutes alone, please?"

"Okay . . . I'ma walk over to my dad's grave."

"Thanks, Brittany."

Once the two of them were alone, Kyzer and his sister's best friend shared a brief moment of silence, before they resumed their conversation.

"Tia, you promised me Sabia would be dead before I came home. You made that promise to me two fuckin' years ago."

"Kyzer, I don't need you remindin' me of the promise that I made, or tellin' me how long ago I made it. I want Sabia dead just as much as you do, if not more."

"Yeah, well, why his mom ain't fuckin' dead yet, then?"

"His mom? What his mom got to do with what he did?"

"She gave birth to that nigga, Tia," Kyzer argued, glaring into the gray eyes of his sister's best friend. He didn't like that her animosity for his sister's killer didn't measure up to his. "Tia, you and I both fuckin' know, if somebody knocked on Sabia's mom door, and blew her fuckin' top off, that shit would have Sabia sick, wherever the fuck he at. You know it. That's the kind of shit you gotta do, once a nigga wanna go into hidin', when it's war time. Shit like that'll bring a nigga from under that rock. You gon' have to choose sides sooner or later, Tia. And I'ma tell you somethin' else . . . ya loyalty to my fuckin' sister shouldn't've died when she did. That's what my mom don't understand. What kind of loyalty is that?"

Taking Kyzer totally by surprise, his sister's best friend slouched over her steering wheel, and started an episode of crying that right away brought a boat-load of guilt to Kyzer's chest. Regretful, Kyzer lowered his head in shame. Then, as if what his mother was feeling, was also being felt by him as well, the sleeping child in the backseat, popped his gray eyes open, and started screaming at the top of his little lungs. The harder his mother cried, the harder he did. It was an astonishing moment for Kyzer. Not able to consciously ignore what was going on, Kyzer did the first thing his heart had inspired him to do.

Nine minutes later, the dynamics of the atmosphere in the Jaguar had altered so dramatically, and in such an unexpected fashion, Kyzer was feeling the overwhelming need to step out of the car, so that he could give his emotions time to regroup themselves. In his lap, Kyzer now had a smiling little boy, who was bouncing up and down, and across from him, in the driver's seat of the Jaguar, now was sitting Brittany, and not his sister's best friend. Kyzer's mother had called his sister's best friend's cell phone, and had asked her to come join her at Kyzer's sister's burial site in the middle of her crying episode.

"We come here everyday."

"For real?"

"Since I been her assistant, we have."

"How long you been her . . ."

When the sudden eruption of loud gunshots started, the safety of the child in his arms was the first thing that Kyzer concerned himself with.

"Stay inside the car, and stay down!" Kyzer ordered, while protectively handing over his sister's best friend's son, to her assistant. His heart was flipping, and flopping with the sound of every gunshot that his ears heard. "If the shootin' stop, get the fuck outta here, before the cops get here! And don't drive too crazy, 'cause that bag got a lot of shit in there, alright?!"

Kyzer and Brittany shared a moment, while brief, it was the act of fate, pushing their lives into a joint venture, that would soon lead to a path of unequivocal madness. In their eye contact, which lasted no longer than a hot second, a silent oath had come into fruition.

Out of the Jaguar, Kyzer moved instinctively, and solely off of his impulses. He took off running at top speed, in the direction of where he knew his mother, and his sister's best friend were. The gunshots were echoing around the entire cemetery, making it impossible for Kyzer to determine where the shooting was actually taking place. More than anything, Kyzer just wanted his loved ones to go unharmed. His knowledge of guns was telling him that four different guns were being used; Three high caliber handguns, and an assault rifle. Almost twenty-seven feet away from the Jaguar, and his mother's Range Rover, three things occurred, causing Kyzer to pause in his tracks for just a moment. He had forgotten to remove a gun from the duffel bag his sister's best friend had given him. While this realization had stalled Kyzer, all of the shooting had suddenly ceased, and in its place, was now the sound of police sirens. On the move again, Kyzer silently prayed for his mother's well being.

After hurdling some erected tombstones, and weaving in and out of the rows of several others, Kyzer ran up a grassy embankment, and came to a stop. Kyzer's brown eyes instantly became cloudy with tears. He had stopped, because waves of shock had begun to crash into his soul, as his eyes slowly began to take in the heart-wrenching scene before him. Had it not been for his peripheral vision, Kyzer would have never been able to memorize the colors, or the models of the two vehicles that were racing wildly for the cemetery's exit.

Skeletons.

There wasn't a surgery team on the face of the earth capable of saving the lives of Kyzer's mother, or his sister's best friend. What had been done to them was more uncalled for, than it was unnecessary. Atrocious was what it was. The two women had never seen their attackers coming from behind, as they cried, while cleaning the area surrounding Kyzer's sister's tombstone. Both women died, crying for the dead.

The cops got to the Southwest Philadelphia cemetery, while Kyzer was crying, and begging his mother, and his sister's best friend to stay alive as he frantically tried to give them both CPR at the same time. Over the gigantic cemetery, a hovering news station's helicopter was feeding the live footage to its news station, for all to see. In the days, and the weeks to come, the streets of Philadelphia was going to learn something extremely important about Kyzer Rogers. That something was going to leave a lot of people impressed for decades.

When killers cry . . .

killers multiply.

Chapter Four

Philadelphia Police Headquarters
8th and Race/Parking Lot
7:17 p.m.

After several hours of some intense questioning, and having his bloody clothes, and both of his hands tested for traces of gunpowder, Kyzer was released from police custody, only to be met outside in the parking lot by his cousin, Idris, two of his aunts, an uncle, Brittany, and a half a dozen local news reporters. Brittany was the only person who took it upon herself to lead Kyzer away from all of the news reporters, and their many cameras, once they tried to make a circle around him.

Heroes.

&

Villains.

As she led the way, Brittany was finding it extremely difficult to hold back her tears as she escorted Kyzer to her boss' Jaguar. It wasn't helping that Kyzer's left hand was shaking inside of hers or that Kyzer was beginning to cry with each step that brought them closer to her boss' car. Brittany felt like she was the blind leading the blind. She had no idea where her inner strength was coming from.

Emotionally, she was bankrupt and feeling like she was on the verge of having a nervous breakdown. Everything that had happened, and was still happening, seemed so unreal to her and too impossible to be true.

All of the news reporters, and even some of Kyzer's family members stopped and froze in their tracks when Kyzer suddenly spun around, and angrily faced everyone that was following him and Brittany. His threatening posture brought tears to the eyes of both of his aunts.

"Get the fuck away from me! Get them fuckin' cameras outta my face!!"

A detective and four uniformed police officers had been standing beside the glass double-doors of the entrance to police headquarters, simply observing the scene as interested spectators, and nothing more, but when Kyzer had yelled, every last one of them had perked up. They stayed alert, until Kyzer and Brittany were both inside of the Jaguar and making their way over to the parking lot's 7th Street exit.

The sun was just starting to drop out of sight, leaving the sky with an orangish-tint as it disappeared. Temperatures had dropped down to the 50s, and had become unseasonably breezy.

A red traffic light stopped Brittany at 7th and Race. There, Brittany and Kyzer both stared blankly at the eastbound Race Street traffic, sharing a moment of silence that was louder than five planes crashing. They were total strangers. A tragic circumstance had stitched their destinies together, with neither of them having a choice in the matter.

"Kyzer, I gotta go back in there."

"Back in where?"

"In there," Brittany answered, cutting her watery eyes at the looming presence of the Police Headquarters' building. When the traffic light ahead, turned green, she took a breath and pressed her Christian Louboutin sneaker down on the gas pedal. "The detectives called my phone. I guess once they learned I was Tia's assistant, they um, I . . . um, sorry."

Overcome with emotion, Brittany pulled over and parked on the opposite side of Race Street, beside Franklin Square Park. Mentioning her boss' name had engulfed Brittany with such an enormous amount of anguish, it had blinded her eyes with tears and had almost caused her to crash into Kyzer's cousin's SUV.

"Can you apologize to him for me?"

"It's cool. Just calm down. Ay, where you take Tia, son?"

With his question, Kyzer pushed the Jaguar's passenger door open, and swung his right leg outside. Kyzer's eyes were bloodshot from anger, crying, and they were almost as red as the bloodstains on his clothes. The look in his eyes and his facial expression could mirror fifty broken hearts and one hundred punished souls.

"I—I did like you—"

Brittany paused and took a deep breath. As she wiped away her teardrops, she looked at Kyzer's cousin's GMC Yukon in the rearview mirror.

"I did what 'chu told me to do. I, um, I left the cemetery as soon as I heard the cops comin'. That's what 'chu told me to do, right? Ain't that what 'chu said?"

Kyzer nodded his head, holding Brittany's stare.

"You know Zay? Tia cousin?"

"Yeah, I know Zay."

"That's who house I went to. She, um, she . . ."

Brittany paused again, and took another moment to take a deep breath. It had been a futile attempt at gathering herself, but it only became the prelude to more crying.

"Zay . . . got Sooly. And I gave her that bag that Tia gave you at the cemetery. That's where I was at when, um, when the detectives called my cell phone."

"Okay."

Kyzer shut the passenger door and walked away from the Jaguar. Brittany watched him in the rearview mirror, as he slowly approached the passenger door of his cousin's truck. For a few seconds, Brittany kept her eyes on Kyzer until the lingering scent of her boss' perfume began to torture every corner of her sanity. Dropping her face down into her hands, Brittany sobbed with an agony that was as strong as the bond that she and her boss had built together.

For little over a minute, Kyzer stood on the sidewalk, facing the passenger door of the Jaguar, watching Brittany as she cried. It was the first time that he was actually able to have a private moment to himself, since all of the responding police officers had surrounded him at his sister's grave. It had taken seven cops to subdue him and drag him away from the lifeless bodies of his mother and his sister's best friend. Two years earlier, more corrections officers than that had been needed, after Kyzer's prison counselor had delivered the news to him that his older sister had been murdered.

The level of grief that Kyzer was feeling was new to him. It was surpassing every anguishing moment that he had ever experienced in his life, while at the same time, destroying every single compassionate emotion he had under his skin. His relationship with his mother was as essential to him as oxygen was to his lungs. His mother was irreplaceable. Her legacy was his.

His next steps would be hers.

Compelled by Brittany's crying, Kyzer got back inside of the Jaguar, and he pulled Brittany into his arms. Their hug lived for a long moment. The hug was an unspoken pledge of allegiance. While their lips said nothing, it was their hearts that were doing all of the talking. Their souls were paying full attention.

Enemies.

Are.

Forever.

Chapter Five

The Philadelphia County prison system was located in Northeast Philadelphia, opposite an I-95 expressway overpass, on State Road and Rhawn Street. In total, there were six county prisons, taking up the entire block of State Road. All of the facilities stood adjacent to one another, beginning with the women's prison first. Over five thousand inmates were being housed on State Road. The intake prison for the men was so overpopulated, on some housing units, three inmates were being forced to share a two-person, jail cell. One of the other facilities was sometimes using its gym as a place for inmates to sleep in, due to it being a shortage of bed space in general population. Three of the county prisons held inmates that had maximum custody levels, while the other three were housing inmates who had medium custody levels, or were in work-release programs.

It was Saturday morning, not yet ten o'clock. Brittany was in the lobby of the women's prison, waiting to visit a female cousin of her boss. Kyzer was down the street, visiting Brittany's boss' husband. In light of the prior day's tragic events, the superintendents at both prisons had permitted the weekend visits, so that Kyzer and Brittany would be given the chance to convey their sad news in a more private setting. The two of them were granted access to rooms that attorneys often used when they came to the county prisons to visit their clients.

"Who got my son?"

"Zay," Kyzer answered, unaffected by the teardrops that were flowing down the face of his old friend. His heart was refusing to let him sympathize with anyone, other than himself, and Brittany. "It was a hit, Splash. The order came from Detroit. They almost got away, but they banged out on 63rd and Cobbs Creek. They shot it out wit' the cops, but they lost. One of the niggaz lived. He the one that told the cops where the other ones was at. They was stayin' at a hotel up on City Line Avenue."

"Detroit?"

"Some general manager for some overseas basketball team had a mistress who was pregnant, and she wasn't tryna get an abortion. Sound familiar? Dude wanted her outta the way, so he got at Tia aunt. Tia shot the chick in her stomach wit' a riot pump five times, right?"

Mrs. Gunplay.

"That ain't happen in Detroit."

"Yeah, I know that. That's where her uncle from, though."

"Her uncle?"

"Yeah, her fuckin' uncle," Kyzer repeated, raising his voice. His anger moved him to rise to his feet. "Splash, her uncle was doin' a bid when that shit happened. They was close. Real close. Soon as he got out, he went right at the general manager dude. Rocked that nigga son . . . his daughter ain't been seen by anybody since. Splash, he had main man so shook, the nigga confessed to him. Dude told ol' head everything, Splash. He even gave ol' head a picture of him, you, and Tia, that y'all took at one of the basketball games his team had in Puerto Rico, a while ago. Splash, ol' head been slow walkin' Tia all fuckin' year. He had them niggaz goin' to ya fuckin' club 'n all 'lat."

"And how the fuck you know all this shit?"

"The cops told me yesterday. They told me everything that dude told them. What they didn't tell me, they told Brittany."

In the past twenty-four hours, Kyzer had learned a lot about Brittany and about a grand scheme that had all of the ingredients for a successful takeover of the streets of Philadelphia. It was a secret campaign, brought to life by his sister's best friend, Brittany, and a female detective.

"Splash, the cop that framed you, is the same cop that rocked Brittany boyfriend."

For several reasons, Splash was once someone who Kyzer had admired. Splash was a man's kind of guy. Not only was he a basketball legend in his North Philadelphia neighborhood, but along with reaching millionaire success with his wife, as a professional hitman, Splash was also the proud owner of one of the liveliest nightclubs that party-goers in Philadelphia had ever been inside of. Splash looked a lot like the famous Philly rapper, Oschino, and was sometimes even mistaken for being him on a lot of occasions. At the moment, Splash was down on the floor, sitting with his back pressed against the wall. The news of his wife's death had taken all of the strength out of his legs. His eyes were reflecting the anguish of a husband that had just lost his better half. Teardrops were streaming down his face as he held Kyzer's stare, and listened to Kyzer speak. The front of his orange jumpsuit was peppered with tearstains.

"Tia was tryna pull a lot of strings to get 'chu home," Kyzer explained, after kneeling down beside Splash. Oddly, he was suddenly beginning to feel a little empathy for what his old friend was going through. "She gotta real psychedelic plan in motion, and it's all to help spring you from this trap. Brittany put me on game last night, Splash. She said Tia ain't want 'chu to know what was goin' on, 'cause her and Brittany got this detective bitch on the team, and Tia was kinda scared to tell you about it. Tia thought 'chu would've wanted to dead the whole situation, once you found out that a cop was onboard wit' the plan she put together, so she kept it to herself. Splash, the detective bitch got beef wit' the cop that framed you. That ain't where shit end, though."

"She probably a fuckin' agent. Bitch probably been wearin' a fuckin' wire around Tia and Brittany, and they ain't even know it."

"I doubt that. Splash, her mom that D.A. from Baltimore. The one who you did your first job for. Brittany called her this mornin', to feel her out, and to see if she still gon' help with what Tia and her daughter got in motion."

"That D.A. owed me a favor."

"And Tia made use of that favor in a real crazy way," Kyzer continued, while standing back up. Splash extended his right hand to be helped back up to his feet as well, so he grabbed him by it, and pulled him up to a standing position. "That D.A. a federal judge now. She—"

"Kyzer, man, I gotta get back to my cell. Tia— What I'ma do wit' out Tia?"

Kyzer's eyes got cloudy with tears at the agony and the pain dripping from his friend's voice. Kyzer was barely managing to subdue his own anguish. He hadn't slept all night.

"Yo, I'm real sorry ya mom got mixed up in me and Tia bullshit. I mean that shit, Kyzer. I really do, man."

Kyzer and Splash locked eyes, both of them crying for their loved ones. The tragedy had momentarily put their most serious issue on the waiting list. Splash's apology had been heartfelt, but Kyzer wasn't about to let it enter his angry heart completely. He couldn't.

"I don't need to know what the plan is, Kyzer. I ain't know all this time. Yo, man, just get me the fuck outta here.

Get me home to my son, Kyzer. Get me home to my son, man."

"I got 'chu."

"I'ma slaughterhouse ol' head, Kyzer. His whole fuckin' family gon' get it. Anybody in Detroit wit' that nigga last name, gettin' put the fuck down. Did Tia give you that stuff?"

"Yeah, she gave it to me. If you can get me everything else I want, I'll have you outta this mu'fucker by ya next court date."

"What 'chu need?"

The room that Kyzer and his friend were in was extremely small. It was one of several official visiting rooms, used by visiting legal attorneys. These small rooms were on the left side of the county prison's main visiting room. The official visiting rooms were the size of small closets. Each room had a window, which allowed one to view the main visiting room. The official visiting rooms were furnished with a small, round desk, and two chairs, for both client, and the attorney.

Kyzer was standing in one corner of the small, official visiting room, and his friend was standing across from him in another. Three and a half feet separated them. While both men were consciously avoiding the true reasons behind why their friendship had come to an end, and why neither of them had spoken in such a long time, the elephant in the room with them was patiently waiting to be addressed.

Two years earlier, Kyzer's older sister was murdered by a cousin of his friend's. If Kyzer and his old friend hadn't've lost their loved ones yesterday, blood, sweat, and tears would have been on both of their faces.

"I need 'ju to get me some blueprints from the Water Department," Kyzer spoke, after a moment of wrestling with his emotions. Giving a voice to his war plans was making him feel wildly intoxicated, while at the same time, it was causing him to become very emotional, because with achieving vengeance, his sacred promises would be kept. "I want the layouts of every sewer line in Philly, Splash. I need the response times for all of the police districts, and I wanna know everywhere they got them police cameras at. I don't give a fuck if that shit in Montgomery County. If it's there, I wanna know about it. And I need 'ju to get me one of them drone helicopters, too. A small one, though. One wit' a camera attached to it, so I can see what it's flyin' over. You got anymore of them hand grenades?"

"Yeah."

"I need all of 'em."

"They yours . . . what else?"

"That's it, for now."

"Kyzer, get a C.O. I'm feeling' diz . . ."

Before Kyzer could make it to his friend, and stop him from falling to the floor, it had already happened. The news about his wife's death had been devouring his essence, and ripping apart his soul, the entire twenty-nine minutes that him and Kyzer had been talking. On his knees, cradling his friend in his arms, Kyzer shouted over and over again, for help, until two male corrections officers came running to see what the problem was.

"Damn, Splash," Kyzer thought, moments later, while watching as his friend was pushed away on a stretcher by the county prison's medical staff. He felt relieved in knowing that his friend was going to be okay, and that he had only fainted, but the incident itself, still had his nerves unsettled. "Splash, if it wasn't for Tia, or ya'll son, I probably wouldn't 've even came to this mu'fucker to see you. Ya fuckin' cousin killed my sister, and you ain't pick up a fuckin' pen and write me once. No messages or nothin'. Ya family introduced betrayal to my family first. We ain't gon' let that be forgotten. I know you know where

Sabia at, too. It ain't no way you don't. We ain't gon' avoid that shit the next time we talk, either. I'm about to show all y'all mu'fuckers what war is. That ol' head from Detroit ain't gon' be alive by the time you touch the streets. Dependin' how shit go, you might not even last that fuckin' long."

With his final thoughts, Kyzer turned and walked away. He was surprised to see that Brittany was sitting over in the visitor's lobby area, as he made his way over to the lockers, where he had to leave his cell phone, money, and other personal items before he was allowed inside to visit Splash.

Despite all of the pressure that was on both of their shoulders, or how difficult it was emotionally, to be out in the public eye, while the two of them were dealing with such an enormous amount of grief, Kyzer and Brittany were both managing to keep brave facial expressions. In Kyzer's presence, Brittany had trusted her intuition, and had turned her life into an open book for him. She forced herself to be transparent, and hid nothing from Kyzer. Her heart had persuaded her to do so. Likewise, in Brittany's company, Kyzer had been himself. He had released his sincerest ideas for redemption, but he had kept his teardrops captive. Brittany and Kyzer were no longer strangers. They were friends now.

Allies.

Death had given life to their friendship. Neither of them would admit it to the other, but deep down in the crevices of their hearts, they both saw the other as all that they truly had.

"How long you been waitin' out here?"

"Not long," Brittany sighed, as Kyzer approached her. She stood up and fell in stride with him as he headed over to the doors that led out of the county prison. "She denied my visit. A guard came out and told me that somebody else told her what happened to Tia already. I called Zay and asked her did she hear from her, or if anybody else in the family get a call from her."

"And what she say?"

"Nobody ain't hear from her, yet. How Splash take it?"

"He passed out."

Brittany's eyes watered instantly, at hearing that her boss' husband had fainted upon him learning that his wife had been killed.

"Not right away, though. We got to talk. He made a real valid point about somethin', too."

"What?"

"Let's wait, til we get back to the car."

The house that Kyzer had inherited from his older sister was located in Yardley, Pennsylvania, otherwise known as Bucks County. The house was the first estate seen, upon entering the affluent community of Melissa Circle. The property was a small palace, surrounded by a lot of tasteful landscaping. The house owned such an impeccable, interior layout, Kyzer had stayed sleepless in it his first night there. After his mother's departure, Kyzer had walked all around the estate, admiring all that his sister had done with the place. Kyzer's older sister had furnished the entire property from its Louis XIV-styled foyer, out to its huge backyard, as if she had been competing for a home decorating award.

For two years, Kyzer had struggled with what he should do with the property, once he was released from prison. While away, his mother had sent him dozens and dozens of pictures, hoping that visual images of the place would persuade Kyzer into not selling it. While the pictures had impressed Kyzer, nothing could have prepared his emotions, or the great admiration that he had suddenly felt for his sister, once he had taken his first steps onto the beautiful estate. Every single detail of the house had fascinated Kyzer. That next morning, a little before dawn,

Kyzer had decided that he was going to keep his older sister's dream house, and that he was going to leave it exactly as it was. The news had left Kyzer's mother elated.

There were a few changes that Kyzer wanted to make to the four bedroom, three and a half bath, 2,234 square foot property. At the top of his list was adding a sophisticated surveillance system. To the garage, Kyzer wanted to include the latest Audi. Lastly, he wanted his house to have a revolving door, flowing with nothing but beautiful women.

At the moment, however, a surveillance system, the newest Audi, and beautiful women, were the furthest things from Kyzer's mind. With some of the toughest days of his life behind him, and presumably an even tougher week ahead of him, Kyzer had only one though floating around his mind.

I.

Deserve.

Revenge.

"Tia told me that the only way this plan would work, was if you agreed to be on our side, Kyzer. Can I believe in you, like she did?"

"Brittany, the question really should be, can you believe in ya' self," Kyzer responded, as he stepped out onto his rear patio, and looked up at the cloudless afternoon sky. What Brittany had expressed was actually mirroring a lot of the concerns that he had deep down in the pit of his stomach. " 'Cause, like, to keep it all the way real wit 'chu, even if Tia was here, none of this shit would work if you wasn't on ya job. Tia knew that. Now that I know the situation, I know that my role in this shit a major factor, but 'chu got more pressure on ya shoulders than I do. Brittany, this plan gotta lot of crazy angles, and like Splash said earlier, ain't no tellin' what page that cop on."

"Outside of her, what angles of the plan concern you the most?"

A squirrel zipping across Kyzer's huge, grassy backyard, paused, then raised itself up on its hind legs as Kyzer and Brittany both sat down on Kyzer's rear patio steps. Done looking, the squirrel quickly took off in the opposite direction, with Kyzer watching its retreat.

Without being too obvious, Brittany appraised Kyzer out of the corner of her right eye. His calm demeanor was the complete contrast to all of the violent stories she had been told about him. Her new boyfriend hated his guts. Her aunt's boyfriend feared him.

Brittany liked him.

"Cee-lo Green got this song called 'Who gon' save my soul, now,'" Kyzer spoke, while looking blankly out at the area of his backyard, where the squirrel he had been watching had disappeared. With a sigh, he rested his elbows on his knees and looked into Brittany's eyes. "I heard it when I was locked up. One night they had him on Vh-1. You know how they be havin' them jawns, like, when the rappers and singers be, like, performin' all of the songs for a small crowd? So, like, he was talkin' in between all of the songs, and, so, then, he started talkin' 'bout how messed up he was when his mom died. And he started talkin' 'bout the song he wrote for her. Brittany, even when he just said the title of the song, that shit got to me. Like, at the time, I ain't know what it felt like to lose a mother. It did have me thinkin' about my sister, though. The words to the song was so crazy, I got up and wrote the name of the song down, 'cause I wanted to listen to it, once I got out. Brittany, now I know exactly how Cee-lo feel."

Thinking of her father, Brittany lowered her watery eyes.

"Brittany, wit' this plan, you the angle that concern me the most."

"Why?"

"Brittany, on our way here, when I asked you how you felt about Maniac, you gave me this funny look."

"My answer didn't satisfy you?"

Just as Kyzer was fixing his lips to answer Brittany, Brittany's cell phone started to ring in her pocketbook, interrupting the moment.

"That's Maniac," Brittany sighed, upon seeing her boyfriend's face on the screen of her iPhone, as she looked down into her watermelon-red, Gucci clutch purse. To display her loyalty, she ignored her ringing cell phone and stopped Kyzer with her hand, when he moved to rise to his feet. "Kyzer, what do you need to hear from me?"

"It ain't what I need to hear, it's what I need to see."

"Okay, so, what are you not seein' in me, that has you feelin' so reluctant to . . ."

Brittany let out a frustrated sigh when her cell phone started to ring again. Rolling her eyes, she dug into her purse and turned her cell phone off, assuming that the caller was her boyfriend again.

"Let's say we can pull this shit off. What do you want most from this?"

"Revenge for my dad and his girlfriend."

"And you wanna get that cop back for killin' ya boyfriend, right?"

"That goes without sayin'."

"You know what I want?"

"What?"

"To be alive."

Kyzer's answer left Brittany surprised, but also riveted at how unpredictable her own future might possibly be. For a moment, she sat there speechless, holding Kyzer's stare. She saw awareness in his eyes; awareness of things she was completely ignorant of.

"Come wit' me."

Brittany grabbed her purse, got up, and followed Kyzer back into his house. Walking by Kyzer's dining room, and as she caught up with him as the two of them walked together down his Louis XIV-styled foyer, Brittany began to wonder about Kyzer's relationship status. She couldn't recall him ever mentioning that he had a girlfriend, or anyone special in his life. All of the phone calls that he had ever gotten had only been from family members, and friends of his. At an upstairs bedroom, Brittany paused, and raised her eyebrows when Kyzer pushed the door to the bedroom open and stepped aside.

"What's in there?"

"Did Tia tell you about the day that my sister got killed?"

"A little. Her and Splash got shot that day, too, right?"

"A lotta people did," Kyzer explained, as he slowly entered the only room in his house that made him feel eerily uncomfortable. The hairs on his neck stood up, once he was completely inside of his guest bedroom. "They say when men make plans, it makes God smile. You ever hear that before?"

Brittany nodded her head as she joined Kyzer inside of his guest bedroom. The odd way that Kyzer was behaving was making her feel uneasy.

"You ever see that movie 'Smokin' Aces'?"

Brittany nodded her head as her eyes took in the guest bedroom.

"Remember how everybody went to that hotel at the end, and started rockin' each other?"

Again, Brittany nodded.

"That's what happened at this house the day my sister died," Kyzer continued, as his eyes slowly looked around at his guest bedroom's uncarpeted floor. When his eyes found the unmistakable large stains of blood, he stepped closer to them. "One of them stains of blood came from my cousin. Him and his man robbed this armored truck down South Philly, and he came out here to fall back. My sister ain't know nothin' about that shit. What's crazy is, I was in jail and I had heard about that shit. I ain't know it was my cousin, though. Me and this nigga was writin' back and forth the whole time he was in the county. His whole thing was, once he got out, he just wanted to get a job and be wit' his son. That's all he used to talk about, Brittany. His baby mom was shittin' on him. Not bringin' his son to see him. Not answerin' the phone. It was around the time that I had just got my appeal lawyer, so I kept tryna tell him to stick to his plans, until I touched. The nigga didn't, though."

"What happened?"

"God smiled at his plans, I guess."

"I don't understand."

"Brittany, just look at how Tia put that wild plan together, and now she not even here to see if it'll work, or not. My cousin got out, and for some reason, he did the total opposite of what he said he was gon' do. My aunt told me that nigga cut his house arrest monitor off his leg, a day after he was home."

Kyzer knelt down beside the brownish stains on the floor. One of them was shaped like South America.

"The cops killed him?"

"Naw, that's the fuckin' crazy part," Kyzer said, standing back up. His eyes fell on the other huge stain of blood that was a few feet away from his cousin's DNA. "Some nigga that was engaged to his baby mom did. Him, Splash cousin, Sabia, and some nigga that got rocked out on my driveway, came here lookin' for my cousin. That ain't the kicker, though . . . that's my sister's boyfriend's blood, right there behind you."

Brittany turned around and dropped her eyes down to the uncarpeted floor. Her mouth went dry at the large, brownish-design of blood, which she had believed to be just a paint stain, when she had initially followed Kyzer into the room. This stain of blood was far bigger than the other two.

"My sister shot him," Kyzer explained, joining Brittany at the border of the old blood stain. His face changed into a mask of resentment, as he rested his angry eyes on the rectangular-shaped stain on the dusty floor. "He was tryna rob my cousin. He the one that Maniac told you about, who was wit' my cousin, Drees, when they set my man, Saan, up. All the time that nigga was fuckin' wit' my sister, I ain't know him and Maniac was related. I ain't find that shit out, 'til after all this shit happened."

"Can we go back out into the hallway?"

"Go 'head."

Kyzer followed Brittany out of his guest bedroom. She had stepped around his sister's boyfriend's blood stain. Kyzer walked over it, wanting to spit on it.

Out in the hallway, Brittany put her back against the wall, opposite Kyzer's guest bedroom, and slid down to the soft, beige carpet. After placing her purse beside her thigh, she gave Kyzer a concerned stare. Her thoughts were all over the place.

"If God smilin' at our plan, Brittany we fucked."

"You think we gon' die?"

Doing like Brittany, Kyzer made himself comfortable down on the carpet. When Brittany placed her head on his right shoulder, Kyzer crossed his legs and let out a long sigh, while his eyes stared into his guest bedroom. To him, the room was a ghost tomb. It was the main reason why he had wanted to sell his sister's house in the first place. Being in the gigantic house all alone wasn't making things any better.

"Do you, Kyzer?"

"What?"

"Think we gon' die?"

"Only God know that."

Kyzer and Brittany sat there silent for a long moment. The thought of death was intimidating.

"Kyzer, I can't speak for Splash when I say this, but I personally witnessed how Tia was dealing with losing your sister. We went to her tombstone all the time. Even when it come to Splash cousin. I was with her when she got his name tattooed in the palm of her hand, Kyzer. I'm the one who picked out what kind of bullet she should put his name in. It's an AK-47 bullet."

Mrs. Gunplay.

"On the way to the cemetery, she was so excited to finally see you. Kyzer, your opinion of her mattered. Tia loved you and your sister. She did."

"Brittany, what made Maniac tell you that my cousin, Drees, gon' line me up for him?"

"To be totally honest, I'm not sure," Brittany answered, while cleaning the teardrops that were trickling down the right side of her face with her hand. Beside Kyzer, she seemed to always feel safe, and protected, and as she continued to lay her head on his shoulder, she soaked in the comfort of being next to the man, who her boss had believed so strongly in. "The day that I met him, I told Tia how animated he was. He too much. It was Marvin's idea that I talk to him. His fat ass gave Maniac my cell phone number. But, like, he be tellin' me all kinds of stuff."

"Like what?"

"Well, for one, him and ya cousin be meetin' down at this park near Penn's Landing. That's where they be goin' over all their secret plans and everything. If you ever hear ya cousin on his cell phone, and he say, 'Meet me at Green Acres,' that's Maniac he on the phone wit'."

"Green Acres, huh?"

"And he be gettin' his drugs sent to him in dirt bikes, too. It be inside of the gas tanks."

"Let me ask you this . . . how the fuck do Marvin expect you to start a war between Maniac and my team? What's supposed to make shit hit the fan?"

"You."

"Me?"

Brittany and Kyzer both tensed up, and looked at each other, when someone started knocking loudly at Kyzer's front door. The loud knocking was echoing all through Kyzer's house. On their feet, Brittany followed closely behind Kyzer as he walked at a fast pace down his hallway, and went into his master bedroom, down at the far end of his hallway. Brittany drew in a deep breath as soon as Kyzer pulled back the curtain to a bedroom window of his, overlooking his driveway. To both Kyzer's and Brittany's surprise, Kyzer's cousin, Drees, was backing away from Kyzer's front door. A few feet away from him, between Kyzer's cousin's black, SUV, and Brittany's boss' Jaguar, stood Marvin. The two men exchanged some words, then Marvin moved his large body over to the Jaguar and took a look inside of the rear passenger window.

"This pussy out of his fuckin' mind. He gon' bring this nigga to my house? Brittany, go hide somewhere."

"Where?"

"Anywhere."

Chapter Six

The first floor of Kyzer's house was a construction of several glass walls, which allowed the open kitchen, dining area, living room, and foyer to all be viewed with one sweeping glance, without any interruptions being caused to the naked eye. It was a vision to behold.

The floors of the dining area and the living room were made of bamboo. In Kyzer's kitchen, the upper and lower cabinets were also made from this same glossy wood. So-Ho furniture decorated the dining area and in the center of the white, marble floors of the open kitchen, there was a rectangular-shaped granite-topped island that was surrounded by ten piston barstools. Like in the kitchen, every window on the first level of Kyzer's house was covered with beaded-aluminum curtains. There was a gun on the dining room table, hidden inside of a black, ceramic vase. At the end of Kyzer's foyer, where it opened into his kitchen, there was a photo booth, and a digital jukebox that had more than a hundred thousand songs stored in it.

One of Kyzer's favorite areas of his house was his living room. This portion of his small palace had 'rich taste' written all over it; thanks to his sister. Under the amazingly high ceiling of the living room, there was a 30 by 30 foot white, mink rug, that was spread out over the bamboo floors. On top of the white animal fur there was a white, leather sofa, a matching ottoman, and two sycamore armchairs, all facing a gigantic movie screen, which hung from a wall that was made from the same material as the hardwood, bamboo floors. Over at the entrance of the living room, with its back to a wall of glass, stood a full body of vintage armor. The suit of shiny metal stood 6'4" tall. To compliment her Louis XIV-styled foyer, while in New York once, at an auction with friends, Kyzer's sister had purchased the armored suit from two Great Britain historians.

Following Kyzer into his living room, Marvin and Kyzer's cousin shared an uncomfortable stare as the two of them walked by the vintage body of armor. After letting them into his house, Kyzer hadn't spoken one single word to either man.

"Shit," Brittany silently cursed, after her aunt's boyfriend and Kyzer's cousin had taken seats on the couch she was hiding behind. The volume of her heartbeat reached her ears as the weight of Marvin's giant body moved Kyzer's couch against her back. "Oh, my God. Oh, my fuckin' God. Please, don't let them look behind this couch. Shit, shit, shit. Out of all the fuckin' places I could've went in this big ass house, why did I have to pick in here? Marvin just seen me leave the house this mornin' in Tia car . . . shit."

Outside, afternoon was becoming evening.

Inside of Kyzer's heart, a storm was becoming a hurricane.

"I been tryna call you all day. Ya phone kept goin' to voicemail, so I–"

"So, you decided to invade my fuckin' space," Kyzer interrupted his cousin, inwardly battling the storm that was evolving inside of his chest. The sight of Brittany's pink, python-skinned stilettos, brought a sudden sweep of calmness across his body, once he spotted her poor hiding spot. "Not only that, but 'chu got . . ."

Kyzer slammed his fist into the palm of his left hand several times, as he purposely walked in Brittany's opposite direction. He wanted to keep the attention on him, but in doing so, he wanted to gain better control of his brewing temper as well. The two men in his company were enemies with toxic intentions, and pretending that he was oblivious to their plans was giving his level of patience a brand new threshold.

"Drees, just so you know, if you ever bring anybody else to my fuckin' spot, you and whoever wit 'chu gon' be in some real deep shit, unless it's Aunt Crystal."

"It won't happen again."

"Why you in my house, Marv?"

Nervously, Marvin shifted his big body on Kyzer's couch and leaned forward. His eyes refused to meet Kyzer's intimidating stare, but instead, they focused on how many glass walls he saw all around him.

"Kyzer, Marvin got somethin' real important to tell you. He wanted to tell you what it was in person."

"Alright, I'm listenin'. Talk."

Behind Kyzer's couch, the act of staying completely still was beginning to feel like a serious workout to Brittany. Her entire body was covered with sweat; some places more than others. Her black, leather pants were sticking to her thighs and calves, and her gray, and pink-sleeved, Ipa-Nima shirt, was stuck to her back like a piece of duct tape. Kyzer's mink rug was crucifying her.

Across the room, Kyzer had his arms crossed over his chest, eyeing his cousin and Marvin closely.

"First off, I apologize for intrudin' on ya space. My bad. I'm sorry to hear about 'cha mom, too."

"It should've been you, right, Marv?" Kyzer asked, uncrossing his arms as he thought about some of his own experiences with Marvin in the past. Aware of what Marvin had did to Brittany's father, and to Brittany's father's girlfriend, it only challenged his attempts of portraying himself as a fool in the eyes of his cousin and Marvin. "Or maybe me, right? Look, Marv, don't say what 'chu think I wanna hear, just spill what supposed to be so fuckin' important. And stop cuttin' ya fuckin' eyes at Drees, 'cause if he joy-stickin' this whole situation, which I'm sure he is, you should already know from the past, the blame game don't work in my court. Now, talk."

"Kyzer, I ain't joy-stickin'–"

"Drees, shut the fuck up. Talk, Marv."

"Okay, look . . . okay, here's the situation. First, is Brittany here? I see her boss' car out in ya driveway."

Brittany held her breath.

"Until the cops release my mom truck to me, I'm gon' be drivin' that. Why? If she was here, that ain't none of ya fuckin' business. She at her boss cousin house, out West Philly. Marv, it's a real thin line between being a fuckin' coward and being clever. Know ya fuckin' lane."

"She's Maniac's girlfriend."

"Who?"

"Brittany."

Kyzer gave his cousin a dramatic look, then shot his eyes back at Marvin, who, too, had cut his eyes at Kyzer's cousin. To further sell his ignorance, Kyzer shook his head in disbelief.

"That's what I was tryna tell you when you came outta 8th and Race, but 'chu jumped in the car with her, before I could warn you. Yeah, she was Tia assistant 'n all that, but that's where shit stop. You won't answer none of my calls. I had to come out here, Kyzer. That ain't the steak 'n gravy of this shit, though. Marv, tell him what 'chu told me. Comin' from me, he probably shrug that shit off."

"The bitch is evil as they fuckin' come. This bitch come to me and her aunt, right? This about two, three months ago. So, she know all about my funeral home being under foreclosure, and everything. It's all I talk about. Guess what this bitch come up with as a plan, Kyzer? Listen, you'd never imagine what she thought of in a million fuckin' years."

"Wait 'til you hear this shit."

Kyzer cut his eyes at his cousin.

"For fifty percent of my business, right? Guess what this bitch told me she could do?"

"What?"

"Start a fuckin' war in the neighborhood."

Aware of the truth, Kyzer chuckled. Shaking his head, he turned away, not before catching his cousin and Marvin cutting their eyes at each other. It was a moment that made Kyzer so badly want to just have Brittany reveal herself.

"Alright, so, let me guess. The war supposed to be between us, and Maniac and them, since they back down Marshall Street, right?"

Kyzer's question got him nods from his cousin and Marvin. Behind his couch, Brittany was fuming, while at the same time, hoping that Kyzer wasn't being fooled by Marvin's lies.

"Did you agree?"

"To what?"

"Her plan? Drees told me about how you was gon' let us do our Janazahs there 'n all 'lat, but this a whole new angle, Marv. You sure this was just her idea, and not yours?"

"I'd never ransom the blood of our neighborhood to make no money."

"You got morals, now, huh?"

"More than that bitch do, that's for sure."

"So, why should this be important news to me, Drees?" Kyzer questioned, looking directly at his cousin. It ached him to his core that his cousin had played a role in their best friend's death, and that he was now trying to bring him the same fate. "You already know what page I'm on. Didn't I make that clear to you at the cemetery the other day? My mom got bullet holes in her fuckin' face. Ya aunt. And what I'm supposed to be leery of Brittany, 'cause she fuck wit' Maniac? Nigga, I got my mom on my fuckin' mind, but 'chut know what? Because I know you, and I know how this fat mother fucker right here get down, I'ma make it easy for both of y'all, since y'all niggaz seem to be havin' a fuckin' problem wit' just comin' out and askin' me what all three of us know gon' happen any fuckin' way. It's just who gon' capitalize off of it. Y'all niggaz know I ain't goin' for Maniac and them niggaz bein' on Marshall Street. Saan wasn't goin' for it, and neither am I. Plays out perfectly for you, Marv. I just wanna see how you gon' get niggaz peoples to bring they families to you. That funeral home ain't been open in like twenty fuckin' years. I know this, though. That fifty percent of ya business you claimin' Brittany wanted, come to me. Now, get the fuck outta my house. Naw, not 'chu, Drees."

Kyzer's cousin paused, after he stood up. Marvin had a tougher time rising to his feet.

"Matter fact, both of y'all stay right there."

Behind the couch, Brittany's eyes grew wide as she daringly flipped over to her back and placed her clutch purse on her stomach. Like Kyzer's cousin, and Marvin, she had picked up on the threat that was mixed in with Kyzer's orders.

"Let's leave, Drees."

"Man, if we do, then we really gon' look suspect."

"This was ya fuckin' idea. I said to wait 'til after his mom funeral. I told 'ju he wasn't gon' like that 'chu brought me here. I'm leavin'."

"If you do, I'ma let Maniac know you fuckin' his mom."

64

"You think I give a fuck about that, compared to ya fuckin' cousin? Move out my fuckin' way."

"Too late."

Marvin and Kyzer's cousin both watched as Kyzer came walking down the length of his glass wall, which separated his kitchen, and his dining room. He was staring at both of them from the opposite side of the glass. He was carrying a gun in his left hand.

"Oh, Jesus."

"Chill, Marv."

Marvin exhaled a long sigh that transcended into a string of whimpers. He had been shot by Kyzer once before.

"Both of y'all come in here!"

Kyzer's command prompted Brittany to rise to her knees. The suspense of what was going on had her nerves panicky and too unsettled to control. The fear that she heard in Marvin's voice had been so gratifying, she was no longer concerned with him finding out that she was there. Since knowing Marvin, she had never witnessed him show any fear for anyone. The moment was epic in her eyes.

In his kitchen, Kyzer was holding one of the guns that his sister's best friend had given him. It was a silver Smith & Wesson, .40 caliber handgun. It was fitted with an extended clip, holding thirty-two, hollow-tipped bullets. The clip was longer than the gun. As Kyzer paced around the center island in his kitchen, he kept his eyes on his cousin and Marvin, as they both slowly made their way to him. Their eyes were begging him for mercy. Past them, Kyzer could see Brittany peeking over the back of his couch.

"You gotta choice, Drees," Kyzer announced, pointing his gun at his cousin, as him and Marvin hesitantly closed the distance between them. Both of the men deserved death, but at the moment he could only do a little harm, because there was a bigger, and bolder picture surrounding them all. "And you only gettin' one minute to make up ya fuckin' mind. Now, just the other day, you was at the cemetery, tellin' me all those nut ass fuckin' reasons why I shouldn't turn shit the fuck up. You remember that conversation, right? How its cameras everywhere. Niggaz sendin' text messages to the fuckin' cops. Remember all 'lat bullshit? Yeah, but here it is, now, though, you show up at my house unannounced and you got this fat mother fucker wit 'chu, and you suddenly seem to have this odd ass change of heart. Like, I'm supposed to just believe that this just came outta no fuckin' where, right?"

"Kyzer, why would–"

"Shut up . . . I'm talkin'. Drees, I always been smarter than you. Saan was smarter than you. Drees, you only move for money. You always been like that. Me and Saan moved for war and money. That's why we was able to keep outsiders outta our fuckin' hood for so long. Drees, under ya throne, all 'lat shit went down the fuckin' drain. It crumbled, and you let it. Tenth and Thompson niggaz back on Marshall Street. Niggaz from Richard Allen got the bar on Eighth and Master. I keep hearin' about how niggaz from Eighth and Diamond just be comin' down, and be robbin' whoever they want, whenever they fuckin' feel like it."

Kyzer paused and glared across his kitchen island at his cousin. His cousin held his stare.

"Shit like a fuckin' invasion. And it's all conveniently fallin' into place, while Marv funeral home in need of money, right? Well, guess what? I ain't a fuckin' pawn on nobody chessboard, Drees. You got that, Marv?"

Marvin nodded his fat face, never taking his eyes off of the intimidating looking gun in Kyzer's hand. His face was wet with beads of perspiration.

"Drees, comin' here, you and Marv both knew my mind was on fire. You knew that shit from our conversation the other day."

"You gon' let me talk?"

"When I'm fuckin' ready to."

The day that Kyzer's suspicions about his cousin had been confirmed by Brittany, it had only been hours after he had identified his mother's body at the coroner's office. It was a truth that was working like poison inside of Kyzer's blood system. It was why he had been avoiding all interactions with his cousin. To know that his best friend had been double-crossed by his cousin, was hurting him much more than the other truth, which was that his cousin had the same intentions planned out for him as well.

"These are ya options, Drees. And like I said, you gettin' one fuckin' minute to make up ya mind. Now, you can either let me shoot 'chu in that hand that got 'loyalty' tattooed on it, or when you make it back down the way, you kick off the war, by choppin' on them niggaz on Marshall Street, or you can air out them Richard Allen niggaz at the bar. And you gotta show ya face. The clock tickin', Drees."

"Damn, you gon' do me like I ain't family, though?"

"A friend wouldn't 've got a choice, Drees."

"And I can't wear no mask?"

"If you do, niggaz won't know who declarin' war. You got forty-five seconds, Drees."

"Alright."

"So, who you gon' bomb on?"

"Richard Allen."

"Why not Tenth Street?"

"I'll leave that to you. Come on, Marvin."

Kyzer smiled at his cousin's back as Marvin brought up his rear, and followed his cousin down his foyer to his front door. When Marvin looked over his shoulder at him, Kyzer raised his gun and pointed it at Marvin's face.

"Should I be concerned that 'chu know where I live, Marv?"

Marvin shook his head, and because he wasn't looking ahead of him, he collided into Kyzer's cousin's back at Kyzer's front door. His big body sent Kyzer's cousin into the door face first.

"Ay, Drees, don't sit up front at my mom funeral, either! Stay in the back, where you fuckin' belong!"

Kyzer's voice echoed throughout his entire house, and quietly disappeared out of his front door, after Marvin had pulled it shut behind him. Not even a second after they were alone again, Brittany popped up from behind Kyzer's couch, looking upset and disheveled. Kyzer left his gun on the island in his kitchen, and met Brittany in the center of his living room.

"Kyzer, you see he chose to go at Richard Allen, and not Maniac and them, right?"

Kyzer shrugged his shoulders, while giving Brittany a serious stare. Her behavior moving forward still had him worried.

"Why you lookin' at me like that? You don't believe all that shit Marvin was sayin', do you?"

"Fuck no."

"Well, what's wrong?"

"Brittany, you survive around killers, by becomin' one yourself. It's about adaptin'. That's the way shit is wit' anything. This plan you and Tia came up with, is goin' into effect as soon as Drees throw that first bullet tonight. If you wit' Maniac and I see you, or any of my niggaz see y'all, fire comin'. This shit might not have a happy fuckin' endin', Brittany."

"Why worry about the destination, when the road is full of snakes?"

Chapter Seven

"A vast Philadelphia-based drug ring, that annually moved more than twelve million dollars worth of cocaine, heroin, and PCP was busted by state drug authorities early this morning. Agents from the Attorney General's Bureau of Investigation filed charges . . ."

Intrigued, Sabia Barnes sat up in his hotel bed, and with the remote control, he began raising the volume on the gigantic plasma television, that was on the far bedroom wall of his luxurious hotel suite. Two of the three naked female escorts in bed with him, stirred in their sleep, but none of them fully awakened.

". . . this morning, against seventeen suspects from Philadelphia, and ten from Pottstown. The operation allegedly distributed more than one hundred kilos of heron annually to lower-level dealers, as far west as Altoona, and Pittsburgh, Pennsylvania. According to the grand jury, the heron was sold under the name 'Devil's Smile,' and was responsible for several residential overdoses that recently occurred in North Phila . . ."

Having heard enough, Sabia thumbed the power button on the remote control and then tossed it aside. With a long yawn, Sabia laid back down and closed his eyes; not to sleep, but to think.

It was a little after ten in the morning, and the temperatures in the city of Philadelphia were down in the low 60s. A wet mixture of hail and rain was falling from the early Monday morning sky. It was September 22nd. For Sabia Barnes, who was an America's 'Most Wanted' fugitive, the cold unwelcoming weather was feeling like a thoughtful gift from God.

Life as a fugitive had given Sabia the opportunity to travel all across the United States. He had even been down into some parts of Mexico. A lot about who Sabia was as a person had changed over the past two years; intellectually, but most of all, physically. To stay two steps ahead of federal, and local authorities, Sabia had invested a substantial amount of money into altering his entire physical appearance. He had paid a California, plastic surgeon, seventy-five thousand dollars in cash, to make his face look the exact opposite of how God had originally fashioned it. Sabia had even gone so far as to have the surgeon purposely reconstruct his larynx, to change the sound and pitch of his vocal tone. He had also spent thousands of dollars on tattoos. His entire body was a canvas of beautiful artwork, exhibiting all sorts of murals, and designs, that were all highlighted on his brown skin with a lot of bright colors. The only places on Sabia's body where, there weren't any tattoos, was his bald head, his face, thighs, and below his ankles.

Besides his green, eye-contact lenses, and the exotic look that they gave him, what Sabia liked most about his new appearance, was the remarkable physical shape that his body was in. He had dropped thirty pounds of fat. A lot of jogging, daily cardio-exercises, and removing red meat from his diet, had trimmed Sabia's 6'4" body down to one hundred and ninety-five pounds.

Sabia's new name was Terrell Matthews. Down in San Antonio, Texas, twenty-eight thousand dollars had gotten

Sabia a whole new identity. Inside of one of his Fendi suitcases, where there was a little under half a million dollars in cash, and a hand-Uzi, Sabia had a driver's license, a social security card, and a birth certificate, that would make it through the toughest inspections known to man.

Despite all of his wealth, and his ability to splurge, and live lavish, as he had grown accustomed to doing, Sabia was still just a 25-year-old, young man, who had lost his way in life. Spiritually, he was a mess. Guilt had his soul handcuffed, and there wasn't a day that went by, where he didn't succumb to an uncontrollable fit of crying. Sabia didn't know how to cope with his predicament some days. The last time he had checked, he was number one on the Philly's 'Most Wanted' list. As of Saturday, he had been moved up to number forty-nine on the America's 'Most Wanted' list. Boldly, no longer committed to trying to outrun his fate, Sabia had returned to Philadelphia, while most of its citizens had been asleep. Sabia had some wrongs that he desperately wanted to right.

The only person aware of Sabia's return, was a male cousin of his. At exactly 10:30 a.m., like they had planned, the male cousin of Sabia's, who was currently incarcerated at a Philadelphia county prison, placed a call to Sabia's cell phone. Sabia answered the phone call in the middle of its first ring.

"Hello?"

"You made it?"

"Yeah, I'm here," Sabia confirmed, after climbing out of his hotel bed. He wanted to put as much space as he possibly could, between him and the sleeping female escorts, so he didn't stop walking, until he was completely out of his hotel bedroom and out on the terrace. "I got here, like, a little after three 'n the mornin'. I gotta suite at the Marriott, down on Market Street. I'm on the top floor, in one of them penthouse suites. Fuck all 'lat, though, you cool? Did they let 'chu go to the funeral?"

"Yeah, I just got back. She had to have a closed casket, Bia. Fuckin'—Man, the fuckin' sheriffs wouldn't even open the coffin for me."

Sabia clenched his jaws as his cousin's voice cracked with emotions on the other end of his cell phone.

"Bia, you sure nobody gon' recognize you?"

"Positive."

"Would I?"

"What?"

"Recognize you?"

"Splash, you'd walk right past me. The only thing the same about me, is my fingerprints."

"If I was you, that would've been what I changed first."

"Them mu'fuckers had my face on the news, not my fingers."

"You right."

"Splash, I had to put priority first."

"Naw, I definitely ... I definitely feel you. You absolutely right, Bia. You made the right move."

Sabia thoughtfully rubbed his left thumb over the tips of his fingers, as he descended the marble stairs of his hotel suite, and made his way down to the kitchen. He knew he couldn't afford to be put in a situation, where he found himself being fingerprinted by the cops. If that moment ever came, Sabia knew that his freedom would be history for him. This meant that any encounters with the Philadelphia police, or U.S. Marshals, would potentially have to end with him holding a smoking gun.

"Alright, so, what situation you want me to handle first?"

"I want 'chu to knock Tia assistant off. Her name Brittany. Slow walk her ass, Bia. She think you a club promoter. Look, though, wait 'til after her and Kyzer pull the strings they pullin' to get me out, then do both of they fuckin' asses dirty. Hurry up and get to the funeral, Bia. It's at that church down the street from my house. Yo, and when Tuna get back from New Orleans, rock his nut ass, too."

"I'm all over it."

Deception is always for sale.

Chapter Eight

"Where you at?"

"Work."

"That thing for ya boss still goin' on?"

"It's just now endin'."

"A lot of people came?"

"Twice as many that came to the funeral."

"How was it?"

"Sad to the tenth power. A lot of cryin'."

"You cool?"

"I'm drunk and depressed," Brittany admitted, sighing sadly, as she switched her cell phone to her opposite ear and sat down behind her boss' office desk. She was intoxicated, but her intuition was telling her that her boyfriend's phone call had reason behind it, and that it had nothing to do with his concern for her current emotional state. "My phone won't stop ringin'. It died on me twice today. All my co-workers wanna know what's gon' happen with the club now. Is the club gon' stay open? What about their jobs? I got people callin' about the parties they booked. Club promoters callin' every five minutes. Maniac, I got so many e-mails this afternoon, and our business website had so much traffic comin' to it, my iPad screen froze up on me. Then, Rock 'n Roll Rhonda called and left me this crazy threatenin' message. My boss son don't want nobody, but me. It's just–"

"Is Kyzer there?"

"Where? Here at the club?"

"Yeah?"

"No, Maniac."

"Damn, was I wrong for askin' . . ."

Brittany removed her cell phone from her ear and thumbed the power button on it, then slid it across her boss' office desk. Her boyfriend had just ruined what little feelings she was starting to develop for him. Her intuitions had proved to be correct. As she lowered her forehead down to her left forearm, the Moscato in her system started begging her to call her boyfriend back, to give him an honest piece of her mind.

It was a few minutes shy of becoming midnight, and the people at the club were just beginning to leave. To Brittany's left, several surveillance monitors showed the crowd thinning on the nightclub's second floor, where the huge dance floor, stage, and bar were. A large portion of the crowd were friends and family members of Brittany's boss. The rest were Brittany's co-workers. They had all been there, since leaving the cemetery. The bar had been open for everyone. To the left of the nightclub, there was a valet parking lot. It was filled to its capacity. Cars and trucks of every model outlined 3rd Street, going up to Market Street, and ending down at Chestnut Street.

The day had exhausted Brittany. It had also put her in a reflective mood about her father, and his girlfriend, and what they had meant to her. Her heart was also with her boss' son. His crying at the funeral had backed her soul into a corner. Brittany wanted to escape her life, if only just for one single moment. Then, there was Kyzer. At the funeral, he didn't speak to her. He spoke to no one, and had simply sat in the first pew, the entire funeral service, staring at his mother's closed coffin. When family members and friends had tried to hug him or speak to him, he had ignored them all. At the cemetery, he stayed after everyone had left for the nightclub. He wasn't answering any of her calls or text messages.

A knock on the opposite side of her boss' office door prompted Brittany to raise her head and rise to her feet. The alcohol in her body had her irritable and in no mood to bite her tongue for anyone. With a sigh, Brittany snatched her boss' office door open, only to see someone who she immediately felt relieved to see.

"Now, you gon' show up? Really, Zay?"

Brittany responded to her boss' cousin's embrace by wrapping her arms around her midsection, and hugging her back just as tightly. Both women fell into a duet of crying. The loss of Tianna Paradise Barnes had rocked their cores. Her role in their lives was vast beyond comprehension.

Inside of the office, after the door was once again closed, Brittany sat down behind her boss' desk.

"So, what's this Detroit stuff you was sayin' in ya text?"

"Me and some sisters flyin' there tonight."

"Why?"

"Because the day of my janazah, if Tia was there for it, she would be on the same page, Brit. That nigga in Detroit took my favorite cousin from me."

Brittany looked across her boss' desk, into the eyes of the only muslim woman she knew. Zainab and her boss were extremely close. Their bond as cousins had more sisterly qualities than anything else. Her boss had always spoken of her with admiration and high regards. On her own, Brittany had come to love her boss' cousin herself. Zainab was beautiful under her face veil, and one of the kindest women that Brittany had ever encountered. However, it was her boss who had always confided in her that Zainab wasn't to be underestimated.

"Are you gonna be okay, while I'm gone?"

Brittany had no answer.

Zainab flipped up her face veil as she stepped to a wall in the office, where there were a variety of pictures. Teardrops escaped her eyes as she approached a particular picture containing herself, her cousin, and two of her cousin's best friends, who were now deceased.

"Tia told me that you reminded her of Camay. Kyzer's sister. She loved you a lot, Brit. Don't let nobody or nothing stand in the way of the plan you and Tia had. Brit, pull it off for her. You and I both know, it's what she wanted."

"Zay, can I ask you a question?"

"What?"

"What Rock 'n Roll Rhonda got against me? She left me this real weird message earlier."

"Brit, Tia was like a mother to Rhonda. If Rhonda could be anybody, it would have been Tia. In Tia's eyes, and Splash's, for that matter, Rhonda can do no wrong. I'll go see her when I get back from Detroit. To answer your question, though, she was jealous of how close you and Tia were. Simply put, that's all it ever was. Then, it don't help that you started messin' with that guy Maniac. I know that was all Tia's idea, but Rhonda and her boyfriend got their own dealings with that guy, and maybe, too much of you is just rubbin' her the wrong way. Leave her to me."

"How will I know you okay in Detroit?"

"You won't, until I get back."

Brittany shared a sad stare with her boss' cousin. Brittany was scared for Zainab, but she couldn't bring herself to express her worries. Instead, she walked around her boss' desk and hugged Zainab tightly. Zainab's braveness invoked her own heart in a way that was unexplainable.

"Nobody still heard from my Uncle Tuna?"

"Nope," Brittany answered, as she released Zainab from her embrace. She, too, was confused as to why her boss' uncle hadn't reached out to anyone, since him and his girlfriend had left for New Orleans two weeks earlier. "His daughter was askin' me about him at the funeral. It's not like him at all."

"Walk me to the door, Brit."

On their way to the nightclub's front exit, the topic of Kyzer came up. It was a conversation that put Brittany's mind back on her boyfriend.

"Like, I know he gotta act like me and him ain't on the same page in front of everybody else, but, like, Zainab how else am I supposed to know what's his ideas? His friends been shootin' at my boyfriend and them for the last two days. Last night, they was shootin' for like ten minutes straight."

"Let him do what he do best, Brit. Trust me, you and Tia needed a war to distract that cop, and ya aunt's boyfriend, and after what happened to his mom, war is all Kyzer gon' know for awhile. He'll contact you when he need you."

"But, that's the thing. What if I need to contact him, Zay. His cousin was at the funeral, textin' on his phone the whole time."

"Brit, the best thing you could have ever did for Kyzer, was let him know that his cousin was a traitor. Our real dilemma, if you ask me, is how we gon' keep him and Rhonda from killin' each other? What she did to his friend, Hasaan, ain't gon' get swept under the rug, Brit. And now that Tia not here, I don't know who gon' be able to get in between them. To be honest, I'm happy Rhonda where she is. She'd monkey-wrench y'all entire plan, Brit. That girl is a wild card for real."

"If you had to pick between Kyzer and my boyfriend, who would you choose?"

Brittany smiled in embarrassment, as Zainab shook her head, while pulling her face veil back down over her face. They had reached the front exit.

"Okay, look, this is why I'm askin'. Earlier, I was talkin' to ya mom. So, somethin' she said been rentin' space in my head all day. It was about sex."

"Sex? On a day like today, she had a conversation with you about–"

"Zay, in her defense, we was at the bar and we overheard one of the strippers sayin' how a aunt of hers told her a long time ago that babies always get made after funerals. You know how, like, people be all sensitive, and–"

"Oh, I get it."

"I don't wanna be with my boyfriend tonight, Zay. We haven't done it yet, and at this point, I doubt if we'll ever get beyond kissin', but I want to be with somebody who'll appreciate me. You understand what I'm tryin' to say?"

"If you had 've asked Tia that question, who would she have told you to choose?"

"Who do you think?"

"Kyzer?"

"Well, there you go. Too bad he not answerin' his phone. Let's be fair, though. I guarantee you, sex is the last thing on Kyzer's mind. Brit, he just buried his mom today. Give him some space. Like I said, let him dictate the pace. Plus, if it get out that y'all up to a triple-cross, like y'all are, it ain't no tellin' what ya boyfriend will try to do to you. Throw yourself into your work, and keep as much distance between you and Kyzer as possible. We can't afford to let this plan go down the drain over a random night of sex, right?"

"Yeah, you right."

"Okay, let me go. I'll see you when I get back."

Brittany and Zainab hugged for a moment, then separated.

"Be careful, Zay."

"Brit, I got twenty-five sisters in Detroit, waitin' for me as we speak. That's what Twitter and Facebook can do for you. That guy that sent them orders to kill my damn cousin about to learn what women of the Sunnah are like, once you cross us. He killed women, Brit. Now, women about to kill him.

12:17 a.m.
"Yes? Hello?"
"Mom?"
"Sabia?"
"Yeah Mom. It's me."
"Oh, my God. Sabia, you sound so different. Are you okay? Where–where are you?"

It had been almost two years, since the mother and son had spoken to each other. The two of them were talking on recently purchased, pre-paid cell phones. The cell phone that the mother had pressed against her ear, had just been dropped off to her house earlier that morning, hidden inside of a box of elbow macaroni, that had been packed at the bottom of a bag of fresh groceries.

"Mom, I need 'ju to listen to me, okay?"
"Okay. Okay, I'm listenin'."
"Mom, Ashley and Honey parked around on Marshall and Oxford, in front of Howard and Bruno's. They in one of them new Nissan Pathfinders, waitin' for you. It's blue. Mom, Ashley and Honey gon' bring you to where I'm at, alright?"
"Okay."
"Now, look . . . as soon as we get off the phone, take the sim card outta that cell phone, break it, and flush it down the toilet. Mom, you hear me?"
"Break it, then flush it down the toilet."
"Yeah. Alright, now, on ya way to Ashley and Honey, drop that cell phone down that sewer hole on the corner of 6th and Cecil B. Moore. I love you. See you when you get here, okay?"

"Okay, I'm puttin' some clothes on right now."

"Mom?"

"Yes?"

"If any car move when you make it to the corner of 6th and Cecil B. Moore, turn around and just walk back to the house, like you forgot somethin'. Keep the phone with you. Once you back in the house, call Ashley cell phone, and tell her what happened. Her and Honey gon' come around to the house and get that phone from you, so we can get rid of it. We'll just try another way, alright?"

"Okay, baby."

"Alright, Mom."

Feeling anxious, Sabia sat his cell phone on his lap and let out an uncomfortable, long sigh. He was seated behind the steering wheel of his level six, bulletproof, aurora-blue 2012 Audi station wagon, and he was feeling more nervous than he would have like to have been. For the hundredth time, Sabia's eyes scoured his surroundings.

"I ain't gon' blame this on nobody, but me, if this move blow up in my fuckin' face," Sabia concluded, while looking around at the parking lot of the Fresh Grocer, where he was parked on 56th and Market. Him meeting his mother in West Philadelphia had been his friend, Ashley's idea. "Alright, lemme go over my 'Jason Bourne' shit again. My name Terrell Matthews. I'm twenty-five. I was born on December eleventh, nineteen eighty-seven. I'm from San Antonio, Texas, and I just got hired to be the new club promoter for the nightclub 'Gossip Alley,' down in Old city, on Third and Market. Yeah, my boss name Rasool Barnes. Huh? Yes, I have my driver's license, and my car registration, and insurance information right here in my glove compartment. Okay, you have a nice day yourself, sir."

As a necessary precaution, in case any potential confrontations with the law turned out to not lean in his favor, Sabia had two guns that were specifically for his car. One was on his right hip, and the other one was tucked beneath his driver's seat. All of the bullets in both Kimber forty-fives had baby, piranha teeth, sealed under a special dissolvent, in the small spaces of their hollow points. Each custom made bullet had cost Sabia fifty dollars a piece. He had five boxes of them.

While smiling, and pushing his shopping cart through the motion-sensored glass doors, of the 24-hour, Fresh Grocer supermarket, Sabia's cell phone began ringing in the pocket of his Gucci, leather jacket. The cool air in the supermarket chilled Sabia's bald head as he pulled out his cell phone, accepted his incoming call, and pressed his cell phone against his right ear.

"Who this?"

"Monica."

"Oh, yeah, from the funeral, right?"

"What other Monicas you know?"

"Lewinsky."

"You expectin' her call?"

"Naw, you the only Monica I'm tryna hear from right now. What's up wit 'chu?"

"Can I watch you fuck somebody tonight?"

Stunned by the request, Sabia stopped pushing his shopping cart and scratched the side of his head. He was standing beside the beginning of an aisle that was lined with canned vegetables, spices, and cooking oil, on its left side, and cereal on its right. Even while it was a late hour at night, the supermarket was still flowing with a generous amount of shoppers.

The woman that Sabia was speaking to was actually a narcotics detective, who had been employed by his cousin's wife to assist in the plan to help get Sabia's cousin out of jail. This knowledge was unknown to Sabia. A simple attraction, which was purely physical, had pulled Sabia and the detective to the same spot, outside of the church, after the funeral services for Kyzer's mother, and his cousin's wife, had ended. Sabia had approximated that the young, white woman was in her early twenties, but she was actually thirty-two. Sabia's other miscalculation was that the pretty, white woman was employed at his cousin's nightclub, as a stripper. They had exchanged numbers quickly, and had smiled the entire time, while doing so.

"To make it easy on you, I have a girl in mind, too. It's Terrell, right?"

"She work at Gossip Alley?"

"How'd you guess?"

"I'm good at guessin'. Alright, so when you tryna make this happen?"

"That's up to you. Listen, how about we do this. I'm going to text you my address. When you're on your way, I'll let the girl you're gonna fuck, know to beat 'chu here. I'll have her hot and wet, and ready for you by the time you make it to my front door. That's a promise, Terrell."

"Consider it a date, then."

"A date it is."

12:46 a.m.

With the night as their cover, silently, Marvin and Detective Baron Konn, both continued to unload their materials out of Detective Konn's rented, U-Haul truck. The orange and white truck was parked on the passenger side of Franklin Street, diagonal from Marvin's funeral home. The materials being unloaded, and taken into Marvin's funeral home, consisted of large bags of cement mix, and kitty litter, which would act as a substitute, instead of family members actually receiving an urn filled with their loved ones' human remains.

From several area hardware stores, broom sticks, pipes of various sizes, and law fertilizer, had been purchased to replace the bones, organs, and potential brains, of all of the corpses, once their lifeless bodies were transported to Marvin's Funeral Home, from the city morgue, and the Medical Examiner' s office.

The war in the neighborhood had begun. As of yet, no one had suffered any fatal injuries, but Marvin and Detective Konn wanted to both make sure that their inventory was substantially stocked. Agreements had already been made with a burn victim center in Portugal. They were willing to pay excellent money for skin of all colors, as long as the skin was in good condition. The doctor there had been calling and e-mailing Detective Konn, since they had spoken three weeks earlier. In a day, Marvin and Detective Konn's mortician from Kingston, Jamaica, would be arriving, which, then would complete their to-do list.

Living.

Dead.

12:52 a.m.

Growing up, Kyzer had been given the privilege of having two neighborhoods, where he was able to roam as he pleased. In South Philadelphia, his family members were valued, and highly respected for their participation in the growth and development of the notoriously known Philadelphia Black Mafia. Because of their involvement, no area in South Philadelphia had ever been unsafe for Kyzer. His mother's side of his family was spread out all over the streets of South Philadelphia. However, unlike a lot of his male cousins, Kyzer had grown up with an unquenchable thirst for earning his own street fame. He lusted it. The desire had blinded him in his teenage years, before he was even out of the seventh grade.

In North Philadelphia, Kyzer had an aunt, who was his mother's youngest sister. This aunt of Kyzer's had three daughters, and two sons, but she had loved Kyzer, and had treated him just like he was one of her very own. Spending most of his summers at his aunt's house had led Kyzer to meeting his friend, Hasaan, and the rest of his North Philadelphia friends. It was in this North Philadelphia neighborhood, where Kyzer had earned his status as a legend. He had proved himself in ways, both dangerous, and intelligent.

It was here, in this North Philadelphia neighborhood, on the night of his mother's funeral, where Kyzer was finding an eerie sense of comfort.

Head down, Kyzer was inhaling the cold, night air, through his nostrils. He was walking north, up Marshall Street, angry, tense, and crying. His mother's Range Rover was behind him, three blocks away, on the other side of Girard Avenue. At Marshall and Master, Kyzer paused, looked left, then he looked right. The streets were empty. Ahead of him, a city block away, the picture was completely different, and would be, until Kyzer got there.

Crossing Master Street, Kyzer began unbuttoning his gray, suit jacket. He started with the top button first. He was still dressed in the same attire he had worn to his mother's funeral, which consisted of his gray, Burberry suit, the white, Burberry shirt beneath it, and the gray, suede, Pierre Hardy sneakers, that he had on his feet. Kyzer's long, individual braids, were swinging back and forth across his face as he walked, hiding his teardrops at times, exposing them at others. Head still down, and still crying, Kyzer continued on his path up Marshall Street. He was on the passenger side of the street. His right shoulder was inches away from a giant wall of red paint, belonging to the Ludlow Recreation Center.

Ahead of Kyzer, on Marshall and Jefferson, crack and heroin were being distributed like they were legal. Kyzer's watery eyes counted at least eleven enemies, subtracting the dope fiends, crack addicts, and the random vehicles that were pulling up, double parking, buying their drugs of choice, and peeling off just as hurriedly as they had pulled up. The chatter of several conversations being had was reaching Kyzer's ears all the way down the street. The fact that he was outnumbered wasn't bothering him. In fact, the fire in his heart grew a temperature hotter, simply because there weren't more of them.

One block north, and four blocks west, stood the infamous intersection of 8th and Jefferson. In this particular neighborhood, 8th and Jefferson was like the United States. Kyzer was one of its leaders; some called him, 'The Enforcer,' while others referred to him as 'The Colonel.' Specific leaders from 8th and Jefferson determined what was allowed, and what wasn't allowed in the neighborhood. One of the foremost prohibitions was that no outsiders were permitted to freelance in the neighborhood, and sell any drugs on any corners, whatsoever.

Decades earlier, this wasn't the case. Between the intersections of Girard Avenue and Cecil B. Moore, and east and west, from the Amtrak bridge on 9th Street, down to 5th Street, was once a large melting pot of various groups. There were no set laws in the 80s, and early 90s, until Kyzer's friend, Hasaan, came up with the idea to rid the neighborhood of all outsiders. It was a plan that worked, and had worked well. Groups like the 10th and Thompson projects were cleared off of the corner of Marshall and Jefferson. Richard Allen projects no longer could freelance at the bar on 8th and Master. All others, who attempted to rely on their family roots in the area, were taxed weekly, and forced to distribute drugs from 8th and Jefferson.

Tenth and Thompson projects was 8th and Jefferson's biggest adversary. Led by Maniac, who controlled almost every housing project in North Philadelphia, 10th and Thompson didn't abandon Marshall and Jefferson, without one of the biggest, and bloodiest wars in North Philadelphia history. After Hasaan's death, in the summer of 2010, 8th and Jefferson had lost its premier leader. Kyzer's absence didn't help matters, and with the help of Kyzer's cousin, Idris, 10th and Thompson projects had reclaimed Marshall and Jefferson. Seeing this, other areas like the Richard Allen projects, 8th and Diamond, and Dominicans, with heavy heroin and cocaine connections, tentatively began to make their return. Every man was for himself. This was definitely the perspective that Kyzer's cousin, Idris, had.

It was the suit that Kyzer was wearing that had caused all heads to turn in his direction. It was also the stance that he had taken out in the middle of Jefferson Street that put everyone on alert. None of them were able to see the L-shaped gun in his right hand, because he had his hand behind his back. For a moment, Kyzer kept his head lowered. In that moment, he memorized everyone's positions, who he was going to shoot at first, and lastly, what direction he was going to take, once he was prepared to disappear from the scene.

"Ay, yo, that's that nigga Kyzer!!"

It was.

Like property,

some wars are inherited.

The percussion of gunshots had shattered the silent night with a range so high, it's violent sounds was being heard as far as Broad Street. All of the weapons being used were handguns, and none of them were under the caliber of a 9mm. Out of the seven men against Kyzer, only five of them had bravely dared to engage in a shootout with him.

The remaining two had taken flight up Marshall Street, joined by an equally as fast trio of dope fiends, and six crack addicts.

The five shooters were criss-crossing each other, and firing at Kyzer from both sides of Marshall Street. Only three faces were familiar to Kyzer. One of them was a cousin of Maniac's. Taught to always instill fear, and to leave lasting impressions in the minds of his enemies, Kyzer advanced a few steps, while he dug the live hand grenade out of the left pocket of his suit jacket. With his right hand, he continued to fire his Smith & Wesson 40. caliber handgun. He was being generous, throwing his bullets in threes. The windows of cars were exploding behind him, and in front of him. Car alarms were screaming with the gunshots.

Certain that his brazen tactic was going to bring federal eyes to the neighborhood, Kyzer brought the hand grenade up to his open mouth, and bit down on its metal pin with his front teeth, and pulled. A bullet flew by his left ear. Three more just missed the top of his head, and his right shoulder, as he crouched, took two more steps forward, and bowled the hand grenade up Marshall Street.

The hand grenade rolled and bounced, until it disappeared under the rear of a parked, silver Cadillac station wagon. The explosion was immediate, giving Kyzer no time to retreat. As he turned to run in the direction he came from, the powerful momentum of the blast lifted him from his feet, and sent him crashing into the windshield of a parked, tan, Ford Fusion.

"Ahhhh, shit," Kyzer grimaced, rolling himself off of the small car. As he fell to the sidewalk, he shielded his face with his left arm as falling debris came crashing down all around him. "Damn. What the fuck was I thinkin'? Ahhh!"

A fiery steering wheel from a car came down on Kyzer's left knee, and wobbled away. The contact left the knee area of Kyzer's suit burned, and exposing his right knee. Kyzer felt disoriented. His ears were ringing, and blood was coming out of them both. Up on his feet, Kyzer stumbled, jogged some, and held his hand against his left ear as he willed his body to take him down Marshall Street. Screams were echoing from houses, and car alarms were sounding off all around the neighborhood. The hand grenade had moved some houses from their foundations. Eight vehicles on the corner of Marshall and Jefferson were in flames, on their sides, and the silver Cadillac station wagon was in the living room of a house, directly on the corner, that no longer had a wall.

There were small fires scattered all over the place. Three of the five men from 10th and Thompson had perished from the blast. A left leg, belonging to one of them, was laying in the middle of Jefferson Street, sneakerless. The surviving two were being breathed on by the angel of death. Their agonizing cries for help were following Kyzer as he made his escape in the opposite direction.

The wails of sirens from responding EMT Units, Fire Departments, and area police cars, were intermingling in unison, and opening up the midnight sky.

At Master Street, while looking back at all the damage he had caused, Kyzer ran directly into the rear passenger door of Brittany's gold, BMW X3. The impact sent Kyzer down to the street, following the pin from the hand grenade, that his teeth had unclenched. Grabbing the pin frantically, Kyzer got back to his feet, and rushed around to the driver's side of the BMW, gun raised, and preparing to shoot at the driver. When he saw who was behind the steering wheel, his eyes reflected a mountain's worth of relief.

Brittany lowered her window with wide eyes as Kyzer lowered his gun. The blood from his ears was peppered across the shoulders of his suit jacket.

"Yo, hurry up and open ya trunk!"

"Why? What's wrong? What the hell–"

"Just do it!"

Brittany obeyed Kyzer's order and pulled the lever that opened the rear of her BMW. She looked into her rearview mirror, as Kyzer limped to the back of her car, and climbed into it with a groan.

"Where you want me to take you?"

"My house."

Chapter Nine

"Brittany, I would never place you in any danger that I couldn't protect you from."

"You mean that?"

"I swear to God, I won't. My funeral will come first, Brittany."

The sincerity accompanying Kyzer's words gave Brittany a sense of assurance that reached down into the bottom of her heart, and settled there. Growing up, honest love and attention had never been shown to Brittany. No one ever showed any real concern for her. Her crack addicted father's antics, and his bad reputation for stealing from the homes of family members, had caused a lot of them to undeservingly look down their noses at Brittany. Brittany's aunt was guilty of this as well. For Brittany's aunt, raising Brittany had been her way of polishing up her own image. She wanted to be seen as a savior in the judging-eyes of her family, while in all actuality, she was just an always-growing, black dot, on Brittany's innocent heart. She had never picked up any of Brittany's report cards, or had ever attended any of Brittany's graduations.

Brittany was as perceptive as she was beautiful. By her early teenage years, she had figured out who her true supporters in life were, and who they weren't. Accepting the cards that God had dealt her, Brittany simply lived her life, letting her odds work for her, and not always against her. Like tonight, for instance, she had left her job, drunk, feeling sexually starved, and wishing she was wherever Kyzer was. She had only been two blocks away from her apartment when her and Kyzer's fates had collided head-on.

"So, what do we do now?"

"Wait."

"For what?"

"For the dust to settle," Kyzer clarified, while stepping back from the fire-pit in his backyard, and handing Brittany his empty bottle of lighter fluid. With a toss of a lit match, his Burberry suit, sneakers, shirt, socks, and underwear, all became a ball of fire. "Give niggaz a chance to pick a side, bow out. That shit gon' get a lotta ink in the newspapers. It's probably on the news right now, as we speak. Yo, what was up wit' that club promoter nigga from Texas? He came over and tried to introduce himself to me, talkin' 'bout 'If you need me for anything, no matter what it is, you can get my info from Splash.' Then, I seen him talkin' to that cop bitch you showed me. I kept catchin' her dumb ass lookin' at me, too."

"I have the slightest idea who he is. Tia never mentioned any club promoters from Texas to me."

Brittany and Kyzer became silent for a moment, and watched as the fire ate up Kyzer's expensive clothes. The reflection of the fire was dancing in their eyes. Plumes of black smoke were feathering up into the dark sky.

Kyzer wrinkled his nose at the smell of the leather and suede burning on his sneakers. His fire-pit was outlined with colored stones, and went into the ground three feet. Five chairs circled it. On a chair closest to Kyzer, was another bottle of lighter fluid, brought in case the first one wasn't enough.

Brittany broke the silence and told Kyzer about Zainab's trip to Detroit, and about the message she had received from her boss' cousin, Rock 'n Roll Rhonda. She also told him about Maniac's phone call, and how Maniac had asked her about his whereabouts.

"Since he think you'd give up that type of information to him, maybe we should use that to our advantage. you can't be hangin' up on him, though, Brittany. I need you to keep that nigga comfortable wit 'chu."

"It's easier said, than done."

"What is?"

"Everything is," Brittany sighed, rolling her eyes and turning away from Kyzer's fire-pit. She dropped the empty bottle of lighter fluid down to the grass, balled her fists, and shook them at her sides. "Kyzer, I'm livin' in the house with the people that killed my dad. I gotta see them everyday. All for a plan that might, or might not work. For all we know, the cops can be on their way here right now, after your Rambo stunt you just pulled. You can't honestly stand there and tell me that, had I not been pullin' up to that stop sign at Marshall and Master, you saw ya self getting' away from the cops. You been ignorin' my calls. My texts. Kyzer, you could've died tonight on me."

"On you?"

Kyzer's question, and his confused look made Brittany catch her breath. She was drunk, and only expressing what she really felt. However, she was unsure of it being a wise choice to reveal to Kyzer that the idea of him and her actually being together had been renting mental space in her head, since they had met.

"Yes, Kyzer," Brittany said, letting her emotions get the best of her. Her eyes were on Kyzer's back, as he moved around his fire pit, while squeezing generous amounts of lighter fluid into it. "On me. On me, Kyzer."

It was windy and cold, but Brittany stood there braving it. She stood there watching Kyzer, wishing he understood her; and perhaps, even wanted her, possibly nearly as much as she wanted him. Tears came.

Hesitancy went.

"Before I even met'chu, my heart wanted you, just from how Tia talked about 'chu. She chose Maniac for me, because she thought you'd appreciate her loyalty more, if she brung Maniac to you on a silver platter. It made sense, so I went along with it, but my heart still wanted what it wanted, Kyzer."

Kyzer was on the opposite side of his fire pit, staring across it into Brittany's eyes. He held the half-empty bottle of lighter fluid down at his side. The wind was moving the fire left and right, and continuously guiding its billowy smoke upwards.

"Kyzer, if you came over here and hugged me, I'd probably wanna stay in your hug for the rest of my life. I'd walk across that fire to get to you. Look at me. Should I be in Maniac's arms, or yours?"

Kyzer looked away into the darkness of his backyard. He had dreamed of Brittany two nights ago.

"I'm where I wanna be, Kyzer. I'm here. If you think the cops comin', gimme a gun. I'll die wit 'chu tonight. I don't have no one else alive that loves me, so what am I livin' for? Kyzer, talk to me. For God's sake, say somethin.' Say anything."

"You want me to talk? Alright . . . leave Maniac, and be with me. Fuck him."

"Leave him when? Like, right now?"

"Startin' tonight. Move out here wit' me. We can get 'cha stuff from Marvin buildin' tomorrow."

"But what about our plan?"

"It just got remixed."

Emancipation.

94

Chapter Ten

"Daddy, why I died?"

No.

God, please . . .

Not again.

"Huh, Daddy?"

"You gon' give me a chance to answer you this time?"

The small child beside Sabia nodded his head as he bit into his lollipop, in a hearty attempt at reaching the bubble gum hidden inside of it. Sabia looked down at the little boy with eyes that were quickly becoming watery.

"And you gotta warn me, if you see Camay or Trixie this time, too, alright?"

" 'Kay."

Satisfied with their agreement, Sabia took his eyes off of the little boy long enough to look around at their surroundings. Sabia turned his head right, as far as his neck would allow, then he looked to his left. There were children of all sizes everywhere. The playground was packed with them. They were on monkey bars, the swing sets, the sliding boards, and even in the swimming pool, behind him.

While it had been a substantial amount of years, since Sabia had been inside of the playground, he still knew it like the back of his hand, and could direct someone around it with his eyes closed. It had once been his most favorite place to play as a child. His grandparents' house was two blocks north of it.

The North Philadelphia playground was called '6th and Master,' by the local residents, because of its location. The playground itself was huge, and it took up two city blocks' worth of space. It stretched from 6th Street, splitting Randolph, going all the way down to 5th, and went from Master Street, up to Jefferson. The top-right corner of the playground was a large, baseball field, complete with a dugout, a long, park bench, and a pitcher's mound. The field was a gigantic sea of green grass. To its left, was a swimming pool, only accessible from an entrance on 6th Street, that had a small building for its lifeguard staff. Behind that small building, ten feet away, was another building similar, that faced two, full-basketball courts. In the top-left and top-right corners of the playground, there were swing sets, sliding boards, and monkey bars. In total, the playground had eleven entrances, and was peppered with benches to sit on throughout.

"Daddy, I got two new friends. Lemme show you."

Philadelphia.

Nightmares.

Sabia's sleeping body jerked slightly in his hotel bed, as his dreaming body slowly rose to his feet, and gave the small boy his right hand. In his dream, Sabia looked like his old self. This is how it always was. There were no tattoos. No bald head. He was a lot heavier, and his eyes were their original color of brown. Before the dream became horrific, as they always did, Sabia looked down at the little boy holding his hand with pleading eyes.

"Where you takin' me, Teek?"

"To Macy and Kyree. My friends. They wanna know why you shot me, too, Daddy. Come on."

The little boy leading Sabia by the hand was utterly adorable. He could easily get by as the child of a Filipino, or Hawaiian couple. His skin was an olive complexion, and he was as tall as Sabia's knees. His small head was full of brown, curly hair, and his innocent, brown eyes, were separated by a tiny button nose. Sabia was the only father that the child knew.

The playground was alive with a myriad of childish excitement. It was an innocent environment, absent of any signs of malice. The combination of talking, high-pitched giggling, and laughter, had the atmosphere in the playground buzzing like recess time at an elementary school. The only unsmiling face in the playground belonged to Sabia. Other dreams had taught Sabia well. His eyes were reflecting concern, and uncertainty, as he reluctantly followed behind Shateek, a child he had murdered by mistake.

Remorse.

"Hold up, Teek."

The small boy stopped, and looked up at Sabia, never releasing Sabia's hand. He was almost done with his lollipop.

"Teek, I'm sorry," Sabia apologized, falling to his knees. Tears started to spill from his eyes as the child he once thought was his son, brung his innocent eyes up to his stare, and held it. "I didn't mean to hurt 'chu, okay? I didn't. You got in the way, Teek. It–It was an accident. I would've never did anything to hurt 'chu."

" 'Cause–'Cause I'm ya son, right, Daddy? Ky–Kyree . . . him said you shot me, 'cause you not my Daddy."

"Teek, I'm not."

Every child in the playground stopped what they were doing, and watched as Shateek dropped his half-eaten lollipop, and released Sabia's hand. It was a moment of sad truth. Raising his tiny hands to his face, the little boy began backing away from Sabia; crying. His heart had been broken by his hero. All of the children started to cry with him. Afraid, Sabia slowly observed what was happening all around him, by turning his face from right to left, as he rose to his feet.

The sky above the playground was becoming dark and cloudy. The children started to cry harder; louder. Their physical features were changing right before Sabia's eyes. Clean clothes of theirs were slowly becoming dirty, torn, and stained with blood. Sabia gasped for air when the vaginal areas of certain little girls began to bleed profusely, showing on the front of their school uniforms and pajamas. They had been raped and murdered. Some of them were never found, remaining in shallow graves, dug by pedophiles. Their screams were the loudest in Sabia's ears.

The little boys' crying, while not as loud as the girls', held deep shame. Many of their stains of blood were dripping down the backs of their pants. They were the victims of molesters, still missing; dead, but not found. Other boys had gruesome gunshot wounds to their heads, bodies, and faces. Innocent bystanders of guilty shootouts, where flying bullets had been nameless.

Sabia brought his attention back to Shateek, who now had his face uncovered. Before Sabia could even take in the unsightly mess he had caused to the little boy's face, a loud crack of thunder shook the cement beneath Sabia's feet, and everything went completely dark.

"You dyin' next, Daddy."

Gulping air, Sabia snatched his eyes open and sat up in his hotel bed, dripping sweat. Shateek's words, 'you dyin' next, Daddy,' were echoing inside of his head. The nightmare wasn't as scary as a lot of his other ones, and Sabia felt grateful that it wasn't as he reached over and grabbed his ringing cell phone.

"Hello?"

"I never had a guy stand me up before."

Distracted by his dream, Sabia had answered his cell phone, without looking to see who the caller was. It was 8:37 a.m., and pouring down rain outside.

"Somethin' came up. My bad."

"Not even a courtesy call?"

Sabia swung his bare feet out of bed and put them on the floor. He was happy to be talking to someone, and grateful for being awoke. Placing his elbows on his knees, he wiped his right hand down his face, giving himself a moment to gather his thoughts.

After spending an hour with his mother, Sabia had returned to his Center city hotel suite, put away the groceries he had purchased at the Fresh Grocer, and he had fallen asleep, while watching Sports Center. It was actually the first time that he had slept the entire night through. Most of his nightmares would have never allowed this to happen. The six and a half hours of undisturbed rest had restored Sabia's body with an abundance of energy.

"How can I make it up to you, Monica?"

"Let's do lunch."

"That's it?"

"For now."

Sabia switched his cell phone to his opposite ear, smiling.

"Since Philly is practically new to you, I'll decide where we'll eat. I'll text you the place, okay?"

"Alright," Sabia chuckled, amused at Monica's belief that the city of Philadelphia was a new place to him. Her misconception of him brought a wide smile to his face. "I'm happy you called me, too, though. You beat me to the punch. Where you at right now?"

"Work."

"Work? This early?"

"This early? Terrell, what kind of work do you think I do?"

Sabia lowered his cell phone from his ear and covered its speaker with the palm of his left hand. He could hear Monica's voice still. Confused, Sabia placed his cell phone back to his ear.

". . . .rell? Terrell?"

"So, you don't work at Gossip Alley?"

"You think I'ma stripper? Terrell, what would make you think that?"

Sabia was speechless.

"Terrell, I'ma cop. I'ma homicide detective."

Chapter Eleven

I am

My own worst enemy.

"At least she not dead. I ain't know what the hell was goin' on up here, the way you was knockin'. Well, she's all yours. Her and his little bad ass."

With rain dripping from her umbrella, Brittany stood in the bedroom doorway of her co-worker's one-bedroom, West Philadelphia apartment, at a complete loss for words. Shock was burgeoning through her system like wildfire. Beside Brittany, to her right, stood her co-worker's landlord. The scene before their eyes was a shameful collaboration of poor motherhood skills, atrociousness, and a strong aura of child neglect.

"Let me get my fat ass to the store, so I can play my lottery. Good luck. What's ya name again?"

"Brittany."

"Good luck, Brittany. You gon' need it. That bitch think she got it all figured out. If she ain't pay her rent on time, I would've been evicted her ass months ago."

"Thanks for lettin' me in."

"Don't mention it."

At the door, the middle-aged, black woman, smoothed out her gray ponytail with her left hand, then, with an angry face, placed both of her hands on her wide hips. She was disgusted. Shaking her head at the mess in her tenant's small kitchen, she blew out a sigh, gave Brittany one final look, then walked out of the apartment, slamming the door behind her.

Brittany backed out of her co-worker's bedroom, and walked over to a window in the living room, where she dropped her umbrella down to the floor, and removed her cell phone from the pocket of her floral, Kate Spade raincoat. The Tuesday afternoon rain was pelting against the window like small rocks. Phone to her ear, Brittany called Kyzer.

"Hello?"

"You busy?"

"For you, I'm not. What's up?"

"I need some encouragement."

"Encouragement?"

"Okay, look," Brittany spoke, after switching her cell phone to her other ear, and taking a needed, deep breath. The sight of her co-worker's apartment had her sick to her stomach, and feeling nauseous. "One of the strippers at the club has a big role in our situation. I'm here at her apartment."

"I thought 'chu was goin' by Marv spot, so you could meet the movers?"

"I rescheduled it, 'til tomorrow."

"Why?"

"This was more important."

"So was getting' ya shit outta Marv spot, but go 'head."

"You'll understand my decision later," Brittany assured, as she flipped up the half-open lid of the pizza box lying on her co-worker's space heater. The sight of roaches backed her heart into a corner in her chest, and sent her back over to the window, where she chose to stay, and stand still. "Kyzer, it's a mess in here. She in her room sleep, dead to the world. Her son got condoms on his arms, Kyzer."

"Condoms?"

"Condoms," Brittany repeated, wanting to cry. The sad atmosphere of her co-worker's living space was overwhelming. "It look like he must've fell asleep playin' with condoms, I guess. Kyzer, it's so dirty in here. Her landlord let me in. She don't even know I'm here. What should I do? Her refrigerator door wide open, and ain't nothin' in it. I see a bottle of spring water, and that's it. Her sink full of dishes. It's roaches everywhere. It don't make sense, though, Kyzer. All the guys come to the club for her. Like, it's been times where the bouncers had to bring out bags to help her collect all her money from the stage. Kyzer, she the one that's gon' help us with the detective at the Halloween party. We need her."

"Wake her ass up, and give her the pep talk of her life, then. It sound like she need one."

"That's it?"

"Or leave."

"Kyzer, I can't just leave. I can't."

"Well, if you gon' stay there, turn into a maid, and do what 'chu gotta do, until ya heart satisfied with ya work. That's the best advice I can give you right now, Brittany. You hear from Zay, yet?"

"No. Splash, either."

"So, what 'chu gon' do?"

"Stay."

"Alright, well, just call me, if you need me. Where you at?"

"West Philly."

"Where?"

"Fifty-second and Ogden."

"Alright . . . call me when you done."

"Okay."

Ending her call with Kyzer, Brittany made one more important phone call. She had someone to thank.

"Detective Best speakin'."

"Monica, you busy?"

"Not really. I'm actually at lunch. Did you get my e-mail?"

"That's why I'm callin'."

"A call from him would have been better, Brit. He owe me. You do, too. What I did was far from easy. That can't happen again, Brit."

"It won't."

"You okay? You sound distracted."

Brittany couldn't keep her eyes off of the roach-infested pizza box, sitting on her co-worker's space heater. The sight of the pillaging roaches kept making every inch of her skin crawl.

"I'm good," Brittany lied, glancing up at the ceiling of the living room for any roaches that might possibly fall down on her. Switching her cell phone to her opposite ear, she walked back over to her co-worker's bedroom doorway, and stopped. "I can't say the same for Honey, though. It's lookin' like she might be a wildcard, Monica."

"Oh, really? How so?"

"Can we meet when you get off work?"

"Where?"

"That bar me, you, and Tia met at, the night we put all of this together."

"I'll text you when I'm in traffic."

"Okay."

"Question."

"What?"

"What do you know about this guy Terrell? I'm havin' lunch with him, and I can't shake the notion that he's not as unfamiliar with Philly as he say he is. Tia ever mention him to you before?"

"Not once."

"Maybe it's just the detective in me, but there's definitely somethin' off about him. He's friends with Splash, right?"

"Well, that's what he told me at the funeral. Said he was from Texas, and that he was a club promoter."

"Okay, well, let me stop being rude. I got him waitin' for me at our table. Do me a favor, Brit."

"What's that?"

"Tell Splash to get in touch with my mom. What happened to Tia really has her upset."

"Got 'chu. And thanks again for that diversion, Monica."

"Don't mention it."

Brittany liked Monica as a person, and as a friend. So had her boss. Monica looked like a blond-haired, Katy Perry. Her eyes were blue and always serious. She was thirty-two, had no children, and had no man. Moving to Philadelphia had been a big step for her, but in doing so, it had given her more freedom from her mother's watchful eyes.

Monica loved to party. Gossip Alley had become her weak spot. She loved everything about the nightclub, and sometimes, she was one of the last people to walk out of its doors, after closing hours.

Off of her cell phone, Brittany gave both Monica and her co-worker, Honey, a moment of thought, as she stood in the doorway of her co-worker's bedroom, and continued to watch as her co-worker and six-year-old son slept. The two women were like oil and water, and both had significant roles to play in bringing Detective Konn to his demise. Brittany wanted Detective Konn's death to be a slow and painful one. He had killed her first love. For Brittany, Detective Konn's death was as important as her aunt's and Marvin's. Still, without Monica, or Honey, the opportunity for revenge would most likely disappear.

Monica Best was a police officer with a criminal mind. Her mother had bred her that way. Monica's father was a politician from Baltimore, Maryland, who was serving nineteen years in a federal prison for the misuse of campaign funds, wire fraud, and for being the brains behind a child pornography enterprise. Although, very wealthy, life hadn't been easy for Monica. Most of her life had been spent as a puppet for her mother; at least, this was the conclusion that Brittany had come to, after hearing Monica's story from her own lips. Becoming a police officer had been forced on Monica. She was a tough detective, but an even tougher woman. Her mother, Patricia Best, was a federal judge in Maryland, who had strong ties with a substantial amount of Republicans in Washington, D.C. To get to her position, Monica's mother had played chess. She had already been respected as a federal prosecutor, and as a no-nonsense woman when inside of the courtrooms, but when she had exposed all of Monica's father's indiscretions, it had cemented her credibility at the federal courthouse, and to most, cast the belief that true justice was extremely imperative to her, and that no one, not even her then-husband, should be exempt of its guidelines.

Monica was torn between her parents. Her personal life was surrounded by following her mother's orders, and waiting for her father's collect phone calls from federal prison. Initially, Monica had dreaded the move to Philadelphia. She had cried and had begged her mother to send someone else instead. After meeting Brittany's boss, Monica understood why she had been needed. Manipulated by her mother, of course, Monica was pulled into a special Homicide Unit that dealt with all of Philadelphia's high profile murders, and narcotics arrests.

Detective Konn was in Monica's unit. He was her command leader, unaware that she was secretly building a federal case against him, and sometimes wearing a wire in his presence. Monica's mother had a corrupt, federal agent in Philadelphia, who Monica reported to weekly.

It was unknown to Kyzer, but Brittany had sent Monica an urgent e-mail, explaining what Kyzer had done on Marshall and Jefferson, hoping that Monica could use her position to keep Kyzer in the clear. Thinking fast, and acting as if she had gotten information from a confidential informant, Monica combined a days-old case she had been working, where a Philadelphia-based drug ring had been indicted on drug trafficking charges. Monica told Detective Konn, her superiors, and the federal agent she knew through her mother, that the drug dealers on Marshall and Jefferson had been targeted, because they were believed to be behind the drug indictment.

At the moment, the intersection of Marshall and Jefferson was off-limits. Jefferson Street was closed from 7th Street, down to 6th Street. The Water Department was trying to deal with a water main break, resulting from Kyzer's hand grenade. Water was flooding the pavement and street, and cascading down Jefferson Street, flowing into the playground. Tow trucks had came and removed the destroyed vehicles, after the Crime Scene Agents had done field tests on them. Most of the scene had been photographed, and dealt with, long before the rain had started to fall from the Tuesday morning sky, hours earlier.

Honey Richardson was nothing like Monica Best. Honey was a woman of a different kind. She was a bull in a China shop, and she had to be protected from herself. Her mouth was unfiltered, and her heart was corrupted by twenty-two years of exposure to the streets of North Philadelphia.

As Brittany watched Honey sleep, she wondered how hard life had been to her. She knew little about Honey, except that she had a son, was in debt with a lot of their co-workers, smoked PCP, and that Detective Konn couldn't get enough of her. Honey had also gotten into several fights with other strippers at Gossip Alley, and was rumored to be illiterate.

Despite being uncensored, and whatever else was said about her, Brittany had never had any problems out of Honey at work. Honey mostly kept to herself, and only held conversations with a handful of their co-workers. Honey's beauty was flawless, and it wasn't under contract, but Honey was actually the face of Gossip Alley. Her profile was on the nightclub's business website, and normally used on all of the nightclub's promotional campaigns. To see that she was living so poorly had Brittany stinging with exploitation.

On October thirty-first, Gossip Alley was throwing a big Halloween party. There, Honey's job was to lure Detective Konn into a bathroom stall, where Kyzer would be waiting. The problem was, from what Brittany was now seeing, Honey appeared to be in no shape to deal with such an important task.

"I can't do this right now," Brittany decided, while backing out of her co-worker's bedroom doorway. Turning to go retrieve her umbrella by the window, two mice darted across Honey's dirty, living room floor, giving her heart a good scare. "Fuck that umbrella. This shit don't make no sense. All that money she make, and she livin' like this. Why? And what did Tia have on her, to make her help with Detective Konn? That's what I need to find out. Maybe Monica know."

On the opposite side of Honey's apartment door, Brittany pulled out her ringing cell phone, as she pulled the hood of her jacket over her head, and began descending the flight of stairs down to the first floor of the apartment building. Brittany frowned at the screen of her iPhone, seeing that the incoming call was blocked.

"Yes?"

"Brittany Simmons?"

"Yes? Who this?"

"Detective Konn."

Brittany paused at the bottom of the stairs and removed her hood from her head.

"I'm here at the funeral home with Marvin. It's time we meet. There's also been a slight change in plans. How soon can you get here?"

"About an hour."

"Be here in thirty minutes. Ignore the red lights. If you get pulled over, call Marvin's phone, and simply hand your cell phone to the cop that stopped you. I'll handle the rest. We clear, Brittany?"

"We clear."

"Great. Now, hurry up."

One of Brittany's strongest qualities was her fearlessness, and her high level of determination. Like any other person, she had her personal faults, but when she gave a goal her commitment, she gave it her all, and she seldom took her mind off of it, until she saw her goal completed. In the wake of her boss' death, Brittany's perception had amplified. She knew that all eyes would be on her at work. She also knew that filling her boss' shoes would be impossible, and that in trying to do so, she would easily become a failure. However, Brittany achingly knew that she couldn't stand by, and just watch as her and her boss' plan lost its life. To allow that, would mean that revenge would never be hers in the end.

In her car, Brittany sent text messages to Kyzer, then to Monica. She let them both know about her meeting with Detective Konn, then started up her car with teardrops flowing down her face. After making a U-turn on 52nd Street, Brittany stomped her right foot down on her gas pedal, and sped across the intersection of 52nd and Westminister, ignoring the red traffic light. Detective Konn's death was her goal; failing at that was not optional.

Dishonor.
Before.
Death.

Tuesday afternoon, sitting across from Jamillah, his friend, Hasaan's sister, Kyzer revealed some of his secret plans. The setting was a place that was referred to by Kyzer and his friend's as the 'Chrome Depot.' It was their headquarters, and had been, for more than a decade.

The Chrome Depot was located on the passenger side of 8th Street, between the intersections of Oxford, and Jefferson. It was once, two abandoned, three-story row houses. During their childhood years, it used to serve Kyzer and his friends as an oversized clubhouse. Wisely, while Kyzer had been away in prison, his friend, Hasaan, had purchased both properties at a sheriff's sale, and then had gone on to invest a large amount of drug money into upgrading the two adjacent buildings into a sight worth admiring. The exterior of the properties looked like typical houses, except for the metal shutters covering all of its many windows, and its security cameras. It was the interior of the Chrome Depot that possessed qualities of amazement, and where even a man like James Bond would find himself appreciating his surroundings.

The Chrome Depot had been made into one domain, by having the adjoining downstairs wall, of both houses, removed creating one large, dining area, and an even larger living room. The remaining walls had been mirrored from floor to ceiling. In the spacious dining area, where there was a small bar, there were hardwood floors. The shelves of the bar held every domestic and imported liquor imaginable. Behind the counter of the bar, standing alone in the left corner, there was a white refrigerator. The refrigerator was stocked with orange juice, cranberry juice, pineapple juice, bottles of water, and in its freezer, there were several bags of ice. To the right of the refrigerator, mounted into the rear-wall, above a shot-glass cabinet, there was a surveillance, split-screen monitor. Each small screen on the monitor showed a different view of the Chrome Depot's exterior.

In the giant, living room, where there was an ocean of white carpet, white leather furniture was decoratively placed all around the room. This is where Kyzer and Jamillah were. The two of them were shoeless. Their footwear were back at the borderline, where the white carpet met the hardwood floors of the dining area.

Upstairs, there were ten bedrooms. Each bedroom had its own personal keypad, entry-lock. On the second floor, a bathroom had been remodeled into a gun collector's fantasy. A total of sixty-three guns outlined all four walls of the room, ranging from assault rifles, shotguns, riot pumps, down to handguns, of all makes and models. The basement of the Chrome Depot was sectioned off into five separate rooms. There was a prayer area, a library, an entertainment room, a bathroom, which was the only one in the entire building, and last of them all, was an exercise room that was complete with everything necessary to keep a man's body in top, physical shape.

In case of a police raid, the evacuation drill for the Chrome Depot was that any and everyone who was inside of the building, had to make it to the third floor, where access to the Chrome Depot's roof was available. Once one got to the roof, it was then necessary for one to make it down to the rooftop of the first house on 8th and Oxford. At this house, there were six weather-proof bags, covering chain-linked, drop ladders, that were mounted into the house's rooftop. Below, parked on Oxford Street, facing west, were two, black, 16-seat passenger vans, which hadn't been driven since their purchases.

City.

Of.

Secrets.

"Kyzer, fuck these streets. If I had one chance to talk to Hasaan, that's exactly what I would tell him. Focus on longevity. Take a college course in somethin'. Out grow Philly, and move—"

"Drees was there when Saan got shot."

Jamillah flipped up her black face veil, exposing her light brown, beautiful face. Her brown eyes held disbelief, as Kyzer's own eyes stared back at her, reflecting truth. Slowly, Jamillah's eyes showed acceptance of her husband's unspeakable betrayal, and as they did, her hands rose to her face, and she started to cry. In that moment, Kyzer wished he could kill his cousin a thousand times.

Kyzer and Jamillah shared a complicated history. They both had an unique nearness to one another, and their bond went as far back as their early teenage years. They had been a couple once. However, their relationship had only lasted one summer. The love the two of them shared had never lost its life, and even years later, when Kyzer's cousin, Idris, moved to Philadelphia from Atlanta, and started dating Jamillah, her and Kyzer still maintained their friendship. Jamillah was married to Idris, and they had a small family together.

"Drees don't know I know, Millions," Kyzer explained, as he sat beside Jamillah, and comforted her by wrapping his arms around her. He was ashamed that him and his cousin shared the same DNA, but, too, hoped that Jamillah's love for her brother would outweigh her love for her husband. "He was there, though. I got proof, Mill. He in bed wit' Maniac, so he can be at the top of the totem pole around here. Why you think I ain't been fuckin' wit' him, since I been home? Come on, that right there should've told you somethin' wasn't right. Mill, look, everything you just said was right. My mom was tellin' me the exact same shit that day at the cemetery. Millions, this whole neighborhood can sink to the middle of the earth, for all I care. I ain't back for none of these fuckin' corners. It's about revenge for me, and that's it, Mill."

Jamillah raised her head and wiped her hands down her face. Kyzer unwrapped his arms from around her and held her stare.

"Who told you?"

"Niggaz was talkin' about that shit at my jail. It got confirmed when I got out."

"By who?"

Kyzer filled Jamillah in on all of the things that Maniac had been confiding in Brittany. His sole intentions for telling Jamillah so much, was in hopes that she would feel no sympathy for his cousin, and feel no need to want to protect his life.

"I'm supposed to be next, Mill."

"Next for what?"

Before Kyzer could give Jamillah an answer, his cell phone began to ring in the pocket of his jeans.

"Hold up . . . this Deen."

Kyzer accepted the incoming call from a female cousin of his, then raised his cell phone up to his right ear. Crying still, Jamillah got up from the couch and disappeared into the Chrome Depot's downstairs hallway.

"Hello?"

"What's up, Cousin?"

"Yo, my bad for callin' you, while you was at work."

"It's okay. It just be a little busy in the mornin'."

Shadeen was one of Kyzer's favorite female cousins. Growing up, she'd always get into fights that Kyzer had with other guys, and fight them as hard as she possibly could. It was near her house, where Kyzer had left his mother's Range Rover the night before.

"Deen, you want my mom truck?"

"Why? What's wrong with it?"

"Nothin'," Kyzer assured his cousin, rising from the couch, and wondering where Jamillah had went. Cutting his eyes at Jamillah's pocketbook, he walked over to a mirrored-wall in the Chrome Depot's living room. "It's parked on 5th and Brown. It's yours, if you want it."

"Yeah, I'll take it. You sure, though, Cousin?"

"Deen, you, Kia, Zack, and Aunt Neecy, some of my favorite women in life. You know how many times I would've got locked up, if I couldn't scramble to Randolph Street to y'all house? I'ma leave the keys in ya mailbox, alright?"

"Thank you, Cousin."

Kyzer could hear the emotions in his cousin's voice, and knew that she was moved by the gift, more because the vehicle had belonged to his mother.

"Alright, Deen, I love you."

"Love you too, Cousin."

After Kyzer returned his cell phone back to his pocket, he stared at his reflection in the wall mirror. His individual braids were frizzy, and needed to be done over. As his eyes lowered down past his yellow, Rag & Bone sweater, and his faded blue, Jaree Foxx jeans, he thought about Jamillah's new pain. Her husband, and father of her two children, had been responsible for her older brother's death. This amount of hurt, Kyzer assumed, had to be a grade above devastating.

Kyzer then thought about Brittany. He had called her, after receiving her text message, concerning her meeting with Detective Konn. Marvin's funeral home was only around the corner, but Kyzer had worry in that Brittany would be by herself, and not have anyone to protect her against Detective Konn, or Marvin, if either of the men chose to suddenly get unruly with her. Jamillah's reflection in the mirror pulled Kyzer out of his troubled thoughts. She still had her face veil flipped up over the black scarf, covering her head. Kyzer kept his eyes on Jamillah's reflection, trying to read her. He needed her to be angry; angry enough to want the father of her son and daughter dead. Angry enough to keep it a secret from his family, her children, and anyone else.

"I went downstairs and prayed. I know you enough to know why you told me what Drees did, and why you ain't tell nobody else. He muslim, Kyzer. We all are."

Kyzer turned his back to his reflection and dug his hands down into the pockets of his jeans. He was muslim, but since his sister's death, he had stopped praying.

"You want me to okay what happens to Drees. Ain't that it?"

"Mill, what's the eighth nullifier of Islam?"

"A muslim helpin' the disbelievers against another muslim. The proof in Surah five, ayah fifty-one."

"Need I say more?" Kyzer asked, watching Jamillah as she returned to where she had been sitting on the couch. He crossed his arms over his chest, and let out a sigh. "He 'posed to be settin' me up next, Mill. That nigga usin' Islam like a bulletproof vest out this mu'fucker. He in bed wit' Maniac. A fuckin' kafir. I'm his fuckin' cousin, Mill. If it wasn't for me, who would've shown him love around here? Our fuckin' moms is sisters. If shit was reversed, and Saan wife had somethin' to do wit 'cha murder, do you think he'd give that bitch a pass? Mill, you know he wouldn't. Fuck Drees. I tell you this, no matter how you feel about what he did, I'm fuckin' him over. That's where I'm at wit' it. And if you second-guessin' shit, 'cause of y'all kids, Saan had kids, too. Jackie got married again, and so can you."

"If somethin' gotta happen to him, I wanna be the one that do it, Kyzer."

"That's right, Millions. Now, we talkin' the same language."

"And I want that bitch, Rock 'n Roll Rhonda, to get it, too. I don't want nobody alive that had somethin' to do with my brother dyin'. Now, sit down and tell me how we gon' deal with Drees."

Kyzer walked over and joined Jamillah on the couch. For a long moment, the two of them sat in silence. The agonies of life had pulled them into a vacuum of morose emotions, from what was to come, and what had gotten them to that moment. Normally, a busy place, the Chrome Depot was quiet. The only sounds being heard were that of the raindrops beating against the Chrome Depot's many windows. The metal shutters covering them, were echoing soft thuds, almost sounding like small rocks were being thrown at them.

"I'm two months pregnant."

Kyzer raised his head, and caught Jamillah as she wiped her left hand down her face to catch a falling teardrop.

"We just picked out some names last night. If it's a girl, we naming her Haneefah. And if it's a boy, we decided on Hasaan."

Kyzer's own eyes became watery. He knew that Jamillah's heart was at a crossroad, and that it had a lot to do with her children she shared with his cousin. Despite his cousin's betrayal, even he couldn't deny that his cousin was an excellent father.

"Kyzer, our children gon' miss him so much. Even I am."

"Mill, I'm gon' miss that nigga like I miss a toothache."

At 4:38 p.m., Kyzer received a phone call from Brittany, while he was walking east down Cecil B. Moore Avenue. After making a left turn up 6th Street, Kyzer put his cell phone to his ear.

"Hello?"

"You ready to get picked up, yet? I'm right here on 8th and Jefferson, if you are."

"Yeah, but I ain't even there no more."

Kyzer switched his cell phone to his right ear, and started looking at the addresses of the houses as he slowly passed them.

"Where you at?"

"Down 6th Street."

"Why?"

"I'll tell you when you get here. I'm between Montgomery and Cecil B. Moore. Ay, yo, what was up wit' Marv and dickhead?"

"When I tell you this shit, you gon' flip. Do you have a umbrella?"

"Nope."

"Are you in a car?"

"Nope. On foot."

"Why?"

Kyzer stopped at the house he was looking for. Its address read seventeen-twelve. Raindrops beat at his upturned face, as his eyes went up to the third-floor windows of the red painted row house.

"I'm on my way right now."

"Alright."

As Kyzer went to return his cell phone back to his gray, Nicole Miller jacket pocket, his cell phone started ringing again. Not checking to see who the caller was, Kyzer accepted the incoming call and pressed his cell phone against his ear, while crossing to the opposite side of 6th Street.

"Yo?"

"Kyzer?"

"Yeah, who this?"

"Terrell. We met at Tia and ya mom funeral. I'm a friend of Splash's."

A confused expression swept across Kyzer's rain-wet face as he reached the opposite sidewalk, and turned to face the street.

"I just came from visiting Splash. He spoke highly of you, and thought that we should get together."

"About what?"

"I don't think that type of business for the phone, Kyzer."

"Yeah, well, I'm busy right now," Kyzer explained, as he looked across 6th Street at Sabia's mother's house. The temptation to run across the street and kick the door in was causing an avalanche in his chest. "The rest of my night kind of busy, too."

"What about tomorrow?"

"What about it?"

Kyzer didn't like Terrell. His initial impression of Terrell at his mother's funeral hadn't been a good one. Their first encounter had only been a quick handshake, with Terrell offering his condolences, and him introducing himself as a friend of Splash's. Even in that brief moment, to Kyzer, Terrell's genuine approach had been anything but. A day later, Kyzer was still feeling the same insincere vibe, resonating from the other end of his cell phone. Little did Kyzer know, Terrell was actually Sabia; his childhood friend. The very man who had murdered his sister.

His sworn enemy.

Brittany's gold BMW made a slow right off of Montgomery Avenue, and fell into pace with the string of cars traveling down 6th Street. The windshield wipers on all of the vehicles were swaying back and forth.

"You tryna link up tomorrow?"

"Where?"

"Well, Splash want me to meet this chick that was his wife's assistant tomorrow. He gave me her number. Her name Brittany."

"Yeah, I know 'er."

As Brittany pulled to a stop in front of Kyzer, Sabia's mother opened her front door and looked across the street at Kyzer. The tension between Kyzer and Sabia's mother quickly became palpable. Despite his slight weight gain, and his face being partially masked by his individual braids, Sabia's mother had recognized Kyzer at first glance. He was her son's best friend; or was. There used to be a time when he had permission to walk into her house, without having to knock on the door.

Thousands of raindrops were falling between Kyzer and Sabia's mother. Hundreds of emotions were coursing through their veins, and the one person who was solely responsible for their contempt, and deep rift, was on the opposite end of Kyzer's cell phone, clueless to the silent confrontation happening between them.

"Splash want me to help Brittany out at the club, 'n shit like that. Make sure it stay afloat. Once I . . ."

Kyzer switched his cell phone to his other ear as he walked around the front of Brittany's car, never once breaking his stare with Sabia's mother.

". . . what her schedule like, you feel like meetin' me there?"

"Yeah, we can do that. Just call me when you there."

At Brittany's passenger door, Kyzer stood with his back to it, and continued his staring match with Sabia's mother, while returning his cell phone to his jacket pocket. His clothes were drenched, but he could care less.

"I ain't gon' do nothin' to you, Miss Steph," Kyzer thought to himself, putting his back against Brittany's passenger door, as some cars coming down 6th Street got closer to where he stood. Sabia's mother's eyes were as angry as he was feeling. "Not yet, anyway. I just want 'chu to feel threatened, that's all. I'm willin' to bet my right fuckin' arm, you and Sabia be in touch some kind of fuckin' way. I know y'all is. Vacations over, now, though, Miss Steph. I'm about to throw you and ya son a real live, middle finger party."

Dripping wet, Kyzer raised his right hand to his forehead and saluted Sabia's mother. As soon as he got into Brittany's car, Brittany greeted him with some bad news.

"They got a hit out on you."

"Who?"

"Tenth and Thompson."

"Let the fuckin' games begin, then. Matter fact, take me through there right now."

"Kyzer, stop . . . wait. There's more."

"What else?"

"Rock 'n Roll Rhonda home. She got out this mornin'."

Chapter Twelve

The still-raining sky was now a black, dreary canvas. Afternoon had become evening, and temperatures in the city of Philadelphia had dropped down to the late 40s.

Sabia was standing at a window in the kitchen of his hotel suite, lost in thought. He was in a dismal mood, and feeling depressed. He had just returned from Northeast Philadelphia, where he had gone to visit his cousin, Splash, at a county prison. The hour long visit had Sabia exhausted mentally, as well as emotionally. What little fortitude he did have remaining, had left him, once he had spoken to his childhood friend, Kyzer, on his cell phone. The phone conversation had brought goosebumps to his skin. Right away, Sabia had sensed Kyzer's distrust in him, and understood clearly, that if Kyzer ever learned of his true identity, death would soon become one of them.

Or them both.

The sudden ringing of his cell phone pulled Sabia out of his deep thinking. Seeing who the caller was, Sabia accepted the call and raised his cell phone to his ear.

"Hello?"

"Where are you?"

"My hotel suite."

"Really? That's a coincidence."

"Why you say that?"

"No, I mean, well, I just got off work. I'm walkin' to my car as we speak."

If not for Monica's phone call interrupting his thoughts, Sabia would have still been standing there at the window in the kitchen of his hotel suite, occupied by thoughts that were gradually bringing on a headache.

"So, how's Splash dealing with losing Tia?"

"It's eatin' him up," Sabia shared, turning his back to the window, as he pulled his right arm out of the sleeve of his pricey, wool-cashmere, Canali suit jacket. Switching his cell phone to his right hand, he shrugged his suit jacket off of his left shoulder and caught it with his left hand. "All Splash see is red right now. He cried the whole visit. I mean, like, we still talked, but 'chu know, like, he even had me cryin'."

"Awwwwww . . . you sound like you really could use an escape."

"I could."

"Care for a suggestion?"

"I'm all ears."

"You can take a vacation in my pussy tonight. And you can stay in it as long as you like."

A smile teased Sabia's lips as he tossed his suit jacket on the back of a chair in his hotel suite's gigantic, living room.

"Well?"

" 'Well', what?"

"You want the vacation or not?"

Sabia heard the sound of a car door slamming on the other end of his cell phone, and pictured Monica scrambling to her car, trying to escape the pouring rain. Their earlier lunch date had left him liking Monica a lot. His attraction to her had matured, and was no longer merely based on the two of them just acting out a sexual fantasy. Over lunch, him and Monica had laughed, and had shared their backgrounds, and while he had told Monica all lies, he still had found himself enjoying Monica's company, and appreciating her opinionated personality. More than anything, Monica was a police officer, and because she was, and more likely than not, had some manner of accessibility to his case file, he thought it wise that he manipulate his fugitive status through Monica as her friend, than as some random fugitive, who she might have crossed paths with on the street.

During his visit with his cousin, Sabia had discovered that there was actually more to Monica's story, than she had led him to believe, and that she had been shielding him from some of her darker truths herself. These truths now known to him, had Sabia feeling suddenly comfortable with his own lies.

In the two years that Sabia had been a fugitive, he had never had any run-ins with the police. Early on, while in Las Vegas, there were episodes, where Sabia wouldn't 've even dared to leave his hotel room for anything. Over time, he gradually became braver; a lot smarter as well. In late 2011, he had turned to online dating services as a way for him to meet single women, who he would travel all across the country to see, and sometimes stay with. In Atlanta, Georgia, Sabia had a fiancé waiting for him to return home to her. She was five months pregnant, carrying his unborn son. She was the only woman of them all, who was aware of Sabia's true past.

"Can I get a nap in first?" Sabia asked, as he began climbing the marble stairs that led to the second floor of his hotel suite. With his free hand, he started unbuttoning his shirt. "I'm tired as shit, Monica. I ain't eat, or nothin'. All I got on my stomach is that salad I ate at lunch. I ain't tryna give you no bad performance."

"I doubt that's possible, Terrell. How about this. I have some business to take care of in about an hour. From there,

I'll give you a call, and see what type of mood you're in. Deal?"

"Deal."

"Okay, bye."

"Alright."

Sabia made it to the master bedroom of his hotel suite, and threw himself onto the unmade bed face down. The events of his entire day started to play itself in his mind, as he closed his eyes, and concentrated on his breathing. It was a stress-relieving method his fiancé had taught him once.

"I'm really gon' have to be on my game wit' Kyzer," Sabia realized, flipping over to his back, as his eyes adjusted to the darkness surrounding him. Before he was able to will them back, teardrops began to spill from his eyes and crawl down the side of his face. "Splash puttin' me all the way in the fuckin' fryin' pan on this one here. This nigga joy-stickin' me. He can think he gon' be pullin' my strings all he want, but I gotta mind of my fuckin' own. I ain't doin' shit to Kyzer, or Brit—"

Sabia's cell phone started ringing beside his left leg. After grabbing it, and answering it, he pressed it against his ear.

"What's up, Ash?"

"We need to talk."

"Why? What's wrong?"

"Me and Honey down in the lobby. Come get us."

"Alright, but first tell me what's wrong. What happened?"

"You'll find out, once all three of us on the elevator. And Honey need to use the bathroom, so you might wanna press fast-forward. She drunk, and ready to make a scene down here."

"What the fuck she doin' drunk this early? It ain't even seven o'clock, yet."

"Seven o'clock is late for Honey."

"Late? When the fuck she start that?"

"The day all of our lives changed. Are we seriously gonna have this conversation right now?"

Frowning, Sabia sat up and swung his legs out of bed. He wasn't in the mood for his friend, Honey, and he definitely wasn't in the mood for the monumental grudge that she had against him.

"I'll see you when you get down here."

"Ash, go to the elevator. I'ma call the desk and let 'em know it's cool for y'all to come up."

"Please do."

Cataclysm.

Over the summer of 2010, Sabia had made some horrible mistakes. Most of them had been impulsive, triggered by too much anger, impatience, and a lot of pride. The local and federal authorities were under the assumption that Sabia's rampage had been sparked, after it was made known to him that another man had actually fathered his five-year-old son. Some believed that the unexpected death of his grandmother might have pushed Sabia over the edge. It was the belief of others, that Sabia had just been a time bomb, waiting to explode. There were many myths hatched from Sabia's 2010 crime spree. However, only a handful of people knew the actual truth.

Ashley Briggs and Honey Myers were included in that handful. The two women had played intimate roles in one of Sabia's biggest crimes ever. Of the two women, Sabia was a lot closer to Ashley, than he was to Honey.

7:27 p.m.

Ashley sat quietly, while Sabia spoke to his mother on her cell phone. Honey was upstairs in the bathroom, on her knees, dry-heaving over the toilet. Her left hand had her long, black hair, fisted into a ponytail, to avoid it from getting any vomit on it. Honey was too drunk to notice that what she was hoping to prevent, had already taken place.

Sabia cut his eyes at his friend, Ashley, as he paced back and forth in front of her. The moment the two of them had hoped wouldn't come, had just arrived, and it was extremely unsettling. By Kyzer going by his mother's house, Kyzer was sending them a clear message. It was a message that Sabia understood crystal clear. After ending his phone call with his mother, Sabia handed Ashley her cell phone and let out a long sigh.

"Ready for some more bad news?"

"What can be worse than what I already heard?"

"Honey pregnant by Detective Konn."

Ashley's news struck Sabia like an unexpected punch to the stomach. For a long moment, Sabia stood there in front of Ashley, speechless, hoping she would break into a smile, and laugh, and tell him that her revelation about Honey had been nothing more than a joke. Instead, Ashley held Sabia's stare, and quietly began to nod her head. The thought of his friend, Honey, being pregnant by the very detective who was largely responsible for his cousin being in jail, was so unfathomable, yet horrendous, Sabia suddenly felt weak.

"That came outta left fuckin' field," Sabia admitted, sitting down beside Ashley. His headache had moved behind his eyes. "Ashley, all this shit my fault. Lookin' back, I'm to blame for why this shit got so spun outta control. Bleach and Moo—"

"Sabia, we all to blame."

"Not as much as me, though, Ash," Sabia disagreed, rising back to his feet, after noticing that Honey was standing on his hotel suite's balcony, looking down on him and Ashley. If his best friend, Bleach, was still alive, he was certain that he would be ashamed of how Sabia had been dealing with his younger sister. "Honey, I'm sorry. I swear to God I am. As much as I try to consider myself bein' thorough, I been actin' the exact opposite wit 'chu, Honey. Can you come down here? Please?"

Touched by Sabia's apology, Honey wiped her watery eyes, then began to slowly make her way down the black, marbled staircase. She steadied herself by holding onto the gold-finished railing on the left side of the staircase. Her right hand would rise to catch her still falling teardrops, while her eyes stayed fixed on her pink and blue printed socks. She had left her Christian Dior rain boots in the bathroom, along with her cell phone, and her pocketbook. Honey was suffering from a deeper hurt than what Sabia, Ashley, her mother, or anyone else could possibly imagine she was dealing with. It was difficult to read Honey, because she had a tough exterior.

Honey had an exotic look. At her height, which was six foot even, she could have easily chased a dream to become a model. She had flawless, golden brown skin, the face of a Brazilian movie star, and long, dark hair that hung below her shoulders. Men loved her beauty, but they loved her body more. Honey had a body type that would make an ugly woman acceptable to almost any man. Her measurements were 34C-26-45. However, while all of her physical traits were reasons why she was a successful, exotic dancer, they, too, were to blame for why she was currently harboring such an enormous amount of despair inside of her heart.

Reaching Sabia, Honey let out a sob, and allowed herself to be hugged by him. Although, he looked nothing like the friend she had known, Honey slowly hugged Sabia back. Her older brother and him had been best friends.

"Honey, I need to know everything that's been happening."

"It don't even matter, now. What's done is done, Sabia. This the bed we made. It's nothin' anybody can do. And now that Tia fuckin' dead, I'm just shit outta fuckin' luck. Like, I swear, you and Ashley have no fuckin' idea what I'm goin' through right now. Seriously."

"Look, we ain't really get to talk the other night, 'cause of the whole issue wit' me tryna see my mom. The little I do know, I got from Ashley in bits and pieces. How the fuck did Tia find out you was Bleach's sister in the first place, Honey? And how Detective Konn get put into the equation, where you gotta be fuckin' this nigga? Wit' no condoms on at that."

"Sabia, he fuckin' raped me! He put somethin' in my drink, and he fuckin' raped me!!"

Honey's confession was so riveting, it silenced Sabia, brought tears to Ashley's eyes, and left them both watching Honey as she joined Ashley on the couch. In a rare moment of vulnerability, Honey helplessly shrugged her shoulders, and began to cry. Sabia sat down beside her. When Ashley moved closer, sandwiching her in the middle, Honey dropped her face into her hands and sobbed harder.

Remember.

"Ashley, this can't get back to my mom. Sabia, what I'm about to say, can't get back to Splash. You can't tell your mom. Nobody. It stays here, alright?"

Sabia and Ashley both nodded their heads in unison.

"Okay, let's take it back to the beginning. So, and this not meant to be a dig at 'chu Ashley, but this whole situation became an issue for all of us, once you and my brother started messin' around. Think about it. Prep might not have been the best baby father, but he was a lot better than a lot of these mu'fuckers walkin' around here today. Ashley, messin' wit' Bleach hurt him. He knew Gary set y'all up. Then, when you and Bleach got engaged, and he had to hear it from his mom, that really pushed him to the edge. You wasn't takin' his son to see him. Wasn't answerin' his calls. Just think how that had him feelin', Ashley.

Ashley let out a sigh and lowered her head. Her eyes had begun to spill teardrops as soon as Honey had mentioned her son's father's name. He was no longer alive, because of her. What Honey was speaking on, were truths that sometimes caused her to lose sleep.

Just recently, Ashley had begun to get her life back on track. Along with moving to Bear, Delaware, with her parents over the summer, Ashley had started mentally preparing herself to go back to college. She wanted to start her own urban, fashion magazine. At twenty-six, with one child, and finally coming to terms with the hard blows that life had thrown at her thus far, Ashley found herself, yet again, standing at a crossroad. Two weeks earlier, after not hearing from him in almost a year, Sabia had sent her an inbox message on her Facebook page, telling her that he was returning to Philadelphia and that he needed her help. Now, here she was; helping.

Ashley was loyal to a fault. Since a child, her heart had never been inclined to turning her back on any of her friends, or disappointing them. How her friends thought of her was important to Ashley. It was a quality that would sometimes spark heated arguments between Ashley and her parents. However, after the summer of 2010, Ashley had come to the sad realization that it was time that she put her son, and her own life, first. It was unknown to both Sabia, and Honey, but Ashley's involvement in what they had going on, as unpredictably uncertain as it was, would be Ashley's final goodbye to them, and the last time she would be extending herself to them as their friend. It was a promise Ashley had made to her parents, the night she had left her son with them, before leaving for Philadelphia.

Like Honey, Ashley was also blessed with good looks. While not as tall or as curvy, Ashley could easily hold her own. She had hazel eyes, and closely resembled the WNBA basketball player, Skylar Diggins. Adding to her status,

Ashley's father was the owner of several furniture stores in Bear, Delaware. Ashley was her parents only child, and to them, returning to Philadelphia, in their eyes, was possibly Ashley's biggest mistake ever.

"Ashley, when Prep mom called you, and told you they was lettin' him out on house arrest, I told you not to go around there. You had to drive around there in Bleach's truck, though. Then you seemed so surprised that he spit in ya face. And you got mad at me, 'cause I ain't want 'chu to tell Bleach. Ashley, I ain't want Bleach to find out, 'cause I knew he would tell Sabia to get involved. And, Sabia, be honest, what I tell you that day we talked on the phone?"

"Stay out of it."

"Did you listen to me, though? No. You went and bailed Bleach out, knowin' the first thing he was gon' wanna do was find Prep. He ain't even call me, or my mom, and tell us he was home. How stupid you think my mom felt, when she tried to go visit him, and they told her he got bailed out? Then, as soon as Prep and Gary robbed that armored truck, and Gary got killed, it was, like, our lives turned into that movie, 'Smokin' Aces.' "

"Honey, how Tia find out you was Bleach's sister?"

Honey exhaled a heavy sigh as she wiped her hands down her face, cleaning away the tears that were streaming from her eyes. Her body language was suggesting that Sabia's question had touched a sensitive spot.

"Ask Ashley."

Confused, Sabia looked from Honey, over to Ashley.

"Well, if you remember, me and Moo wife was still at that house in Wildwood, waiting for you, Bleach, Moo, and Trixie, to come back. Once we saw the news, Moo's wife called her friend to come and pick us up. Little did we know, her friend was Tia's cousin."

"Which one?"

"Zay."

"Zainab?"

Ashley nodded her head.

"But still, how—"

"Sabia, Moo's wife was so messed up from seeing that Moo got killed on the news, and I wasn't no better, so the whole time we on our way back to Philly, and we talkin' about everything that happened, Zay was just takin' it all in silence. Sabia, she could've pulled over on the highway and just killed us, and nobody wouldn't 've known shit. Zay ain't say nothing,' until we got to my apartment. Because Moo's wife was muslim, Zay told her she was givin' her a day to get out of Philly.

"What she say about 'chu?"

"Why you think I moved to Miami with my aunt? If it wasn't for that money Prep told Gamble to gimme, I would've had to call my mom and dad. And they would've been askin' me all kinds of questions, which, I mean, like, once it all came out on the news, they found out anyway. It was just a mess. This what Zay told me and Moo's wife, though. Of course, she was, like, Tia wasn't gon' care that Prep, Bleach, or Moo died. She said Tia wasn't gon' even care about what 'chu did to her aunt. It was what 'chu did to Kyzer's sister that she was, like, Tia was gon' want all of us dead."

Sabia sat back.

"Ashley told me to stop dancin' at the club, 'cause Tia knew, so instead of me quittin',' I just went in her office one day, and I just put everything out on the table. I told her it was all a big mistake. At first, she just wanted to know if I knew where you was. This was, like, a week after she got out of the hospital. The same week as all of the funerals. Sabia, she went to all of them. She even came to Bleach's, and introduced herself to my mom. That's the day she told me about her plan for Detective Konn, and how, once she had it all in place, I had to be the one that lured him into her trap."

"Let me ask you this...how much do the chick, Brittany, know about all of this shit?"

"Sabia, she might as well be Tia. Why?"

" 'Cause, Splash want me to meet her tomorrow. I'm meetin' her and Kyzer at the club. My role gon' be as the new promoter for the club."

"Kyzer can't know I'm here, Sabia. I'm not comin' to that club."

Sabia and Honey looked at Ashley.

"Y'all don't understand."

"Look, just hold up," Sabia pleaded, angered at the threat that Ashley felt of Kyzer. Brought back to what Kyzer had done outside of his mother's house, earlier in the day, he hoped that the decision he was about to make, wouldn't be one that he would live to regret. "I want both of y'all to move into this suite wit' me, until all this shit is over."

"Ashley can, but I can't."

"Why not?"

"Two words . . . Detective Konn."

"Yeah, but 'chu still ain't get to how he connected to—"

"Tia made a deal wit' him, Sabia."

"Which was?"

"Look, for awhile, nobody knew what really happened at Kyzer's sister's house. It was just a lot of speculation. For example, and Ashley know this, we ain't know it was you that killed Trixie, or Kyzer's sister. The news was sayin' it, but, like, we ain't wanna believe that was the truth. They was even sayin', you, or Bleach shot Moo."

"Why the fuck would we shoot our own man?"

"Well, who did? Nobody still know?"

"When we first pulled up, we saw these niggaz sittin' in this truck in the driveway. Mind you, we ain't have no fuckin' idea it was Camay's house. So, Bleach just took the curb, mashed across the lawn, and we jumped out, thinkin' we caught Prep slippin'. The whole time it wasn't even him.

The niggaz started choppin' back at us. Moo got hit right in front of me. I know the nigga face, if I see him. I was chasin' this nigga, but then like, it-shit just got crazy. The garage door shot up. Bleach ran into the house. Moo was layin' right there. I heard shootin' comin' from inside the house. Trixie pulled up on me, while I was chasin' dude. We ain't shoot Moo."

"That's what Detective Konn think. After stuff died down, he started to come by the club, once he found out Tia was runnin' it. At first, her uncle, and his girlfriend was doing everything. It was like, once Tia showed up, he showed up. I seen him come out of her office a few times. Supposedly, he was trying to extort her. Sabia, from her own lips, Tia told me that she was just outthinkin' Detective Konn. Lettin' him think he had the upper hand. She promised me fifty thousand dollars, if I went along. He told Tia he wanted her best stripper."

"So, she was just gon' put all 'lat other shit that happened at Camay spot in the past?"

"That's what she said. She did want me to tell her, if I ever heard from you, though."

"Did she ever tell you about a cop that's suppose to be in on her plans?"

"No. All I know is, on Halloween, Detective Konn was supposed to be gettin' killed in a bathroom at the club, while our Halloween party goin' on."

"Who pullin' the trigger?"

"That, I don't know. I'm just supposed to have Detective Konn thinkin,' I wanna get fucked in the bathroom. Once I get him to the bathroom, my job done."

Permanent.

Mistakes.

8:36 p.m.

"That was a gutsy move you pulled last night."

"This phone we on cool?"

"I wouldn't be on it, if it wasn't, Kyzer."

Kyzer switched his cell phone to his other ear, as he walked over to his bedroom window, and pulled the curtain aside.

"Kyzer, should I be concerned about 'chu doin' somethin' to my aunt?"

"Should you?" Kyzer questioned, as his eyes cut right, then left, checking the outside of his house. The darkness of the night, mixed with the falling rain, gave him little comfort, in that, the cops or patient enemies, could possibly be waiting for the right moment to converge on his house. "I knew she was goin' to call you. I was hopin' for a call from your cousin, though. That's what that was all about. I want her to call Sabia."

"What would make you leave her alone? I mean, like, not goin' by there. No phone calls. None of the shit that'll intimidate her, Kyzer. She a innocent party."

"So was my fuckin' sister. You forget that, Splash? So was my fuckin' sister."

"What if I can deliver Sabia to you?"

"Do that, and Miss Steph'll never see my face again. When, though?"

"Gimme a month. One month from now, Kyzer."

"What about that shit I asked you about?"

"It'll be at my club tomorrow. Did my man, Terrell, call you?"

"Yeah, I heard from him. We gon' meet up tomorrow."

"He a good dude. Plus, he somebody you could use—"

"He ain't needed," Kyzer declined, looking at his cell phone, after it had alerted him that he was receiving another call. Stepping into his master bathroom, he pressed his cell phone back against his ear. "Look, I got somebody else callin' me, Splash. On that bargain you just mentioned, though, if you not true to ya word a month from now, all bets off the table. Even the one wit' Detective Konn."

Staring at his shirtless reflection in the mirror, Kyzer ended his call with Splash, and accepted the second incoming call.

"Hello?"

"As Salaamu Alaykum."

"Wa Laykum As Salaam . . . who this?"

"Kyzer, seriously? It's me, Rhonda. People call me, Rock 'n Roll Rhonda now."

Skyfall.

9:03 p.m.

Brittany looked across the restaurant table at Detective Monica Best, impatiently, waiting for her to bring an end to her conversation, she was having on her cellphone with Terrell, the club promoter from Texas. A moment later, roles were reversed, and it was Monica watching Brittany, as she whispered most of her conversation to Kyzer, as if Monica overhearing what was being said would suddenly bring the world to an end. After stuffing her cell phone back into her clutch purse, Brittany looked around the crowded restaurant, until her eyes fell upon a set of creepy eyes that flashed a hint of humor, as soon as it dawned on Brittany, just who the set of creepy eyes actually belonged to.

"Monica, you'll never believe who's fuckin' here."

"Who?"

"Detective Konn. Oh, my God."

Slowly, Monica followed Brittany's stare across the sea of restaurant tables, until she, too, came eye to eye with Detective Konn. Grinning, Detective Konn waved hello. He was seated at a booth.

Monica politely waved back, then turned her attention to her plate of food, calmly using her fork to bring a piece of her yellow-finned tuna up to her open mouth. As she chewed, Monica was thinking. While Monica was chewing and thinking, Brittany was watching her from the opposite side of their restaurant table, with panic written all over her face.

"How can you sit there and eat at a time like this?"

"Do I look calm?"

"Too fuckin' calm, if you ask me."

"Good."

"Good?" Brittany asked, horrified from what was happening. She couldn't dare herself to look in Detective Konn's direction again. "Monica, we caught. How do we explain us being together?"

"No, the question is, how the fuck do he explain that? Look who just came from the ladies room, Brittany."

Brittany shot a glance in Detective Konn's direction, only to see someone who she would have never expected to see with Detective Konn in a hundred years. Smiling, and carrying her oversized body like she was a size two, and on a hot date, there was her aunt, blushing in Detective Konn's face, as she squeezed her frame into the booth, opposite him. Detective Konn was saying something to her, causing her aunt's smile to slowly disappear.

"Apparently, we're not the only ones up to no good. Let's go over there."

"Sounds good to me," Brittany agreed, pushing her chair back and standing. The sight of her aunt smothered fear, and uncovered courage. "Remind me to take a picture of them, too. It might come in handy one day. Monica, look how she lookin' at me. Bitch. Ruined her entire night."

"Somethin' tells me he knows the truth about your dad. For her to be with him, something's off."

"Or they're plotting against Marvin."

Brittany and Monica continued talking, as they closed the distance between them and Detective Konn's booth. In that moment, Brittany felt many things, while following Monica's lead through the Upper Darby Restaurant. Brittany looked around at all of the faces in the restaurant, privately remembering their faces, who they were with, what they were eating, and what they were all wearing. She felt more alive in that moment, than she had the moment she was born into the world.

"Monica, what if she told him I was Sean's girlfriend?"

"If he knew that, Brittany, trust me, he would've been spoken on it. Smile, and follow my lead. Let me do most of the talking."

Brittany held her aunt's stare. In her aunt's eyes she saw skepticism. This helped Brittany's smile come with ease, as her and Monica approached the restaurant booth. Detective Konn regarded them with an unintimidated facial expression, while patting Brittany's aunt's fat hand reassuringly.

"Mind, if me and Brittany join y'all?"

"Not at all. Be my guest."

Monica slid into the booth, choosing to sit beside Detective Konn. With no other choice, Brittany sat beside her aunt.

"You sure this a road you'd like to go down, Detective Best? Your mom's not here to hold your hand, you know."

"Let's keep my mom out of this discussion. We both know I'm a big girl. Not quite as big as your date, but we all know what I mean."

Brittany's aunt didn't appreciate Monica's insult about her weight. Her right hand reached for her salad fork, and held it threateningly. Her angry eyes met Monica's. Detective Konn and Brittany started their own tense stare. For a moment, no one spoke. The silence only broke when Brittany's cell phone started to ring in her clutch purse. As soon as Brittany had her cell phone in her hand, and saw who she was receiving a call from, she hurriedly excused herself from the restaurant booth, and found some privacy.

"Zay, you okay?"

"Brittany, where you at? You home?"

"No. Why? Wait, are you back?"

"I'm leavin' the airport as we speak. Brit, meet me at the club. And bring Kyzer, too. I found out where Sabia is."

"What? Are you serious? Where is he?"

"He right under our nose. Brittany, the club promoter from Texas is Sabia. Terrell is Sabia, Brittany."

Chapter Thirteen

So much had been happening. There had always been an important phone call to make; or, there was always an important phone call coming in that couldn't be ignored. At other times, the idea itself just didn't seem appropriate. There never seemed to be enough time in a day. Not one single, private moment.

Until.

Now.

Brittany rolled over and faced Kyzer. Their faces were on the same pillow. It was morning. Random places in Kyzer's master bedroom were lit with streaks of sunlight, mostly around the areas where the giant windows were. It was serenely quiet. With reasons to be concerned, Brittany looked deeply into Kyzer's brown eyes. She could still see the traces of what Zainab's news had done to him. She thought it remarkable that Kyzer had stayed in bed with her the entire night, until morning. She was proud of him. However, his eyes were dangerously alive with an emotion she could only describe as being nuclear.

"You okay?"

"Brittany, last night showed me how weak I was," Kyzer expressed, blinking his eyes as Brittany raised her hand and tenderly began to stroke the side of his face. Her affection made his heart move in his chest. "All this time, Splash and Sabia had one up on me. I knew it was somethin' about that nigga I didn't like. His fuckin' voice don't even sound the same. Zainab was right. Now that Tia gone, Splash all for self. He showed that last night, when he offered to hand Sabia over to me. So, that must mean in a month from now, Sabia gon' be expendable to him. Splash specifically asked me for a month."

"The Halloween party a month from now. Maybe it's that."

"Yeah, but think about it. Sabia don't have no hand in that. It's gotta be somethin' else. Who side that cop on?"

"Which one? Monica?"

"Yeah."

"Mine, as far as I know. Yours, too. Kyzer, she went through a lot to clean up what 'chu did the other night. Be thankful those guys that got away chose to deal with it the street way. Kyzer, Monica is our Tia with a badge. And just in case you wonderin', she don't know Terrell is really Sabia."

"You sure?"

"Kyzer, I'm positive," Brittany assured, rubbing the pad of her thumb over Kyzer's thin eyebrow. She fought away the thought to kiss his lips. "She in the dark, just like we was. I agree with Zay. Right now, our main concern should be using what we know now, as ammunition."

"Against who, though? I don't know what situation to deal with first. I got that shit lined up for my cousin, Drees, later on. I suppose to meet Rhonda at the masjid with Zay. That situation alone, got my mind somewhere else. This shit wit' Sabia, though."

"Kyzer, I've been carrying around the truth of what my aunt and Marvin did to my dad, and every day I wake up with it, it makes me question how much I really loved my dad. Kyzer, use what Splash and Sabia don't think you know against them. If I can do it, you can."

"You see how I am, Brittany. I wear my emotions on my sleeve. I been like this all my life."

"You was able to do it with your cousin."

"Brittany, I know me. It ain't no way I'm gon' be able to face Sabia, and pretend I don't know who he is. He shot my sister in her face, Brittany."

"Marvin killed my dad with the gun my dad gave me for my birthday. Detective Konn killed my boyfriend, and I listened to the whole thing. If you not ready to deal with all this shit today, stay home, then. We can stay in and figure things out together. Let's cut our phones off. Kyzer, you not weak. You far from it, if you ask me. They just don't know who they're fuckin' wit', that's all. They don't see what I see, Kyzer."

"What 'chu see?"

"The kind of father I want my daughter to have. A man that I want my son to be like. Kyzer, I see a man that can go far in this world, as long as he keep a woman like me by his side."

"You'd marry me?"

Brittany nodded her head, as she studied Kyzer's handsome face. His perfect nose. His thin eyebrows. Those passionate, brown eyes, beneath them. The fiery emotions they held. Those kissable lips, and the strands of hair under the center of his bottom lip, that reached down to that patch of fine hair on his chin. Brittany looked deeply into Kyzer's eyes, and knew that she was the woman for him, and he was the man for her.

Inspired by the moment, Kyzer inched his face across the pillow and softly kissed Brittany on the lips. Brittany met the kiss with an eager tongue, and moistened lips, as Kyzer grabbed her by the waist beneath the sheets, and pulled her body closer to his. After the death of her boyfriend, Sean, Brittany had believed that there was no way that she could ever enjoy an act of intimacy with another man again. Because of their schedules, her brief relationship with Maniac had been nothing more than dinner dates, and random, hour-long phone calls. They had only kissed twice, and on both occasions, Brittany had felt nothing; not even a spark. Kissing Kyzer, Brittany quickly recognized that she had been wrong. She was not only enjoying her and Kyzer's intimate moment, but the sensuous flow of their kiss, and the sheer experience of being kissed by a man who she knew felt the same way about her, had Brittany feeling like she was a traveler visiting her favorite places across the world.

Shoe stores.

Exotic beaches.

Cloud 9.

Paris, France.

Kyzer climbed on top of Brittany, still kissing her. The moment he was between Brittany's legs, he felt his body temperature triple. Hot, and nearly breathless from their kissing, he took his kisses down to Brittany's neck, as she opened her legs wider, accommodating his weight. His hard dick was sandwiched between them, pressing against her clit. All ten of Brittany's metallic-polished fingernails, clawed into Kyzer's upper back when he lowered his hips, and positioned the head of his dick at the opening of her pussy. The thin material of Kyzer's Tom Ford pajamas, and the laced-fabric of her white Line & Dot panties, kept the magic from happening.

"Play some music for us."

"Huh," Kyzer asked, slightly confused, bringing his kisses back up to Brittany's lips. Her request suddenly resonated as she kissed him back, and ran the palms of her hands up his shirtless chest. "What 'chu wanna hear?"

Kisses.

Licks.

"Play a song you liked, while you was in jail."

Strokes.

Thinking of a song, Kyzer watched Brittany's fingers as they slowly began unbuttoning the top to his black pajama set, which Brittany had chosen to go to sleep in. As his eyes followed her fingers, lower and lower, and it became noticeable to him that she wasn't wearing a bra, he wondered what her bare chest would look like. His mouth watered with hungry anticipation. At the final button, Brittany paused, teasingly.

Brittany's delay helped Kyzer memorize the moment, as he dragged his eyes back up to her face. He remembered being in jail, and sometimes wondering to himself, what his first moments with a woman would be like, once he was actually free. He remembered wanting the woman to be exquisitely beautiful, yet nasty. There was nothing that could be said about Brittany's beauty. Even early in the morning, without yet washing her face, or applying any make-up, she had a look about her that was undeniably enviable. If Brittany wasn't nasty in bed, Kyzer could care less. As Brittany unbuttoned his pajama top, and exposed her chest to him, Kyzer recalled a song, absolutely sure its lyrics would magnify the mood, and indirectly let Brittany know exactly what he thought of her.

"Play, 'King,' by Alicia Keys."

At Kyzer's command, the wall-speakers inside of his master bedroom came to life, bringing into the huge space a tremendous, love song.

Touched, Brittany cupped Kyzer's face with her hands, and guided it back down to hers. His chest and stomach felt hot against her skin, as they kissed again. His individual braids were hanging, hiding both of their faces like curtains. His song choice was reaching down into her soul. A king couldn't afford what her and Kyzer had; no one could.

"You my girl, right?"

"Yessssss," Brittany declared, losing breath, after Kyzer licked small circles around her left nipple, then took it into his warm mouth. Before she was able to catch her breath, his mouth was over her right nipple, licking, sucking, teasing. "I'm your girl, Kyzer. I'm all yours, okay? All . . . yours."

Brittany had never been so wet in her life. Her clit was obscenely swollen, and alive, it seemed. As if he knew her cravings, Kyzer pushed his hand down between them, and moved her underwear aside. A moment later he was fumbling with the draw-string on his pajamas, until he had his dick fisted in his hand, and was pushing it deep inside of her. Kyzer's eyes came to hers, as she raised her hips to greet his stroke. She wanted his entire body inside of hers. His dick was going further than Sean's ever had.

Right away, Kyzer knew that he was in trouble, and was quite possibly fighting a one-sided battle. He hadn't had sex in over five years. Besides an occasional wet dream, and those times where he had masturbated to an adult magazine, he was otherwise a born-again virgin. Luckily for Kyzer, he was in great physical shape. In jail, he ran for miles in the yard, lifted weights, and spent a lot of time doing push-ups, and did just about any exercise that would lead to him being in excellent shape. Still, with no further to go in Brittany's pussy, Kyzer knew that there wasn't a workout routine discovered that could ever prepare him for what Brittany owned between her legs.

"It's been awhile."

"I feel like I'm in kryptonite," Kyzer joked, slowly pulling his dick out of Brittany, as she nibbled on his left earlobe. Sighing, he willed away a rushing orgasm, and slowly pushed his dick back into Brittany's wet, warm pussy. "Damn. Hold-Hold up. I can't . . ."

"What's wrong?"

Kyzer climbed off of Brittany and got out of bed, fixing his pajamas, after he was on his feet. Biting her bottom lip to stop a smile, Brittany sat up.

"You know you wanna laugh. Go 'head."

"Kyzer, we got all day."

"That shit should have a 'Warning' sign on it."

The compliment made Brittany smile broadly. Her pussy was a hundred miracles, divided by one rainbow. Her boyfriend, Sean, was the only person she had ever been with sexually. Since his death, there had been no others. She didn't like sex toys, and she had never tried masturbation.

"Get back in bed."

"We outta pocket, anyway. I ain't even have no condom on."

"Alright, so, put one on and get back in bed."

"I ain't got none," Kyzer admitted, feeling embarrassed, as he stuffed his hand down into his pajamas, and grabbed his dick. Brittany's eyes followed his hand expectantly, causing his dick to get even harder. "You got some?"

"Nope."

"So, what we gon' do?"

To Kyzer's question, Brittany peeled off his pajama top, then stood up on the bed. Her nipples were the color of pink roses, matching her lips. She had breasts that were full. Her long hair was in one single, French-braid, gathered behind her right ear. There was shyness in her eyes as she hooked her thumbs into the waistline of her panties, and slowly pulled them down.

"Don't blame me, if you get pregnant, Brittany."

"Why you talkin' from over there?"

Brittany threw her underwear at Kyzer. He caught them with his left hand, unable to take his eyes off of her clean-shaven pussy. It was his new weakness. Smiling, Brittany watched Kyzer, watching her.

"You nasty on the low, ain't 'chu?"

"Come find out."

"Naw, hold up. Let's talk for a minute. That was my mistake last time."

"Alright, let me choose our next song."

"Go 'head. Nothin' corny, either."

"Shut up."

They were bonding; getting to know each other. Becoming comfortable as a couple, yet discovering the other's sexual identity, so that what they learned would further their chances of combining to have great sex.

"Take those pajamas off."

"Choose our next song first."

"I'm tryna think."

"I'm tryna fuck."

"So am I."

"Hurry up, then."

Brittany pouted her lips, and began turning her naked body counter-clockwise to follow Kyzer as he walked around to the opposite side of his bed. Somewhere, along the way, he had dropped her panties down to the floor.

"Alright, while you thinkin' of a song, what's ya favorite position?"

"From the side."

"That's it?"

"And layin' on my stomach, with, like, a pillow, or somethin' underneath me, so my butt can stick up."

"Regular, or you mean, like, anal?"

"Both."

Kyzer felt his dick stiffen, as he picked his cell phone up from his nightstand. After powering off his cell phone, he sat it back down, then picked up Brittany's. The screensaver on her Louis Vuitton, encased, iPhone was a picture of her late boss, holding her smiling son. For a moment, the endearing photo took Kyzer's mind back to that fateful day at the cemetery. His hand tightened around the cell phone. He could see himself over Tia, and over his mother, crying, and begging them both not to die, while desperately trying to give them both CPR. Blinking away the still-painful memory, Kyzer powered off Brittany's cell phone, and placed it back on the nightstand, beside his.

"Is that weird?"

"Is what weird?"

"That I'm into anal sex, and I've only been with one person? Sean . . . I don't know. He talked me into tryin' it once, and it hurt at first, but once I got past the initial pain, I liked it."

"So, you just like it a little bit, or you like it, like it?"

"Kyzer, I love it. It makes me cum so hard. Especially, if you pull my hair, and talk dirty to me."

Kyzer could hear the addiction for anal sex in Brittany's voice as he dropped his pajamas to his ankles, and stepped out of them. Brittany was his cup of tea.

"I thought of a song. Play 'Love,' by Musiq Soulchild."

"Come here," Kyzer ordered, slowly stroking his dick with his right hand, as Brittany's song request filled his entire master bedroom. When Brittany got to him, he grabbed her waist and helped her down from the bed. "We gettin' it in all day. Our phones off. It ain't gon' be no distractions. It's just you and me."

"Talk dirty to me."

"Turn around and bend over."

The command made Brittany bite her lower lip, as she obeyed Kyzer, and turned her back to him. She inhaled breathlessly, and let out a shuddering sigh when he pressed himself against her. His thighs were warm against the back of her legs. Licking her lips, she bent over on the bed, becoming wetter between her legs, as Kyzer grabbed her French-braid in his hand, and gave it a little pull.

"Where you want my dick, Brittany?"

"My ass."

"Beg me."

Brittany swallowed, but just as she was preparing herself to beg, Kyzer started guiding his dick into her wet pussy, without warning. His stroke was slow. She could feel the blood pulsing through the veins on his dick, as its thickness stretched her pussy walls.

"Why you not beggin,' yet?"

"I'm-I'm sorry," Brittany apologized, arching her back to get every inch of Kyzer's dick into her pussy. She grabbed two handfuls of bedsheets and lowered her face to the bed, as Kyzer began to stroke her deeper and faster. "I'm so sorry. Baby, please fuck me in my ass. Oh, my God. Yes, Daddy. yes. Take it outta my pussy, and put it in my ass, Kyzer. I'm beggin' you to. I'm ready for that fat dick in my ass."

"Turn around and get on your knees."

Brittany turned around and knelt. Kyzer held her French-braid as if it was a leash, and brought her face to his dick.

"Open ya mouth, and swallow all of it," Kyzer groaned, as his orgasm rushed up his thighs and shot out of his dick. Brittany opened her mouth, catching his first spurts of semen, then she took his dick into her mouth, licking, and swallowing. "That's right. Yeah, get all of it. Yup. That's right, baby. That's my girl. Shit. There you go. Yeah, there you go. Good girl. Ain't no more?"

Shaking her head, Brittany licked every trace of Kyzer's semen from her lips, as she brought herself up to her feet, and climbed back into bed. Before she could get far, Kyzer grabbed her by the ankle, and pulled her back to him. The silk bedsheets felt like rose petals against her skin, as her body was dragged over them. Brittany swallowed, still able to taste the saltiness of Kyzer's semen in the back of her throat.

"Where you think you goin'?"

"Nowhere."

Allowing herself to be pulled across the bed, Brittany closed her eyes for a brief moment, and listened to the messages that her body was sending her. The nerve endings inside of her pussy had become an orchestra. Her clit was pulsating, nearly to the point that it seemed to be aching with a hungry need. Kyzer stopped pulling, and her body became still. It was then that she realized that the music had stopped playing. The silence seemed to soothe her. She opened her eyes, only to catch Kyzer gazing down at her.

"Turn over."

Brittany rolled over to her stomach, and Kyzer straddled the backs of her thighs. His weight pressed her into the mattress, as he leaned forward, and removed her long, French-braid from her back. She sighed when he kissed behind her left ear, then moaned when he used his hand to sit his hard dick between the crack of her ass. She could feel his balls on the back of her pussy. He had her back tingling with the tormenting way he was peppering tantalizing kisses across her upper back. She couldn't stop her body from shuddering.

"Stay still."

"I can't."

"Yes, you can."

"Finish talkin' dirty to me. You had me so wet."

Kyzer placed a hand on both sides of Brittany, then moved his body lower, until his face was hovering above her ass cheeks. Sitting up, Kyzer used his hands to separate Brittany's ass cheeks, and ran his tongue from the back of her wet pussy, and over her asshole. Brittany let out a satisfying moan, then hummed her appreciation as Kyzer pressed his thumb against her asshole and started to trace small circles around it, using the pad of his thumb.

"Is it tight?"

"Yes."

"What if my dick too big?"

"Try and see. Please?"

"My dick too fat for it, Brittany."

"I still want it. Gimme just the head."

"Just the head?"

"Yes."

"What if I wanna give you more?"

"I want all . . . of—"

Brittany went breathless when Kyzer pushed his thumb into her ass. When she shut her eyes, the room spun a thousand times. Slowly, she circled her hips, and placed her palms on the bed. Kyzer pushed his thumb in deeper. She arched her back, pressing her palms into the bed for support.

"We gon' fuck everyday, alright?"

"Yes."

"Grab a pillow, and put it under you."

Brittany reached and grabbed a pillow. She was on a sensual high. Kyzer pulled his thumb out of her ass, and slowly reentered her, this time, letting a string of saliva fall from his mouth, and into the crack of her ass. Using his saliva as a lubricant, he eased his thumb deeper into her ass, and started to stroke her with it. Brittany's throaty moans became a string of exotic notes. Her pussy was wetter than a swimming pool; wetter than a thousand raindrops. The pulse in her clit had a staccato rhythm to it.

"You think you ready?"

"Yes," Brittany moaned, on the verge of convulsing. She pushed her hips back, again, and again, and kept her back arched, as Kyzer continued thumb-fucking her ass. "Baby, I want more than the head. I want all of it. I'm-I'm ready. Fuck me in my ass. Please . . . I want it."

Kyzer pulled his thumb out of Brittany's ass and sat up. His breathing was labored. Another orgasm was mounting in his legs, and slowly gathering momentum.

"Kyzer, keep talkin' to me."

"You better not just lay there."

"I'm not."

Using his left hand to spread Brittany's ass cheeks, Kyzer guided the fat head of his dick into her ass with his right hand. Instantly pleasured, Brittany brought her thumb to her mouth, moaning in pure delight.

"You want more?"

"Yes, gimme more."

"How much more? All of it?"

Kyzer spread Brittany's ass cheeks apart further, and pushed more of his dick slowly into her tight ass, as Brittany nodded her approval. Remembering what she liked, Kyzer grabbed a handful of her hair, and gave it a tug. He needed a distraction. The tight feel of Brittany's ass, and how dangerously close he was to filling it full of his hot semen, he willed himself to help Brittany get to her orgasm first. Inching back, he grabbed Brittany's French-braid with both hands, and forced her to rise to her knees.

"Stay face down."

Brittany couldn't hear. She was in her own world, absolutely in love with the way that Kyzer's dick was stretching her ass. It had her full, rubbing against every sensitive nerve in its path. She wanted more.

"Gimme all of it."

"Work for it."

Biting her bottom lip, Brittany pushed her hips back, meeting Kyzer's stroke. It was magic. Every inch of Kyzer's thick, nine inch dick, disappeared into Brittany's ass, and it sent Brittany into a cloud of lust. Beads of sweat started appearing on her back, as she slammed her body into Kyzer. His dick was pumping into her ass, sending explosions of pleasure and pain up her spine. Their skin was slapping together, echoing all over the bedroom, and coming back to her ears, a thousand decibels louder. He still had her by the hair with both hands.

"That's right. Get it."

"Kyzer, I'm gon' cum so hard. I feel it comin'. Oh, my God."

Brittany's confession made Kyzer tighten his grip on her hair, and increase the force behind his strokes. He could feel Brittany's ass gripping his dick tighter and tighter. He was sweating. He was so close to exploding, but he fought it away.

"Kyzer, here it come! Here it come!"

Kyzer released Brittany's hair, and grabbed her by the hips, and pulled her roughly against him, once, twice, then again, and again, sending his sperm deep into Brittany's ass, until he had no strength left to keep their bodies joined. Gasping for air, he fell on Brittany's back, and she melted under his weight. Beneath Kyzer, Brittany was trembling, struggling to catch a decent amount of oxygen, while her pussy and ass both climaxed at the same time. That had never happened to her before. The power of it scared her. As the walls in her pussy and ass contracted, she reached back and fondly patted Kyzer on the thigh.

"Can that be my breakfast, Kyzer?"

"It can be lunch and dinner, too."

"Everyday?"

"You serious?"

"With the drought we both been on, shouldn't we be like porn stars up in here?"

Kyzer slid off of Brittany, and let out a groan, as the need for sleep pulled at his senses. Brittany rolled to her side, staring at him with love in her eyes.

"Am I too nasty for you?"

"You perfect, Brittany. My mom and my sister would've liked you."

"My dad would've liked you, too."

Love.

Chapter Fourteen

"... her badly, decomposed body was found by two joggers in Fairmount Park, earlier this morning. Detective Monica Best had been missing for almost a week. She was last seen ..."

As calm as he could possibly be, Sabia spun his barstool around, and slowly started walking to the only available exit in the West Philadelphia bar. At one point, while passing a young black couple, Sabia nearly reached out and grabbed the back of one of their barstools to prevent himself from falling down to the floor. Behind him, the bartender was using the remote control to raise the volume on the bar's gigantic, plasma television. Sabia didn't want to hear anymore.

Outside, Sabia covered his face with his hands, and stood still for a long moment. The moon above him looked like a thumbnail. It was a few minutes shy of becoming midnight, and the night air had a nippy bite to it.

"Oh, shit," Sabia thought, suddenly panicking, as the grim realization that his cell phone number was stored in the call log of Detective Monica Best's cell phone, including all of the text messages he had sent her. Cell phone in hand, he rushed over to the southeast corner of the 61st and Market Street intersection, and tossed his cell phone down the sewer hole. "Soon as they see how much me and her was talkin,' they gon' wanna know who the fuck I am. I'ma be a suspect from the rip. They gon' think I did that shit. Damn, Monica. What the fuck happened?"

Sabia started walking fast. Crossing 61st Street, he regretted that he had just gotten rid of his cell phone so quickly, without first making some important calls. There were phone numbers he didn't have committed to his memory. The only number he was certain of was his mother's home number, and calling her was completely out of the question. The thought of going to his Center City hotel suite, packing his suitcases, and leaving Philadelphia, became prevalent in Sabia's mind, as he crossed to the opposite side of Market Street, and closed the distance between him and his Audi station wagon.

In the past week, Sabia had been put through some extreme tests. Kyzer had begun to trust him, and they were now spending a lot of time with each other. Then, there was the issue with Monica. On her way to his hotel suite, she had suddenly disappeared, and was never heard from again. Then, there was his cousin, Splash, who was continuously pressuring him into killing Brittany.

Sabia got into his car, and after starting it up, he sat there, not knowing where to go, or what to do next. The thought of abandoning Philadelphia again, was echoing in the back of his mind. He thought of his fiancé, and their unborn son. He thought of his mother; Ashley, Honey, Kyzer.

Camay.

Jen.

Shateek.

He then thought of Monica.

Sabia started to sob uncontrollably, and melted against his steering wheel. As he cried, he made up his mind on what he would and wouldn't do. He wasn't leaving Philadelphia until he knew who killed Monica Best. He owed her that much. He also wanted to ensure that his mother was safe from Kyzer.

Chapter Fifteen

"Do I have to stay here and referee this?"

Brittany and Rock 'n Roll Rhonda cut their eyes warily at each other, then looked at Zainab, shaking their heads. Zainab returned their stare, noticeably doubtful about leaving the two women alone together.

"We okay, right, Brittany?"

"Look, this Tia's house," Brittany answered, looking at her late boss' cousins, who both instantly seemed to show a visible sadness in their body language, at her mentioning their deceased cousin's name. Her boss' memory was the only common ground that the three of them stood on. "Couldn't nothin' or no one, get me to disrespect it. And I'm damn sure not raising my hands to nobody that shared the same blood as her, unless I got to. I'm here to talk."

"You and me both. You can go, Zay. Me and Brittany gon' be okay in here by ourselves."

"I'll be upstairs."

Left by themselves for a moment, Brittany and Rock 'n Roll Rhonda just sat in silence, neither knowing how, or where to begin. Tia's death had vacuumed away all of their resentment.

"You think Sabia killed that cop?"

"At first I did," Brittany admitted, uncrossing her legs and sitting up. She was dealing with so much inner-turmoil, because not only did she know who was personally responsible for Detective Monica Best's death, but she was even in possession of evidence that could prove it. "I mean, it ain't like he don't have a pattern of killin' women. Sabia didn't do that to Monica. Detective Konn did that to her. I got proof . . . look."

Thumbing and swiping away at the screen of her cell phone, Brittany rose to her feet, and walked to the center of her late boss' home theater, and paused. The home theater was Brittany's favorite place in the entire house. Facing a 14-foot wide movie screen, were five rows of tomato red, leather seats. There were four seats in each row, with two-step drops at the start of each one. Above the home theater, a plexi-glass ceiling gave an amazing view of an office, and a guest bedroom. In the rear of the home theater, in the far right corner, there was a sports bar, and a concession stand. Standing over in the far-left corner, near the arched entrance, leading out into the foyer, a huge, bamboo birdcage stood. There was an African gray parrot inside of the birdcage, busy at preening its colorful feathers. The floor of the home theater was an expanse of plush, white carpet.

As the movie screen lit up, and slowly began to display a series of video captions, Rock 'n Roll Rhonda walked over and joined Brittany in the center aisle of the home theater.

"Your cousin was the smartest woman I ever met."

"What's those?"

"Video footage from this funeral home, where I used to live," Brittany explained, swiping her index finger down the screen of her cell phone, until she saw the option she was looking for. That handled, she walked back over to the last row of theater seats, and sat down, then gestured for Rock 'n Roll Rhonda to also have a seat. "Trust me, you're gonna need a seat for this. Okay, so, before I play any of those videos for you, I have to fill you in on some stuff first."

Glancing inquisitively at the movie screen, Rock 'n Roll Rhonda returned to where she had been sitting, and over the next hour, she sat quietly and listened as Brittany filled her in on all that she had been unaware of. A probation violation had recently landed her in an all-female, county prison, for eleven and a half months. In Rock 'n Roll Rhonda's absence, a lot had taken place.

Rock 'n Roll Rhonda, as she was notoriously known, wasn't an easy person to get along with, and she was well aware of this. On most days, she was temperamental, and to her, love meant war. This sad understanding came from all of the domestic violence she had witnessed at home as a child. Rock 'n Roll Rhonda's parents had been a match made in Hell. Her father was a traveling con artist, and her mother had earned her money by dating successful drug dealers, who she would later set up to be robbed by her older brothers. During the late night hours of Thanksgiving 2002, while Rock 'n Roll Rhonda had laid in her bed, listening to her parents argue, and fight, Rock 'n Roll Rhonda's father had strangled her mother to death, then, shortly afterwards, he had put the barrel of one of his guns into his mouth and had committed suicide.

The emotional, and psychological impact of that incident had turned Rock 'n Roll Rhonda into an always angry, pre-teen, who none of her remaining family members could control. Rock 'n Roll Rhonda was pretty, and she had a calmness about her, in the way that she carried herself, and even in how she behaved around others. One would be left with the impression that she was a sweetheart. She was as feminine as the next girl, but she was insanely dangerous. By her seventeenth birthday, she had been in dozens of shootouts, and had been questioned by the homicide detectives more than five times. She was responsible for the deaths of eleven people.

At the moment, Rock n' Roll Rhonda was dealing with an inner-storm, fueled by guilt, anguish, and some deep, unresolved emotions that reached back to her childhood. At twenty-years-old, Rock 'n Roll Rhonda felt lost and alone. Two months before her probation officer had issued a warrant for her arrest, she had rolled over, and had smothered her three-month-old daughter, while the two of them had been asleep in the middle of the night. While at the county prison, Rock 'n Roll Rhonda had become muslim. Guilt had given her humility, and had turned her soul into a repentant one. Her spirit was broken in a lot of places. The death of her cousin, Tia, who she had loved to no limit, had her more concerned with her spirituality, and how she could increase her faith in her newfound religion. She was afraid to meet her Creator, and have to answer for all the sins she had committed.

While talking to Rock 'n Roll Rhonda, Brittany had been privately scrutinizing her; mostly for Kyzer's sake. Rock 'n Roll Rhonda was dressed in the traditional, all-black garments, which most of the muslim women in Philadelphia wore on a daily basis, but Kyzer was unsure of Rock 'n Roll Rhonda's truthfulness. Now knowing that Rock 'n Roll Rhonda was actually Tia's younger cousin, and the same cute, little girl, who he had once saved from drowning at an amusement park swimming pool, Kyzer now felt himself at war with yet another difficult decision.

The complexity of it all, and the potential damage Kyzer's unmade decisions could have on all of their lives, had Brittany feeling torn, and afraid for all of the futures belonging to each and everyone involved. For this reason alone, after Rock 'n Roll Rhonda had suddenly excused herself to deal with a family-related issue, Brittany had anxiously retrieved her own cell phone from her pocketbook, and had called Kyzer.

"Hello?"

"Did I catch you at a bad time?"

"Kinda, but what's wrong, though? You alright?"

Before answering Kyzer, Brittany glanced in the direction of the home theater, where Rock 'n Roll Rhonda had disappeared through an exit, that led to the kitchen. Brittany let out a fleeting sigh as a moment of trepidation came and went.

"Okay, so, I'm here at Tia's."

"Yeah."

"With Zay and Rock 'n Roll Rhonda," Brittany explained, keeping her voice at a moderate tone, so that it wouldn't travel far. Turning her body forward, her eyes went up to the movie screen, and swept across the ten files of video footage she had yet to play for Rock 'n Roll Rhonda. "So far, everything seems to be okay."

"I doubt that."

"You doubt what?"

"That everything okay. I can hear it all in ya voice, Brittany. Why you whisperin'?"

"That's not important right now," Brittany insisted, provoked by a sudden urge to look upwards. The plexi-glass ceiling of the home theater granted her an uninterrupted view of Rock 'n Roll Rhonda, who was pacing the see-through floor of the guest room, while she appeared to be having an upsetting conversation on her cell phone. "Look, I—"

"Do I need to stop what I'm doin' and come out there?"

"No."

"You sure?"

"I'm positive, Kyzer. You tell Jamillah about Rock 'n Roll Rhonda, yet?"

"Not yet. I'm still at the Chrome Depot. Once Neef, Uzi, and Leek show up, we headin' out Montgomery County to handle that 'Drees' situation. Jamillah gon' meet us there."

"Sabia still with you?"

"Yup."

The silence that followed Kyzer's curt answer was heavier than the Empire State building. Brittany held her cell phone against her ear, momentarily at a loss for words. Since learning that Terrell was actually Sabia, all of them had been challenged with a new facet of immeasurable odds, but none of them more than Kyzer. His fight was on an emotional battlefield. His challenges were a lot deeper, and much more personal.

Deliberately, Kyzer had forged an unauthentic friendship with Sabia, and had been spending a lot of time with him. Kyzer's plans for Sabia, Brittany thought, were tantamount to possibly being the best revenge plot anyone had ever conceived. His plot had actually given Brittany the resilience she had needed to go on, because days earlier, after Detective Monica Best's body had been found, Brittany had confined herself to the bed, crying all that day, because her path to redemption, seemingly had been unearthed as she was taking her final steps.

"So, you sure you okay?"

"Yes," Brittany answered, her eyes becoming watery. Since Kyzer had begun to spend time with Sabia, her concern for him had heightened, and she now had a cryptic intuition that kept bothering her spirit. "Once we both at home tonight, together, I'll feel so much better. It seems like that's the only time I can relax. I want you to be careful, okay? And remember what we talked about this mornin', Kyzer."

"I got 'chu. Look, Uzi, Neef, and Leek just got here."

Brittany listened as Kyzer spoke to the arriving people, wondering if him and the men had shared any conspiratorial stares, due to Sabia being in their presence.

"Call me, if you need me, alright?"

"Okay . . . Kyzer?"

"Yeah?"

"I love us."

"I love us, too."

"We got Sabia, Tia," Brittany quietly celebrated, while returning her cell phone to her pocketbook. Glancing above her, she saw that Rock 'n Roll Rhonda had left the guest bedroom, so with dragging her eyes back down to the movie screen, her thoughts came back to her late boss. "Splash wasn't being honest with you, Tia. He knew where Sabia was all that time. I wish you was here. Stuff is gettin' so crazy. Detective Konn killed Monica. But thanks to you, I have the proof that it was him. I just wish you could be here, Tia. We need you. What do we do about Splash?"

Brittany wiped away some involuntary teardrops as she lowered her head sadly. No longer able to hold it back, and tired of trying to, Brittany raised her hands to her face and began to sob. Behind Brittany, over at another entrance of the home theater, different from the one she had gone through earlier, Rock 'n Roll Rhonda stood watching.

It was October 8th; Brittany's birthday. She was now twenty-three. To live to see twenty-four was the only wish she had in her heart.

To hide her own teardrops, Rock 'n Roll Rhonda pulled down her face veil, before walking over to Brittany, and sitting down beside her. At Rock 'n Roll Rhonda's return, Brittany straightened up, and while fishing inside of her pocketbook for some tissue, she shook her head, feeling slightly embarrassed.

"Tia ever tell you she got kidnapped before?"

"No."

With her answer, Brittany's hands stopped moving inside of her pocketbook. Eyes still watery, and her face still wet with her tears, Brittany turned to the side in her seat and looked at Rock 'n Roll Rhonda's veiled-face. She sat her pocketbook in her lap, stunned by the tears in Rock 'n Roll Rhonda's eyes, but also by the admission that her late boss had been kidnapped once, and that it was her first time ever hearing about the incident, until now.

"Me and Zay got her back, though. We got some help from these muslim sisters Zay knew."

"When was this?"

"Two years ago."

Brittany opened her mouth to ask another question, but when Rock 'n Roll Rhonda put a hand beneath her face veil to wipe some tears from her face, she offered her a kleenex she had found in her pocketbook. Rock 'n Roll Rhonda accepted the kleenex, but instead of using it, she curled her fingers around it, and held it in her lap.

"How y'all get her back?"

"Bayyinah made this du' a."

"What's that?"

"It's—It's a personal supplication to God. Like a prayer. We was all at Zay house. Bayyinah kept gettin' up, while we was talkin' and she would go over to the corner and pray, then she would raise her hands. I wasn't muslim at the time, but I knew what she was doin.' I had Zay in my ear, tryna get me to take my shahada, since I was little, so a lot of the stuff I already knew. Remember them Mexican girls blew that house up down South Philly, and killed all 'em cops, and they threw them heads of them people out the window?"

Brittany shook her head, remembering the incident. She had watched it unfold on her television.

"That was Bayyinah house."

"She was one of the ones that got her head cut off?"

"Yup."

Brittany and Rock 'n Roll Rhonda became quiet for a long moment. In that moment, Rock 'n Roll Rhonda used the tissue and wiped her face. Brittany remembered her late boss mentioning Bayyinah once before, but she couldn't recall why she had done so.

"She got mixed up in some stuff her brother and her old boyfriend had goin' on. A few days before that happened, Bayyinah gave me my shahadah over the phone. Brittany, it was the happiest day I ever spent in jail. Bayyinah and Zay came to visit me that next day, and they was so excited for me, and just smilin' at me through the entire visit, it had me feelin' special. I can add it to one of the times that I honestly felt true love. Brittany, I denied ya visit that day when you came to tell me about Tia, because—Brittany, I knew already."

Brittany watched sadly as Rock 'n Roll Rhonda flipped up her face veil. Her eyes held unspoken apologies.

"I knew, and I didn't want it to be true. Brittany, I just had talked to her that night before."

Brittany lowered her eyes when Rock 'n Roll Rhonda lowered hers. Tears came down both of their faces, in memory of a phenomenal woman who had meant so much to them.

"When that happened to Bayyinah, Tia and Zay came to visit me that afternoon, and Wallahi, I felt like I was gon' have a heart attack. I apologize for leavin' you that message. At the time, I just—"

"I personally know how much Tia loved you, Rock 'n Roll Rhonda. When she hired me, she told me not to let 'chu intimidate me if you called her office, while she wasn't there. She had me so scared, I ain't know what to think."

"I was jealous."

"That's what Zay said."

With sad smiles, Brittany and Rock 'n Roll Rhonda both wiped their eyes and their faces.

"Now, the whole thing with Maniac was Tia's idea," Brittany clarified, handing Rock 'n Roll Rhonda another kleenex from her pocketbook, and removing one for herself. As she used the kleenex to wipe under and around her eyes, she continued. "I already knew who he was from the neighborhood. Once me and Tia knew what kind of plan Marvin and Detective Konn had, I deliberately started, like, walkin' all around the neighborhood, so guys would see me, or whatever. Detective Konn was throwin' his two cents in, just tryna throw his weight around at the funeral home, but he ain't know me and Tia was already ten steps ahead of his little, ugly ass. I let him and Marvin think they was pullin' my strings, and makin' my decisions for me, but I had to, so it'll all seem organic. So, anyway, Maniac came to the club one night, and I just made Lucia, our bartender, act like she needed a break."

"And let me guess . . . he started flirtin' with you?"

"As soon as he seen me," Brittany confirmed, rolling her eyes. She was happy that Maniac was out of her life. "I can say, though, if not for him, and his big mouth, I wouldn't 've known about Drees, how much of a slimy bastard he is, or, that they had plans to kill Kyzer. For him to have the status he got, he talk entirely too fuckin' much."

"2 Chainnzzz!!"

Startled by the outburst, Brittany and Rock 'n Roll Rhonda both turned and fixed their eyes on the huge birdcage, over in the far-left corner of the home theater. The African, gray parrot, whose name was Gunna, hadn't said anything, since the death of its owner. A smile spread across Brittany's face. Rock 'n Roll Rhonda got up and walked over to the birdcage, smiling as well.

"Hey, Gunna."

"2 Chainnnzzz!!"

Rock 'n Roll Rhonda looked over her shoulder and smiled at Brittany, who had risen to her feet. Brittany quickly joined Rock 'n Roll Rhonda at the tall birdcage, standing beside her, anxious to hear the parrot mimic something else. For five minutes, Brittany and Rock 'n Roll Rhonda, both stood there, trying desperately to get the parrot to speak again, but he simply preened his colorful feathers, and ignored them both.

"Alright, so, let's address why we're really here," Brittany suggested, as she held her pocketbook against her lap and sat back down. She waited until Rock 'n Roll Rhonda was also seated, before she continued. "You do understand why Kyzer don't want you and Hasaan's sister to meet yet, right?"

"Brittany, here's what I understand. I was right beside Zay when she talked to Kyzer on the phone last night. Look, shouldn't my apology come from my lips? Shouldn't Hasaan's sister get the chance to look me in my eyes, hear what I have to say, and sense if I'm being genuine on her own, instead of all these walls gettin' put up between us? Brittany, Hasaan had a kufi on his head when I shot him. Do you have any idea how that makes me feel, now that I'm muslim? I wish I could undo it, but I can't, Brittany. I can't go back and change nothin' I did in the past. All I can do is beg Allah for forgiveness, and never repeat those sins again, Insha Allah. I understand that people not gon' be able to just get over all the stuff I did, but am I supposed to let my guard down, and be out here, and not protect myself? Brittany, that's never gon' happen. I'm not lettin' nobody do nothin' to me."

"And if I can do anything about it, nothin' will," Brittany added, lowering her eyes down to her pocketbook in her lap. She hoped to God that a peaceful resolution could be made, because if one wasn't, several funerals were on the horizon. "Zay don't want nothin' to happen to you, and neither do I. Kyzer's not sure what he wants. If you were just some random girl he didn't know, his decision would have been made already. He has a lot to deal with right now. Then, there's the colossal issue with how do we deal with Splash, and this shocker, that Terrell has been Sabia all this time. He's bottling it all up, and—"

"I didn't know Hasaan was his friend, Brittany. Wallahi, I didn't. As far as I knew, Kyzer only hung down South Philly, and that's it. How was I supposed to know he had started bein' up Eighth and Jefferson? From the age of ten, until I turned sixteen, I lived down South Carolina with my gran'mom. The last time I seen Kyzer, I was like nine-years-old. Brittany, he know this."

Brittany could do nothing but exhale a sigh. Hearing Rock 'n Roll Rhonda speak, and able to sit there and discern how honest she was actually being with her, it provoked her to believe that Rock 'n Roll Rhonda truly felt remorseful. Still, Brittany knew that Rock 'n Roll Rhonda's regrets, for what they were worth, had to be inspected by Kyzer, and lastly, Hasaan's sister, Jamillah.

"Brittany, when I came back to Philly, Kyzer was in jail."

"Maniac never mentioned his name to you, while all that stuff was goin' on?"

"Not to me . . . maybe to my ex-boyfriend. All I heard about was Hasaan, and he would mention some other people, here and there. If I would've heard him say Kyzer name once, I would've wanted to know if it was the same Kyzer I knew. Don't nobody else got that name in Philly, Brittany. I'll kill Maniac for Kyzer, if he asked me to."

"What about Splash?"

"My loyalty to Splash died with my cousin. My loyalty to Maniac died, once I took my shahada, and he told somebody I was still goin' to Hell. My loyalty is to Muslims, Brittany. I wanna talk to Hasaan's sister. I'll find her on my own, if I have to. Bayyinah told me when I took my shahada, days like this was goin' to come. I have to trust in Allah. Brittany, people know the old me. With Allah's help, Philly about to see a serious change. If they think Zay a problem, wait 'til they see what her little cousin comin' with. I don't make no weak du'a's, either. Bayyinah was one of the tightest sisters in Philly, and that's why Zay as sharp as she is. Bayyinah taught us how to get our du'a's answered, Brittany. That's how Zay found that out about Sabia, while she was out Detroit. One answered du'a, Brittany, and Detective Konn, Splash, Sabia, ya aunt, and her boyfriend, can all be brought to our feet."

"Let's not forget Maniac."

"I don't want Maniac brought to our feet. I have somethin' special planned for him. That phone call I got earlier was from my ex-boyfriend."

"What he say? I looked up, and I saw you in the guest bedroom."

"Well, as of today, I'm on this so-called, hit list, Maniac just put together. My name is right under yours."

"Under mine?"

"Supposedly, some Latin Queens are on their way here from New York today. It's five of them."

For a brief moment, Brittany sat there frozen, looking into Rock 'n Roll Rhonda's eyes, feeling scared and afraid. A moment later, her fear quickly began to subside, once she thought about the threat made on her life. Calmness came with her knowing who her boyfriend was. Calmness came with her sitting there, and remembering that she, in fact, had been the apprentice of Mrs. Gunplay herself, Tianna Paradise Barnes.

Rock 'n Roll Rhonda raised her eyebrows as Brittany's face slowly softened, and displayed a big smile.

"What?"

"I know how to get in Tia vault upstairs."

"Stop playin'. Are you serious?"

"I was her assistant," Brittany reminded Rock 'n Roll Rhonda, as she took off running out of the home theater. Rock 'n Roll Rhonda was right behind her. "She got these

Kevlar, bulletproof vests, that come all the way down to your knees. Some guy in Japan made them for her. It's two of them. They fit like dresses."

"We should empty it so Splash won't have no arsenal to come home to, anyway."

"Good fuckin' idea."

Chapter Sixteen

"This shouldn't take longer than an hour," Kyzer explained, while looking around at all of the faces that were staring back at him. Purposely, with disgust, and bottled hatred, surging inside of his chest, he avoided locking eyes with Sabia, and his cousin, Idris, who were standing to his far left. "It might not even take that long. For the most part, I wanted all of y'all to get familiar with everybody's names, and to be able to put them to faces. My plans was to do this when I first got out, but as y'all know, a lot been goin' on. Alright, so this farm, and all these acres belong to a real good friend of mine. Now, let me show y'all why we here. Follow me."

Everyone followed Kyzer into the gigantic barn, except for Sabia. After dropping a knee down to the grass, and pretending to tighten the laces on his left, Louis Vuitton sneaker, Sabia casually stole a glance over his right shoulder, and looked at all of the parked vehicles off in the distance, including his own.

Excluding Sabia's Audi station wagon, there were four SUVs, five cars, and one motorcycle, all parked randomly, on both sides of the long, dirt path that stretched back down to Providence Road. The Montgomery County property was desolate. There were only trees and grass to be seen. The tall trees were beginning to shed brown leaves, and the grass was about an ankle's length. The huge barn, and the dirt path leading to it, were the only two things the thirteen and a half acres consisted of. Above the farm, strong winds were sending the clouds east. It was a brisk, fifty-three degrees. The sun was visible, but on this early October afternoon, it seemed to be even too cold for the sun.

Rising to stand, Sabia wiped away some dirt from his right knee, as he ran his eyes across the dark windshield of Kyzer's new, black, 2013 Cadillac ATS. Sabia sensed that there was someone inside of Kyzer's car, hiding behind the tinted windows. His gut was telling him this, and had been, since their departure from Philadelphia. Kyzer had chosen to drive alone, and had ordered Uzi, Haneef, and his cousin, Malik, to drive with Sabia. The three men had stayed silent the entire drive.

Sabia walked into the barn, feeling overtaken by anxiety. Despite what Kyzer had just told him, and everyone else, this meeting was showing all the signs of it being a trap.

The group of eighteen men, and three women, all began to fan out, giving each person ample space, as their eyes widened in wonderment, and their mouths fell open in surprise. Kyzer stood several feet away from them all. When Sabia's eyes came to his, for a moment, he forgot to breathe. A second later, remembering his ultimate goal, he looked away. Kyzer casually brought his eyes to Uzi, Haneef, and his cousin, Malik, and with a nod of his head, the three men went into action.

"Everybody move out the way!" Kyzer barked, as Uzi, Haneef, and his cousin, Malik, circled his cousin, Idris, with their guns drawn. The moment of revenge had the blood in his veins, feeling like liquid fire, as Idris slowly raised his hands, and turned to look at him with questioning eyes. "Bring him over here."

Justified.

The thirteen and a half acres belonged to the famous Philadelphia rap artist, Freeway. Before Freeway's rise to stardom, he had played an active role in Kyzer's push for power and control in the North Philadelphia neighborhood, where Kyzer's aunt lived. While Kyzer had been away in prison, him and Freeway had stayed in touch with each other. Both men had some powerful plans brewing.

While the outside of the barn appeared to have seen better days, and its surrounding land looked forgotten about, and barren, the inside of the barn closely resembled the location where Rob Dyrdek filmed his MTV show, 'Fantasy Factory.' Entering the barn, there was a regulation-sized boxing ring to the left. The background of that area was a mirrored-wall. Further down, along the same wall, Freeway's giant, black tour bus was parked, commanding most of the space in the rear left corner of the barn. Along the back wall, on the opposite side of the big metal, roll-up door, presumably necessary for bringing in Freeway's tour bus, there was a flight of aluminum spiral stairs, leading up to the second floor of the barn, where there was a recording studio, a bathroom, and two offices, all lining the upper level of the barn's right-side wall. The lower half of the exposed brick wall was outlined with a long string of arcade games that stretched to the rear of the barn, where the aluminum spiral staircase was.

At the front of the barn, behind Kyzer's small assembly, there were a few dirt bikes, some four wheelers, and two motorcycles. Kyzer's back was to the best attraction of the barn, which was located in its center, beneath a thick slab of plexi-glass. Under the rectangular-shaped plexi-glass, there was an alligator tank. The tank was thirty feet in width, fifty feet in length, and ten feet deep, and had an intimidating appearance. The water was murky and dark.

When visiting Freeway's barn, few people dared to step one foot onto the plexi-glass, fearing it would collapse beneath their feet; Kyzer wasn't one of those people. As Idris was brought to him, Kyzer backed further onto the plexi-glass, until he stood in its center. His eyes had become dangerously violent.

"Right there cool," Kyzer instructed, prompting Uzi, Haneef, and his cousin, Malik, to back away from his cousin, Idris, whose hazel eyes were in a daze, as they stared down at the huge alligator tank beneath their feet. Satisfied, he looked over his shoulder at everyone else. "Make a circle around us."

"Kyzer, what's this about?"

Kyzer ignored his cousin and removed his Gucci field coat, and let it fall down to the plexi-glass floor. He was done talking. He was in a volatile area of his mind, where bad thoughts evolved into terrifying sins. As the group began circling him and his cousin, he thought about what had led him and his cousin, Idris, to this moment, and it pinched at the corners of his heart, more times than he would have liked. Kyzer knew then, that he had to speak.

"Confess, Drees."

"To what?"

Beneath them, the murky water started to ripple. There were murmurs from the group, as their circle became complete. Sabia stiffened when the Puerto Rican girl to his right grabbed the sleeve of his leather jacket, as an alligator came to the surface of the dark water beneath them. The other two Puerto Rican girls spoke in hushed-Spanish, for no more than a few seconds, then put their eyes back on Kyzer and Idris. Every chest in the circle owned a rapid heartbeat, and eyes kept dropping down to the plexi-glass floor, because more alligators were beginning to rise to the surface of the water below.

"Die wit' some dignity, Drees," Kyzer suggested, while handing his cell phone to his friend, Shiz, whose facial expression was as grim as his. Next, he walked a few steps, and stopped in front of his friend, Mel, and took off his double-shoulder holster, which had his two Glock 45s, and handed it over to Mel's waiting hand. "Drees, I know you was wit' Saan. I know everything. I know I'm supposed to be next, 'n all 'lat. I'm just askin' you to admit it, that's all. Confess."

After looking around at all of the faces surrounding him, and seemingly accepting that his life had reached its expiration date, Idris let out a long sigh as his hazel eyes came back to Kyzer's face.

"Confess, Drees."

"Fuck you and Saan."

Those vile words stabbed Kyzer in the heart five times. He charged his cousin with his shoulders squared, and his fists clenched, guarding both sides of his chin. The crowd circling him and his cousin vibrated as the first punches of the fight were thrown. Idris opened up with a wild left hook, and an even wilder, overhand-right cross. Neither punch had met their target. Kyzer had taken a knee at the very last second, before spitting in Idris' face. One punch to the groin caused Idris to double over, and melt down to the plexi-glass floor.

"Fuck me?!" Kyzer snapped, back on his feet. Crouching over his cousin, he rained down punches to his face and head, then stepped back, and started to kick him in the chest and ribs. "Nigga, fuck Saan?!! We made you! Who you ever would've been wit'out us?!"

"Let—Let me get back up! Lemme stand up!!"

"Oh, you ain't done?!"

The shouting echoed around the barn, causing no one to hear or notice that someone else had come into the barn.

Sabia could feel his heart slamming against his chest. The fight between the two cousins wasn't the first one he had witnessed. They had fought in his bedroom once. Watching Kyzer fight anyone had always been entertaining to him, because he knew that few men could outlast Kyzer for long. Kyzer's father had been a professional boxer, who had almost turned Kyzer into a prodigy at an early age. As both cousins squared off again, Sabia felt his heartbeat soar, as Kyzer peeled out of his sweater, and the shirt beneath it. It was about to get good.

"You never could beat me, Drees."

"That was back in the day."

"If you thought I was a problem back then, I'ma— Drees, I'ma show you ya own fuckin' eyeball. Come on . . . let's get it, pussy."

Like lions, Kyzer and Idris charged at each other again, only this time, after a quick exchange of punches, Idris grabbed a handful of Kyzer's individual braids with his left hand, and rammed his forehead into the bridge of Kyzer's nose. Idris then brought his right hand to Kyzer's throat, squeezed, and lifted Kyzer off of his feet. Gasps came from the crowd. Those that didn't gasp, stood there, involuntarily, clenching their fists, wishing their arms were attached to Kyzer's body, as he was slammed down to the plexi-glass floor.

A groan escaped Kyzer's lips, as his back made contact with the plexi-glass floor. The back of his head made contact next, and Kyzer felt pain shoot down his spine. A moment of dizziness paralyzed his entire body.

"Kyzer, get up!!"

Kyzer heard the command, but he had no idea who the voice belonged to. He started shielding his face, blocking punches, and listening, as his cousin said dark words. Time seemed to stop, as he was being punched. He could hear more people from the crowd encouraging him to fight back, to get up, to do something. He could feel his own blood pouring out of his nostrils. Idris had gotten stronger, and he had underestimated him. A hard blow got through a space between his forearm and his right shoulder, and it brought stars to the back of his eyes. Another moment of dizziness came.

Sabia couldn't believe what he was seeing. Beneath him, the alligators were becoming agitated down in their tank, and there was Kyzer, losing a fight to his cousin, Idris.

Teardrops began to slide out of Kyzer's eyes. Time started to move once more; the dizziness subsided. Shame that he was even on the floor, was parallel to the rage he started to feel as every dead person he loved, spoke to him, and begged him to finish what he had started. In prison, those same voices had helped him run more miles, at times when he had wanted to stop and walk. Like his father had taught him, Kyzer calmed himself, and thought four moves ahead, then he rolled from beneath his cousin, and slowly stood. His teardrops were still spilling from his eyes, almost blinding him. The blood from his nose had made it down to his bare chest.

Kyzer opened and closed his fists, then raised them up to both sides of his chin again. Idris did the same, but more warily, because he knew that when Kyzer cried, his ferocity knew no bounds.

This time, Kyzer assumed a southpaw stance and moved forward, relying on instinct alone, and nothing else. In four moves, if he didn't have his cousin defeated, he was going to grab his gun, and finish their fight that way. Considering that option made him angrier. Close enough, he fainted with a jab, just to see what kind of reaction it would earn him from his cousin.

Like Kyzer had assumed, after feigning with his jab, Idris had tensed, and had thrown a looming, overhand right cross. A tactician, Kyzer moved fast and methodical, sending a punishing jab to his cousin's chin, then turned that jab into an uppercut with the same hand. After raising Idris' chin with his uppercut, Kyzer threw a fierce right cross at Idris' Adam's apple. Three moves down, as soon as Idris melted down to the plexi-glass floor, clutching his throat, Kyzer was all over him.

It was then, that Jamillah, made herself visible to everyone, by clearing her throat as she approached the circle, surrounding Kyzer and Idris. Today, she wore no face-veil; only her black head scarf, and her flowing, black, over-garment.

Idris began to yell and scream as Kyzer dug his right thumb into his left eye-socket. Both cousins were wrestling, and tossing and turning on the plexi-glass floor. Idris' loud screams were echoing off of the walls in the barn, and the more he yelled and protested in pain, the more the alligators got excited down in their tank. No one had noticed, but in the far-right corner, where the plexi-glass ended, and the cement began, there was a handle. The handle, if pulled up, opened a small, circular, plexi-glass door, held by two brass hinges. The alligators were fed through this opening.

"What the fuck I tell you?!!" Kyzer shouted, rising to stand, more enraged from a fight than he had ever been in his whole life. He had his cousin's left, bleeding eyeball in his right hand and the victory of having it, and being able to show it to his cousin brought glory to his veins. "Pussy, what I tell you?! Look!! You fuckin' snake! After all the shit Saan did for you, you gon' cross him like that! Millions, kill that nigga!!!"

Teardrops rolled down Jamillah's pretty face, as she crossed her arms, and dug her hands into the hand-stitched openings beneath the armpits of her black over-garment. She was wearing a double-shoulder holster under it. Shocked that she was there, Idris watched her from the floor, holding a trembling hand over his empty, bleeding eye-socket.

"Babe, no. Look, listen—Babe, listen to me. What about the babies? Think about our babies, Mill."

"I did."

Jamillah moved forward with her words, aiming one of her Glock 380s at her husband. The one in her left hand was down at her side.

"Mill, my blood halal! Don't this! Kyzer, stop her. Leek, you just gon' stand there and let them do me like this?!"

Sabia watched the brief eye exchange between Kyzer and his younger cousin, Malik, then looked away, pretending not to notice. Suspicions confirmed, Sabia looked back at Jamillah, who now only stood a few feet away from Idris. It all began to make sense to Sabia. Jamillah had been the person inside of Kyzer's car. Her and Kyzer had set this stage for Idris. Relieved he wasn't in any danger, Sabia picked Kyzer's sweater and shirt up, then walked over and handed them to him.

"Wait 'til you see what I got for you," Kyzer thought, accepting his stuff from Sabia, after tossing his cousin's eyeball aside, and wiping his bloody palm across the front of his jeans. Looking back at Jamillah and his cousin, he fed off the energy that revenge brung. "One down, and a few more to go."

The gunshots sounded like several small buildings were imploding inside of the barn. After Idris' hand fell away from his injured eye, his body began to twist and jerk violently, as his wife peppered his stomach and chest with a series of hot bullets. As spent shell casings ejected from her gun, and fell to the plexi-glass floor, Kyzer walked over to where they had fallen, and retrieved every last one. Everyone watched the murder in silence, as the walls in the barn caused the sound of the gunshots to reverberate for along moment.

Once Idris laid lifeless, and his crimson blood began to appear from beneath him, staining the see-through floor, he was dragged over to the feeding-hole by Uzi, Malik, and Haneef.

"Hold up," Kyzer spoke, cutting his eyes at Jamillah as he passed her, and knelt down beside Idris. He removed Idris' cell phone from his pocket, and then stood and backed away, until he was standing beside Jamillah. "Alright, go 'head."

"Oh, shit," Sabia thought, after Uzi had grabbed the metal handle on the plexi-glass floor, and lifted it up. A cold wave of fear tickled his heart, as Haneef and Malik slowly moved Idris's dead body over to what he now realized was a feeding hole for the alligators. "These mother fuckers trippin.' Damn, Drees. I really gotta stay on point around these niggaz. They damn sure ain't gon' rock me to sleep like that. Wait 'til I tell Splash this shit."

Chapter Seventeen

"Two days ago, my cousin had to get subtracted from this movement," Kyzer mentioned, while glancing down at the screen of his cell phone, and reading a new text message sent from Brittany. Returning his cell phone back to his pocket, he looked around at all of the faces in the living room of the Chrome Depot, then exhaled a sigh before continuing. "It had to happen. While I was locked up, I knew that I could've made a call or wrote a letter, but I wanted it to be somethin' that I dealt wit' personally. Plus, I ain't wanna just be workin' off speculation, so once I got out, I did my homework. Drees was fuckin' wit' Maniac for a minute. For like three years. Could've been longer than that . . . who knows? The point is, Maniac had eyes on the inside all that time. We lost Saan because of it, and I was next in line. Crazy, right? My own fuckin' blood. So, since Maniac been such a thorn, from tomorrow forward, we in attack mode on him, and everybody else who seem to think this fuckin' neighborhood is Candy Land. No picks. If they ain't runnin' wit' us, I want them mu'fuckers runnin' from us. But first, though, let me formally introduce everybody, since we ain't really get to do that shit the other day. I ain't know them alligators was gon' have niggaz throwin' up 'n shit."

Dangerous minds.

Think alike.

One by one, Kyzer started introducing each person in attendance, starting with his younger cousin, Malik, first. Malik lived in walking distance of the Chrome Depot. He had arrived on a four wheeler. He was 17-years-old, but wise beyond his years, and any enemy of Kyzer's, was an enemy of his. Haneef, Uzi, Rashad, Wakil, F.L., and Aleem, all shared Malik's view as well. They were all teenagers who had been born and raised in the neighborhood. Before his death, Hasaan had started to groom the seven teenagers into reputable, young men. Sadly, under Idris, this grooming had ended. He had merely mishandled them, and treated them condescendingly. Kyzer was about to give them an opportunity to make history.

The closeness of the teenagers reflected in their body language. All of them were in one area of the Chrome Depot's living room, either sitting, or standing up. Some of them weren't comfortable with the new faces among them.

One of those new faces belonged to Mel. Kyzer and Mel had met at a state prison. Mel was from Brooklyn, New York, but he also had a lot of family in Reading, Pennsylvania, where he spent a lot of his time. Mel was 23-years-old. With him, were three beautiful, Puerto Rican women. Their names were Dolly, Paloma, and Genesis. As Kyzer introduced Mel and his female friends, he pointed out that Mel and the three women, already knew who Maniac was, and what he looked like.

Next, Kyzer pointed to the quiet guy standing to his right. His name was Dame. Dame was from 15th and Erie in North Philadelphia. The two had met at a county prison, while Kyzer, had been awaiting his sentencing date. Dame, Kyzer mentioned, had a dangerous team of his own, who he would be utilizing when it was necessary. Kyzer then pointed at Shiz, who was standing to his left. Shiz, Mel, and

Kyzer, had all been housed on the same block at a state prison in Huntingdon, Pennsylvania. Shiz had a fearless nature about him, and he had proven his loyalty to Kyzer on more than one occasion. Shiz was 25-years-old, and was a member of the infamous North Philadelphia group, Young and Deadly.

The last three faces belonged to Mikel, Tauheed, and Ern. The three men were in their early twenties, and had traveled to the Chrome Depot from South Philadelphia, where they had been born and raised. Looking at the three men, Kyzer felt assurance.

For two and a half hours, Kyzer and the group talked about strategies, concerns, and for the new faces, a tour of the Chrome Depot was even given. After everyone had departed, Kyzer got into his car and drove down to 6th and Cecil B. Moore. Killing the headlights, he parked across the street from Sabia's mother's house, and dialed Sabia's cell phone number. A long moment passed, before Sabia picked up.

"Hello?"

"Rell, what 'chu up to?"

"Shit . . . here at the club, helpin' the DJ set all his music stuff up. It's supposed to be crazy in here tonight. You comin' through? Ay, yo, I thought we was gon' get together earlier?"

"Somethin' came up," Kyzer lied, glancing up at his rearview mirror, then looking back over to Sabia's mother's house. He frowned as he shrugged his shoulders uncomfortably, in an effort to ease the discomfort of the bullet-proof vest he was wearing. "Yeah, I'll be there, though. Ay, remember when we was talkin' the other night and I was tellin' you about the nigga that did that nut ass shit to my sister, a few years ago? Splash cousin?"

"Yeah."

The wavering in Sabia's voice made Kyzer curl the fingers on his left hand into a tight fist. As much as Kyzer wanted to believe that he had the situation with Sabia under control, there had been moments where every single emotion inside of his body had begged him to just end the mind games with Sabia, and simply avenge his sister's death. Kyzer began tapping his fist against his steering wheel, as he fought to suppress his rage.

"I'm parked across the street from main man, mom's house, as we speak," Kyzer revealed, after switching his cell phone to his opposite ear. His eyes shot up to his rearview mirror, and stayed there, upon noticing a slow, traveling police car, coming down 6th Street. "Rell, I been doin' this shit for the past two weeks. Just parkin' up, and watchin' her crib. Guess what Splash offered me, if I left her alone?"

"What?"

"This between me and you, right?"

"No question."

Kyzer smirked devilishly. He waited until after the police car had turned left on Cecil B. Moore Avenue, before he cut on his headlights and pulled out of the parking space. At Cecil B. Moore Avenue, he made a right and drove, until a red light stopped him at 7th Street.

"Splash gon' line his cousin, Sabia, up for me, Rell," Kyzer announced, wishing he could see the expression on Sabia's face. Sabia's silence urged him to pour more salt into his wound. "At first, I ain't believe him. Then, like, I had to sit back and really think about Splash whole take on all this shit. Right now, his main concern is his freedom, and his son. That nigga know I hold all the pieces if he tryna beat that case. Feel what I'm sayin'? He ain't got Tia out here no more."

The traffic light turned green, and Kyzer moved his new Cadillac across 7th Street, pressing on the gas pedal lightly. The reflection of the half-moon was visible on the car's trunk, as it traveled west up Cecil B. Moore Avenue.

"Splash don't want no more innocent blood on his hands," Kyzer explained, as he made a left at Franklin Street, while wondering what type of thoughts were spinning through Sabia's mind. Since Sabia and his cousin, Splash, were playing war games with him, he had decided that he would do the same with them both, but just more cunningly. "Plus, like, his cousin done brought enough shame to their family name as it is. You know Splash like I do, Rell. He always been a man of his word. If he told me that he'd give up his cousin, as long as I leave his aunt alone, that shit written in stone."

"He said where his cousin at? I mean, like, in what state, or whatever?"

"Naw, not yet. He will, though. He got two and a half weeks left. Ay, yo, I'ma see you when I get to the club, though, alright?"

"Alright."

Kyzer dropped his cell phone down to his lap, then tugged at the collar of his bulletproof vest beneath his plum-colored, Paul & Shark sweater. Him, Brittany, and Rock 'n Roll Rhonda, had all been taking extra precautions the last few days, fully aware that at any moment, death could call. Kyzer's attention was being divided between so many issues, it left him with few moments to actually give each dilemma its due assessment.

Oddly enough, after pulling over and parking at the corner of his aunt's block, on Randolph and Thompson, Kyzer seized the opportunity to do some serious thinking. His first thoughts were about his cousin, Idris. His family was starting to ask questions. So far, Jamillah was keeping a brave face, and acting as clueless about Idris' disappearance as everyone else. He still hadn't found the courage or the energy needed, to talk to Jamillah about Rock 'n Roll Rhonda yet. He was still having a hard time accepting that the same shy, little girl, who he had once known, was now a cold-blooded killer, and the female he had heard people talking so much about, while he had been away in prison. At times, he thought of just killing Rock 'n Roll Rhonda himself, and not telling Jamillah anything. However, the night that Zainab had returned from Detroit, and had revealed that Terrell was actually Sabia, Zainab had tearfully begged him to spare Rock 'n Roll Rhonda's life, and to give Rock 'n Roll Ronda a chance to explain herself and apologize.

Not ending there, with Brittany watching, Zainab had then begged him to begin practicing Islam again, and to start making his five daily prayers. That night, Kyzer had laid in bed, unable to sleep. As Brittany had slept beside him, he fought with his mind, his heart, and his soul, unwilling to alter his plans for anyone, or anything; at the moment, he saw no need to.

Zainab had made some convincing points that night, even sharing with him and Brittany, how God had been answering a lot of her prayers. Zainab explained to them that one of her specific supplications to God had been that He continuously expose the deceitful people around her, and protect her, and her loved ones from their harm.

While in Detroit, Zainab had met several muslim women, who had all assisted her in avenging her cousin's death. The younger sister of one of these women, had divulged some shocking news to Zainab, as she was being driven back to the Detroit Airport days later. Earlier that year, the younger sister had met Sabia on an online dating service. After weeks of sending e-mails, text messages, and doing a lot of talking on their cell phones, Sabia had visited the younger sister in Detroit for a week. On one particular night, Sabia had fallen asleep, forgetting to log-off from his iPad, and bitten by curiosity, the younger sister had used the moment as an opportunity to possibly learn why Sabia seemed to be so secretive about his life as a club promoter, or why he only turned on his cell phone, after he believed she was asleep at night.

Before dozing off, Sabia had been sending and receiving instant messages from his friend, Ashley. Upon realizing that Terrell Matthews was a false identify, the younger sister explained to Zainab how she had locked herself in the bathroom, and had read all of Sabia's instant messages, and had gotten into his e-mail account, and had read all of them as well.

Luckily for Sabia, the younger sister was the granddaughter of an old, Detroit, drug kingpin. That next morning, she didn't reveal to Sabia that she was aware of who he really was, and she continued to refer to him as Terrell. She had even prepared breakfast for him. Afterwards, however, she told Sabia that he had to go, because her son's father was coming home from jail that afternoon, which was just a lie to get Sabia out of her house. The younger sister had only shared the story with Zainab, simply because Zainab was from Philadelphia. She had been totally unaware of Zainab's closeness to Sabia. Zainab cited the experience as God answering her invocations to Him.

"That was crazy," Kyzer thought, recalling Zainab's experience in Detroit, as he looked around at the houses lining Thompson Street. His eyes went up to his rearview mirror, then fell back on his digitized-dashboard. "Zay thorough as shit. If it wasn't for her, Sabia and Splash could be rockin' me to sleep right now. She ain't have to tell me that shit. Unless that was her way of softenin' me up, so she could get me to hear her out about Rock 'n Roll Rhonda. All this shit crazy. I'm gon' have to tell Leek that Terrell is Sabia. I can't keep this shit to myself. Now, I just gotta find out where Sabia hidin' Ashley the fuck at."

Kyzer pulled out of the parking space, and sped up Randolph Street, until he reached Girard Avenue. As he made a right turn, his cell phone started to ring. The number on the screen of his phone was strange to him, but he still accepted the incoming call, as he brought his car to a stop, obeying a red traffic light at 6th and Girard.

"Hello?"

"Is this Kyzer?"

"Yeah, who this?"

"Tamika. My attribute is Haneefah. Idris told me if somethin' ever happened to him, to point my finger at 'chu. We got married two weeks ago. I haven't heard from him in two days. He not answerin' my calls, or none of my text messages, and as of yesterday, his phone been goin' straight to his voicemail."

Rattled, Kyzer drove across 6th Street, after the traffic light had turned green. He held his cell phone against his ear, thinking, and not knowing how to respond to the strange woman on the other end of his cell phone, who was claiming to be his cousin's wife. That his cousin had told the woman to blame him, if something was to ever happen to him, was unsettling every fiber in his body.

"How you know he not with his first wife?"

"Well, is he?"

"Listen, you can save the attitude for somebody else," Kyzer argued, as he drove west up Girard Avenue, unaware that he was being followed by a dark-colored, Chevy Impala. The conversation with the strange woman had him distracted, as he drove to nowhere in particular. "Where Drees at is his business. And why the fuck he told you, if somethin' happened to him, I had somethin' to do wit' it?"

"You tell me? And you're right, where he is, is his business, but I—"

"But nothin' . . . don't call my phone again. I ain't Drees keeper."

After ending the phone call, Kyzer scrolled down the names in his phone, until he got to Jamillah's number. As he waited for Jamillah to pick up, he pulled his car into the gas station on Broad and Girard, and pulled beside a service pump. Holding his cell phone to his ear, Kyzer's breath caught in his chest as he came eye to eye with Maniac, and two of Maniac's male cousins. The three men had attempted to go unnoticed, as they sat in a four-door, black, Chevy Impala. He remembered seeing the car in his rearview mirror at 9th and Girard.

"Kyzer?"

"Mill, these niggaz got the drop on me."

"Who?"

Kyzer switched his cell phone to his opposite ear as he stepped out of his car, and watched as Maniac and his cousins made a slow, right turn on Broad Street. Maniac was in the front passenger seat, holding his stare. The two men had been foes, since their teenage years. Maniac was equally as dangerous. He was a tall man, standing six feet six inches tall. He had a cocoa brown complexion, curly hair, and had a muscular build. He normally wore his beard full, but today he had it neatly trimmed into a goatee.

It was 10:45 p.m., and the night sky above the busy intersection of Broad and Girard was lit with stars, and a glowing, half-moon. The mid-October temperature was chilly and unwelcoming, and as Kyzer inhaled the cold air into his lungs, he wondered if it would be his night to die. He was outnumbered, outgunned, and after only being home for one month, he had done so much, but he had also done so little.

Broad and Girard was one of the busiest intersections in North Philadelphia. There were police surveillance cameras above the traffic lights on all four corners. One corner housed a CVS pharmacy, and across from it there was a Checkers, fast-food restaurant, as well as a KFC. People were standing on both corners, waiting for transit buses, and every eleven minutes people would pour out onto the sidewalk, after climbing the stairs, leading from the underground subway stations. Kyzer was on the busiest segment of Broad and Girard, where there was a gas station, and a McDonald's, sharing the same corner. The drive-thru at the McDonald's was outlined with cars as usual, and other than Kyzer's Cadillac ATS, the gas station was empty.

"Mill, send somebody to pick up my car from the gas station on Broad and Girard," Kyzer instructed, as he closed his driver's side door, and backed away from his car. Maniac and his cousins were turning off of Broad Street, and entering the gas station from its other entrance. "Call Leek."

"Kyzer, what's—"

Kyzer ended his call with Jamillah and stuffed his cell phone down into the pocket of his jeans. At the sidewalk on Girard Avenue, he looked right, left, then across Girard Avenue at Watts Street. His heart was slamming against his chest, as the sounds of car doors slamming behind him echoed all around him. A quick glance over his shoulder showed Maniac and his cousins walking away from their car, which they had parked facing his. There was no going back. Walking faster, Kyzer started crossing Girard Avenue, heading towards Watts Street. Maniac and his cousins quickened their steps as well, as all three men simultaneously raised their weapons, and started firing their guns.

"Pussies!" Kyzer cursed to himself, as he made it to Watts Street, and put his back to the wall of a corner store. Breathing heavily, he withdrew his Glock 45, as Maniac and his cousins shot at him recklessly, not even able to see where he was. "Them niggaz don't even dig, they on fuckin' camera. I gotta make it down to Popular Street."

Watts Street was a narrow block that was dark and long. Its darkness was masking Kyzer, but him not shooting back, had incited Maniac and his cousins to continue their pursuit of him. They believed Kyzer was running for his life, and had no gun on him. When the three men made it to the top of Watts Street, still shooting, Kyzer was nearing the bottom of the dark block, looking back at them. The echoes of the gunshots were deafening.

A moment of clarity came to Kyzer as a hot bullet ripped into his right elbow. God came to his mind, and all things sacred to him, began to flash in his thoughts, as a second bullet slammed into his back and a third one hit him in the back of his left thigh. Kyzer stumbled, grimacing, sure that he was experiencing his final moments alive. A fourth bullet slammed into the lower right side of his back, and burned its way through his stomach, before chipping his right hip, and making its exit. The momentum of the fourth bullet sent Kyzer stumbling to his right a few steps. Maniac and his cousins were sending a firewall at him.

Done running, Kyzer raised his gun as he turned around. Bullets were whistling past his body. Staggering forward, he aimed and squeezed the trigger of the Glock five times, then sent another volley of bullets. He wanted to die with valor. Days earlier, his uncle had suggested that he mix some ammonia and bleach together, and pour it in the hollow-tips of his bullets. Kyzer had done so; so had his cousin, Malik. The clip in Kyzer's Glock was filled with a lot of them.

As he shot back, Kyzer believed he could hear the sounds of dirt bikes and four wheelers off in the distance. He wondered if it was his help coming. He felt weak as he suddenly noticed that Maniac and his cousins were gone, and he was shooting at nothing. The immediate silence on Watts Street made his ringing cell phone sound magnified, as he turned and slowly made his way to the corner of Watts Street. Every place where he had been shot hurt like hell, and he knew he had just escaped death. Pain brought him down to his knees. On all fours, he started crawling, making it out into the middle of Popular Street. He refused to abandon his empty Glock, knowing it was now useless to him. A cab came to a screeching halt, just as Kyzer was losing consciousness in the middle of Popular Street. Up at Girard Avenue, a second shootout was happening, and several teenagers were on four wheelers and dirt bikes, shooting at Maniac and his cousins, while their eyes desperately searched for any sign of Kyzer. One of them, who had came to the scene on the back of a four wheeler, had made it to Kyzer's car successfully, and had pulled away in it.

Meanwhile, Kyzer's life was hanging in the balance, as the cab driver stood over his bleeding, motionless body, not sure if he should pull out his cell phone and dial 9-1-1, or drive Kyzer to the nearest hospital. With seconds vanishing, and the background being shattered by so much gunfire, the young, Albanian, cab driver, chose to rush Kyzer to the hospital, instead of informing the authorities, or leaving him there to die on the street. It would be a deed that would one day save his own life.

Favors.

Chapter Eighteen

Brittany sat inside of her car, staring blankly through her windshield at the rear window of Sabia's Audi station wagon. Her emotions were finding freedom in the teardrops spilling out of her eyes. It had been two days since, Kyzer's now-epic shootout with Maniac and Maniac's cousins, and no one still had the slightest idea of where Kyzer might possibly be. The speculation that he was dead, and maybe buried in a shallow grave somewhere, was being whispered all across the streets of Philadelphia. In just two days, Kyzer had become a household name. The surveillance video from Broad and Girard, of him being shot at, and chased, had received national attention, but it was Kyzer's disappearance shortly thereafter, that seemed to be holding the most intrigue.

All of the social media sites were alive with gossip, and local, and national, news stations alike, were continuously airing the old, news footage, of the massacre that had occurred at Kyzer's sister's house, along with video footage of Kyzer at the Southwest Philadelphia cemetery, as he was desperately attempting to save the lives of his mother and Tia, by giving them both CPR next to his older sister's gravesite. Parts of the world had fallen in love with Kyzer's story. His face was on the front page of the Philadelphia

Daily Newspaper, with the caption above it reading, 'How Did Kyzer Vanish?'

After a sigh, Brittany reached over and grabbed the folded newspaper from her passenger seat, then unfolded it before placing it on her lap. Crying still, Brittany stared tearfully down at Kyzer's picture. She didn't like that the newspaper had used an old arrest photo of Kyzer.

"Kyzer, where are you?" Brittany wondered out loud, raising both of her hands up to her face, and wiping her eyes. The last two days had been heavy on her shoulders, and even heavier on her mind and heart, but to her own surprise, she was still managing to hold it all together. "You're not dead. I can feel it. You—Kyzer, you somewhere alive, and I know it. We just need to know where, so we can come and get you, and take care of you. Baby, where are you?"

Brittany was parked behind the Chrome Depot, on Darien Street. The narrow block was gridlocked with cars, SUVs, dirt bikes, and four wheelers. At the corner of Darien and Jefferson, there were four, moving trucks. The trucks were parked one behind the other, stretching back to 9th and Jefferson. More than thirty people were inside of the Chrome Depot. All of them were waiting for Brittany to arrive, so they could get their meeting started. Brittany was expected to arrive at 10:00 p.m., but Brittany had chosen to show up early.

It was 9:30 p.m., and the skies above Philadelphia was dark, displaying a bright, full moon. Cold winds were whispering all around the city.

Brittany grabbed her pocketbook from the backseat, and fished her cell phone out of it, after it alerted her that she had just received a new text message. After quickly reading the text message, Brittany dug into her pocketbook and pulled out a second cell phone that she had purchased earlier in the day, from a cell phone store in West

Philadelphia. Taking a deep breath, Brittany dialed a number into the new cell phone, then waited for an answer. Who she was calling picked up on the first ring.

"Can I safely assume that this phone you're calling me from can't be traced back to you or me?"

"Yes."

"Good. Now, let's discuss this e-mail I received from you last night."

Brittany snatched her car keys out of the ignition and stepped out of her car, leaving her pocketbook behind. After shutting her car door, she stood still for a moment, undecided of which direction she should walk. Her eyes cut right to left, as she held her cell phone to her left ear. Her eyes went to the rear door of the Chrome Depot, but with looking there, she thought of everyone inside, and knew that she could never get anyone inside of there to comprehend her reasoning for being on the phone with a federal judge.

"Tia and Monica were my friends," Brittany expressed, as she began to walk south, down the middle of Darien Street. On this night, she knew that revenge would be met, and it was her goal to be prepared when she came face to face with it. "Mrs. Patricia, Tia and your daughter taught me things no one in life has ever taken the time to show me. My mother died giving birth to me. And I can't credit my aunt for shit . . . nothin'. Mrs. Patricia, I had to learn how to be a woman from life. Life, and all the bullshit that come along with it. What will always stay with me, that I learned from Monica and Tia, is that no matter how big the obstacles in front of you might be, you won't know you can get over it, until you make the effort to try. Mrs. Patricia, all of the great women in history are remembered, because they all dared to do what other women wouldn't. Tonight, I want you to help me be one of them."

"By doing what exactly?"

"By being the mother you can't be to Monica anymore, Mrs. Patricia. Insulate me tonight with your power and influence. Monica and Tia would want that for me."

"Does this have anything to do with your missing boyfriend?"

"Mrs. Patricia, tonight my goals have something to do with all of us," Brittany clarified, after squeezing between two parked cars, and stepping up on the sidewalk, where there were several four wheelers parked. After glancing back up Darien Street at her own car, then looking again over at the rear door of the Chrome Depot, she took a seat on the four wheeler closest to her, and let out a sigh, before continuing to speak into her cell phone. "With your help, I can satisfy the motives that got this whole thing started, Mrs. Patricia. We won't get Monica and Tia back, but we'll definitely give them something to smile about in their graves. I can promise you that."

"What help do you need from me?"

"Connections."

Brittany's eyes blurred with fresh tears; not from the gusty winds blowing all around her, but from the overwhelming sense of relief that was washing across her body, due to her knowing that Patricia Best's decision could have gone either way. With that to worry about no longer, Brittany still had an enormous amount of anxiety sitting on her shoulders. The moment had come for her to tell Patricia Best that she knew who was responsible for Monica's death. Brittany caught a teardrop with the back of her hand, before it could fall from her left eye, then looked up and down Darien Street, over the roofs of all of the parked vehicles, until finally resting her eyes on one of the rear, muddy tires of the four wheeler she was sitting on.

The night that Brittany and Monica had unexpectedly bumped into her aunt, and Detective Konn at the restaurant, it had exposed to Detective Konn what her and Monica had been trying to keep hidden from him all along. In retrospect, Brittany wished that her and Monica had never confronted her aunt and Detective Konn that night. Instead, she wished they had've just left the restaurant before they were noticed.

Remembering that night, and remembering that it had been the last time that she had seen Monica alive, Brittany got emotional for a moment, but quickly got herself together. In memory of Monica, she decided that the identity of Monica's killer would be a secret from Monica's mother no longer.

"Mrs. Patricia, I know who killed Monica. I have a recording of their confession."

"What?"

Suddenly nervous, Brittany took in a deep breath and switched her cell phone to her opposite ear. She hadn't known exactly how Patricia Best would react to hearing this unsettling news from her, since she had just denied knowing anything about Monica's death, days earlier. On Monday morning, Patricia Best had visited Philadelphia, and had given an emphatic speech outside of City Hall, with the mayor of Philadelphia, and the police commissioner standing closely behind her, as she faced dozens of news cameras, vowing that she wouldn't rest until the killer of her daughter was found. That afternoon, Brittany had joined Patricia Best for lunch at a Center City restaurant. The two women had spoken in detail about the days leading up to Monica's disappearance, and ultimately, her body being found days later.

Patricia Best was a callous women, driven by the strong urge to one day become the governor of Maryland; from there, she wanted to run for president. In the political world, there had been rumors that she had once been involved with an ex-Navy Seal. Their relationship was believed to be a mutual agreement of one helping the other. Patricia Best wanted political power. The ex-Navy Seal wanted a seat in the Senate.

Monica's death had fractured Patricia Best's core. Unresolved issues with Monica were now haunting her, and chipping away at the cold layer of ice surrounding her heart. She had expressed this to Brittany while they had sat and ate lunch that afternoon.

"Detective Konn did it, Mrs. Patricia," Brittany tearfully admitted, rising from the four wheeler, and standing there on the sidewalk for a moment, unsure of what to do, or where she should go next. When Patricia Best let out a sob on the other end of her cell phone, and began to cry, the older woman's moment of vulnerability awakened an old, painful memory inside of her heart. "I have the proof right here inside of my phone. Mrs. Patricia, don't think you can't trust me, because you can. I—I couldn't—The same detectives who questioned me when Tia died, was the same ones who questioned me about Monica. Detective Konn got eyes and ears all over this city, Mrs. Patricia. I had to keep what I knew to myself. I had to."

"From me?"

"Not for why you might be thinkin,' Mrs. Patricia."

"I sent my daughter there to help you and Tia."

"And Tia really appreciated that. I did, too, Mrs. Patricia. Monica was my friend. She became both of our friends. Look, if I would've exposed to the detectives how close I was with Monica, or all that I really knew about her, it would've led back to me and Tia's involvement with you. Why you think I told you not to come by Splash's club? Mrs. Patricia, I didn't tell you what I knew, because I wanted to be the one to kill Detective Konn personally. I didn't want you to take that power from me. Mrs. Patricia, he killed my boyfriend and got away with it.

"Hide, Brittany."

"What?"

"Run for your life. Detective Konn won't be getting the same warning. I'm giving you one, simply because you let me know who murdered my daughter. Hide."

Patricia Best abruptly ended the call before Brittany could respond. A long moment went by with Brittany just standing there, staring at the screen of her cell phone, as the night air whispered all around her. Brittany had known all along that she was taking a great risk in withholding the truth about Monica's death from her mother, but she had never once thought that it would put her own life in danger for her doing so. The entire time she had been looking over her shoulder, hoping that Detective Konn never found out that she was in possession of the truth. Until a few moments ago, Brittany's only enemies were Detective Konn, Marvin, her aunt, Maniac, and Sabia. Now, she had to add Patricia Best to her list.

When someone announced Brittany's arrival, everyone on the first floor of the Chrome Depot grew silent. Brittany was six minutes early. The people in the dining area and the kitchen, all began to slowly move in the direction of the Chrome Depot's crowded living area, where Brittany was headed.

Sabia was already in the living area, sitting quietly in a chair, observing everyone, and everything that was going on around him. He had the black hood of his Nike sweatshirt over his bald head, with its strings tied tightly. When Brittany brought her eyes to his, Sabia casually nodded his head to acknowledge her. Unlike everyone else in the Chrome Depot, Sabia was glad that Kyzer was no longer in the picture. He hoped to God that Kyzer was indeed dead, because this meant that his mother's life would no longer be in jeopardy. His friend, Ashley, shared the same hopes, but refused to believe that fate would be that kind to them.

At the moment, while those close to Kyzer desperately wanted him to be alive, and not be dead, them coming together on this night was specifically about them sending a message to the 10th and Thompson housing projects. The aroma of vengeance was being inhaled inside of the Chrome Depot, and Brittany was breathing it into her lungs the most.

"We all know why we're here, right?" Brittany questioned, doing a slow circle in the center of the living area, meeting the eyes of each and every person staring back at her. She wanted them all to know what Kyzer meant to her, and what he should have meant to them. "Don't we? Well, if you didn't get the memo, let me tell you why we're all here. We here, because loyalty is a fuckin' verb. Drees didn't show it to Kyzer, and Sabia didn't, either."

Sabia's heart plunged down to his stomach.

"Tonight, none of us will fail Kyzer," Brittany continued, hoping her comment about Sabia had his veins feeling like they had acid flowing through them. For Kyzer's sake, tonight, she had every intention of using Sabia like a pawn, and she was going to reveal his true identity to Kyzer's cousin, Malik, after she shared some other important matters with him. "Tonight, I want Tenth and Thompson to know they made a mistake. They have to."

"So, what's the plan?" Someone asked.

Kyzer's cousin, Malik, stepped forward, joined by Uzi. Both young men were dressed in black clothing, and the expressions on their faces were deadly. Like Brittany, everyone in attendance knew that Malik and Uzi were who Kyzer would have chosen to lead any attack, if he was absent. Malik stayed silent, as Uzi uncrossed his arms and began to speak.

"We all splittin' up into teams. We gon' hit these mu'fuckers on four wheelers. We poppin' up from underground on 'em. We walkin' down on them pussies.

Anybody try to run, chase 'em the fuck down, and put a fuckin' hole in they fuckin' ghost. Like Brittany said, loyalty is a fuckin' verb. Tonight, you get to show what Kyzer meant to you. Last night, we unloosened the sewer drains on Randolph and Thompson, Tenth and Jefferson, Eleventh and Master, but we might just nix that one, because that shit might be a little iffy. We got the blueprints from the Water Department, though, so niggaz will know how they movin,' 'n shit like that. Neef grabbed a bunch of walkie-talkies from Radio Shack this mornin', too. Everybody gon' have one. Stay with ya fuckin' group. If somebody get hit, carry they ass the fuck back. Them niggaz out there deep tonight. We got three hand grenades. Them jawns only gettin' used, if the cops try to box one of us in a fuckin' corner."

"And if you on one of the four wheelers, and some shit go wrong on it, you get hit, or whatever might happen, that's what 'cha walkie-talkie for. Ain't nobody gettin' left behind," Malik added, before cutting his eye at Brittany, who was wiping away a falling teardrop as she stood to his left.

Sabia looked around at all of the faces. Counting himself, there were thirty-four people present. Some faces were unfamiliar to him. Seated to his right and left, were two of the Puerto Rican girls who had been at Freeway's barn the day that Kyzer and Jamillah had killed Idris. Tonight, the young women weren't sparing any smiles. Sabia could feel the anticipation for violence resonating from both of their bodies, as he sat quietly between them.

"Niggaz in the streets, sayin' Maniac got hit that night," Someone commented.

"I heard he went to a hospital over Jersey, and they cut his leg off. Mu'fuckers goin' around sayin' Kyzer had ammonia 'n bleach in his bullets."

"I heard it was rat poison."

"That's what I heard."

The living area of the Chrome Depot quickly began to buzz with questions and answers, and a lot of speculations. The only ones who remained silent, were Brittany, Malik, Uzi, Sabia, Haneef, and those that actually knew the truth. Brittany excused herself when her cell phone began ringing in her pocketbook. To her surprise, Patricia Best was calling her back.

"Hello?"

"Brittany, I owe you an apology."

"Mrs. Patricia, hold on for one second, okay?"

Brittany reached the staircase, leading up to the second floor of the Chrome Depot, and started climbing the stairs with haste. Her heart was doing flip-flops in her chest as she held her pocketbook under her left armpit, and the cheap cell phone she had purchased specifically to speak discreetly to Patricia Best, against her right ear. Before coming into the Chrome Depot, for a moment, Brittany had considered tossing the cell phone into the tall grass at the mouth of a vacant lot, adjacent to the rear of the Chrome Depot. Now, she was happy that she hadn't. Up on the second floor of the Chrome Depot, Brittany looked up and down the hallway for an open room. Seeing that all of the doors were closed, she stopped at the end of the hallway, beside the bottom of the staircase, leading up to the third floor. Hopeful, Brittany swallowed nervously, before speaking.

"I'm ready for my apology."

"So is Monica's father. A lot of people are. Brittany, to get to my position, I did what I thought was useful. Politics are no different than what goes on in the streets. We're just carrying briefcases, and wearing suits, Brittany. My mother was a weak woman. She let my father stifle her. Brittany, my mother never spoke up for herself. Not once. On her death bed, she shared with me that she wished she had've.

Earlier, you spoke on making history, and you reminded me of a day when my mother had told me to do just that . . . make history. I have. In doing so, I betrayed my marriage vows, and I dictated every choice my daughter made, from who she went on her prom with, to what career she chose. Brittany, Monica was happy to go to Philly. Happy to put distance between us. How could I blame her? I was a tyrant to her."

Patricia Best was crying, and Brittany's heart ached as she listened to the older woman speak. Her own eyes had brimmed with tears.

"My main goal in life was never to be weak. Not as a wife, a mother, or as a woman, Brittany. I molded Monica the same way. I stole my daughter's life from her. What I said to you was wrong, and inappropriate. You were Monica's friend. I understand why you made the decision you did. Now, tell me how I can help. Earlier, you mentioned that you wanted me to be the mother that I couldn't be to Monica, tonight. What's so special about tonight?"

"Mrs. Patricia, can you hold on one more time?"

"Sure."

"Thank you."

Brittany lowered her cell phone from her ear and pressed it against her chest. The sound of voices and footsteps had prompted her to bring a pause to her conversation with Patricia Best. Looking down the hallway, a second passed, then Brittany's eyes met with Haneef's. A string of people had followed him upstairs. Brittany counted eight heads. The small group of men followed Haneef down to the other end of the hallway, and stopped, after Haneef twisted the doorknob on a door of a room, then disappeared into it. A moment later, Haneef was back at the door, and passing the men assault rifles, two at a time. After accepting the weapons, the men walked back to the staircase, and disappeared back downstairs. Some of the men had looked down the hallway at her; some hadn't. A moment passed, then more men came upstairs, and went to the room, where Haneef was waiting, holding more assault rifles. This cycle went on for a long moment, with Brittany staring down from the opposite end of the hallway, watching it all happen. Brittany didn't return her cell phone back to her ear, until after Haneef had pulled the door to the room shut behind him, and had gone back downstairs.

"Mrs. Patricia, you there?"

"I'm still here."

"I'm sorry," Brittany apologized, as she began to walk down the hallway, curious to see the room Haneef was just inside of. She had only been inside of the Chrome Depot once, and on that occasion, she hadn't gone further than the first floor. "It's a lot goin' on right now. Mrs. Patricia, my boyfriend has a lot of friends. Deadly ones. Young, dangerous, and don't care about shit. We're all upset. None of them are aware of the relationship I have with you, or the one that I had with Monica. I've crossed a line they'd never consider. My boyfriend was the same way. He wanted nothin' to do with Monica. He was aware, though, that all of what we were doing was in efforts to help us get Splash out, and to get Detective Konn, not just for all the bullshit he took Splash and Tia through, but for what he did to my boyfriend. Kyzer has a big heart, and he's a good person, Mrs. Patricia. I love him. You don't have to care anything for him, because that's not what I'm askin' of you."

Brittany reached the room where Haneef had been distributing the assault rifles. Switching her cell phone to her opposite ear, she twisted the doorknob and pushed the door open, then slowly entered the room.

"Isn't your boyfriend the guy that tossed a hand grenade at somebody in North Philly? I recall Monica telling me about him."

"That was him," Brittany confirmed, as she did a slow circle, taking in the sight of the Chrome Depot's arsenal room. Looking at all of the gun cabinets, and seeing all of the bulletproof vests, reminded her of the secret room at Tia's house. "That was the night of his mom's and Tia's funeral, Mrs. Patricia."

"I was half asleep, but I was the one who gave Monica the idea of how to throw the cops and the FBI off of his scent."

"You came up with that?"

"Half asleep. Listen to this . . . my best friend is on the Grand Jury in Pennsylvania. She was Monica's godmother. All day she had been sending me all sorts of e-mails. A member of this cartel had reached out to her. Discreetly, of course. I can't go into details with you, but him and my best friend came to an understanding. A profitable one. So, when Monica woke me up in the middle of the night, wanting some advice, the cartel thing being already in my head, was the first option that came to mind. I mean really, who's really throwing hand grenades these days? Once Monica told me the guys were into drugs, it made sense to attach them to that big drug indictment, where those guys were selling some heroin called 'Devil's Smile.' I told Monica to say she got the tip from an informant of hers. It worked, too. Once the FBI hears, 'Cartel,' Brittany, their dicks get hard."

"Can you make it look like that cartel came back tonight?"

"And did what?"

"Came through the sewer tunnels. Had Puerto Rican girls shootin' machine guns from the backs of four wheelers. Movie shit, Mrs. Patricia. It can work, and make a lot of sense, because we're going against the same people my boyfriend went at that night."

"Will hand grenades be involved?"

"Only if the cops come."

"Sounds like you have the kind of friends I might use one day. Listen, for me to glue both stories together, a hand grenade will have to be thrown, even if it's just for shock value, and nothing more. How soon will this be happening?"

"Before midnight."

"Is that it?"

"I'm going to send you Detective Konn's video confession. There are more videos, too. I want you to make use of them, a day after Halloween, Mrs. Patricia. I want to be the one who brings death to him. If you let me do that, without interfering, I'll owe you for the rest of my life. Can you promise me you'll let me deal with him my way?"

"You have my word. What else?"

Brittany stepped out into the hallway, pulling the door to the Chrome Depot's artillery room closed behind her. Going no further, she stepped aside, and put her back against the wall. Thinking about what other help she needed from the federal judge, she tapped her pocketbook against her right thigh.

"Brittany, why haven't you mentioned your aunt, and her boyfriend, yet?"

"What 'chu mean?"

"Monica told me what they did to your father, Brittany. I know about what they're doing in that funeral home, too. What's your plan for them?"

"I wanna kill 'em, Mrs. Patricia."

"What's stopping you?"

Tears flooded Brittany's eyes.

"You deserve revenge, just like your boyfriend do. Just like Tia. And just like Monica. Think of what's owed to you, Brittany. You want me to act like I'm your mother tonight? Do you really want my help?"

"Yes."

"Okay, well, while all of your friends are raising hell, why not pay a visit to your aunt and her boyfriend? And don't do any talking, Brittany. I can have someone clean up the mess. Just make sure you e-mail me those videos tonight. What's the address to the funeral home?"

"Fourteen-Eleven, North Franklin Street."

"Fourteen-Eleven, North Franklin?"

"Yeah."

"Go avenge your father, Brittany."

Brittany took in a deep breath, and exhaled it out of her nostrils. Her stomach had become a bundle of knots, as she began to think about the intensity of the moment, once her aunt and Marvin realized that she had arrived to kill them. Kyzer came to Brittany's mind next. She had always assumed that he would be by her side for this moment. Teary-eyed, Brittany knelt and sat her pocketbook down on the floor, then, with her cell phone still pressed against her left ear, she returned to the Chrome Depot's artillery room. Moments later, Brittany came back out into the hallway, carrying a chrome, pump-action shotgun. The tears in her eyes had gone away.

"Tia's cousin, Rhonda, got locked up yesterday," Brittany spoke into her cell phone, after kneeling down again, and fishing her other cell phone out of her pocketbook. She sat her other cell phone on the floor, face-up, beside the shotgun, and activated the app on her iPhone, which gave her access to the surveillance cameras Tia had gotten installed inside of Marvin's funeral home. "Mrs. Patricia, I need her out here with me. Somebody called her probation officer, and told her probation officer that she had a gun in her car."

"Did she?"

"Yeah . . . she had two of them."

"And let me guess, they dropped a probation detainer on her?"

"And they gave her a crazy bail, too."

"E-mail me the name of her Judge, and give me a day to look into it."

"I really need her home, Mrs. Patricia. Look, give me a minute to get to my car, and I'm going to send you all of the videos, and everything, okay? It's a lot of footage, Mrs. Patricia. Stuff from inside of the funeral home, and everything."

"Do you know where all of the cameras are in there?"

"Yeah."

"Make sure all of them are removed before you leave. Will that be a problem?"

"No."

"Call me once you're done. I'd feel a lot more comfortable knowing you're okay, Brittany. Be careful. Make Monica and Tia proud of you. Your father, too."

"I will, Mrs. Patricia. I most certainly will."

"Make sure you call me as soon as you're done."

"It'll be from my other phone. After this call, I'm gettin' rid of this one."

"Smart girl. Okay, now, before you go. I have some associates in Center City. While we were talking, I sent them an e-mail, explaining your situation. They'll be entering the funeral home, upon your exit, Brittany. Walk by them, and do not speak a word."

"Okay . . . thank you, Mrs. Patricia. Thank you so much."

After ending the call with Patricia Best, Brittany thumbed the power button on the cell phone, then put it inside of her pocketbook. Her eyes then returned back to the screen of her iPhone. The knots in her stomach slowly began to unloosen themselves, as she stared down at the images of her aunt and Marvin, who were both seated at the table in Marvin's kitchen, feasting over some shrimps and crabs. Marvin's wide back was to the tiny, hidden camera that was installed above an old, dusty picture of Marvin's grandfather. The black and white photo was nailed in the upper right corner of the front wall, in Marvin's living room. The beige-painted wall was covered with dozens of framed pictures. Brittany felt rewarded, as she watched her aunt and Marvin eat in silence. A single teardrop crept from her right eye and dropped on the screen of her cell phone.

"I need somebody to come with me," Brittany realized, as she grabbed her pocketbook and cell phone with one hand, and grabbed the shotgun by its rubber-gripped handle, with the other. Rising to her feet, and heading for the stairs, someone came to mind. "Zay told me I could call her if I needed her. I need her to get the cameras in the funeral home, while I'm upstairs. It'll be quicker that way."

Downstairs, while heading for the rear door of the Chrome Depot, Brittany made eye contact with Malik, and signaled for him to follow her outside. In the few moments that she was alone, Brittany was piecing her plan together, and preparing herself to commit a double-murder. As the cold winds greeted her outside, she tilted her head and looked up at the dark sky, and wondered if killing Marvin and her aunt would be viewed by God as a sin, or a justifiable act. This was important to Brittany. Since the age of twelve, Brittany had always believed in God, and that all people would one day have to answer for their deeds in life. Her father had explained this reality to her, one day, while the two of them had been on their way to the Philadelphia Zoo. Brittany had detailed that day with her father in one of her diaries; in large part, because before dropping her back off at her aunt's house, her father had taught her a special prayer, that she had never forgotten.

"God, please forgive me for my sins," Brittany prayed, still staring up at the night sky. The sound of the rear door to the Chrome Depot being closed behind her reached her ears, but she didn't let it distract her from her prayer; not even when Malik came and stood beside her. "The ones I forgot, and the ones I haven't done, yet. Please make me better as a person, and never give up on me . . . Amen."

"Who about to be on the receiving end of that?"

Brittany glanced down at the chrome, pump-action shotgun in her right hand, then looked up into Malik's eyes. His question had traveled on a saddened voice. Out of everyone in the Chrome Depot, she knew Malik truly was suffering emotionally, from not knowing if Kyzer was actually alive or not.

"I'm about to go kill my aunt and Marvin."

"With that? Brittany, that shit gon' wake up the whole fuckin' neighborhood."

Brittany started walking to her car, with Malik following her. At her car, Brittany turned around and faced Malik, while raising her cell phone up to her ear. She had called Zainab.

"Want me to go wit' chu?"

"No, but I do need a walkie-talkie. And I have somethin' to tell you, too."

"I'll be right back."

Malik turned and jogged back to the Chrome Depot, disappearing around the tall tree that stood beside the cemented path, leading back to the rear door of the Chrome Depot. When Zainab answered her cell phone, Brittany turned away and opened her driver's side door. Leaning in, she released her pocketbook from her armpit, letting it fall to her driver's seat, then leaned in further, and laid the shotgun across her passenger seat.

"Zay, you busy?"

"Not really . . . what's up?"

"Are you home? Because if you are, I might have to call some—"

"Brit, don't play with me. What's wrong?"

"Can you go with me to visit my aunt?"

"Like, right now, you mean?"

"Right now, Zay."

"Where are you?"

"Around the corner."

"Gimme ten minutes. I'm at Broad and Erie."

"Call me when you get to 7th and Master. Take 6th Street, Zay. Park on 7th and Master, and walk around to me."

"Okay."

Brittany looked down Darien Street, as Malik came jogging back up to her. He had a walkie-talkie in his hand, and a hand-Uzi, with a suppressor attached to it, in his other. Malik stopped in front of Brittany, and offered her the hand-Uzi first.

"If you insist," Brittany sighed, accepting the hand-Uzi with her right hand. The gun wasn't as heavy as the shotgun, and as she raised her left hand up and held it beneath its squared-frame, she saw herself shooting Marvin in his fat face with it. "You can take that other gun back. Malik, what I'm about to tell you is for you to know only. Don't ask me why Kyzer ain't tell you, because it's not for me to explain all of that."

After Brittany was in her car, and had handed him the shotgun, Malik took in a deep breath. His body language suggested that he was preparing himself to hear some unsettling news. He looked up and down Darien Street twice.

"Malik, Rell is Sabia."

"What?"

"That's him," Brittany assured Malik, staring up at him from her car. She could see the confusion in Malik's eyes, and felt so sorry for the emotional war her news was causing him, but tonight she knew that it was information that Kyzer would have wanted his little cousin to be equipped with. "He got plastic surgery somewhere, and he got them to change his voice. That's him, Leek. Kyzer knew."

"Why he ain't tell me?" Malik questioned tearfully, racking the shotgun.

"Ask Kyzer that."

"But—"

"No, Leek."

Brittany refused to hear anyone say that Kyzer might possibly be dead. It would destroy all of her hopes; hope was all she was holding onto.

"Don't count him out, Leek," Brittany insisted, using her hands to wipe away the instant tears started by Malik's insinuation that Kyzer might, in fact, be dead. Keeping in mind that Zainab was on her way, she started up her car, then looked back up into Malik's own watery eyes. "Don't be like them. They don't know Kyzer. We do. Fuck what they sayin' in the papers. Leek, my baby alive. And tonight—Leek, tonight we gon' show them how we feel about ours."

"I'm leavin' Sabia down in one of them sewer tunnels."

"I hoped you would. Let him kill for us first, though. Once I'm done around the corner, I'm gonna let you know over the walkie-talkie."

"Want us to wait, 'til after you done?"

Brittany nodded her head.

"How long you think you gon' take?"

"Gimme fifteen minutes. Go in there, and start telling everybody to get ready, though. All these cars and four wheelers out here don't look good, anyway. Who you gon' be with?"

"Uzi, Wakil, F.L., and Leem. Rashad comin' wit' us, too. Sabia was goin' wit' Mel 'n Shiz, but I'm about to go in there and switch shit up. Go handle ya business, and be careful. We waitin' on you. Yo, where you goin,' after that?"

"Back to Kyzer house."

"We tryna make it to I-95, and see if we can make it to Free barn."

"Y'all will."

"Insha Allah."

Malik stepped back, and watched for a moment, as Brittany reversed her BMW back out of Darien Street. When she reached Oxford Street, and disappeared going west, Malik turned and started jogging back to the Chrome Depot with the shotgun down at his right side. In memory of his cousin, Camay, Malik was intent on Sabia meeting his death violently, and suddenly.

Beware.

Of.

Me.

Until Kyzer, no man in the city of Philadelphia had ever been avenged by so many people, in such a daring fashion. As everyone slowly began to spill out of the Chrome Depot, and divide up into small teams, the significance of the moment could be felt by them all. Tonight, many more significant moments were going to present themselves, and not all of them would be in favor of Kyzer's avengers.

Unfortunately.

Chapter Nineteen

Brittany unlocked both locks on the front door to Marvin's funeral home, then slowly began twisting the doorknob, but just as she was about to step up and use her left shoulder to budge the door open, something passing by in the sky caused her to pause momentarily, and look upwards. Zainab was standing a step below Brittany, and had also been compelled to look up at the flying object up in the dark sky as well.

"Brit, is that what I think it is?"

"Yup," Brittany confirmed, training her eyes on the drone helicopter, flying west up Master Street, heading towards Eighth. Before turning her attention back to the funeral home's front door, she glanced across Franklin Street at the dark-windowed, black, Dodge Charger, certain that Patricia Best's help was occupying the unfamiliar vehicle, and quite possibly, returning her stare. "Kyzer made Splash get that for him. Whoever controllin' it, can see whatever it's flyin' over on they cell phone. Alright, come on, Zay. Why my heart gotta be beatin' so damn fast?"

Zainab followed Brittany inside of the funeral home, shut the door, locked both locks, then turned to face Brittany with her answer in a whispered-tone.

"It's your adrenaline. Once you get upstairs, and see them, it'll get worse. It's natural, Brit. It happens to me all the time. Open this door, so I can get those cameras in there. Brit, go up there, do what'chu gotta do, and meet me back here. Don't forget the cameras, either."

Brittany took in a deep breath, settling her rampant emotions, then nodded her head as she exhaled. Before her emotions had a chance to siege her system again, and embarrassed that Zainab was witnessing her appear weakened by the gravity of what was next to come, she thought of her father, and all of their stolen moments, and she began to move methodically. This was her moment, and she wouldn't' allow it to be lost. Stepping around Zainab, Brittany singled out a silver key on her key-ring, and unlocked the door, which led into Marvin's funeral home. Brittany left the job of opening the door to Zainab, and went walking down the hallway in a hurry.

At the end of the narrow hallway, Brittany turned right, and started taking the splintered-wooden, flight of stairs in twos. Some of the steps made noises under her weight, as they often did, so many times in the past. Marvin had never cleaned the hallways, or the stairs. On the second floor, Brittany walked by the closed door to her old apartment, refusing to look at it. It had once been her safe haven in life. All of her things were now at Kyzer's house; he had made his home hers. As Brittany began climbing the stairs that led up to Marvin's apartment, she pulled her iPhone out of the pocket of her dark purple, Ascot Chang, leather jacket, while also digging her right hand down into the Ugg pocketbook Zainab had suggested she use to conceal her hand-Uzi.

The sound of soft music was escaping beneath Marvin's apartment door, joined by the stale smell of cigarettes, seafood, and what Brittany suspected to be marijuana. Proving true, Brittany stared down at the screen of her cell phone, and there was her aunt, and Marvin, still sitting at Marvin's kitchen table, passing a marijuana cigarette back and forth. Both of their faces were wearing sheepish grins, as their heads nodded to an old, Isley Brother's song. With a swipe of her left thumb, the screen of Brittany's iPhone momentarily went completely blank for about a second, then lit back up, and showed a vision of Zainab in the morgue section of Marvin's funeral home, slowly peeling back a white sheet from a small corpse, lying on a metal table.

"Zay, you said you wouldn't' look, "Brittany thought, quickly stuffing her cell phone back into her jacket pocket, because she was too afraid to see more. With a deep breath, she readjusted the thick strap of Zainab's pocketbook on her left shoulder, then, after knocking several times on Marvin's apartment door, she withdrew the hand-Uzi. "Aunt Tanya?! Marvin! Open the door! Somebody just robbed me at the Chinese Store! They took my car! Hurry up!!"

Brittany knocked five more times, this time more urgently, then put her back to the wall, opposite Marvin's apartment door. Someone was coming, cursing under their breath. Brittany wanted it to be Marvin, but it wasn't.

As soon as the door opened, Brittany held her breath, squeezed the trigger of the hand-Uzi, and started stepping forward. The horror she saw in her aunt's eyes satisfied her need for revenge a thousand times, but in that fulfilled moment, Brittany reminded herself why she was there. As her aunt went stumbling backwards into Marvin's apartment, swinging her arms wildly, Brittany advanced, thinking of her father, and no one else in the world. Her aunt's eyes were wide and engaging, staring at her in total disbelief. Marvin's eyes held the same emotion when she looked to him, after his coffee table had shattered beneath her aunt's falling body. Brittany felt the floor shudder under her feet.

"Brittany?! What the fuck you do?!"

"The bigger they are, the harder they fall, Marvin, "Brittany answered coldly, while walking up to her aunt's lifeless body. Aiming with the hand-Uzi, she sprayed her aunt's wide back with another barrage of bullets, making sure her aunt's demise would be true, then turned and started walking towards Marvin, who now had a knife in his right hand. "My dad and his girlfriend didn't even have that to defend themselves, and you still shot them like dogs. Marvin, that was me my dad was talkin' to on his cell phone.

Marvin dropped the knife, backing away, until his kitchen sink stopped him from going any further. His lips were trembling, at moments trying to form some words. He was sorry, and his eyes weren't lying.

"Why you do it?"

"She told me to. I ain't wanna do that, Brittany."

Brittany shook her head at Marvin, as her eyes brimmed with threatening tears. When Marvin attempted to say more to her, she held her breath, and pulled her index finger against the trigger of the hand-Uzi. Her entire body vibrated as the gun coughed and jerked in her hand. For what seemed like a long time, the momentum of all the hot bullets helped keep Marvin standing on his feet. The kitchen cabinets behind him were splintering, and the dishes and glasses on their shelves were all breaking, and flying out in shards. Dead on his feet, Marvin's giant body fell face-first to his kitchen floor, and his blood quickly began to pour out from beneath him. Brittany hadn't noticed that she was crying, or how heavily she was breathing, until she took a step back with her right foot, and the heel of her purple, Nike, wedge-sneaker, came down on one of the many shell casings, littering Marvin's apartment floor.

Emotions running rampant again, Brittany took off running to the back of Marvin's one-bedroom apartment, while stuffing the hand-Uzi back into Zainab's over-sized pocketbook. In Marvin's bedroom, she went to where a tiny, hidden-camera was located, and ripped it out of its hiding place, pulling wires out with it. Out in Marvin's living room, after hurdling over her aunt's bleeding body, she stepped up on the arm of Marvin's couch, and ripped out the last hidden-camera in Marvin's apartment. Leaving, Brittany felt a surge of emotions build inside of her chest, as a song playing on Marvin's stereo system followed her down the stairs. It was Cee-Lo Green's song, "Who's going to save my soul now?" It was the song Kyzer had told her about once. Gripped by all that she had gone through in life, and by what she had just done, Brittany was to shaken up to speak coherently into the walkie-talkie Malik had given her, as she ran by the door of her old apartment on the second floor. She could barely breathe.

At the end of the hallway, and turning to take the last flight of stairs, Brittany looked down the steps at Zainab and felt her legs prematurely paralyze themselves. Zainab was leaning against a wall, cradling the dead body of a small girl, whose hands and feet were missing. There were tree branches, still bearing tiny leaves, protruding from the child's wrists and ankles. A sob exploded from Brittany's mouth, and echoed through the hallways of Marvin's funeral home.

"Brit, come on. Come on . . . we gotta go. I couldn't leave her in there. They so fuckin' wrong, Brit. I got all the cameras for you. Brit, come on."

When Brittany and Zainab came walking out of Marvin's funeral home, and paused on the top step, a gust of wind caused the long, black hair, of the dead girl in Zainab's arms to sail and flutter, along with Zainab's black, overgarments. Zainab's face-veil was wet from the teardrops still spilling from her eyes. She was intent on making sure that the little girl's body was buried properly, and perhaps, also prayed over. As Brittany and Zainab walked down the steps, and both tearfully began to walk slowly towards Master Street, the front doors of the dodge Charger, parked across the street from Marvin's funeral home opened. Two, serious-looking, white men, stepped out, and after glancing at the departing backs of Brittany and Zainab for a moment, they both quietly crossed Franklin Street, and entered Marvin's funeral home like the three-story property had been in their family for years.

At the corner of Franklin and Master, while watching Zainab walk down Master Street to her car, Brittany squeezed the call-button on her walkie-talkie, and raised it up to her mouth. For a moment, she was unsure of what she should say. Sparing a second to wipe away her teardrops, she thought of something that would affect the hearts of each and every last person that was about to hear her voice echoing out of the speakers of their walkie-talkies.

"Even if Maniac got shot that night, a half a leg shouldn't satisfy none of us. Loyalty is a fuckin' verb. Make them have to fill up half a fuckin' cemetery."

Foo, an older male cousin of Kyzer's, was standing on the center of the Chrome Depot's rooftop, busy controlling the navigation of the drone-helicopter with his iPhone, when Brittany broke the silence of his walkie-talkie with her message. Everyone had been waiting on Brittany. Most of them were just minutes away from their designated marks, and making some last-minute preparations, moments before Brittany had spoken. Others were just getting ready. The intensity of the invasion had tensions mounting high inside of everyone, except for Sabia.

As Malik and their small group walked ahead, Sabia was walking slowly, using his flashlight to look at the concrete walls overhead, and on both sides of him. The sewer tunnel beneath Thompson Street had Sabia mesmerized, and feeling like a small child inside of a museum. He felt like he had finally been let in on one of Philadelphia's biggest secrets, and the wait seemed well worth it.

The sewer tunnel was eight feet high, and its floors were coated with a mixture of water and sand. It hadn't rained in weeks, so there was mostly sand underfoot. The darkness of the sewer tunnel was unforgiving, and the most challenging for everyone. While all six men were equipped with flashlights, walkie-talkies, and assault rifles, all of it was meaningless against the struggle of seeing what was ahead of them. Malik was in the lead, and Sabia was a few steps behind, bringing up the rear. Haneef, Merk, Brill, and Freck, were in the middle, all using their flashlights to see ahead of them, and on their sides. They were just making it to Marshall Street.

"Alright, we got four more blocks to go," Malik spoke, after shining his flashlight down the shafts, leading right and left. "This Marshall Street."

Four blocks ahead, beneath a loosened-sewer drain, on the southwest corner of Tenth and Thompson, Tauheed, Ern, Khalid, Russell, K.P, and Meatball, were all standing in silence, with their weapons drawn. They were waiting for Malik and his group to join them. All six men were from South Philadelphia, and this kind of attack was nothing new to them. Khalid and Russell were brothers, but also cousins of Kyzer's; Meatball was a cousin of Kyzer's as well.

Two blocks north, on the northeast corner of Tenth and Jefferson, there was a slight problem happening, and Keenan, another cousin of Kyzer's, was reporting it to Malik, over their walkie-talkies.

"This mu'fucker at his front door, smokin' a cigarette, and he keep lookin' up at the fuckin' drone."

"Do something about that, Foo."

"Send that shit towards Broad Street," Mel suggested, as he walked up and joined Genesis, who was standing on the corner of Tenth and Oxford with a baby stroller. "Look, me 'n Genesis gon' walk down the same side of the street ol' head on, and try to distract him. Keenan, as soon as we get to the front of ol' head house, put the truck in reverse, and back up a little bit, and that should give Uzi 'n 'em enough time to hurry up and make it down the sewer hole. Here we come."

It was almost midnight, and the night sky was a beautiful, dark blue. The clouds were thin, and moving to the west with the winds, seeming to follow the drone-helicopter, in its flight to Broad Street. A half moon was witnessing it all; seeing the initial stages of an attack formation.

The drivers of the moving trucks had been given the most responsibilities. Each driver had to first pull beside their designated sewer hole, and position the moving truck at the corner, so that no one would notice as people from the truck, first removed the sewer drain, then, one by one, began to disappear down into the manhole. The driver's job was then to secure the sewer drain back over the manhole, and proceed to his next mark, where he had to exit the truck once more, lift up the rolling-door at the rear of the truck, which would give freedom to the two people on the four-wheeler, armed with handguns and an assault rifle.

"Ay, Tauheed, we almost there," Malik reported over his walkie-talkie. "Y'all should be able to see us comin' in like two minutes."

"We waitin' on y'all. It's niggaz standin' right over top of us."

"I'm at my spot," Sherman added, after killing the headlights on the moving truck, and bringing it to a stop at Ninth and Thompson.

In total darkness, with the chattering over the walkie-talkies continuing, Kyzer's cousin, Juice, breathed calmly, as he sat silently on the four–wheeler. Paloma was behind him, sitting with her back to his. They knew nothing about each other, and were strangers, but there was a sense of comfortability in the back of the moving truck with them, and they both were appreciating it. Paloma had her long, dark, hair pulled into a ponytail. Her brown eyes had been made evil by her thoughts. As Manny Yunk made a right turn off of Girard Avenue, and began driving north up Eleventh Street, she arched her back against Juice's and sat up as straight as she possibly could, while readjusting the leather strap of the AR-15 across her right shoulder, and over her chest. In Reading, Pennsylvania, she was known as the Mexican Mamba.

In the rear of Keenan's moving truck, Ant-Ant and Paloma's sister Veronica, were also quiet, as they both sat on their four-wheeler. They were listening to all that was being said on their walkie-talkies, and just waiting for their moment. In the rear of Sherman's moving truck, Mikel and Dolly were exchanging small talk to pass the time. They were talking about Mikel's newborn son.

There was a police car crossing Diamond Street, slowly traveling south on Hancock Street, and another one stopped by a red traffic light at the intersection of Broad and Master, waiting to travel west. On the opposite side of Girard Avenue, there were two, unmarked cars, driving around the Richard Allen housing projects, simply looking for any suspicious conduct. None of this was being captured by the drone-helicopter, as Foo used his iPhone to fly it back east. The drone-helicopter was only able to capture an aerial view of what it was flying over, as well as some partial images of what was surrounding it. At several thousand feet in the dark sky, the drone-helicopter went unnoticed, as it flew quietly over a Rite Aid on Twelfth and Girard.

From the rooftop of the Chrome Depot, Foo watched as Hoose, Shizz, Mal, and Dame, all climbed on their four-wheelers down on Darien Street, and started them up. The sudden sounds of the four-wheelers coming to life brought a wry smile to Foo's face, as he squeezed the call-button on his walkie-talkie, and raised it up to his mouth to speak.

"Tear they asses up."

The sewer tunnel on Tenth Street, between Jefferson and Master, was dark, and smelled like damp air and wet sand, with an undertone of sewage. The smell of the sewer tunnel was horrible, but Uzi, Rashad, F.L, Wakil, Aleem, and Shaka, were in too much of a rush to pay it any mind, while desperately trying to reach their mark, before Mel and Genesis got to the corner of Tenth and Master, above ground. Uzi was leading the way, using his flashlight to see ahead of him. The wet sand on the floor of the sewer tunnel wasn't easy to run on, but the six teenagers were covering the distance rather quickly. Above ground, Mel and Genesis were ten feet behind, and appeared to be just a young couple out on a late night, walking with their small child in a baby stroller. Mel and Genesis were wearing smiles, as they looked down at the Tenth and Thompson housing projects, both anticipating the bloody violence that would soon awaken, once they closed the gap between them, and it.

The Tenth and Thompson housing projects was one of the few, still-standing high-rises. Its height soared up into the sky several stories, and the face of its domineering structure was speckled with dozens and dozens of windows. Going back to its beginning, the Tenth and Thompson housing projects had always been the home for some of North Philadelphia's most reputable men; and women too.

The spray of the machine gun happened suddenly, taking Mel and Genesis both by surprise, as the two of them were preparing to reach for their guns. In that one vital moment, those intending to kill, and those unwilling to meet their deaths as cowards, all, knowing it, or not, had just added themselves to a pivotal episode in Philadelphia's history books. In Maniac's absence, his cousin, Jus, and his younger brother, Kamal, had taken charge. It had been Kamal's decision, that for a month straight, they would be paying one thousand dollars a night, to any man willing to serve as their personal security, while their drug operation continued up into the following morning. Tonight, twenty-five men had arrived, and all of them had gotten paid in advance.

Sabia was last to climb the steel ladder, and make it out of the manhole on Tenth and Thompson. He was immediately met by the heel of Malik's boot. The kick to the face left Sabia stunned and dizzy, and caused him to lose his footing. He went falling back into the manhole at an awkward angle, and after Malik made a quick advance on him, and stood over the open manhole, spraying his assault rifle down into it, Haneef hurriedly replaced the metal lid back over the manhole, then, like Malik, turned to face the madness.

And madness it was.

The frightening and unpredictably cruel kind.

There were people shooting assault rifles from various dark windows of Tenth and Thompson's high-rise. The bright muzzle flashes of their weapons were sparkling all across the front of the giant building. Down on both sides of Tenth Street, the doors of parked cars, and SUVs, kept opening randomly, and exiting them all, were brave-faced men, who all quickly began to trade gunfire with any trespassers they saw. This preparedness on their part had removed any facet of the element of surprise that Malik and Uzi had been hoping to achieve. After providing some cover for Mel and Genesis, everyone had emerged from the sewer tunnels and manholes and quickly found a safe place to regroup for a moment.

"Where the fuck y'all at on them four-wheelers?" Malik barked into his walkie-talkie, as he scrambled behind a parked car breathless, followed by Haneef, Freck, and Brill. "Hurry the fuck up!"

"Cousin, they a second away," Foo's voice responded out of everyone's walkie-talkie.

"Yo, Genesis got grazed," Mel reported, "We up here near Master Street. Leek, throw one of them fuckin' hand grenades at that buildin'!"

Ten seconds in, the intensity of the shootout rose several notches higher, because like some twist of bad karma, exposing its ugly face, Juice, Mikel, Ant-Ant, and all of the other four-wheeler drivers from Darien Street showed up, and so did two, unmarked police cars. Someone announced the arrival of the cops into their walkie-talkie, and it echoed out of Sabia's walkie-talkie loud and clear, as he crawled north, up the Tenth Street sewer tunnel. Sabia could hear everything that was going on; the different calibers of all the guns being fired, the four-wheelers, the faint sound of police sirens, coming from somewhere off in the distance, but of all that Sabia heard, Malik's voice echoed in his ears most.

Sabia stopped crawling when the pain became too intense for him to go on. He had been shot in both legs, and was bleeding profusely. Letting his face rest on the wet sand of the sewer tunnel, Sabia tried to find a reason why Malik would have wanted to kill him, and couldn't find none. There, as a wild shootout took place above him, Sabia imagined dying where he laid, and his corpse going unfound. The idea of that kind of ending caused him to sweat even harder, as he lifted his face, and groaned out in agony. He had no flashlight, and no cell phone. His car was parked on Randolph and Master, beside a schoolyard. Sabia started crawling again, crying in pain with every movement, and whispering prayers to God for a little bit of help.

Ironically, the spot in the middle of Tenth Street, where Malik had stopped, and had thrown his hand grenade, was exactly where Sabia had taken a moment to rest, inside of the sewer tunnel. Their fates would collide once more. As would the fates of a lot of the others.A brief moment of silence had followed the deafening explosion of Malik's hand grenade. For many, some seconds had been needed to actually process what Malik had done. The presence of the undercover cops had inspired everyone to move north up Tenth Street, while still trading gunfire. Those defending Tenth Street were either scattering in the direction of the high-rise's lobby, or heading for Master Street. Malik had thrown the hand grenade at the lobby, and while back away, and running up the middle of Tenth Street, had continued to shoot down at the undercover cops blocking Thompson Street. The shooters in the windows of the high-rise had all stopped spraying their assault rifles, and were looking down at the cement structure of the now-crumbling, front lobby, in total shock. Composure regained, they began shooting again.

At Tenth and Master, the gun battle became deadly. Trying to provide cover for Genesis, as she climbed aboard Dame's four-wheeler, Merk ran out into Master Street, shooting his AK-47 at the small group of men, fleeing west around a string of parked cars. One of the men bringing up the rear shot wildly, hitting Merk in the center of his chest, and twice in his neck.

Uzi ordered Rashad, and Shaka to get Merk's body, as he went running after the men with his assault rifle. Juice and Paloma sped by Uzi on their four-wheeler, carrying the same vengeful intentions.

Seeing what had happened to Merk, Ern, Tauheed, and Leem, ran across Tenth Street to the other sidewalk, forming a line. Malik and Wakil ran up on the hoods of two parked cars, and F.L climbed up on the hood of a SUV, and together, they all sprayed their assault rifles at the last wave of men trying to get away from the undercover cops, and away from the damaged lobby of the high-rise. On the opposite side of the street, Mikel and Dolly flew by on their four-wheeler, and turned east on Master Street. Ant-Ant and Veronica were right behind them. Foo, Semaj, and Moosey, were waiting for everyone to ditch the four-wheelers, and for the ones on foot, to make it to Ninth and Jefferson. It was here, where Semaj and Moosey were waiting behind the wheels of the two, 16-seat passenger vans. Foo had made it there first, after landing the drone-helicopter on the roof of the Chrome Depot. He was in the van Semaj was driving.

"Come on! It's over! Make it to the fuckin' vans!! We out! We out!!" Foo shouted into his walkie-talkie, as he frantically helped Rashad and Shaka place Merk's bleeding, lifeless body into the van.

They.

Died.

Fighting.

Minutes later, as the two, 16-seat passenger vans drove north up the I-95 expressway, and all were silent, and some were crying, the two people absent among them had a police helicopter hovering above them, and nowhere else to go. Their fates had run out of time; or, at the moment, it at least appeared to be that way.

"How you tryna do this?" Ant-Ant asked, glancing up at the police helicopter in the sky, then down American Street at the line of police cars, blocking Dauphin Street. "Whatever judge we go in front of , we gettin' the fuckin' library thrown at us."

"Over my dead body."

Ant-Ant shifted on the seat of his four-wheeler when Veronica unhooked her left arm from around his waist and climbed off the back of his four-wheeler with her AR-15.

He tried everything possible, but had been unable to get them away. The police helicopter had been relentless in its pursuit of them. Saying nothing more to him, Veronica raised her assault rifle and fired off a volley of bullets at the hovering, police helicopter, then started marching up the middle of American Street, spraying her gun at the windshields of the cop cars blocking York Street. The cops immediately began to return fire.

Looking over his shoulder, giving Veronica one final stare, Ant-Ant removed his Glock 45 from his shoulder holster, then climbed off of his four-wheeler. As soon as his feet touched the cement, his face twisted into a mask of contempt, and he started running towards the line of cops down at Dauphin Street, firing his Glock with his right hand. Ant-Ant never got to see how far Veronica was able to make it in the opposite direction. Both of them had died bravely, killing three police officers, and injuring two more. Those that had gotten away would remember them, and the fearless stand the two of them had taken on this night, and would never let any notion of their memories be in vain, or lost to the vanishing moments of the past.

RIP . . .

Merk, Ant-Ant

And Veronica.

Chapter Twenty

Fourteen years earlier . . .
September 7th, 1999
7:31 a.m.

The front of the elementary school at the intersection of Frankford and Ontario was gridlocked with people, cars, and school buses. The school buses were continuously pulling up to the front of the school, allowing the school children a moment to unload, and hastily pulling away. The sidewalks were overflowing with children of all sizes, and parents were pit-stopping their vehicles wherever they possibly could, and some weren't pulling off, only, and until after their children had disappeared behind the front doors of the school.

The morning air had a nippy bite to it, but the clear, cloudless sky, and the sun, seemed to be promising much better weather for the afternoon. At the moment, however, it was a chilly, sixty-one degrees.

While it was the first day of school, and an exciting day for Kyzer, it was also the very first time that Kyzer got to witness teardrops fall from his father's eyes. Kyzer was sitting in the passenger seat of his father's white Ford Taurus. Him and his father were down the street from his new school, parked behind an idling, school bus. Kyzer had his book bag on his lap, and an unsharpened pencil in his left hand. Seeing his father cry had Kyzer's little heart crumbling to pieces.

"Kyzer, it ain't a father nowhere on this earth, who love his son more than I love you. You know that, right?"

Looking over sadly at his father, Kyzer nodded his head. His own eyes had gotten watery, and were beginning to spill teardrops down his face. Seeing his father cry was playing wicked games with Kyzer's heart. Kyzer wanted to know what was causing his father's tears, but he couldn't bring himself to ask his father that question.

"Kyzer, from here, I'm goin' to the airport. I have to go back to Panama City. Uncle Santos need me to take care of somethin' for him. It's some real important stuff that only I can fix."

"Can I go?"

"Not this time."

"Why?" Kyzer asked, using the back of his right hand to catch a falling teardrop.

"It's the first day of school, Kyzer."

"My mom don't have to know. If-If we leave now, we can be back, before my school let out, and we can pretend like I was in school all day. Dad, I won't tell."

Kyzer couldn't see it, but his father was having an extremely difficult time with masking his emotions. The teardrops sliding down the front of his face were just a prelude to what was actually brewing inside of Kyzer's father's heart. In his hometown of El Chorrillo, in Panama City, there was a violent war taking place. His return could quite possibly bring an end to his own destiny. However, fully aware of this, losing his life, or the potential threat of it, wasn't what was bothering Kyzer's father. He wasn't a man easily intimidated by anything or anyone.

Roberto Medina was known as the Panama Ghost. As a teenager, to evade the Panama authorities, he once stayed in the unforgiving jungles of Panama for five months. No one had thought that he was still alive, until he had showed his face at his father's funeral. In his late twenties, Roberto Medina had arrived on the United States' soil, by crawling with a pack of illegal immigrants, through a miles-long, underground tunnel, that started in Mexico, and ended in the basement of a house in Southern California. In the book bag on his back, Roberto Medina had brung with him, one kilo of heroin, and a nine millimeter. His fee to use the underground tunnel, had been that he kill the man leading their group, as soon as their group reached the house in the United States. Instead of waiting, Roberto Medina had choked that Mexican man to death inside of the tunnel, then, after giving a tyrannical speech, he had led the small group the rest of the way. The journey had taken eleven grueling days; unprepared, two Dominican men had died from heat strokes, and dehydration. The rest of the men had arisen in the Southern California home on a Thursday evening, exhausted, but alive and eager for all that America had to offer. From that day forward, Roberto Medina's only focus had been to become powerful, rich, and respected.

In one year, Roberto Medina had met all three of his objectives. Visiting a drug connect of his in Philadelphia, Roberto Medina had met Kyzer's mother at a popular, South Philadelphia bar. Their chemistry pulled their hearts together, but it was Roberto Medina's constant trips back to Panama, and his refusal to give up his dangerous lifestyle, which had ultimately pulled their hearts apart.

Over the past summer, Kyzer's parents had separated. Kyzer and his older sister, Camay, had been blindsided by the split, and internally, had been blaming their mother for their father's decision to move out of their home. The absence of his father had been pivotal in how Kyzer had begun to behave, once his temper would flare. It was less about attention, and more about Kyzer actually just missing his father being at home.

At 7:45 a.m., Kyzer's father glanced down at his watch, then turned to face Kyzer, with a grim expression on his face. The moment had come for him to be completely honest with Kyzer, about his life, his relationship with Kyzer's mother, and why Kyzer had been transferred to a school in North Philadelphia, miles away from his home in South Philadelphia. In silence, Kyzer listened to all that his father said. In silence, Kyzer cried. In silence, Kyzer returned his father's hug, holding onto him tightly, never wanting to let go. In silence, Kyzer watched the back of his father's Ford Taurus, as it disappeared down Frankford Avenue, and turned left at Allegheny. That was the last time that Kyzer had seen his father.

In silence, Kyzer had went through his entire day at his new school, only speaking when his teacher had called on him. It was a day that Kyzer had never forgotten. It was that day, at the age of eleven, Kyzer had changed irrevocably.

Oddly, it was that altering moment from Kyzer's tumultuous past, that followed him into consciousness, as he let out a low, agonizing groan, while blinking his eyes open to the four white walls, of a small, unfurnished bedroom. Immediately attracted to movement, Kyzer caught a glimpse of the back of a small child, making a quick exit through the bedroom door.

"Where the fuck I'm at?" Kyzer wondered, swallowing, after taking in a deep breath through his nostrils, and exhaling it slowly out of his dry mouth. Turning his head left, he gazed weakly at the vital-signs machine, beeping his stats, beside the bed he was laying on, then he looked down at the IV-line attached to his left forearm. "Ahhh, shit."

Kyzer squeezed his eyes shut, and while grimacing in pain, dug the back of his head into his pillow, as his attempt to sit himself up, brought his entire body extreme, physical pain. Eyes closed, he didn't notice he had company.

"See? Told you he woke up."

Kyzer opened his eyes and became still. His chest was rising and falling as the shocks of pain, resonating in his body became increasingly unbearable by the second. Breathing was now hurting, and he now knew that any slight movement on his part, would quickly invite tidal waves of unwanted agony to his body. Still, more curious, than cautious, Kyzer slowly turned his head to his right and fixed his eyes on the little boy and woman, who were approaching him. There was an unmistakable hint of admiration in the both of their eyes, and this helped Kyzer feel a little at ease. The child and woman were both middle eastern, and looked more like brother and sister, than mother and son.

"Where I'm at?"

"My grandfather's masjid. This is an upstairs room, we sometimes use for people with nowhere to stay. My grandmother should be here soon. She wasn't sure, if you were allergic to any pain medications, so after she did surgery on you—"

"She did surgery on me in here?" Kyzer asked, looking at the pretty, middle eastern woman, then looking around at the small bedroom. He brung his eyes back to the middle eastern woman, and the small boy, standing closely by her side. "I'm not allergic to no pain medicine. How did I get here? Who brung me here?"

"My brother, Nasir."

"What's y'all names?"

"I'm Hakeema, and this is my little brother . . ."

"Tariq."

Kyzer looked at the smiling, little boy, then returned his eyes back to the boy's older sister. He wanted answers.

"You got hurt really bad. My brother brought you here three nights ago. You were shot four times. My grandmother said three of them passed through, and that one is still behind your left thigh. Well, one, I mean was stopped by the bulletproof vest you were wearing. The impact broke some of your ribs. You might want to stay still, until my grandmother gets here."

"So, I been here for three days?"

"Tonight makes three."

"Where my cell phone at?"

"You'll have to ask my brother and grandfather. I don't think it's here. They were concerned that someone would trace your cell phone here, so—"

"Kyzer, you're famous. Tell him Hakeema. I'll go get the newspapers."

"What he talkin' 'bout?" Kyzer questioned, as the little boy scrambled out of the bedroom with a huge smile on his face. Some scenes from the night he was shot flashed in his mind, as Hakeema held his stare. "I need to use a phone. Why ya little brother said I was famous? What he talkin' about?"

"My grandparents ordered us not to let you use any phones, if you were to awake, while they weren't here. You'll understand their concerns, once Nasir gets back. A lot of people think you're dead. Actually, everybody does. My grandfather thinks it's an untruth, that may prove useful to you once you're well enough to leave."

Kyzer closed his eyes, thinking, seeing the back of his father's Ford Taurus, as it drove away from his school, so many years ago. That day was like today, in many ways; change had come.

I'm.

Dead.

Chapter Twenty-One

"The employees here at Gossip Alley..."Brittany paused purposely, taking a breath to find the words she thought her co-workers needed to hear from her, but to also give her nerves a moment to subside. By default, she had become the new boss of the nightclub, until Splash was to decide otherwise. "We are family. That's how Tia saw us. That's how she treated every last one of us in here. Like family. It didn't matter if you were a bartender, one of the dancers, or on the security team. I want things to stay that way around here. It has to."

Transparency.

Brittany looked around at all of her co-workers. They all stared back in silence. She had asked all of them to join her on the second floor of the nightclub, where she had ascended the stage, and had nervously approached the microphone stand. Tia, there late boss, used to speak to them at their meetings, from this same position. After this morning, Brittany wanted every woman and man present, to know she was in charge, in control, and that she could be trusted by them, and believed in. Most of all, Brittany wanted to clarify to everyone that Gossip Alley was not closing down, or as the rumors had it on social media, being sold to a group of Center City investors.

Brittany believed she could conquer the loyalty of everyone in attendance. Everyone had shown up on time, and appeared eager to hear what she had to say. Looking out at them all, she thought of her late boss.

Mrs. Gunplay.

"Until Splash sends a message from jail, Gossip Alley is ours," Brittany clarified, feeling an angry thrill sweep through her body. In honoring her late boss, and seeing their pact to its completion, anger and conviction would have to stay her primary emotions. "The survival of the club is on our shoulders. We'll get what we invest in it. Don't believe that shit on social media, or none of the blogs. For one, it should be understood that we'll have the discussion amongst us first, if any changes were being made. Tia ran a tight ship. Her absence is the only change we have to adjust to. I want that to be clear. If it's any matters that need more clarity, with how the next magazine layout will be, who will be in it, see me at the office later, or call me. As far as our routine around the club, nothing is changing. Are we clear?"

Everyone nodded their heads.

"Any questions?"

"What's goin' on with Tuna and Victoria?" One of the female exotic dancers asked, from a barstool at the bar.

"Good question," Brittany responded with a sigh, wishing the question hadn't been raised. Her late boss' uncle and his girlfriend hadn't been heard from, since the two had traveled to New Orleans, and neither of them were answering their phones, or responding to none of the e-mails she had sent them, going back to the day Tia was killed. "As y'all know, so much has been going on. And I really do apologize, because I know a lot of what's goin' on in my personal life has been affecting my concentration here at the club. What we can do is this . . . if Tuna isn't back by the Halloween party, we'll replace him temporarily, and let somebody else fill the manager's position. It won't be someone new, though. There won't be any new hires for a nice little while. So yeah, we can deal with that next week. Any other questions?"

No one else had any other questions for Brittany. With the relief that their jobs were definitely secure, and that Brittany seemed to have everything under control, everyone, except for Honey, began heading towards the stairwell that led down to the 1st floor of the nightclub. It was only a little after ten in the morning; sleeping hours for most of Gossip Alley's staff. On a normal day, many of the nightclub's staff wouldn't be making any arrivals to the nightclub, until the setting of the sun.

Alone, Brittany and Honey eyed each other for a moment, as Brittany came down the short staircase at the rear of the stage. Both women had dangerous and deceptive thoughts brewing in their minds.

"Brittany, why that guy, Rell, wasn't here for the meetin'?"

Brittany dismissively shrugged her shoulders as she walked ahead of Honey across the huge dancefloor.

"He still work here?"

"You still do, and that's all you should be worryin' about."

"Really, Brittany?"

"Yes, really. We goin' to the office, so we can talk about this Halloween party, and what we gon' do with Detective Konn. I have somewhere I need to be in thirty minutes."

"You'll be late."

Brittany stopped and spun around. The gun in Honey's right hand was being aimed at her chest, and slowly rising. With her free hand, Honey thumbed the screen of her cell phone, then pressed it against her left ear, glaring at Brittany with a malicious intent in her brown eyes.

Sabotage.

"Splash, I got her."

Chapter Twenty-Two

A day later . . .

Rock 'n Roll Rhonda tilted her face up to the small shower head, and let the warm water mix in with the teardrops, falling from her brown eyes. Her day at court hadn't turned out the way she had hoped it would. Despite a long-winded attempt by her attorney, the judge had refused to lift her probation detainer, which would have then allowed her to pay bail on her new case and go free. After the prosecutor's rebuttal, and some unsatisfactory comments from her probation officer, the judge had gone into a fifteen minute tirade of his own. He had vehemently expressed how he had been far too lenient with her a year and a half earlier, and that at her original sentencing hearing, he should have been a lot more stricter with her and not fooled by her age and innocent appearance. Now that she had gotten arrested with two more guns, while already on probation for a gun, the judge had decided to postpone her probation violation hearing in front of him, until the outcome of her new charges, which were being heard in the courtroom of another judge.

Lowering her head, allowing the water to wash over her long hair, Rock 'n roll Rhonda raised her hands up to her face and began to sob uncontrollably. She was back in jail again, and feeling useless to the people who needed her home the most.

"Tia, I'm so sorry I failed you," Rock 'n Roll Rhonda cried, as the sudden thought of her deceased cousin came to mind. The privacy of the prison shower stall kept her sobs limited to her own ears, as she pressed her back against the rear wall, and continued crying. "I'm so, so sorry, Tia. And I only got to see Sooly twice. Stuff just so weird . . . Splash been lyin' to you about Sabia all this time. All this time, he-I can't trust him no more. It might come to us goin' at it, Tia. I'll raise Sooly, if I got to. I miss you so fuckin' much. What do I do, now, Tia? What do I do, now?"

On the opposite side of Rock 'n Roll Rhonda's shower door, stood two, muslim women. One was reading her Noble Qur'an, while the other held Rock 'n Roll Rhonda's towel, bathrobe, and black scarf, she would immediately want to cover her head with, as soon as she was done drying off, and stepped out of the shower. The all-female, county prison, was located in Northeast Philadelphia. Months earlier, Rock 'n Roll Rhonda had left the prison a legend; she had returned one still. While Rock 'n Roll Rhonda was well known by inmates, and corrections staff alike, she wasn't one to throw caution to the wind. Her safety was always a priority to her, and others were well aware of this, so her closest associates, and even some corrections staff, made sure that her back was always watched. It was understood, that if something happened to Rock 'n Roll Rhonda, something could potentially happen to everybody.

Decisions.

A half an hour later, Rock 'n Roll Rhoda was sitting in her jail cell, talking on an iPhone, that was recently brought to her by a corrections officer. She was in the dark, still crying.

"Liberty, voodoo, though? Where are you gettin' this from?"

"My computer. Where else? Rhonda, look her up for yourself, as soon as we get off the fuckin' phone. That bitch did somethin' to my dad. I can feel it. Why haven't none of us heard from him. Victoria did somethin' to my dad, Rhonda. It say her whole family into black magic, and how she got these aunts down New Orleans, who own—"

"What's her last name, Lib?"

"Beauvais... Victoria Beauvais. That bitch did somethin' to my dad."

"Okay, let me look into it. I'll call you back. I need to call Zay first, though, alright?"

"Okay, I'll be up there tomorrow, so we can talk some more. I love you."

Rock 'n Roll Rhonda thumbed the screen of the iPhone, ending her call with her younger cousin, Liberty, then sat the cell phone beside her on her pillow. She felt exhausted, and the need for sleep was pulling at her. After a sigh, and staring through the darkness at her jail cell door, she used her left hand to wipe away her tears and reached for her new cell phone with her right. It had come as a gift from her cousin, Zainab. Tearful again, Rock 'n Roll Rhonda dialed her cousin's number, then pressed the cell phone against her ear. With each ring, the momentum of her emotions were quickening.

"Cousin?"

"As Salaamu Alaykum, Zay, "Rock 'n Roll Rhonda greeted her cousin, as her eyes blurred from her tears. After her cousin returned her greeting, she took in a breath, and sadly shook her head as she exhaled. "You see how that judge was talkin' to me, Zay? What me havin' on a kimar and overgarments had to do with why I was there? Wallahi, I hope his brakes give out on his fuckin' way home. My court date for this new case ain't until January, Zay."

"That might be a blessing. Stop cryin'. Have faith in Allah."

"I am."

"I stored all the numbers I thought you might want in that phone. Liberty wanted to talk to you first, that's why I had that guard give you that message. Look we gon' be okay out here. We just need you to—"

"You still got Sooly?"

"Wanna talk to him? Hold on."

Tia, Rock 'n Roll Rhonda and Zainab's deceased cousin, had left behind a 17-month-old son. His name was Rasool Barnes, and he was a junior. It was an unspoken pact, but the remaining living, female cousins, which were Zainab, Rock 'n roll Rhonda, and the youngest of the three, Liberty, were all dedicated to the idea of making sure their cousin's son be well provided for, and taken care of. As for Splash, the little boy's father, if at any moment, fate was to free him from the county prison he was currently at, where he was fighting a murder charge, the three cousins were of the opinion that he should die immediately.

Rock 'n roll Rhonda felt much better, after speaking to her little cousin. He knew her voice, and had even began to cry when Zainab had removed the cell phone from his ear. While she had been at the county prison the last time, a week hadn't gone by, without her cousin, Tia, coming to see her. During all those visits, Rock 'n Roll Rhonda would hold her little cousin, and sing to him. His young heart had memorized her voice.

"Why wasn't Brittany in the courtroom with you, Zay?"

"That's really why I got that phone to you."

There was an eerie tone to her cousin's voice, and it immediately made Rock 'n Roll Rhonda feel sick to her stomach.

"Nobody knows where she's at, Rhonda. I went by Kyzer's house . . . she's not there. Her phone keeps goin' to voicemail. She didn't—"

"What about the club?"

"No sign of her there, either. She was there yesterday morning, but she didn't show up last night."

"Anything new on Kyzer?"

"Nothin' still."

"Zay, what does your gut tell you about Brittany bein' missin'? And be honest, Zay."

"Keep her in your du'a, Insha Allah."

"No, Zay. That's not an answer. Don't sugar coat it, 'cause I'm not out there. What is your gut tellin' you, Zay?"

"Whoever called your probation officer, is the same person responsible for Brittany bein' missin'."

"Got any ideas?"

"Rhonda, who mad at us the most right now? Who mad at the world right now?"

"Splash?"

"It's either Splash, or Maniac. And I say him, 'cause of that hit he put on you and Brittany. I say Splash, because of him and Sabia—"

"What's goin' on with him anyway? Brittany told me he gotta middle finger party when they hit Tenth Street. I gotta get him, Zay."

"Sabia should be where he need to be, Rhonda. Dead. Look, right now, we need to find out what's goin' on with Uncle Tuna. Lib found all this stuff about Victoria that's raising a lot of eyebrows, Rhonda. I'll keep you posted on Brittany and Kyzer. I'm thinkin' about visitin' Splash."

"Spit in his face for me."

"Cousin, if I send anything to his face, it won't be spit. I'm here at his house."

"That's Tia house, Zay."

"That's another conversation. Tia not here anymore, Rhonda. Our concern has to be Sooly from here on out, Insha Allah. You got that phone. Make some calls. I love you, okay?"

"I love you, too. As Salaamu Alaykum. Zay, be careful."

241

"I will, Cousin. Wa laykum As Salaam Wa Rahmatullah."

It was October 27th, days before Halloween. The sun had set, and the sky was a shade of blue that appeared purplish. The early evening had come with a chilly wind. At a Northeast Philadelphia Masjid, this nippy breeze was going ignored by Kyzer, as he sat quietly in his wheelchair.

Vanquish.

"Kyzer, with the temper you have, how long do you expect to stay alive?"

"Come on, Mr. Zubair," Kyzer complained, frowning his face at the elderly, Albanian man. They had been sitting in silence, until the question had interrupted his deep thinking. "I thought we had an understandin'? I don't use cuss words around Tariq, which I haven't. I stop askin' for a cell phone. I fell back on everything you asked me to stop doin', Mr. Zubair. Not once, have I broken our agreement. I asked Hakeema to push me out here, so I could get some fresh air, and so I can think. Out here, we agreed that I would be given some privacy. I ain't even say nothin' when you first came out here. How could I? If it wasn't for ya gran'son bringin' me here, and ya wife operatin' on me, I'd most likely be dead. I respect you, Mr. Zubair. At the same time, what I do wit' my life is my decision. You gotta respect that. From day one, we both understood that we viewed life differently. And I don't mean on the Islamic tip. I'm talkin' about our personal opinions. If you ask me, havin' a temper is priceless. I bet 'chu, if you used yours, these white people, or whoever the fuck it is, wouldn't keep paintin' them Nazi signs on the door of this masjid, or keep throwin' fuckin' pig feet all over the sidewalk. Even ya wife wanna do somethin'. Maybe y'all should switch tempers."

Mr. Zubair rushed Kyzer, grabbing him by the collar of his sweatshirt with both hands. Kyzer didn't flinch. He simply held Mr. Zubair's angry stare, quickly recognizing emotions in the elderly man's eyes that had been hidden before. Mr. Zubair did have a temper; one just as unruly as his, if not more. As the brisk air whipped around them, and through the small gap of space, separating their faces, and Kyzer held his grip on the armrests of his wheelchair, a hand tentatively came from behind and grabbed Mr. Zubair by the shoulder. The contact caused the anger in Mr. Zubair's hazel eyes to return to the place it had come from.

"My gran'son should've left you to die."

It was a whisper, left unheard by Mr. Zubair's granddaughter, Hakeema. Kyzer's soul was struck by the comment. He watched the short, gray-bearded man as he stepped around his granddaughter and headed back to the rear door of his masjid. Silent, Hakeema watched Kyzer, watching her departing grandfather. Their altercation had put confusion and concern in her eyes.

"Let me see ya phone, Hakeema."

"I can't."

"You can't, or you won't?"

"To call who?"

Kyzer thought of his girlfriend, Brittany. He had to call her first. She needed to know that he was okay and still alive. He missed her. He then had to call his cousin, Malik, to tell him that Terrell was Sabia. He also needed to speak to Jamillah, to tell her about the mystery woman, who was claiming to be Idris' second wife. He wanted a meeting. He wanted all of his bullet wounds to heal quickly.

"You know what? Tomorrow, Hakeema. I'm outta here as soon as the sun come up. I'm gon' shake up the whole fuckin' city, early in the fuckin' mornin'."

"In a wheelchair?"

"When I die, I'ma do it from my grave."

Immortal.

Influences.

At exactly 8:55 p.m., Sabia opened his eyes to nothing but darkness and the faint sounds of traffic, coming to him from a nearby sewer drain. He could hear voices. Remarkably, despite all of the blood he had lost from his gunshot wounds, he was still alive. His refusal to die alone, undiscovered, had helped him crawl almost a mile from where he had begun. He was now beneath the intersection of 7th and Montgomery. Believing that he was still being pursued, instead of crawling in one direction, Sabia had made left and right turns, as he encountered different sewer tunnels.

As fate would have it, during his random moments of unconsciousness, his cell phone would ring in the back pocket of his jeans. Sabia was hanging on to a thread of life, and was gradually releasing his hold of it. He had no strength left to crawl. Closing his eyes, Sabia began to think of his mother, totally unaware that he was only a block away from her house. As the edge of unconsciousness creeped closer, the low sound of his ringing cell phone made his heart leap in his chest, and encouraged him to fight off the swallowing sensation of blacking out again.

With a deep groan, Sabia reached behind him and dug his cell phone out of his jeans. The effort it took drained his energy to keep his eyes open. The moment Sabia placed his cell phone to his ear, it stopped ringing, and then, a second later, it alerted him that a voice message had been left. Sabia turned his face away from a rat, he had felt nibbling at his left ear. His dark mind showed him a gruesome image of his dead body being feasted upon by dozens of rats, as he weakly thumbed the screen of his cell phone to redial the number that just called him.

"Hello?"

"Nigga, you can't be serious? Now, you wanna answer ya fuckin' phone? Sabia, man, where the fuck you at, dog?"

"Ro?"

244

"Yeah, nigga. Man, where the fuck you at? I been in Philly for three . . . hold on, ya folks got some holla for you."

Sabia turned his head to the left, then to the right, in an effort to keep the rats off of him. More of them were starting to come. He felt them nibbling on his bloody legs and crawling on his back, so he shook his legs the best he could and slowly turned to his side. The darkness of the sewer tunnel seemed like a dungeon some place far away. He was sprawled out on a bed of trash and filth.

"Sabia, where are you?"

"Down in one of the sewer tunnels, Honey, "Sabia answered, swiping at the rats nibbling at his left thigh. He knew his fight with the rodents wouldn't last long. "They lined me up. They know-They know who I am, Honey. Them niggaz know. Give Rohan back the phone . . . hurry up."

"Okay, but, Sabia, turn the GPS back on ya phone, so we can find you. Do you know where you at?"

"No . . . give Rohan the phone. Now, Honey."

"I'm here, dog. Give me instructions. This one of them moments we already talked about. I talked to ya cousin, Splash. Shit in rotation as we fuckin' speak, dog. Stay in control of ya destiny. Talk to me."

Like Sabia, his friend, Rohan Saint Pierre, was an America's 'Most Wanted' fugitive, and was wanted for multiple murders. He was a Haitian native. The two had met at a nightclub in Houston, Texas. A bar fight with some local men had bonded them. Under Rohan's tutelage, Sabia had gotten his new identity, and further persuaded into getting all of his cosmetic surgeries done. Rohan had been eluding the authorities for almost two decades, without ever stepping foot out of the United States. His guidance meant a lot to Sabia, because thus far, it had yet to disappoint him once. Sabia spoke, swiping away at the rats on his chest and shoulder. He could feel them chewing at the gunshot wounds above his right knee and left thigh, but his strength was to drained to shake the rats off of him. "I got hit in both my legs. I can't stand up. I started crawlin' from the sewer tunnel on Tenth and Thompson. I'm not that far from there. Probably a couple of blocks, Ro. My car parked on Randolph and Master. It's an extra set of keys in my left, Gucci sneaker, in the, um, in the closet. Some kind of . . . shit. These rats fuckin' me up, Ro. They eatin' me alive, dog. They all over me."

"Concentrate. Who shot'chu?"

"Leek. It was Leek."

"Who that?"

"Kyzer cousin."

"Where he be?"

Tears escaped Sabia's eyes as he fought away the rats that kept coming close to his face. They were nibbling at him everywhere.

"Sabia, stay wit' me. Where the fuck is this nigga? Talk to me, dog."

"Eighth and Jefferson, Ro. Put down anybody you see comin' outta this fuck-ahhh, shit."

"Comin' outta where?"

"It's two houses put together, Ro. You can't miss it. They use the back to go in 'n out, Ro. Tell my mom I love her, alright?"

"That ain't how we talk, dog. You gon' tell her ya fuckin' self. Now, hang up and turn ya GPS on."

"Ro, I can't."

"That word ain't in our vocabulary."

"I'm too weak, Ro. These . . . fuckin'-Ro, these fuckin' rats, man."

"Are they worse than ya nightmares?"

"Naw."

"Alright, then. Dog, me 'n Honey got the bitch, Brittany. If we don't find you, you can fuckin' guarantee, they'll never find this bitch. Look, we about to blitz Splash house for him, and run down on his wife cousin. Some muslim bitch that got his son. He want us to take his son to ya mom. I need an hour at the most. Can you stay alive for that long?'

"Yeah."

"Alright, now situate that GPS on ya phone for me, and leave the rest to me. No retreat."

"No surrender."

Ultimatums.

After several knocks on the front door, and ringing the doorbell twice, the handsome man in the dark suit took a step back from the small palace in Chestnut Hill, Pennsylvania, and readjusted his expensive tie. He then took a glance at his watch. Zainab watched the man's movements closely. As she kept her eyes glued to the surveillance monitor, in her cousin's kitchen, she made a call on her cell phone.

Zainab found something odd about the stranger's unannounced visit to her cousin's house. It was close to nine 'o clock in the evening, and she wasn't expecting anyone. Her first concern was that of her little cousin, who she had just gotten to fall asleep a half an hour earlier.

"As Salaamu Alaykum . . . what's up, Zay?"

"Wa Laykum As Salaam Wa Rahmatullah . . . Hook, are y'all locked down, yet?"

"Naw, we still out. Why? What's up?"

Hook was the husband of Zainab's friend, Jamillah. He was from Southwest Philadelphia, but currently incarcerated at a Philadelphia county prison. He was a giant, standing well over 6'4" tall, and weighing over two hundred and seventy-five pounds. Coincidentally, Hook was being housed on the exact same unit as Splash, Zainab's cousin's husband, whose house she was in. The coincidence had become Zanab's way of keeping a watchful eye on Splash's everyday temperament.

"I need to talk to Splash, Hook. Right now. Can you do that for me?"

"So, you ready to expose ya hand, huh?"

"Only some of it."

"The nigga got the whole block out in the yard, watchin' him and this guard play one on one in basketball. Supposed to be for ten stacks."

"I need to talk to him, Hook. It's very important."

"These niggaz about to be hot at me. Alright, this what I'ma do, though. I'ma slide in his cell and put my phone under his pillow. You gon' have to hold on, and just wait for the nigga to get to it."

Zanaib let out a sigh.

"Zay, make sure you tell that nigga to get my jack back to me, before we lock in."

"It'll be the first thing I tell him, Hook. Shukran."

"Afwan . . . As Salaamu Alaykum."

"Wa Laykum As Salaam."

The Philadelphia county prison system was a corrupt one. Most of its staff, from the medical departments, food services, and its corrections officers, participated in smuggling contraband into the inmates. Zainab made it her personal business to know which ones were successful with getting cell phones inside. She was a woman with connections, and a fear for nothing, but her Creator.

"This better be fuckin' important, Zay."

It had taken Splash seven minutes to make it to the cell phone. For a moment, while still looking at the stranger on the surveillance monitor, Zainab wondered what Hook had said to Splash, and how surprised Splash must have been upon realizing that Hook knew who she was.

"Splash, who this at 'cha front door? He's tall, dark skin, and he's wearin' a suit. He's not a friend of yours, or Tia's."

Silence.

"Sooly here, Splash."

"Don't 'chu think I fuckin' know that?"

"Why is he here?"

"To kill you, bitch. To kill you, and take my fuckin' son."

Mr. Gunplay.

After completing her group, text message, and sending it, Zainab pocketed her cell phone, pulled down her face veil, then walked out of her cousin's kitchen. The thought of her little cousin, who was upstairs in his bed asleep, and what his young life meant to her, she knew there was no way she would allow anyone to remove him from her presence; not even someone that had been sent by the child's father.

"Oh, Allah, send me your angels," Zainab prayed, as she cut through the home theater on the lower level of her cousin's massive home. The threat on her life, or the idea that it could be moments away from being cut short, was only angering her, and increasing her hate for her cousin's husband. "As many as I need to help me protect Sooly. I never miss my chances to please you, and I never neglect my salat, Allah. Splash is a kafir. Bring humiliation to any plan he ever make, and let this man at the door die with his regrets on the tip of his tongue . . . Ameen."

Zainab was a petite woman, standing exactly five feet even. Beneath her black, face veil, and the black, overgarments, covering her body, she was in possession of a beautiful face, and a curvy frame. Her eyes sometimes changed colors from a light brown, to an almost perfect blend of walnut-brown and hazel.

Home.

Alone.

There was a dangerous calm about Zainab's demeanor when she came walking out of her cousin's home theater, and stepped out into the large foyer. Zainab's mind was moving as fast as the rhythm of her heartbeat; maybe faster. Her eyes cut up ahead to the front door, where her new enemy was waiting on the opposite side. With no fear, she started her march down the marble-floored foyer.

Rohan could see Zainab approaching through one of the glass sides in the front door. He began to smile, and his eyes became lit with amusement. The man who had sent him hadn't given him a true account of Zainab's heart.

Die.

Brittany's exhale paused in her lungs when she saw the front door of her boss' house open. The pace of her heart immediately quickened. She was in the backseat of Rohan's Chevy Suburban, being guarded by Honey, who, when not watching her, was also watching Rohan.

"This just keep gettin' easier and easier."

"Don't open that screen door, Zay," Brittany quietly thought, after Honey's comment. Her mouth was covered with duct tape, and her hands were handcuffed behind her back, and the seatbelt was being used as an added measure of precaution. "Close that fuckin' front door, Zay, or shoot through it. He Sabia friend. Don't believe shit he sayin', Zay. Splash sent him."

The moment of her kidnapping, Brittany had started cherishing each and every second that she was alive. The constant threat of death had made life her biggest desire. A teardrop escaped Brittany's right eye, then her left, then both teardrops crept down her cheeks and over the duct tape covering her mouth. Her face was scarred and bruised from the many slaps and punches Rohan had given her. Just an hour earlier, he had ordered Honey to pull over on the expressway, and he had climbed into the backseat with her and had assaulted her and brutally raped her. Afterwards, he had spit in her face and laughed.

Brittany could feel Rohan's semen oozing out of her vagina, and every single pore on her skin was crying out in humiliation. As Brittany stared out of Rohan's dark-colored SUV, she silently wished for two things; an extension on life, and for Kyzer's return. By her boyfriend's side, she wanted to burn Sabia, Rohan, and Splash, to the ground.

After.

The.

Fire.

Chapter Twenty-Three

The same night . . .

"I'm here to pick up Splash son. He want me to take him to his aunt."

"Who are you?"

It was then, as Rohan went reaching into the inside of his suit jacket, that Zainab noticed the stains of blood peppered across the torso and chest area of Rohan's striped shirt. Before Rohan's right hand could fully disappear and reach for whatever he was going for, Zainab reacted.

The panes of glass on the screen door exploded into pieces the moment Zainab lifted her guns and started shooting. The sleeves of her overgarment had been hiding the guns in her hands. After diving for cover, from his back, Rohan began shooting his own gun. He believed he was shot, but the pain he was experiencing on his right jawbone was only a graze wound. When Zainab stopped shooting, Rohan crawled a bit, shot a few more times at the doorway of the house, crawled some more, then scrambled to his feet and began running across the lawn, holding his hand against his face. He was furious.

The lights of neighboring homes started coming on. The brief gun battle had shaken the hearts of everyone living in the small, upscale neighborhood. The first gunshot had prompted many of them to dial 9-1-1.

Honey's eyes were as fearful and wide as Brittany's as Rohan came running up to his SUV. His next move took both women by surprise. After, he had pulled Brittany out of his truck and through her down to the ground, Rohan began to viciously beat her in the head and face with his gun. At one point, he paused just to kick her when she tried to shield herself from the attack.

"You dumb, bitch!" Rohan yelled, looking over his shoulder at the door of the mansion. He did a circle around Brittany, making eye contact with Honey, then turning his head to the sound of approaching police sirens off in the distance. "We gon' meet again, bitch! And when we fuckin' do, you done!! You hear me?!! You fuckin' done!!!"

Rohan looked down at Brittany with eyes that could unnerve the devil. When Brittany dared to meet his stare, he spit in her face, then aimed his gun at her forehead and pulled the trigger twice.

Chapter Twenty-Four

Thursday morning came with mild temperatures and a gray sky. As October was finishing up its last week, it was gradually becoming more and more apparent that Winter was on its way.

Kyzer had met the morning eagerly, and with a little skepticism. As promised, Hakeema had gotten her cell phone to him, while her grandparents had been preparing for the early morning prayer, and getting her little brother ready for school. Kyzer hadn't slept all night. Thoughts of his father, sister, and mother, had put his mind on his younger years, while his heart had been consumed by the emotion of making sure that his every moment counted for something. Beside his wheelchair, Tariq stood quietly, fidgeting with the zipper on the side of his book bag. There was a sadness about his behavior and Kyzer, doing a much better job at hiding his, could find no words to say to the little boy, before he left for school.

"Kyzer, what if them guys try to kill you again?"

"My enemies bring out my strength, Tariq."

"Like—Like the Incredible Hulk?"

"Worse," Kyzer answered, returning the little boy's smile. Him and the seven-year-old boy had developed a strong bond, and he was going to miss him a lot. "Tariq,

I'm comin' back. I owe y'all. It ain't no way I could ever forget you and ya family. You my little homie, Tariq. If anybody ever bother you, all you gotta do is call me, alright?"

The little boy nodded his head sadly, as he stared down at his sneakers. When the dark SUV pulled up at the curb, he looked at Kyzer with tears on his eyes.

"As Salaamu Alaykum, Kyzer."

"Wa Laykum As Salaam."

While hugging Tariq, Kyzer looked at the front door of the masjid, where Hakeema and her grandparents were standing. Him and Hakeema had already said their goodbyes earlier; her grandmother had asked him not to leave, while her grandfather had listened in silence. As the passenger and driver's side door opened on the SUV, Kyzer and Tariq ended their hug, and as Tariq started his walk to school, he curiously watched the men who had come to pick Kyzer up.

Kyzer wanted to capitalize off of the media, and somehow manipulate its engine into helping him shape an idea of his into an unstoppable dream. Instead of calling Brittany, or any of his family members, he had used Hakeema's cell phone to contact the famous, Philly rappers, Oschino, and Peedi Crakk.

"Everything set up?"

"That was the easy part, "Oschino commented, as he steered Kyzer's wheelchair down the sidewalk and over to the rear passenger door of the Infiniti SUV.

"What's the hard part?" Kyzer questioned, as Peedi Crakk opened the rear door, then helped him rise to his feet. He felt pain shooting all through his body, but it was his broken ribs, and the gunshot wounds to his hip and elbow, that made his face tighten with anger and discomfort. "We legends in this fuckin' city. Our old heads should've made this kind of move. If them old heads from the Black mafia would've won, shit in this city definitely would've been different for us. Both of y'all got more power in this city, than all of the state reps put together. Trust me, I know they gon' bite."

The scene at City Hall was tense and chaotic, as Peedi Crakk turned right and blended his SUV with the southbound, Broad Street traffic, as the flow of cars began to circle City Hall. All three men stared out at all of the news crews set up, awaiting Kyzer's rumored appearance. Above the statue of William Penn, in the east and west skies of Market Street, there were two local, news helicopters, hovering, and sometimes flying away for a short distance before returning.

"Kyzer, don't get me wrong, this idea you got make a lot of sense."

Kyzer stared at Peedi Crakk's rearview mirror to make eye contact with him, as Peedi Crakk came to a red light at 15th and JFK Boulevard.

"Here's the thing, though, and I think this what O was trying to say. The easy part was gettin' the media to show up. As soon as me and O got them messages from you, we both took that shit to social media ASAP. In no less than a minute, the internet went ape shit, Kyzer. I had to cut my fuckin' phone off. That's how crazy shit got. Look at all these fuckin' cops out here."

As Peedi Crakk stopped at another red light, on the south side of Broad Street, him, Kyzer, and Oschino, all looked out at the scene continuing to unfold. There were police all over the place, some in small gatherings, and some eyeing the scene themselves. Adding to the tension, were all of the people that seemed to be showing up. City Hall had been converged upon, by Philadelphia citizens, police, local news crews, and journalists. As they moved through the green light, and came around the east side of City Hall, Peedi Crakk let out a long sigh, then began talking again.

"This the stage you asked for, Kyzer. Good thing is, if any of the niggas you beefin' wit' showed up, all these mu'fuckin' cops gon' have them niggaz second guessin' shit. So, look, we wit'chu, though, alright? Insha Allah, this vision you got gon' reach the desk of the fuckin' president."

With those words, Peedi Crakk pulled his Infiniti SUV over to the curb and parked. Oschino made his exit first. Alone, Peedi Crakk turned in his seat and gave Kyzer a serious stare.

"Any last words of advice?"

"Fuck that wheelchair. Leave that shit in here."

"Why?"

"Kyzer, everybody know what 'chu just been through, so let these mu'fuckers see you on ya feet, and not sittin'. Stand like a leader, young'n."

Kyzer felt his heartbeat accelerate when Oschino snatched the door open. He looked beyond Oschino, into the swelling crowd, and reminded himself that this was all his idea. At the sight of him, The news reporters and camera men took off running. Unaware of how he would be arriving, and certainly unsure if the entire thing would turn out to be just a hoax, the police officers had no real way of being prepared, so when all of the commotion began, the police officers who were making eye contact with where Kyzer actually was, had no other option, but to use their walkie-talkies and share the confirmation of Kyzer's presence, and his location.

Kyzer was wearing an outfit that Hakeema's grandmother had purchased for him. The Nike sweatsuit and sneakers had been her gift to him. Hakeema had braided his hair for him that morning, after he had shared his idea with her. As the news reporters closed the distance between him and them, and got a lot closer with there cameras and microphones, with Oschino and Peedi Crakk's help, he climbed out of the SUV and planted his feet on the sidewalk. Reminded of Peedi Crakk's final words, he forced himself to ignore every shock of pain that was attacking his body and stepped forward to become the future vanguard of his city.

"Kyzer, where have you been?"

"What made you choose here as your first appearance?"

"Were you kidnapped?"

"Kyzer, how many times were you actually shot?"

"Do you know those men that tried to murder you? Were they the same men who killed your mother, Kyzer?"

"Kyzer, how did you disappear that night?"

"Where were you staying? Were you with Oschino and Peedi Crakk?"

"Kyzer, do you think your life is still in danger?"

For a fleeting second, Kyzer became lost in the moment, and simply stood there, blinking at all of the news reporters, watching them watch him. Their barrage of questions made him view them as vultures. The mention of his mother had derailed his train of thought, and had him feeling angry. His eyes stayed fixed on the face of the Asian, female reporter, who had asked him the question. Beyond the small circle of camera men and news reporters, the crowd was growing larger by the minute. There were people recording with their cell phones and taking pictures, and the police presence had Kyzer feeling slightly uncomfortable, because he was certain that he was wanted for questioning, and that he was definitely going to be pulled aside by one of them.

Oschino and Peedi Crakk stood to Kyzer's right and left, wearing serious facial expressions, with their arms crossed. Above the scene, the two, news helicopters, were recording everything, and streaming it live.

"I'm here to talk to the mayor," Kyzer announced as his moment of speaking immediately caused all of the news reporters to step closer to him, and work for a better spot, as they all aimed their recording devices and microphones at his face. Today, he was going to catapult his status a hundred notches higher. "Him and y'all had a lot to talk about, after I got shot up. Everybody was comin' out wit' opinions."

"So, you were reading the newspapers? How about the news?"

"Kyzer, what was it that you didn't agree with?"

"I saw everything that came out," Kyzer assured the reporter, then let out a sigh. He could see the police presence was becoming more increased on the scene. "How y'all been tryna paint the picture, like, it's because of the youth, Philly so out of control. How about y'all tell the mayor to stop shuttin' down all the rec centers, so the kids that's tryna stay outta the dumb stuff, can have somewhere to go? This a peaceful situation, but look how many of these cops got they hands on they guns. The blame gotta be shared by everybody. In the last month, I can count on all of my fingers, how many unarmed, black people, got killed by a cop. That don't build trust with us in the hood. So, that's directed at the person, who wrote in the paper, about my first thought should've been to call the cops. How that make sense? I'ma call the people that's gon' pull up 'n pull they guns out on me, too? Hell no. And I'm speakin' for probably every black man all over this country. We know racism ain't went nowhere. Just because we gotta black president, it don't bring no safety to us in the ghetto. When my mom got killed, they had me down Eighth and Race, and wanted to know, if she had any enemies I was aware of. Kindness was the only enemy my mom ever had. She was nice to everybody. And no, I wasn't shot by the same people who shot her. I don't know who shot me. Y'all saw the video. I ran."

"Kyzer, how many times were you shot?"

"Four times."

"Where did you go?"

"None of ya business. I'm alive, and that's what should be important."

"How do you know those guys weren't involved with what happened to your mother?"

"Do you know somethin' I don't?"

"Well obviously—"

Oschino chuckled.

"Kyzer, why do you want to speak to the mayor?"

"Because my mom would've wanted me to," Kyzer admitted, shifting his weight to his other foot and putting his arm on Peedi Crakk's left shoulder for support. Beads of sweat had peppered across his forehead, as the pain he was trying to hide dug at his willpower. "She wanted me to do somethin' more serious wit' my life when I came home. So, I wanna be the best Kyzer Rogers I can be, and change some of my goals. We share Philly. So far, all I seen was opinions and nutty comments, but nobody ain't tryin' to come to the people that got the most influence. The people- The people, who all of the youth gon' give they undivided attention to."

"Kyzer, who are these people?" A news reporter asked.

"Them."

After gesturing to Oschino and Peedi Crakk, Kyzer stole a moment to stare around at the still-growing crowd of spectators, then he returned his attention back to the news reporters. In that one glance at the crowd, he had found an imminent threat lurking. Kyzer's eyes flicked back to the area on his far-right, where he had just been looking, and came eye to eye with Maniac, who was giving him a stare of death.

There would never be peace, between Kyzer and Maniac; too many lines had been crossed, and far too many lives had been lost. As both young men engaged in their stare, going unnoticed by all around them, what was a passing moment, seemed like forever and a day. Maniac was dressed in black, with a baseball hat pulled low over his eyebrows. His beard had grown some, and he looked to be a few pounds heavier. Standing still, one would have no idea of the personal struggle he was having with his own pain. Maniac was standing on a prosthetic left foot, and the physical agony he was dealing with was killing him. The buzz of Kyzer's reappearance had rocked him to his core, and to see for himself, if all of the talk on social media was actually true, and now, seeing Kyzer with his own two eyes, standing there, with seemingly the city at his feet, and staring at him daringly, Maniac knew Kyzer's threat as an enemy was about to become timeless. His only satisfaction left, was the heartache he presumed Kyzer was experiencing, due to Brittany's recent death.

"Everybody else had their turn," Kyzer spoke, after Maniac slowly began to blend back into the crowd of onlookers, until he could no longer be seen. While the confrontation with Maniac had been sudden, in secret, and a challenge to every reason he considered himself to be a man worth fearing, the familiarity of danger had felt like a mild intoxicant. "The crooked politicians had theirs. So did all these crooked cops. I think the mayor and city council should sit down with us. The ones the youth gon' listen to. Let us run the rec centers. We got all these rappers, singers, comedians, and ball players, comin' outta Philly... why not put them in the position to stop this violence that everybody claim to want? If O and Crakk showed up at any rec center in the city, it'll be standin' room only. All of these cops out there put together couldn't do that. It's about influence. So that's what I wanted to say today. Every mayor in this country need to let the balance of power shift. Give some to the people that really got the streets. Print that in y'all papers."

Kyzer turned his back to the news reporters, and only made it three steps, before several police officers, and some detectives, surrounded him. Still standing beside him, Oschino handed over his cell phone, with an urgency that Kyzer needed to take the call, before he was taken into custody. Holding the cell phone to his ear, as one police officer grabbed him by the arm, Kyzer heard a revelation from Freeway that made him sick to his stomach.

"Brittany got killed last night."

No.

No.

As Kyzer handed Oschino his cell phone, and was surrounded by more detectives and cops, then quickly ushered over to the curb, where an unmarked police car had been waiting, his thoughts were on one ultimate goal . . .

Euthanasia.

Chapter Twenty-Five

For Kyzer, the weeks that followed Brittany's funeral were a blur. The autopsy had revealed that Brittany had been five and half weeks pregnant and carrying twins. Kyzer had fallen into a routine of depressive behavior. He rarely left his house, and with the unwelcomed sight of random new reporters, each time he cared to look out of one of his windows, it only encouraged him to submerge deeper into his pool of grief and depression.

In three and a half weeks, Kyzer had only been out of his house a total of five times, and two of those occasions had happened on the same day. He had gone to the airport one Thursday morning, to meet and talk with Zainab, before her flight to New Orleans, and that afternoon, he had gone to West Philadelphia, to visit the mother of Brittany's old boyfriend. Him and his attorney had been summoned to police headquarters twice in one week, where Kyzer, again, had refused to say where he had been, after being shot, and who the men were that had chased him and shot at him. Besides that, Kyzer's only other reason for leaving his house, was to throw a Molotov cocktail through the upstairs window of Honey's apartment in West Philadelphia.

There was an arrest warrant out for Honey. The surveillance footage from the cameras inside of Gossip

Alley had clearly shown her involvement in Brittany's abduction, and a camera outside in the parking lot had captured images of her and Rohan forcing Brittany into the back seat of his SUV, then pulling out of the parking lot erratically.

Brittany's death, the mysterious man responsible for it, and the impact of Kyzer's unexpected return, had all become the perfect ingredients for several conspiracy theories to begin. There were now so many truths, woven into the ugly fabric of lies, gossip, and speculations, the detectives handing Brittany's homicide, were sharing information with the detectives that had been given the tumultuous task of figuring out why so many people had lost their lives at Kyzer's sister's house two years earlier. Gossip Alley had been closed down, and its employees, since video footage had shown Brittany speaking to them all, moments before Honey had kidnapped her, were all now under close watch, and being questioned about anything, and everything, that had to do with Gossip Alley, and its owner.

Zainab was released, after several hours of intense interrogation. Her gun permit, and the surveillance footage from her cousin's house, had prevented the detectives from charging her with anything. Brittany's death had stolen all of her resilience. Aware that the horrific night was all her cousin's husband's doing, but revealing none of this to the authorities, it was only when Kyzer had returned that next morning, did she decide to meet Kyzer, and confide in him all that she had known.

With everyone's intentions exposed, and new odds facing them all, certain streets of North Philadelphia were now tombs with traffic lights. A group of teenagers from the Tenth and Thompson housing projects had designated themselves Maniac's new breed of killers, and were leaving behind some gruesome crime scenes. A week earlier, a young mother and child were found dead in the neighborhood playground on 6th and Jefferson. Both had been strangled and placed on the swings. An older lady had gotten curious at the sight of the mother and child, because at almost three in the morning, with the temperatures dipping lower and lower, it had seemed odd to the woman that the mother and child would still be swinging on the swing set, without being one bit bothered by the chill of the night air. That next day, a young couple were shot to death at the neighborhood Chinese store. That afternoon, a girl from the neighborhood was found dead in a bathroom stall at an area high school. She had been stabbed twenty-nine times, and the number ten had been carved into her forehead.

On Halloween, while riding their four-wheelers beneath the 9th Street bridge, Malik, Haneef, Uzi, and Rashad, had crossed paths with seven, young women, who were all wearing Halloween masks. The one wearing the Nicki Minaj mask had opened fire on them as the four-wheelers sped by, and began their turn down Master Street. A three minute shootout had ensued, with no one being hit by a bullet.

A mobile-police unit had been placed in front of the Tenth and Thompson housing project. There were several scaffolds standing against the face of the high-rise building, and four porta-potties were at the curb. A construction crew had been on the sight, and working most mornings and afternoons, since the now-infamous attack on the housing project.

While the streets in Philadelphia were dangerously unsafe, and seemingly getting worse, since Kyzer's speech at City Hall, the entire nation had responded to his suggestions with favorable views. He was wanted on talk shows, and radio stations, and on social media, more and more music artists all across the country were expressing their willingness to participate in his vision. Sadly, since Brittany's funeral, Kyzer wanted nothing to do with anyone, or anything. The losses of his sister, Camay, and his mother, had become mixed with the despair he felt from him losing Brittany. All of her things at his house had gone untouched, even the sheets on his bed. Every trace of Brittany was exactly the way she had left it.

After Brittany's private funeral, Kyzer had been clear with everyone in attendance, that he wanted no contact with anyone. He had made an exception with Zainab, and that was only because he had wanted a description of Brittany's killer, and so he could learn as much as he could about Splash's motives. As Kyzer was lamenting, he was also subconsciously getting himself prepared for the inevitable journey he had to take down the path of retaliation.

Chapter Twenty-Six

A month later . . .

Kyzer pretended not to notice all of the stares, and the finger-pointing, as he approached the front desk in the county prison's visiting room, and handed over his pass. His face was serious and unreadable. The two corrections officers, and everyone else in the crowded, visiting room, kept their eyes on him as he used his cane to walk down to the last aisle. He was favoring his right leg, and moving at a moderate pace.

There was a puzzled expression on the inmate's face, who Kyzer stopped and slowly sat beside. The inmate looked to the prison guards at the desk, then around at everyone else, then put his eyes back on Kyzer, who, for a very long moment, kept his eyes staring ahead.

"Fam, I think you made a mistake."

"I'm here, 'cause you made one," Kyzer clarified, still staring forward. He waited until the tears in his eyes vanished, and his hands stopped their shaking, before he turned to look the man in the eyes, who played a part in his mother's death. "Instead of pressin' pause, when you 'n ya man 'n 'em saw my mom was wit' Tia, y'all still went ahead and did the job y'all ol' head sent y'all here to do."

The man from Detroit became tense. His eyes cut to the corrections officers, and his hands became fists in his lap.

He was ready to fight, if he had to. When Kyzer switched his cane to his other hand, he turned in his seat, and eyed Kyzer warily.

"When you call home tonight, ya mom gon' tell you she gotta guest from Philly at the house. You gon' let her know he's there to protect her. Now, sit the fuck back and relax, because while I'm fuckin' talkin' to you, you ain't gon' be sittin' there, like you about to throw some fuckin' punches at me."

After the man from Detroit unclenched his fists and sat back, Kyzer took his own moment to force himself to calm down. He didn't want his temper to derail his reasons for being there, because if that was to happen, plans he had for the future would never see the light of day.

"So, this my position," Kyzer said, as he laid his cane across his lap and cleared his throat. There was fear in the man's eyes, and it made him feel good. "That hit wasn't on my mom. What Tia and her husband did to ya ol'head peoples was business, just like what y'all did to her was business. I mean, like, what happened to my mom wasn't personal, right?"

The man from Detroit shook his head.

"Good answer," Kyzer commented, taking a moment to study the man beside him. The orange jumpsuit was several sizes too big on the man, and he assumed they were close in age, but it was the need for a haircut, and a trim to his moustache, that made the man from Detroit appear to be in his mid-thirties. "Business, or personal, y'all killed my mom, man. Now, I know you already know what happened to ya ol'head. That wasn't my work, though. Believe it or not, chicks did that shit. I gotta little satisfaction, but it ain't nothin' like hurtin' the mu'fuckers who put in the work. Hurtin' they peoples 'n shit like that. I'm about fairness in that area. My mom . . . ya mom. And trust me, the nigga I got in that house on Cherry Lawn

Street, can get real psychedelic when he want to. So, if you tip, it's gon' turn into a hostage situation, and ya mom ain't gettin' saved. Her life depend on you right now, and how well you can convince me that you're sorry for killin' my fuckin' mom, and that you can pull this favor off that I need from you."

"Dog, listen, I—"

"Kyzer . . . my name Kyzer."

"Kyzer, look . . . not my mom. She a pastor. I'm sorry. Okay? We fucked up. We been here for a year. We started gettin' tired of Philly, and-My man uncle said we couldn't come back to Detroit, 'til we handled the job. My mom all I got."

"How much do her life mean to you?"

"Everything, man. That's my mom. She mean everything to me."

"You think ya mom worth more than mine?"

"That ain't . . . naw, that's not—"

"Nigga, a million of ya fuckin' mom don't equal one of mine. Know that pussy. Y'all killed her by my sister grave. It took all of y'all to rock two women? Nigga, I can make this whole jail close in on you tonight. I can promise a nigga in here a fuckin' lawyer, and he'll down you in ya fuckin' sleep."

True.

"Who you got in Detroit, that'chu can get to travel to Philly?"

"All I got is my mom. My name dirt in Schoolcraft, now that niggaz know I ain't stand tall on this shit."

"I need 'ju to think of somebody."

"I ain't—"

"Listen to me," Kyzer demanded, becoming frustrated. He let out a sigh as he placed his cane on the floor and moved forward in the seat, preparing himself to stand. "When you get back to ya cell, you gon' think long and hard of somebody you can get to come here. It gotta be a nigga. Let 'cha mom life be ya fuckin' motivation. Now, when that fuckin' lightbulb go off in ya head, and you think of somebody, write 'em and tell then you need 'em to get to Philly ASAP."

"For what, though? If you give me an idea of—"

"So, they can come here wit 'chu."

"Here? You—"

"I need them to come here and catch a meatball case."

"You want me to get somebody to travel all the way here from Detroit, so they can go to jail? Ain't nobody tryna do no shit like that for they own mom, let alone mine."

"It's twenty-five thousand in it for 'em."

"What's in it for me?"

"Nigga, ya fuckin' mom. How the fuck she mean so fuckin' much to you, but soon as you hear about some paper gettin' passed off, you forgettin' why it's a stranger in her house, ready to do her dirty. Whoever you get to come, gettin' twenty-five stacks, and ya mom get to live."

"I just thought of somebody."

"Who?"

"My cousin, Tone. He'll come. Why you want him here, though?"

"I'm playin' somebody in chess, and I need ya cousin to be one of my pieces in here."

"Why can't it be me?"

Kyzer used his cane to rise to his feet. The man from Detroit remained seated. He wanted to finish negotiating.

"You on a protective custody block," Kyzer reminded the guy, as he took a moment to glance around at the different people in the visiting room. He was getting stares again. "One of the most dangerous niggaz in this city is here, and you here for killin' his wife. That's the real reason they got'chu where you at. Mark my words, he gon' hear that I was here to see you. They was tryna put us in that little room, but I paid to keep that from goin' down. I needed us to be seen. Like I said, I'm playin' chess. When ya cousin get here, I'm gon' position him on the same block as the nigga I'm talkin' about. Eventually, they gon' become cellies. Eventually, he gon' think he can trust ya cousin. He gon' mention you."

"How you know?"

" 'Cause, I'ma visionary. I know dude. His wife meant as much to him, as ya mom mean to you, and my mom meant to me. That's the weakness I'm gon' use against him. It's gon' seem random, but when he open up to ya cousin, ya cousin gon' offer to take protective custody, so he can get close to you, and rock you to sleep. The plan gon' get that nigga dick hard. The whole time ya cousin in there, though, ya cousin gon' be doin all the cookin', and lacin' his juice wit' anti-freeze. He'll be dead in a month. "

"Damn."

"One of the guards gon' slip my number in ya cell tonight. Send it to ya cousin, and tell him to call me when he get here. If this shit go any further than me 'n you, ya mom death on ya hands, and I'm gon' have half the jail tryna take protective custody, just to get close to you. Oh, yeah, stop drinkin' that juice main man in seventeen cell keep givin' you. That shit ain't taste funny to you?"

The man grabbed his stomach as Kyzer slowly walked away with his cane. A look of panic was on his face as he stared at Kyzer's back. His thoughts came to his mother, her safety, and his own, then to the white inmate on his unit, who had suddenly began to be nice to him days earlier, by offering him large cups of Hawaiian Punch with ice. Over at the exit, another visitor held the door open for Kyzer, as he made a point to make final eye contact across the giant visiting room with the man from Detroit. As he backed out of the door, Kyzer held his cane like it was a shotgun and aimed it at the guy from Detroit, and with everyone in the visiting room watching, he pretended to rack it and shoot it, until the door closed and he was gone.

Outside, in the county prison's parking lot, Kyzer stopped beside the driver's side door of a white, Chevy Impala. When the window came down, Kyzer handed over five, one hundred dollar bills.

"Anytime, okay?"

Kyzer nodded his head at the female, corrections officer, and walked away. She was pretty and looked to be his type, but she was the daughter of a staff sergeant at the county prison, and that was the only real reason Kyzer was interested in her. She was just another one of his chess pieces; actually, she was his queen, thanks to Zainab.

That afternoon, Kyzer had visited the Southwest Philadelphia cemetery, where his mother and older sister were buried. He had left behind flowers for them both. Before leaving, he had gone to Brittany's gravesite, and had done the same thing. However, it was over Brittany's gravesite, that Kyzer left a promise, and several tears.

As Kyzer pulled Brittany's BMW to a sudden stop, he sighed at the unwelcomed sight of his aunt's car in his driveway. Her car was parked behind his, and she hadn't come alone.

"I know that ain't Millions wit' 'er," Kyzer wondered, as he put Brittany's car in reverse, and slowly backed out of his driveway, and down to the street. The muslim woman in his aunt's passenger seat, seemed to have the impression that he was pulling away, and was lifting her face veil as she hurried out of his aunt's car. "Who the fuck is that? Why the fuck she all hype?"

Kyzer stepped out of the car, and stood there at the bottom of his lawn, as his aunt and the unfamiliar woman stormed down his driveway and cut across his lawn towards him.

"Ask him, Miss Angie! He probably can't even look you in ya fuckin' eyes!!"

"Where is Idris, Kyzer?! I wanna know what'chu did to my fuckin' son!!"

Kyzer and his aunt locked eyes as she brought her angry face within inches of his, and snatched his cane from his hand. The smell of alcohol was on her breath, and the traces of cocaine in her nostrils, made Kyzer put his eyes on the woman standing behind his aunt. There was traces of cocaine in the woman's nostrils as well. Eyes back on his aunt, Kyzer made a reach for his cane, but his aunt held it away.

"Where is my fuckin' son?"

"Aunt Ang, gimme my cane," Kyzer demanded, as he made another attempt to take his cane back. After this try, his aunt pulled the cane back and held it as if she was ready to hit him with it. "Don't hit me wit' that cane, Aunt Ang."

"Why won't 'chu answer ya aunt fuckin' question?"

"Bitch, mind ya fuckin' business! You need to pull ya nikab back down, and hide them fuckin' sins you got in ya nose! Aunt Ang, gimme my cane, man!"

"Where is ya cousin, Kyzer? Tell me."

"I don't know!"

"Tamika, get my gun out the car."

Heeding to Kyzer's aunt's request, the muslim woman backed away a few feet, then ran up and across Kyzer's lawn, and over to his driveway, where his aunt's car was parked. Kyzer looked at his aunt in disbelief as he pushed pass her and started walking up his lawn. He had a gun on his waist, but the last thing he wanted to do, was get into a shootout with his aunt. He thought that if he made it to his house fast enough, and was inside, maybe his aunt would think twice about doing whatever her intoxicated mind was considering.

"Don't run now, Mr. Bad Ass! No! Tamika, hurry up!"

Kyzer's aunt stumbled as she threw Kyzer's cane at his back. Limping and only steps away from his front door, Kyzer frowned in pain as he fumbled with his house keys. The gunshot wound to his right hip was sending waves of discomfort up and down his leg as he limped closer to his front door. Unfortunately, he wasn't nearly as fast as his aunt, or the woman coming with the pearl-handled, chrome, 38 pistol.

There had always been bad blood between Kyzer and his aunt. She was his mother's youngest sister, but there had always been some speculation that she may not actually be the true daughter of Kyzer's grandfather. After divorcing his grandmother, his grandfather had moved to Locust Grove, Georgia, and had remarried. The family skeleton, after Kyzer's grandfather's death, was that his grandfather's wife had already been three months pregnant, and that his grandfather, so much in love with the southern woman, had chosen to claim the unborn child as his very own. On his death bed, Kyzer's grandfather had shared this truth with Kyzer's mother.

Kyzer had overheard the conversation, while he had been sitting outside of his grandfather's bedroom. From the young age of ten, Kyzer had been successful at keeping the secret, not once even mentioning it to his mother, but when his aunt and cousin, Idris, had moved to Philadelphia, and his cousin had made a joke about Kyzer's father being in jail, upset, Kyzer had attacked his cousin, and had yelled out their family secret for everyone on the basketball court to hear. That evening, Kyzer's mother and aunt had gotten into a heated argument of their own. From that day on, the rift between Kyzer and his aunt only grew wider, because her son couldn't stay out of Kyzer's shadow, no matter how hard she tried to keep them apart. Her own life was in disarray. There was no disputing the fact that she was a beautiful woman. In the mid-1980s, she had married a popular, Jamaican, drug dealer, named Owen, who, after a year of them being married, had suddenly disappeared from the face of the earth. Kyzer's aunt hadn't been the same since. Her crowd of friends always changed, according to her choice of drug that month.

Inside of his house, and slightly winded, Kyzer disarmed his home alarm system, then turned to face his aunt. She was tapping her gun against her thigh, and appeared to be considering what to do next. To even the stakes, and clarify how far he was willing to let things go, Kyzer exhaled a long sigh and pulled out his own gun.

"You the bitch that called me that night I got shot," Kyzer acknowledged, glaring at the woman, standing beside his aunt, who, now that he had a gun in his hand, seemed a lot more calmer and respectful. He then leveled his stare on his aunt's bloodshot eyes. "So, you gotta daughter-in-law, you can get high wit' now, huh? If I shot 'chu right now, Aunt Ang, you think she'd wanna die wit 'chu? Aunt Ang, this what I do. I fuckin' guarantee you, if I tore ya stomach up with this forty, and stood over you, and gave you everything else to ya face, this bitch'll be on her fuckin' knees, beggin' for her fuckin' life. Did 'ju talk to Mill about Drees? How this bitch word hold more rank, than the daughter-in-law, who gave you gran' kids? Ask Mill where the fuck Drees at."

"I did. I did, before I met Tamika. I did, because I felt it in the fuckin' pit of my goddamn stomach, that something was wrong with my fuckin' son."

Teardrops began to spill from Kyzer's aunt's eyes.

"Kyzer, make me understand, how my only child . . . my only fuckin' child, after never missin' a day of not callin' his mother, could go for almost two months, without callin' me? And-And another fuckin' thing, why in the hell would he tell Tamika that if somethin' ever was to happen to him, to blame you? That just fuckin' baffles me. And you really wanna know what else fuckin' baffles me? That Jamillah ain't makin' a big deal about where Idris is. Guess who the fuck is, Kyzer? She is . . . her. That's why her word is above anything Jamillah might say right now, and yours. Now I'ma ask you one more time. Where is my fuckin' son?"

"I don't fuckin' know."

"You see?"

"I see what?"

"Just how you don't seem to give a fuck. You can hold some fuckin' press conference about – About some gun violence in fuckin' Philly, but not for one second, did 'ju care to mention that Idris was missin'."

"Aunt Ang, why would I, when I didn't think somethin' was wrong with him! So, because me or Mill ain't actin' all goofy like you, that make us less credible in ya eyes?! Man, you trippin'! What we need to be doin' some lines of cocaine wit'chu, to appear innocent?! Man, get the fuck outta my house!"

"This shit far from over Kyzer. I swear . . . I'll go to the police."

"You can go to the fuckin' pope," Kyzer argued, as his aunt gave him a malicious stare, while she ushered her daughter-in-law over to his front door. He limped behind them slowly. "And you, naw, hold the fuck up. Let me see ya ID. You not gon' know where the fuck I live, and I'm not gon' know where you lay ya mu'fuckin' head at."

The woman looked cautiously at Kyzer's aunt, then to Kyzer, as Kyzer's aunt snatched open the front door.

"My pocketbook out in the car. It's in there."

"Get it, then."

As the woman stepped by Kyzer's aunt, and went out the door, there was a new concern in her eyes. While going across the lawn, she pulled her face veil down to hide her fresh tears.

"Kyzer, I'm serious about what the fuck I said. I'll go to the cops."

In his doorway, Kyzer ignored his aunt and stared out at the center of his lawn, where his cane was. He hoped his aunt was only bluffing, and internally, wanted to say more to convince her that he had nothing to do with his cousin's disappearance. But he was too mad to say anything more to her. When her daughter-in-law returned, he took her driver's license, memorized the address, then threw it as far across his lawn as he could, before slamming his front door on their faces.

Mistakes.

Chapter Twenty-Seven

Awakened by the sound of someone knocking incessantly at his front door, Kyzer climbed out of bed and stormed over to a window in his bedroom that provided a view of the front of his house. When he moved the curtain aside and parted the blinds with his fingers, he got the shock of his life. The sight of the mayor of Philadelphia, standing there, knocking on his front door, as two men in dark suits, who were obviously his security detail, stood a few feet behind him, gave Kyzer's skin goose bumps, and a quick heartbeat.

Since Kyzer's impromptu speech at City Hall, the mayor had been silent, at least to the public, about what he personally felt about Kyzer's idea of bringing some peace to the city of Philadelphia. Despite Kyzer's own silence afterwards, he was still in high demand, and many people in high places were now intrigued to hear more of what he had to say.

The paradox of it all now, as Kyzer knew full well, was that he was in no mood for peace, or being an advocate for it. For a moment, he considered ignoring the mayor's knocking, and climbing back into bed, but the curiosity of what the mayor wanted with him eventually got the best of him.

Challenges.

"This is a really nice house."

"My sister left it to me."

"I'm sorry to hear about what happened to her . . . and your mother. Your story, and what you had to say last month has a lot of people raising some new questions, Kyzer. That's why I'm here."

"Why you ain't come here last month?" Kyzer asked, looking over his shoulder to watch as one of the men with the mayor admired the tall suit of armor, standing over at the entrance of his living room. His partner was a few feet away, keeping a close eye on him and the mayor, and after making eye contact with him, he turned his attention back to the mayor, who was seated across from him on the couch. "And I'm only askin' that, 'cause, like, to be honest wit 'chu, after what 'chu just said, I'm left to assume you only hear to holla at me, 'cause other people gettin' in ya ear. Is that what it is?"

The mayor of Philadelphia was in his mid-50s, black, and had an approachable demeanor about him. His name was Phillip Reed, and he was born and raised in North Philadelphia. He was a Democrat, and many of the citizens in the city gave him good approval ratings, but like with any politician, certain decisions he had made, since he had been in office as mayor, wasn't sitting well with everyone. One in particular, was his choice to remove the funding for a majority of the neighborhood swimming pools and recreation centers.

Mayor Reed was a man with a vision of his own for Philadelphia. He recently returned from a mayor's conference that was held in South Carolina, and even there, a questioner had raised the question of how successful he though Kyzer's ideas would be, if his city, and others, were to enlist a handful of their local music artists, as go-betweens to reach the youth.

The mayor's response, then, as it was when the same question was introduced at a forum with Philadelphia's city council weeks earlier, had been the same; it sounded plausible, and worth giving some serious consideration.

Politics.

"My job as the mayor comes with a lot of huge responsibilities. Day in and day out, even before I started my term, my goals have always been to ensure the citizens in our city of some form of hope. I visit shelters, hospitals, churches, senior centers . . . small business owners. Kyzer, I come from a single-parent home. I saw my mother struggle. Me and her shared peanut butter sandwiches for breakfast, lunch, and dinner, for a week straight. I'm not just some mayor, who's walking the walk. I was born and raised on 18th and Master. This city means a lot to me. So understand, while I may agree with your suggestion, and care enough about Philadelphia to pretty much try anything, why should you be the person I hand over that kind of control to? I spoke to the police commissioner last night, Kyzer. He thinks it's a bad idea. I'm not particularly sold on you being the face of this idea myself, and I'll tell you why."

"You ain't even gotta waste ya breath."

The mayor raised his eyebrows and gave Kyzer a quizzical stare. He let out a short sigh of exasperation.

"I been off that idea," Kyzer spoke, slowly rising from his ottoman, and standing up. He stuffed his hands into the pockets of his bathrobe. "And I'm definitely not gon' let 'chu fuck up my mornin', by runnin' down all the reasons why you ain't feelin' me. Not in my house. Not gon' happen. See, if I wanted to bring the kind of peace to this city, you and the commissioner tryin' so hard to get, I could do it on my own. I know wit' corners beefin' wit' each other. I know the dudes who run the streets ya cops can't get out on in the middle of the night, wit' out back up. That's the influence I got. I'm decent wit' the rappers. And if I don't know 'em, I know somebody that do. I can jump on social media right now . . . chaos. You seen my work. I ain't in it for the fame, or the glitz. Look at my house. I'm good. I was in it for the city. It's cryin'. What's sad is, you or the fuckin' commissioner ain't got what it take to stop the tears. Have a nice day, Mayor Reed."

The mayor stood, then after a long look at Kyzer, and his security detail, who were still admiring the things in Kyzer's Louis XIV-styled foyer, a war of thoughts seemed to bother him as he sat back down. His eyes stayed on the spot of the white, mink rug, between his shoes, until the heat of Kyzer's stare got the best of him, and he looked up.

"I received an e-mail from a federal judge in Maryland last night. Patricia Best. If you recall, her daughter was a detective here, and her body was found in Fairmount Park a few months back. She spoke highly of your girlfriend, Kyzer. It appears that her daughter, your girlfriend, and the woman, who was killed with your mother, were in possession of some evidence that a detective in the police de—"

"Hold up," Kyzer interrupted, holding up his hand to stop the mayor from continuing. He was past ready for the mayor and his two employees to get out of his house. "Ain't none of what 'chu sayin' any of my business. None of it. I didn't know that detective, and I don't know her mom. Whatever my girl and her boss had goin' on wit' them, wasn't none of my—"

"You're misunderstanding me. That's not—"

"The door that way."

"Hear me out."

"Man, the door that way."

The mayor stood.

Kyzer stared at his hand when he extended it for a handshake. Kyzer kept his hands inside of the pockets of his bathrobe, and held the mayor's stare.

"Since my face ain't good enough for progress, neither is my hand."

Chapter Twenty-Eight

"How long I been sleep?"

"Two hours and some change. You need the rest."

"Damn," Sabia groaned, slowly turning to sit up straight in the passenger seat of his Audi station wagon. He clenched his jaws, until the unbearable pain in his legs subsided enough for him to stare over the dashboard and out at the road ahead. "Yo, where the fuck-Rohan?! Why the fuck you drivin' back to Philly?! Yo, take me the fuck back to Jersey, to my fuckin' mom, dog! Ay, Rohan?!"

"Let me do me, Bia."

Sabia knew Rohan too well, and knew that under his calm response, a rage was on the horizon. Still, Rohan's temper and wishes for revenge could end both of their legacies as fugitives. Sabia was grateful to be alive, grateful for Rohan's loyalty, and grateful that Rohan had gotten his mother out of Philadelphia safely. In his eyes, Rohan had done enough.

In Rohan's eyes, he hadn't. The agony his heart had felt the night he had finally found Sabia's unconscious, rat-covered body, and had thought that he had gotten to Sabia too late, and had failed him, it had triggered some past memories deep down in this soul. His yell had echoed through all of the sewer tunnels in North Philadelphia.

Rohan had killed some of the rats with his bare hands. To him, Sabia was much more than just a fugitive bother. To Rohan, since his path had crossed Sabia's, Sabia had unknowingly become the reincarnation of the younger brother he had lost back in Haiti during the devastating earthquake, years earlier.

The early morning clouds were peppered across the blue sky, and the sun was giving off a bright shine, as Rohan drove Sabia's Audi station wagon over the Walt Whitman Bridge into Philadelphia. It was November 6th, and it was windy and cold. In three days, seven people had been murdered; one, a grandmother, unloading her groceries from her car, outside of her home.

"Ro, I promised my mom I'd introduce her to Kim. She wanna be there wit' me when my son born, Ro."

"Bia, it'll still all happen."

"Not if you don't take the next exit, and turn around. Fuck them niggaz. Ro, we got more to lose, than any of them mu'fuckers."

"I want Kyzer."

Sabia gave Rohan an incredulous look. His eyes became watery as he accepted what he knew Rohan failed to realize. An attempt to kill Kyzer was going to be far from easy, given that he was certain of Kyzer's instincts becoming much more sharper, after his near-death experience. Him and his mother had watched Kyzer's speech at City Hall together. Sabia's own instincts were warning him that, if him and Rohan went looking for trouble, it was going to find them first.

As his tears rolled down his face, Sabia stared to his right, and looked out at the Delaware river. He thought of his mother, his fiancé, and their unborn son, who he was sure he would never get to meet.

"Where my gun at, Ro?"

"Still under ya seat."

Sabia let out a sigh and closed his eyes. He wasn't in any condition to do anything. The doctor Rohan had taken him to in Lawnside, New Jersey, had saved his life, but there had been no saving his legs, or his lower, left arm. His two legs were only mid-thigh now, and his left arm ended at his elbow. When he had spoken to his wife, she had cried long and hard, and only wanted him back home with her, and no where else. She promised to take care of him and his mother. The sweetness of her promise made more tears spill as he closed his eyes and wondered which parent his son would look like.

"Go to they headquarters, Ro."

"Indeed."

Life is a gift.

Death is a promise.

As Sabia and Rohan were entering Philadelphia in Sabia's bulletproof Audi station wagon, Kyzer was at home, preparing to leave. After using a rubber band to gather all of his individual braids into a ponytail, he stopped at the bottom of his bed and stared once more at the large map of Philadelphia. His eyes focused on a spot in South Philadelphia. As he stood there, in deep thought, he readjusted the straps on the right side of his bulletproof vest, then he walked around to the side of the bed, where Brittany's open diary was.

"Last night, I had a dream Kyzer came back," Kyzer read, after picking up Brittany's diary from the night stand. His eyes blurred with tears, as he followed Brittany's cursive handwriting. "When we hugged, he held me for so long. It seemed so real. I could feel his tears falling on my neck. He kept telling me how much he loved me, and how much he missed me. He made a promise to never leave me again. I knew he meant it. I know Kyzer alive. I don't care what nobody else think or say. Okay, well, let me start my day. I got everybody meeting me at the club this morning. I need something to distract me. I think I'm going to finally tell Zainab that I'm pregnant. I know she'll be excited to hear the good news."

Some tears splashed on the diary as Kyzer returned it to the night stand. Walking away, Kyzer gave his bedroom one sweeping glance, as he put on a zip-up, Rock, Paper & Denim hoodie, covering his thermal shirt, and bulletproof vest. Out in the hallway, while walking, he answered his ringing cell phone.

"Yo?"

"Ya chess piece from Detroit just landed. I got him on the other line."

"Alright, stick to the script. I changed my mind on the location. Make it Fifth and Carpenter."

"Ain't no eyes in the sky there, either?"

"Naw, plus I wanna watch how everything go, after y'all pull off."

"Say no more. See you in a couple of hours."

"Alright."

Kyzer pocketed his cell phone as he headed down the steps to the first floor of his house. He winced as an explosion of pain shot down his leg. He had been walking without the cane for a few days, but at random times of the day and night, the pain of the gunshot wound to his left hip would remind him that, although his wound had healed on the surface, he still wasn't fully back to being in perfect shape.

At the end of his foyer, Kyzer stopped and stuck his feet one at a time in his blue, Brooks, track sneakers. Stepping away, he looked down at Brittany's own similar pair, remembering the day she had purchased them on-line, while they had been eating dinner in bed.

Outside, Kyzer pulled out his cell phone as he took the path that led to his driveway. The fresh air was cold and unforgiving to his skin, and he thought for a second about going back into his house for a winter hat, but ignored the urge at the sound of his cousin's voice.

"Yo, cousin?"

"Leek, let everybody know I'ma be at the Chrome Depot at nine, and it's important for everybody to be there, alright?"

"I'm on it. My mom cussed Aunt Ang out this mornin'."

"Yeah? What happened?"

"She came by, tryin' to turn my mom against you."

"Aunt Neece ain't goin' for that."

"You already know. Aunt Ang left steamin'."

Kyzer switched his cell phone to his opposite ear as he walked by his Cadillac ATS. He considered parking it inside of his garage, as he got to the driver's door of Brittany's BMW, and pulled it open.

"So, you back, huh?"

"Like I never left, Leek," Kyzer answered, while pulling the driver's door shut. The aroma of Brittany's still-lingering perfume scrambled all of his thoughts momentarily, until another urgent matter pushed its way into his mind. "Remember I told you about the situation wit' Brittany old boyfriend mom? And what I was thinkin' about doin'?"

"Yeah, I remember. What 'chu tryna set it in motion?"

"In a way I am, but, then, it's like, I'm still—"

"Faheem and Wakil wit' me. Neef is, too. All you gotta do is press the button, and we all over it.

"Alright, we'll talk tonight."

"Nine, right?"

"Niggaz gon' be snappin'. My mom told Aunt Ang you our new family hero."

"That's 'cause Aunt Neece played a big part in groomin' me. She know what the fuck I'm made of, Leek. Yo, I'ma see you at nine, though, alright?"

"Alright, cousin."

After starting Brittany's car, Kyzer reversed out of his driveway. On the I-95 expressway, he activated the Bluetooth in Brittany's car and accepted the incoming phone call from Rock 'n Roll Rhonda.

"Rhonda, what's up?"

"You alone?"

"That's the new story of my life, Rhonda. Besides my niggaz, and my family, and I mean the ones that's really for me, it's just me 'n my gun."

"Kyzer, they found my uncle body last night. Zay just met my cousin, Liberty, at the airport, down New Orleans. Kyzer, I need a favor."

"Let's hear it."

"Okay, so this bitch full name is Victoria Beauvais. Her sons on her top. She got they dad kidnapped 'n rocked. His body ain't never been found, but ol' head definitely outta here, though. His oldest son took over his business. The youngest son got sent out Boston. This bitch come from this family that's into voodoo 'n all'lat crazy shit, Kyzer. Think about it . . . my uncle never, ever, fucked wit' black chicks. Like, never. A couple times, me 'n Tia talked about how weird my uncle used to be about this bitch. Kyzer, she got this lipstick . . . she kiss you, you under her spell."

The right corner of Kyzer's mouth turned up in disbelief, as he continued to drive south on the expressway.

"Uncle Tuna was under her spell. Kyzer, they took all of his insides outta his body. Zay said . . . "

Kyzer let out a sigh when Rock 'n Roll Rhonda started to cry. He knew that her uncle had been like a father figure to her, and felt some sympathy for what she was going through. However, there was no way he was allowing himself to believe that her uncle's girlfriend was in possession of lipstick that could put someone under her control. It was too movie-like for him.

"Kyzer, the oldest son gotta hair salon on Marshall Street."

"Marshall and what?"

"Girard . . . it just opened. His name is Baseer."

"Baseer?" Kyzer echoed, trying to place a name to a face, as he moved over into the next lane on his left. He knew a Baseer from South Philly, but hadn't seen or heard anything about him since he was in his teens. "I know a Baseer, but he from South Philly. He definitely not from North."

"This one from South Philly."

"Which side?"

"The lower numbers."

"He got green eyes and freckles on his face?"

"I'm not sure, but I can find out. Kyzer, can you go by that hair salon for me?"

"And do what?"

"Find out what 'chu can about that bitch, Victoria. See if you can find out where she at for me. Zay should be back in a few days."

"What's the name of the salon?"

"That, I don't know. Just ask for Baseer. His girlfriend name is Breen."

"Baseer and Breen?"

"Thank you, Kyzer. We really appreciate it."

"Don't mention it. Just hurry up 'n get 'cha ass back out here. I could really use your help."

"I'm workin' on it. I'll call you later, okay?"

"When you do, I should have some answers for you."

Done with the phone call, Kyzer concentrated on driving and thinking. He had a real busy day ahead of him. The lingering scent of Brittany's perfume had his heart singing sad tunes, and the gun on his waist had all of his demons cheerful of what they all hoped would come.

With the night, came even colder winds and an alarming dip in the temperature. The sky had become a dark curtain, and the moon itself, was just a glowing dot in the distance.

Kyzer was standing in the doorway of an old friend's house on Carpenter Street, closer to 6th, with his cell phone to his ear. Down at 5th and Carpenter, his friend, Dame, was sitting in his car, speaking with Tone from Detroit, who was under the impression that Dame was him. Dame had his cell phone in his lap, with its speaker activated, so Kyzer could hear what was being said.

"So, who this nigga you want me to get close to?"

"His name Splash. He on A-two-one. You gon' be on quarantine for a minute, though."

"Damn, how long I'ma have to be on that shit."

"About a week . . . I got some folks who gon' speed up ya process. I'm gon' position you on this nigga block."

"How he look?"

"Trust me, you'll know who he is, once you get to the block. This ain't gon' be a rush job. I need'ju to get comfortable. Treat him like you treat everybody else, alright? He a boss. He used to niggaz bein' on his dick. I got five stacks for you to go in wit'. That's for commissary 'n shit like that. Once he see you got'cha own, and you ain't pressed to get in wit' his circle, that'll earn you a little respect from him. Not much, though. He good. You know how to fight?"

"Do I need to? I Can, but I ain't no mu'fuckin' Floyd Mayweather, or no shit like that. Why?"

"Dog, this Philly. Our county jails worse than some of our state jails. You goin' to the "F". You need to know how to fight, dog. It's a must."

Kyzer stared down the street at Tone as he stood outside of Dame's white, GMC Terrain. Tone was a small guy, in height and weight. Kyzer estimated he was about one hundred and forty pounds at the most, and was no taller than five feet four inches tall.

"I gets it in, Fam. Ask my cousin, if you think I'm not about my work."

"This not Detroit. See, what 'chu might consider work where you from, might not even scare one of our fuckin' gran'mothers. Alright, so, look . . . here go the five stacks. Pocket that."

Kyzer watched Tone accept what he knew was the five thousand dollars he had given Dame an hour earlier. Tone stuffed the money into his jacket pocket. He was shifting from foot to foot, trying to keep warm.

"I gotta guard that's gon' get 'chu a jack, as soon as you get out in population. Now, I need you to pay attention, and listen to me closely. The nigga wife got killed by ya cousin. He might wanna down you the first second he find out you from Detroit. You was here, 'cause you met this little Rican bitch on Instagram, alright? When you got to the bitch spot, she tried to line you up."

"What the fuck that mean"

"Dog, the bitch tried to get 'chu robbed."

"And?"

Kyzer held his breath for what he knew was next to come. He grinned as Dame stuck his gloved-hand out of his driver's side window and pointed the barrel of the 38 revolver up to the night sky. Kyzer lowered his cell phone from his ear when the gunshots began. Taken by surprise, and at first, believing that Dame was going to shoot him, Tone had cowered down to the street, and had remained there, until Dame had fired off the last and final bullet.

"Yo, what the—"

"Stay here, 'til the cops come."

Dame tossed Tone the gun.

"Stay here, 'til the cops come?"

"Ain't that what the fuck I just said? Stay here, 'til the fuckin' cops come, nigga. I'll be in touch."

As Dame pulled off, Kyzer watched Tone closely as he stood there, holding the gun at the intersection of 5th and Carpenter. The sound of police sirens suddenly became a part of the distant noise, and while watching Tone and his reaction to hearing the police sirens himself, Kyzer raised his cell phone back to his ear, and listened as Dame laughed on the opposite end of his cell phone.

"Is the nigga still there?"

"Yeah, he a trooper, Dame," Kyzer smiled, watching as Tone talked to himself, while pacing back and forth down the other end of the street. He had to give credit to his chess piece from Detroit, he hadn't turned into a runner, as he had speculated he would. "The nigga down there pacin' back 'n forth, talkin' to himself. He probably like, these niggaz in Philly is shot the fuck out. Alright, oh, shit, yo, here go the cops. Let me blend back in Annie house. I'ma holla at 'chu later. Good lookin'."

"Anytime."

Two hours later, Kyzer stood in the company of men that he most certainly knew loved him, and who he loved back just as equally. The Chrome Depot was packed to its capacity, and it was standing-room only, but no one was doing any complaining. Kyzer's presence was inspirational for some, and for others, it was only an act a legend could manage. It was still difficult to believe that he had never died, and all along, had been somewhere, recuperating, and planning his ultimate return.

"I want more for us," Kyzer shared, as he used Uzi's shoulder to support himself as he stepped up on a chair, so he could be seen by everyone. The intent stares he quickly received fed ambition to every vein running through his body. "Because I do, I have to learn to be a better leader. No matter if I think y'all might not agree wit' my vision, or not, I still gotta keep-I gotta keep us focused, is what I'm tryna say. This neighborhood is somethin', but this shit ain't everything. Some of y'all ain't never been on a fuckin' airplane . . . a yacht, jet skis, one of them fuckin' exotic islands. We got muslims in here, who never made Hajj. All the paper gettin' made, just goin' right back into the hood, and what's bad is, this the only property we can truthfully say is ours. What else belong to us in this neighborhood? Let's keep it a buck, don't none of these corners really fuckin' belong to us. The cops show up, niggaz gotta bounce. We need stores around here. Barber shops, daycare centers . . . fuckin' houses. Look how Temple buyin' up everything for they students. Them mu'fuckers all the way down Thompson Street."

Kyzer became silent for a moment, and looked around at all of the faces that were staring back at him. Many of them were in there late teens, and early twenties, like him.

"We need to tighten up," Kyzer continued, hoping that what he was saying was reaching the hearts of everyone listening. He was responsible for them, because all of them trusted in his leadership and influence. "Some of us ain't cut out for this street shit. You might need to be in a lawyer's office. Who are we? Are we just some neighborhood gang, who can kill shit 'n sell drugs? Is that what we want our sons to grow up 'n be? Do we want our daughters to grow up 'n fall in love wit' a nigga, and his main goal is to control this fuckin' neighborhood? Won't none of us admit that's what we want for ours. None of us. I wanna take us to another level. I got they attention. I want every last one of y'all wit' me, while I put this city on my fuckin' back. I'm settin' up some social media pages tonight. I'm reachin' out to all the rappers 'n singers. The comedians, too. We about to go corporate. We gon' switch up our hustle, and we gon' invest some paper into commercial property. I need niggaz to get on some positive shit. By next summer, nobody should be under fifty stacks, and no fuckin' body should be standin' on none of these fuckin' corners. To do this, we gotta get these wars over wit', so we won't keep gettin' distracted."

"How we do that?" Somebody questioned.

"Tomorrow, we gon' make a list, and we gon' kill everybody on it. No more shootouts. We gon' take a page outta them Italian mu'fuckers book. We run down on 'em, take 'em wit' us, and we bury the mu' fuckers ourselves."

Kyzer.

Maniac.

Sabia.

Many of the neighbors on 8th Street were well aware of the Chrome Depot's presence, and were familiar with the faces that occupied it. Its domain actually made some of the neighbors feel safe. They never had to worry about a burglary, or having one of their vehicles stolen, or deal with the anxiety of someone trying to rob them as they walked to their front doors. The men who frequented the Chrome Depot were security in the neighborhood, who went unpaid for their services. Unfortunately, the comfortability of the neighbors on 8th Street, Darien Street, Franklin Street, and 9th Street, and even those who lived on Oxford and Jefferson, who also shared in this cycle of relaxation at home, were all oblivious to the silent invasion, taking place.

As Rohan steered Sabia's Audi station wagon across Cecil B. Moore Avenue, his eyes spotted several crouching figures, rushing across 8th Street, almost a block away. A second later, another group followed behind the second.

"Bia, you see that?"

"What?"

"When we get to this corner, just peep out the whole scene. Dog, niggaz out here on some swarm shit."

Alert, and forcing away other thoughts, Sabia cut his eyes from right to left, as Rohan made a slow stop at the intersection of 8th and Oxford. He didn't see anything out of the ordinary. When Rohan flexed the fingers of his hand around the handle of the gun in his lap, he shifted uneasily in his passenger seat.

"Bia, keep ya eyes on both of these lots. On ya side and mine."

Sabia took a deep breath as he pressed his head against his head-rest and cut his eyes from right to left, as Rohan drove at a normal rate of speed down 8th Street. His Audi station wagon was built to prevent any damage from handguns, from 45 caliber handguns on down; even his tires and windows. This assurance did nothing for Sabia's nerves, the moment his eyes spotted movement in both abandoned lots Rohan had mentioned.

"You see them niggaz?"

"Yeah," Sabia confirmed, leaning forward some to look at his side-passenger mirror. As Rohan neared the intersection of 8th and Jefferson, he watched as at least fifteen, crouching figures, hurried across 8th Street, to join the first group. "These niggaz out here deep, Ro. The lights on in the Chrome Depot, too. If we go back around, we gon' look suspect. That ain't Kyzer 'n 'em, 'cause them niggaz would've let off on us soon as they seen my wheel. Go down to Master and make a right, then cut up Ninth. I wanna see this shit, Ro. I wonder who them niggaz is."

As Sabia's car was making the turn up Master Street, Kyzer and everyone else was beginning to file out of the rear exit of the Chrome Depot, and disperse in the direction of their cars and SUVs. Darien Street was a narrow block, and with the way some vehicles had been parked, others were unable to move their vehicles, until the cars and SUVs closest to the top and bottom of Darien Street were moved first. The silence of the night had become undone by the chatter of numerous conversations, cars and SUVs coming to life, and when everyone seemed engrossed in the moment, Maniac came running out of an abandoned lot, followed by more than thirty men, all who were unmasked, angry, and carrying machine guns.

The choreography of the attack seemed elementary to Kyzer, until the bottom of Darien Street suddenly became blockaded with the Halloween mask, wearing females, and all of them began running up the block, shooting and trampling up the hoods of some of the parked cars.

Instinctively, Kyzer went down to a crouching position and pulled his gun off of his waist, while looking at everyone, watching, assessing. When his peripheral vision caught a glimpse of Sabia's Audi station wagon coming to a stop down at the bottom of Darien Street, believing his own eyes were lying to him, he remained frozen for another second, then he ran into the center of the shootout, with Uzi and Malik yelling at his back. His brazenness brought them concern. Their yells only made him angrier as he ran up the back of a bullet-riddled car, and over its roof, shooting in all directions that showed him enemy faces. Back down on the sidewalk, Kyzer aimed down the street of Sabia's car and shot four times, then sent a few at the young woman with the Nicki Minaj mask, as they ran around Tauheed's Buick Enclave. The windows on the SUV exploded as their bullets flew through them, one of them only missing Kyzer by mere inches.

Rohan jumped out of Sabia's Audi and returned Kyzer's fire, leaving Sabia behind. His fatal mistake was not staying inside of the bulletproof vehicle, and not questioning Sabia about the Chrome Depot, and why it was named exactly that. Trading gunfire with Kyzer, and standing out in the middle of Darien Street bravely, it was only when Rashad began shooting at him from the roof of the Chrome Depot, did Rohan start to retrace his steps and scramble back to Sabia's car.

Up at the top of the block, Uzi, Malik, Haneef, Wakil, and Aleem, were all running through lots and trading shots with

Maniac and his men. In the middle of the block, using cars and trucks for cover, Dame, F.L, Ern, and Tauheed, were dealing with the women in Halloween masks. In all of the chaos, only Shaka had been hit. Still, he was standing beside the open driver's door of his SUV, throwing bullets at anybody that wasn't on his side, while holding his free hand against the right side of his stomach, where he had been shot.

Sabia could only watch the chaotic scene, and do nothing more than wish Rohan would hurry back to his car in one piece. Suddenly, Rohan's body was slammed violently into the driver's side door, and as his body began to slide downwards, Rohan stared at him blankly. The sound of police sirens started piercing the night air, and Sabia started to hyper-ventilate as he moved into action.

Rashad swiveled the machine gun left and sent a line of fire at the windshield of Sabia's station wagon, causing it to crack into pieces. Seeing that Rohan was still alive, he swiveled the machine gun back right and ripped up Rohan's legs as he managed to climb back into Sabia's Audi and close the door. The sound of approaching police sirens was reason for everyone to start their paths to escaping an arrest. Rashad rose quickly from the roof-top of the Chrome Depot and as he backed away, he spotted Kyzer running west up Jefferson Street. Down below, gunshots were still being exchanged, but now with longer pauses in between them. The sound of cars and trucks speeding away were part of the symphony too.

"Ro, hit the brakes!! Hit the fuckin' brakes!!!"

Rohan took his final breath with Sabia's pleas echoing in his bloody ears. His body slumped forward, and his death grip on the steering wheel sent Sabia's Audi station wagon crashing into the cement face of the Chinese store on Franklin and Jefferson. The impact sent Rohan through the windshield, and Sabia into the backseat. Kyzer witnessed the crash as he raced Brittany's BMW down to the accident, hoping he could beat the cop car he saw racing across the intersection of 5th and Jefferson. Passing 8th Street, he saw cop cars coming in both directions. At Franklin Street, Kyzer reversed Brittany's car into the block and fishtailed it quickly into a parking spot.

Kyzer had believed Sabia was dead. It was one of the only sweet facts Malik had given him at Brittany's funeral. As he ran down Franklin Street and stepped out on Jefferson Street, Kyzer stopped the speeding cop car in its tracks at 7th and Jefferson, by throwing several gunshots at its windshield. Wasting no time, he hurried over to Rohan's lifeless body and put five bullets in his face, then squatted beside Sabia, who had managed to open the back door of his station wagon, and crawl out onto the sidewalk. The sight of Sabia's body made Kyzer stand in shock, but not remorse. Gratified, and feeling Sabia had been dealt the fate he had given so many others, Kyzer smiled and left him alive. Sabia's facial expression became a mask of horror when Kyzer turned his back and took off running. He wanted to die. The thought of going to jail, in the physical shape he was now in, would be harsh and tormenting. He yelled for Kyzer to kill him, but Kyzer never looked back.

In the middle of Franklin Street, Kyzer jumped a fence and ran to the other end of the yard. There, he climbed the fence that faced 7th Street, and winded, and tucking his gun back on his waist, he jogged up to the corner of 7th and Oxford, and met the Septa bus just as it was stopping.

Forcing calmness upon himself, Kyzer walked to the back of the mildly crowded bus, while staring out of its large, rear window. He stared down 7th Street at the cops, as they knocked on doors, and were searching under parked cars with their flashlights. A smile teased Kyzer's lips as he took a seat and bent forward to wipe some grass away from the front of his left sneaker.

If only they knew . . .

Chapter Twenty-Nine

In the early morning hours of Tuesday, November 6th, 2012, heavily armed officers raided Kyzer's Bucks County home, and arrested him for the murder of his cousin, Idris. After his arraignment at police headquarters, Kyzer was then shipped to the intake-county prison, in Northeast Philadelphia, where he was processed, then sent to one of the quarantine units.

Through every stage of the process, Kyzer had been silent. When other inmates, or the prison guards acknowledged him, as he carried his bedroll, he simply nodded his head their way. It was almost two in the morning when he pulled open the door to his assigned cell, and stepped inside. His arrival had awakened his cell mate, who was on the bottom bunk, beneath his blanket and sheets.

"Back to this bullshit," Kyzer thought, after placing his bedroll on the top bunk and walking back over to the door. After pulling the cell door shut, he stood there and looked out at the quarantine, housing unit. "I gotta get a fuckin' phone. This Aunt Ang work. Damn . . . I wasn't even home six fuckin' months."

"Yo, you can cut the light on, if you want."

Kyzer turned and faced his cell mate as he swung his legs out of bed. His voice had sounded oddly familiar. Kyzer flipped up the light switch, and when he saw who his cell mate was, a wave of humiliation washed over his entire body. His cell mate was his chess piece from Detroit; Tone.

"My name Tone."

"I know."

"How you know my name already?"

"Because I hired you. I'm the reason you here. Now listen up."

Espionage.

Sneak Read of . . .

ROCK & ROLL

Coming in Spring 2017

Chapter One

"So, what should I do, if I see Mommy somewhere?"

"What? Party, man, what kinda fuckin' question is that? You better try to blow that bitch head off, if . . ."

With a sigh, Party switched his cell phone to his opposite ear, as he flipped over on his bed, from his side, to his back. For a moment, Party just stared blankly up at the ceiling fan above him, not even paying any attention to the ranting his older brother was doing on the other end of his cell phone.

" . . .Yo, I can't believe you just asked me some nut ass shit like that. Fuck that bitch over. Shoot her in the face as many times as you fuckin' can. Yo, you hear me?"

"Yeah, I hear you, but—"

"But?! Man, it ain't no fuckin buts!"

"Sab, I'm not 'chu!" Party snapped, sitting up in bed. Bottled up emotions started saluting his heart, as words that he had buried deep down inside of his chest, since he had been a child, started to escape his lips. "There, I said it! I'm not 'chu! That's what 'chu wanna hear me say?! You happy, now?! You feel better?! Just 'cause I don't wanna kill Mommy, don't mean I don't hate her as much as you do! That's how you feel, though, right?! Ain't that what 'chu told Uncle Sko yesterday? Sab, he told me everything you said!"

"So, what?! I ain't tell Uncle Sko shit different, than what I always tell you! And stop fuckin' hollerin' at me! Party, I ain't the fuckin' enemy . . .Mommy is."

It was February 9th, 2013, thirty-seven minutes shy of midnight. The dark sky was clear, except for the bright display of a full, shimmering moon. The city of Philadelphia had just recovered from one of its coldest days, and according to local, weather experts, no relief was in the week to come.

For Party, whose real name was Pierre Anderson Jr., the cold temperature felt eerily appropriate. His life had been turned upside down, and inside out, on a cold, rainy day. Cold and rainy days were when Party was emotionally vulnerable the most. Only the people closest to him were aware of this.

"Party, do you want Mommy to do to you, what she got done to Daddy?"

"No."

"Alright, well, you gotta act like it, then, man. Party, this shit ain't no game. You Daddy second comin', Party. Don't 'chu see him when you look in the mirror? You look just like him."

"I know."

"Party, man, we owe it to Daddy, to get Mommy back. It's up to us. Us, Party. Nobody else. I know you don't like how we been livin' our lives the last ten years."

Party caught a falling teardrop with his left hand.

"Party, I don't, either. This the cards we been dealt, though. Like, and trust me, I know more than anybody else, that all this nut ass shit is a lot for you to have on ya shoulders at eighteen, but-like, what other options we got, Party? We not goin' to the fuckin' cops. We definitely not givin' Mommy Daddy money. Party, we talked about this shit a million times. I keep tellin' you what it's gon' come down to. Our lives ain't gon' never be normal again, until we find Mommy, and rock her crazy ass."

"You think she still might be in Philly?"

"I doubt it, but then, like, who knows? That's why you gotta keep ya eyes open, and be on point at all times, though, Party. This shit not just about 'chu not bein' me. Party, Mommy know she ain't gotta snowball chance in Hell, if she ever cross my fuckin' path. If she cross yours, and you don't kill 'er, her whole angle gon' be to use you as leverage to get Daddy money. Party, she gon' torture you. She gon' have you somewhere, where ain't nobody gon' be able to hear ya screams. She gon' be doin' that voodoo shit on you 'n all 'lat. And even if I give her Daddy money, she still gon' kill you. So, like, if you ain't ready to put on ya fuckin' war paint, then go back to Boston wit' Uncle Sko, until I come home, before Mommy make the score two to nothin'.

With a sigh, Party slammed his left fist into one of his bed pillows, before stretching his six foot frame across the middle of his bed. Party's thoughts were starting to race. Wherever his mother was, he wanted her to stay there. Just talking about a potential encounter with her had him feeling suddenly anxious, and extremely uncomfortable.

"Party, you begged me to let 'chu come back to Philly for the past ten years. Now, you got what 'chu been askin' me for. You there. Party, help me keep Daddy legacy goin'. Show me this wasn't a mistake, by bringin' you back. Party, I want 'chu to show fuckin' Mommy what 'chu made of."

"I am," Party vowed, feeling inspired by his older brother's words and sentiments. Thoughts of his father brought along emotions of anger and sadness, causing teardrops of frustration to pour from his eyes. "I been waitin' for this moment, since I was eight, Sab. I ain't goin' back to Boston. You the one that made the decision for me to go stay wit' Uncle Sko, not me. Sab, that shit was like boot camp."

"Yea, but 'chu a problem, now, though, Party. Yo, if you apply all that shit that 'chu learned in Boston from Uncle

Sko, and use that shit in Philly, Party, Mommy, or nobody else, won't be able to fuck wit 'chu. Not only that, but 'chu got access to anything you want."

"I know."

"Alright, look, let's finish this conversation another time. I gotta call Breen, and make sure she still comin' to see me tomorrow."

"She told me she was when I spoke to her earlier."

"Yeah, but, I'm tryna get my celly a visit, too, though. I'm tryna get Breen to bring up his babymom 'n his son."

"Sab?"

"Yo?"

"They still gon' let 'chu go next year?"

"Hopefully . . .my minimum February twenty-fourth. I ain't got no write-ups, so it shouldn't be no reason why they don't gimme the green light."

"Is what Uncle Sko told me true?"

"What he say?"

"That, if one of them guards catch you in there wit' that cell phone, it's gon' mess up ya chances of comin' home."

"Man, tell Uncle Sko to fall back."

"Will it, though?"

"Party, let me worry about that. Everything cool. Trust me, I'm comin' home. Ay, did Breen give you ya own set of keys to the hair salon, like I told her to?"

"Yeah, I got 'em right here. She gave 'em to me, before she left."

"Alright, well, look, I'ma holla at'chu tomorrow, alright?"

"Alright."

"Alright, I love you."

"Love you, too."

Ten years earlier . . .
January 7th, 2002
8:47 p.m.

Something.
Wrong.
"They killed Daddy, Party!"

After his soul crippling confession, Sab pulled the rear passenger door to his car shut, then frantically began unbuckling Party's seatbelt. Sab's clothes were drenched from the pouring rain, and his eyes were wet with tears.

"It was Mommy. Party, she—That bitch got Daddy kidnapped, and they—"

The moment his older brother's uncontrollable sobbing started, seemed more defining to Party, than the news his older brother had just given him about their father's fate. Party was only eight-years-old, so his young mind was unable to fully grasp the reality, or the sheer magnitude, of what his older brother had just revealed to him. Due to this lack of comprehension, Party only became emotional, and began to cry, because his older brother was himself. Party was the youngest of two children. His brother, Baseer, who everyone called 'Sab', was ten years older than him. Party was their father's exact replica; just a tinier version, minus the beard. Like their father, Party was even allergic to cats, and seafood, and he loved butter pecan, ice cream. It was Sab, who had their mother's looks. Sab had her green eyes, the same light complexion, and he also had a sprinkle of freckles on both cheeks, and on the tip of his nose.

Pierre Anderson, Party and Sab's father, was the combination of a mother from Portugal, and an African American father from New Orleans. His parents had stumbled upon love at a coffee shop in Montreal, Canada. Pierre was born in Montreal, but was raised in New Orleans, where he, himself had found love, during his senior year of high school. In his mid-twenties, Pierre had come to the decision that he wanted him and his then-pregnant wife, to move to the city of Philadelphia, where he had an older brother. The move had also been inspired by Pierre's underworld ties to an Italian, drug kingpin, by the name of Salvatore Masino. With the backing of Salvatore Masino, it had only taken Pierre one year to establish himself in the streets of Philadelphia. It took him an additional three years to proclaim himself a self-made millionaire. However, while the drug trade had been being kind and generous to Pierre, life at home with his wife had become a living hell.

Party and Sab's mother had a soul that was darker than the mouth of a train tunnel. She was 'Revlon' beautiful, but she owned a wicked personality that was 'Donkey Kong' ugly. Party was afraid of her. Her name was Victoria Beauvais.

Sab hated everything about her.

He even hated that he looked so much like her.

Victoria Beauvais practiced witchcraft. It was her religion, and a strong piece of her family's heritage. In New Orleans, her family roots were legendary. She had two sets of twin aunts, who specialized in all kinds of black magic spells. These four aunts, who were the younger sisters of Victoria's father, had invested a lot of their lives into teaching Victoria everything that had been taught to them. Pierre had been Victoria's first project. In her possession, Victoria had intoxicating perfume that, if smelled once by any man, the fragrance would leave Victoria in total control of that man's decisions, as long as that man and Victoria had sex. To simply inhale the aroma, would only leave a man feeling light-headed, and disoriented, hours afterwards.

During the summer of 1999, the decades-long spell that Victoria had had over Pierre had become lifted. Ironically, it was by Victoria's very own undoing. She had contracted an STD from someone else, but in her rage, she had immediately placed the blame on her husband. The problem was, after an emergency visit to the health clinic, it was revealed that Pierre was actually STD-free. Following a toxic war of words, Pierre had moved out of his and Victoria's house, and the very next day, had hired a divorce lawyer.

It was Party, who had suffered the most from his father's absence at home. His mother had seemed to always find reasons why he needed to be punished, or chastised, and she was always angry and upset. Even more confusing to Party, was what his mother had done to their basement. She had transformed it into her own personal, voodoo cavern. On all of their basement's walls, there was unreadable, cryptic writing, and all sorts of drawings, ranging in all colors, which glowed, and sometimes appeared to move, whenever the lights were out. The floor of the basement was stained with blood. There were animals of all sizes locked in cages. Party had, through crying eyes, watched as his mother drunk the blood of exotic animals he had never seen, and sometimes she had even bathed naked in the blood, after many of these animals' sacrifices. Like always, after all of these bizarre episodes, Party's mother would grab him violently by his little face and threaten him with certain death, if his lips were to ever utter one single word of what he had been witnessing at home, to his father, Sab, school teachers, or to anyone else.

Sab had moved out of the house a week after his father left. He was his father's second-in-command, and at the young age of seventeen, had seen, and touched, more money than a bank teller ever would.

Something.

Wrong.

At the ringing of his cell phone, Sab freed Party from his embrace, then ordered his girlfriend, who was sitting behind the steering wheel of his silver, Dodge Intrepid, to kill the engine on the car. Sighing, Sab took a moment to wipe his face clean of his teardrops. Sab's girlfriend was watching him through the rearview mirror. Party's watery eyes were staring at Sab's ringing cell phone.

"That's her?"

Sab nodded his head at his girlfriend, as he raised his cell phone to his ear. For emotional strength, he put Party beneath the wing of his left arm, and answered their mother's phone call. Sab met his girlfriend's eyes in his rearview mirror from the backseat.

"Hello?"

"Are you ready?"

"Mom—Mommy, I-I only got six hundred and eighty-five thousand. That's all I could get together."

"And what the fuck am I supposed to do with that, Sab?! Huh?! Tell me that!"

Victoria Beauvais had a voice that could scare the shit out of a ghost. It was always kept at a few levels above a whisper, and sounded like something that would come out of the mouth of a female zombie in a horror film. No feelings, or sensitivity, was ever attached to it. Victoria Beauvais' voice was lifeless and dark; like her heart.

"Mommy, man, why you doin' this to us?"

"Sab, do you wanna see your father the fuck alive again, or what?"

"Yeah."

"Okay, well, then, I advise you to get me what the fuck I asked for."

"Can I talk to Daddy again?"

"Once was enough. I want the address to that fuckin' house, too."

"What house?"

"Sab, don't play with my intelligence, okay? I been doin' this shit long before you was born. You know damn well what fuckin' house I'm talkin' the fuck about."

Pierre Anderson owned a house in Gladwyne, Pennsylvania, that had a little over fifteen million dollars in cash in its guest bedroom. The money was hidden in the drop-ceiling, in the denomination of one hundred dollar bills. The money was being kept inside of twenty, leather, Fendi suitcases. Only Sab knew where this house was located. Anybody, who was somebody, knew about the role that Sab played in his father's drug enterprise. Sab had more intelligence of what was actually going on in the streets of Philadelphia, than some DEA agents, who had been employed by the government, far longer than Sab had been alive. Both Sab, and his girlfriend, Sabreena, held intricate positions in Sab's father's drug dynasty. The two of them were money couriers for him. Both of them were equipped with fake driver's licenses, and had access to dozens of cars. Sab and his girlfriend also had Sab's father's permission, to shoot at anyone, who either of them perceived to be a potential threat. Up until now, nothing had ever arisen, where it called for either one of them to respond with any kind of deadly force.

Until.

Now.

"Mommy, I'ma have everything you want in an hour."

"You got thirty minutes, Sab. Thirty fuckin' minutes. And if you try anything slick, I'm sendin' somebody after Party."

"That's—He—Mommy, he ya son, though."

"I can always have another one. And don't think I don't know about Sabreena pickin' Party up from the neighbor's house. Make sure you let her know, if she interfere with my business again, she gon' have hell to pay."

Before Sab could respond to his mother's cold, and insensitive comments, she abruptly ended their call. The clock was now ticking.

"Sab, what she—"

"If I don't give her what she askin' for, in thirty minutes, she gon' send somebody after Party."

"Well, she can forget that, 'cause he with us now."

"She wanna know where my dad house at, too."

"Which one?"

"Breen, which one you think? The house out Gladwyne."

"So, what we gon' do, then?"

Sab looked down at his left wrist, checking the time on his watch. He had twenty-seven minutes left.

"You gon' give her what she want?"

"Fuck no . . .Breen, I'ma give this bitch hell. Her, and whoever she got ridin' with 'er."

"And you sure she killed your dad already?"

"When I asked her to let me talk to him again, she wouldn't let me."

"Sab, that don't mean—"

"Breen, I can feel it. He dead. I can feel it in my heart that he gone."

"This is so crazy. Oh my God. I can't believe—"

"Look, this what we gon' do."

For a little over ten minutes, Party sat quietly, listening attentively, as Sab and his girlfriend, planned, and went over several different scenarios, until they both agreed on an option that seemed to be less difficult, than all of the rest. While Sab and his girlfriend had been talking, it had begun to rain a lot harder. The raindrops had gotten heavier. They were beating on the roof of Sab's car with a steadier rhythm, than before. Sab's car was parked on the corner of 5th and Morris. His girlfriend's white, Mazda 929, was directly across the street, parked beside a Cambodian-owned, laundromat.

"Party, I'ma need 'ju to grow up real fast," Sab insisted gently, while hugging his little brother's body as tight as he possibly could. His teardrops were spilling down into his little brother's low-cut, curly hair. "It's a lot of stuff goin' on right now, Party. Stuff that 'chu probably won't be able to really understand, until you get older. Party, I had to, um, get Breen to pick you up from Ms. Lindy house, 'cause Mommy got somethin' bad done to Daddy, and I wasn't tryna let the same thing happen to you. Party, Mommy got Daddy kidnapped. She want Daddy money, and she wanna know where Daddy new house at. That's what me 'n her was just talkin' about. Party, I was gon' give her what she wanted, but when she called me earlier, and she let me talk to Daddy, Daddy told me not to give Mommy nothin', 'cause Mommy and her friends was gon' kill him anyway. You understand what I'm sayin', Party?"

Party truly didn't understand what was going on, but he still nodded his head anyway. The only thing clear to him, was that his heart had him desperately wanting to see his father. After another tight hug, Sab released Party from his embrace, and quietly exited his car. In his absence, his girlfriend cried loud and hard.

So did Party.

Together, their crying was one of the saddest duets ever performed. It was melodic, yet dynamically sympathetic. At times, Party's crying had gotten so uncontrollable, it sometimes sounded like he was having a hard time breathing. For this reason, Sab's girlfriend had Party climb up front to the driver's seat with her, and had placed him on her lap.

When Sab returned, he reentered his car with the same silent aura he had left with. He had changed out of the wet clothes he had been wearing, and now had on a black, two-piece, rain suit. In his left hand, he was clutching the straps of a large duffel bag, and in his right hand, he was gripping the handle of an Italian-made, automatic shotgun. His facial expression was murderous as he tossed the duffel bag over this shoulder into the backseat. He could feel his girlfriend and little brother studying his every move. Their attention inspired him not to cry. In their eyes, he had to be brave.

Fearless.

Fearsome.

Sab dug down deep within himself, and tapped into the strength he was going to need to outthink his mother, and avenge the death of his father.

"We gotta go to the park on 4th and Ellsworth."

"The dog park?"

Sab nodded his head as he leaned over and removed Party from his girlfriend's lap. Once he had Party settled on his own lap, he turned his attention back to his girlfriend.

"She called me again."

"And said what?"

"That she want me to go to the park on 4th and Ellsworth. She told me to go there by myself, and to call her when I get there."

"But . . ."

"Breen, we still stickin' to our plan. Tauheed and Ern on they way. They gon' meet us there."

Sabreena wiped her eyes and face clean of her tears, then she started up Sab's Dodge Intrepid. Fresh teardrops replaced the old ones as she cut on the headlights, and the windshield wipers.

"Let's switch cars, Breen."

"Okay."

"Go to the Escallade."

"Which one?"

"Where you leave the black one parked yesterday?"

"4th and Dickerson. The white one around the corner, on 6th Street."

"Naw, go to the black one. For this shit, I want us to be in somethin' bulletproof."

In war . . .

The wise shall prosper.

9:59 p.m.

Something.

Wrong.

"Breen, pull over right there."

Obeying Sab's instructions, Sabreena tapped on the brakes and pulled the black SUV over to the northeast corner of 4th and Washington Avenue. It was still raining, but it had slowed down to a slight drizzle.

"Alright, go 'head, Tauheed . . .what 'chu was sayin'?"

"Yo, look at that fuckin' blue, mini-van. That shit been circling that playground, since me 'n Ern pulled up. Watch that shit turn up 5th Street when it get to the corner."

Sab switched his cell phone to his opposite ear, and focused all of his attention on the mini-van, traveling west up Ellsworth Street. The windows on the mini-van were tinted, preventing Sab from seeing exactly who was inside of it. Like his friend had predicted, the mini-van made a right turn at the corner of 5th and Ellsworth.

"Sab, now, watch that shit bang another right when it get up to Washington Avenue. Then, when it get down to 4th, it's gon' bang another right, right the fuck in front of you. It's just circling the playground. Sab, that's them. It's ya call, cuz. Me 'n Ern ready to rock 'n roll."

"Alright, hold up. Let me see what this mu'fucker do."

Again, like Tauheed had predicted, Sab witnessed the mini-van make a right turn as soon as it reached Washington Avenue. It was moving at a snail's pace. The closer the mini-van got, the hotter Sab could feel his blood getting inside of his veins. His hand that was holding his cell phone against his ear had begun to shake.

"Y'all ready?"

"Cuz, let's get it. This shit for ya fuckin' dad."

A second after Sab and his friend ended their phone call, Sab's mother called. At that exact same second, as Sab was answering his mother's call, Sab instructed his girlfriend to drive out into the middle of 4th and Washington's intersection, to cut off the slow-moving , blue, mini-van.

"Hello?"

"Sab, my fuckin' patience is runnin' the fuck out. Where are you?"

"Mommy, shut the fuck up!" Sab snapped, glaring at the windshield of the mini-van. His heart was doing flip-flops in his chest as he cracked the Escallade's passenger door, and dropped the heavy duffel bag down to the rain-wet street. "I got everything you fuckin' asked for. Tell whoever drivin' this fuckin' nut ass mini-van, to get out and get that shit. It's right there. The address to Daddy house in the fuckin' bag wit' the money."

By no means, was Victoria Beauvais a dumb woman. She was as innovative, and ingenious, as she was evil. She had been planning her ex-husband's kidnapping for months. His schedule had become hers; so had Sab's. She had been able to stay several steps ahead of Sab and his father, because she had someone close to them both, helping her along the entire way. That person was behind the steering wheel of the mini-van.

"Sab, how stupid do you think I am?"

The question came from Sab's mother, just as Sab's girlfriend was reversing the bullet proof, Cadillac Escalade, away from the duffel bag, and the mini-van. She stopped the SUV, once she was enough feet away from the mini-van to watch it closely.

"I knew you couldn't be trusted, Sab. You showin' up in that bulletproof truck shows me where your head is. That van was just a fuckin' decoy. And I seriously doubt that whatever is in that fuckin' bag, is what I asked for. Sab, you failed. You fuckin' failed and because you did, your father will never get the proper fuckin' funeral you'd like for him to have. This not over, Sab."

As soon as the driver of the mini-van hopped out, and made his attempt for the duffel bag, he quickly realized that he had made a grave mistake. As Tauheed and Ern came running out of the 4th and Ellsworth park, raising their assault rifles, the driver of the mini-van slowly began to unpeel his ski-mask. Sab climbed out of the Escallade with his automatic shotgun, leaving behind his cell phone. In the backseat of the SUV, Party was taking in the entire scene. When Sab's girlfriend also exited the truck, Party hurriedly unbuckled his seatbelt and climbed up front, wanting to get a better look at what was happening, but to also see the face of the man removing his ski-mask.

Once the driver of the mini-van had his ski-mask off, and his face was completely exposed, Sab and his girlfriend had two totally different reactions. Sab's girlfriend lowered her gun and began to cry. Sab, however, kept his automatic shotgun pointed at the unmasked man, but had started going ballistic. Ern and Tauheed began to back away, with looks of disgust and disbelief on their faces.

"Sab, I'm sorry, man."

It was an apology that blurred Sab's eyes with tears. Standing there, under the drizzling rain, with his girlfriend crying beside him, seeming to want to issue an apology of her own, Sab was inwardly hating the power of his mother's manipulation, as he leveled his automatic shotgun at the face of his girlfriend's identical twin brother, then pulled the trigger. Sab's mother had assumed correctly. The duffel bag contained nothing of value. It was stuffed with broken pieces of dry-wall, sheetrock, and an old doorknob.

Beside Sab, his girlfriend was sobbing uncontrollably, devastated and stricken to her core, by her twin brother's betrayal, and at the fact he had just been killed by her boyfriend. Her parents could never learn the truth.

Sighing restlessly, Party blinked away the ten-year-old memory, and sat up in bed. Everything wasn't okay. Nothing was.

After ten years of craving the day he would return to Philadelphia, Party felt disappointed in it, now that the long-awaited day had arrived. The only things that met his expectations, were the gifts his brother had his girlfriend buy for him. Outside, he had an icy-gray, 2013 Range Rover Sport, that was bulletproof, from the tires, up to the roof. The three-story house that he was in, looked like something out of an Architectural digest magazine. In the master bedroom, hiding behind the gigantic, flat-screen TV, there was a safe in the wall, holding one hundred thousand dollars in cash, four Glock 40 handguns, and a collection of very expensive watches, once worn by Party's father himself. Tonight, the only item Party had removed from the safe, was the automatic shotgun, that Sab had used to kill his girlfriend's twin brother. The gun had become Sab's trophy.

Sab was currently in prison, serving two to four years, on an unrelated drug charge. He had gotten arrested with seventy-five bundles of heroin, that he had been dropping off to an associate of his in West Philadelphia.

"Maybe, I should've listened to Uncle Sko, and just went to college," Party thought, after closing his eyes, and laying back down. As he slowly inhaled through his nostrils, he flexed his fingers around the pistol-gripped handle of his brother's automatic shotgun. "At least, I could've lost my virginity at college. Probably would've been meetin' all kinds of girls...from all over, too. Wouldn't 've had to fuckin' worry about Mommy findin' me, or none of that bullshit. I could've been havin' fun right now. That's crazy, how I'm fuckin' eighteen, and don't even know what pussy smell like. That's Party...the fuckin' eighteen-year-old virgin. My life suck. I gotta show Sab I can hold shit down, until he come home. If I kill Mommy, before he get out, he'll really be proud of me."

Wishes.

About The Author

KHALIL MURRAY was born and raised in Philadelphia Pennsylvania. Along with being a successful book publisher, and an accomplished, best-selling author, Khalil Murray is also a gifted songwriter, and has a large volume of music available. With each of his novels, from his ten-book series (City Of Secrets), there are personal soundtracks for each book. Those soundtracks have R&B music, comedy skits, business advertisements, special guest features, and a variety of music from some of your favorite rap artists. Next on Khalil Murray's agenda, is to transition all of his books to screenplays, and straight-to-DVD movies, as well as taking out the time to publish other aspiring writers. The Equal Team Publications is always looking for new bookcover models; both, male and female, as well as graphic designers, music producers, music artists, and film directors.

For previews of upcoming books by Khalil Murray, and more information about The Equal Team Publications, visit;

Facebook/Khalil Murray

Instagram/Khalil_Murray

Facebook/The Equal Team Publications